VANESSA'S MEN

Psychological Thrillers by Jason Starr
Cold Caller
Nothing Personal
Fake I.D.
Hard Feelings
Tough Luck
Twisted City
Lights Out
The Follower
Panic Attack
Fantasies
Too Far
The Next Time I Die
Vanessa's Men

The Pack Series by Jason Starr
The Pack
The Craving

Crime Novels Co-Written with Ken Bruen
Bust
Slide
The Max
Pimp

Novel Collections
The Manhattan Trilogy (collecting *Cold Caller*, *Hard Feelings*, and *Twisted City*)
Supermax (collecting *Bust*, *Slide*, and *The Max*)

Film and TV Tie-In Novels by Jason Starr
Ant-Man: Natural Enemy
Gotham: Dawn of Darkness
Gotham: City of Monsters

Graphic Novels by Jason Starr
The Chill
Punisher Max: Untold Tales
Wolverine Max: Volume 1
Wolverine Max: Volume 2
Wolverine Max: Volume 3
The Returning
Red Border
Casual Fling
Silicon Bandits

Short Story Collections
Bloodlines: An Anthology of Horse Racing (co-edited with
Maggie Estep)
Outlawed Ink (Jason Starr's Short Stories)

Praise from Writers

"Some of the best new writing there is."

– Lee Child

"Darkly funny and a pure pleasure to read."

– Bret Easton Ellis

"Starr's got a hip style and an ear for crackling dialogue."

– Jeffery Deaver

"*Panic Attack* is the ultimate page turner – a thriller that brilliantly blends psychological and physical suspense. It's rare that you get either in a book, but Jason Starr delivers both in spades."

– Michael Connelly

"Jason Starr is the real deal in a world where a lot of people are faking it."

– Laura Lippman

"*The Follower* puts Jason Starr up there with some of the greats of psychological suspense."

– Joseph Finder

"*Lights Out* has the New York sound, the energy, dialogue that's on the beat…Read it and you'll go hunting for Jason Starr's other books, I promise."

– Elmore Leonard

Praise from Critics

"Starr's writing is slick and his plotting is second to none."

– The Guardian (London)

"Sizzles with streetwise dialogue and furious emotional energy."

– Library Journal

"Extremely chilling."

– Marilyn Stasio, *The New York Times*

"Jason Starr is such a polished writer that once you start reading it's painful to tear yourself away."

– John Freeman, *Time Out New York*

"A pitch perfect sense of storytelling that never fails to surprise."

– Bookreporter.com

"A literary tour de force."

– The Baltimore Sun

"You can't stop reading."

– Newsweek

VANESSA'S MEN

Jason Starr

Published by Jason Starr Books
New York

www.JasonStarr.com

First Jason Starr Books Edition

ISBN: 979-8-9937118-7-4

For Jana and Bernie

ONE

On the corner of Fifty-Eighth and Eighth, I had my right hand outstretched, index finger up, but the taxi zipped by me to pick up the handsome, well-dressed guy a half block away.

"Seriously? You fuckin' kiddin' me?"

Though I'd been living in Manhattan for my entire adult life, I'd always be a Staten Island girl, and I didn't take it lightly when somebody screwed me over in any way, which included stealing my cabs. As my husband Michael often reminded me, "*One of these days that mouth of yours is gonna get you killed, Vanessa,*" and he was probably right.

"Hey, you! Yeah, you, dickhead!"

I marched into the gutter, going as fast as I could in my three-inch platform sandals. I'd just had a great client meeting with Angie Ferguson—a friend of a friend of a friend—who'd hired me to reorganize her daughter's bedroom, and now I was heading uptown to opening night for my oldest son Harrison's first major role: Connor in his after-school theater program's *Dear Evan Hansen*. I guess I could've tried to hail a different cab, or gotten a Lyft, but now this was a matter of principle.

Still glaring ahead at the taxi as I began to jog toward it, I shouted, "Yeah, *you*! Who the hell do you think you are, you son of a—"

Then I stopped, not because I was willing to let go of the cab that easily, but because I suddenly recognized the guy stealing it.

Holy shit, this can't be happening. It's not possible.

He was still almost a block away, and I could only see his profile for an instant as he got into the cab and was about to close the door. Still, I'd gotten enough of a glance to know that I didn't need any more proof.

It's him.

His close-cropped afro had receded, with a faint bald spot, but this made sense since the last time I'd seen him was nineteen years ago when he'd left for "a quick swim," not far from the house we were renting out east, on Shelter Island. He was twenty-seven then, but all in all he'd aged well. He still had the same square jawline, strong cheekbones, and broad athletic shoulders. He'd always been a stylish dresser, and that apparently hadn't changed. He was in dark slacks, a black T-shirt, dress shoes, and a thin, designer black leather jacket.

But how could it actually be—

"Colin!"

I was petite, barely five-one, and had a high-pitched voice, but I could get loud when I wanted to. He was far away, though, and there was a lot of city noise—honking horns, a distant siren, other people screaming—so I didn't think he'd heard me. The door was shut, and the cab was pulling away. I had to get closer. Maybe I could even catch up to it and bang on the back.

"Colin! Colin!"

There was too much noise, including a nearby ambulance siren, and with the windows of the cab shut I knew he probably couldn't hear me no matter how loud I yelled.

I also knew I might never have this chance again.

As the cab veered toward Central Park South, I unleashed the loudest scream I could muster: "Colin! Wait, Colinnnn!"

I was semi-aware of people gazing at me, like I was some crazy woman—screaming, chasing after a cab around Columbus Circle. I knew there was no way I could reach it in time, but I also knew I had to do *something*. Stopping in the middle of the street, I had my phone out. I opened the camera app and tapped "video," then the red record icon. Now he turned to his right, so that his profile was visible again, just for a second, and then it happened.

First, I heard a loud screech, then I felt the impact. During that maybe one second, from the moment the car hit me to the moment when my body slammed onto the pavement, I thought: *Is this really how I'm going to die? Hit by a fuckin' car on Columbus Circle while chasing after my supposedly dead ex-fiancé?* This was wrong; *so* wrong. I'd always envisioned dying at home when I was in my nineties, surrounded by my children and grandchildren. I couldn't die like this—alone, with strangers.

Then it became obvious that I wasn't dead because, well, I was thinking, *and* because a surge of pain hit my left side, especially my left hip. I felt extremely awkward and embarrassed with all the unfamiliar people staring at me. I just wanted to get up and run, but a woman was saying, "Don't move, don't move," and a Spanish-accented guy said, "Sorry, I didn't see you, lady. You came outta nowhere. I'll call nine-one-one. I'm really sorry, please be okay, I didn't know you was there, I swear."

I had sharp pain in my left shoulder too and the hip pain had gotten worse. I also noticed that my lacy black blouse had a tear in it.

"It's okay, it was my fault, not yours," I said to the driver. "Don't worry about it, I'm fine, really."

I made it onto my knees, then stood with my Coach handbag dangling from my non-injured shoulder.

"I'm so sorry," the driver said. "Really, I'm sorry."

I looked at him for the first time. He was middle-aged, had a gray beard. He appeared as nervous and scared as he sounded.

"It's okay," I said, trying to get up. "Don't feel bad, it wasn't your fault. I got distracted."

"She shouldn't stand," the woman who'd spoken before said.

"Maybe…maybe you should wait," the driver said.

But I was already up. My hip hurt but the other pains didn't seem so bad anymore.

"Hey, is this your phone?"

Another woman with curly red hair was holding my iPhone.

"Oh, thank you so much," I said, taking it from her.

"Don't go," the driver said. "Just wait till nine-one-one gets here."

"It's okay, really. Go on with your day, and I won't sue you, I promise."

I limped away, past the people—mostly tourists—who'd gathered on the sidewalk or stopped on their CitiBikes to see what the hoopla was about. I was trying to act like nothing was wrong, ignoring the gazes that were laser-focused on me.

My hip hurt a lot, and I noticed that I had a bad scrape on my knee with blood oozing.

"Fuck me," I muttered.

I was upset—not about my blouse or bruised hip, but because I didn't get to that cab in time. Was it really him? Was he really *alive*?

I hailed a cab, and we headed across town. Sitting made the pains seem worse, but with a Starbucks napkin I found in my handbag I got the bleeding to stop and used some Purell to disinfect it. I was thinking mostly about Colin, or the guy I'd thought was Colin. Now that he was gone, that I was out of the situation, I had more perspective and the whole thing seemed insane. I was angry at myself for believing a scenario that he could be alive, and that I risked my life because of it. What was more likely, that Colin was alive or that I'd *imagined* seeing him? It wouldn't have been the first time I'd had a Colin sighting and mistook him for someone else. I'd thought I'd spotted him dozens of times over the years and had been wrong every time. Well, probably wrong.

The video.

I'd gotten a clear shot of the taxi, but it was taken from almost a block away and it was hard to make out any details. I paused the video and took a screenshot. Then I expanded the screenshot with my thumb and forefinger and zoomed in on the man's profile.

"Holy fuckin' shit," I muttered. "It's you. It's actually *you*."

TWO

At least my hip wasn't broken. If it were, I wouldn't be able to walk—well, that's what I told myself anyway as I struggled to get out of the cab and limped along Third Avenue.

Actually, all in all, I felt okay. Aside from my bruised hip and shoulder, I'd probably have nasty black-and-blue marks, but the pain wasn't worsening, and now I was more concerned with how I looked than how I felt. I didn't want to show up as a total mess, distracting from Harrison's big night. My jeans had a tear in the right leg, but it was okay because it might look like I'd bought them that way. The rip in my blouse near the shoulder area was a bigger problem because I didn't have anything to cover it with. Also, I noticed that both knees were bruised, and my bruised shoulder was bleeding slightly. Thankfully the blouse was black, so the blood was hard to see.

I checked myself out in the hazy reflection of a store's window. I fixed my lipstick, fluffed up my highlighted hair a little, and smoothed out my blouse. Well, it was the best I could do.

At Eli's, I bought the biggest, most beautiful bouquet of mixed flowers they had, then limped a few blocks to the St. Jean Baptiste Church on East Seventy-Sixth Street near Lexington Avenue where the Encore Theater School rented rehearsal and performance space in the basement. When I entered through the side entrance, I approached my friend Cara who was taking tickets tonight.

"Hey, Vanessa."

"Did it start?" I must've sounded frantic.

"Just about."

"Shit." I rushed inside.

I glanced at my phone: 7:24, and the showtime was 7:30. Thank God. Harrison had a small cameo in the opening number, and I would've felt awful if I'd missed it.

Michael was waiting with my in-laws in the lobby, but most people had already gone into the theater. I approached, managing to hide my limp by sucking up the pain. As Michael gazed at me, he appeared to be smiling, but within the smile was a look that only I could see—a disappointed glare that I knew meant, *Where the hell have you been*?

"Hey." I kissed him hello, noticing how stiff and dry his lips felt.

Forcing a happier expression, I said to my mother- and father-in-law, "How are you, guys? Thanks so much for coming."

"For me?" Joe joked, pretending to take the flowers.

I laughed politely, then kissed Joe on the cheek and air-kissed Stella. I saw that Stella's gaze was fixed on my bouquet, obviously noticing mine was prettier and more expensive than the smaller bouquet that she was holding.

Stella and I had been butting heads for years. She had been against Michael marrying me because I came from a lower-middle-class Staten Island Italian family, and Stella and Joe were upper-middle-class "Jersey Italians." Even after her grandchildren were born, her underlying attitude was that her son was slumming and could've done better. She hated that I hadn't raised my kids Catholic, saying ad nauseam, "Can you believe my own grandsons haven't even had Holy Communions?" Out of respect for Michael and my children, I always tried to be cordial around Stella, but this was often a challenge. Her normal expression was a downturned mouth and a slight sneer—classic resting bitch face. Whenever I spoke, she looked even more irritated; I often caught her shaking her head or rolling her eyes. I'm sure I gave her looks too, since she always seemed to be searching for opportunities to get digs in. After insulting me, she usually claimed she was "just being honest," but the truth was she had no filter. She'd been a vice principal at John F. Kennedy High School in Paterson, and she often bragged about how many of the students hated and feared her. Since she'd retired, about five years ago, her nasty edge had intensified, maybe because she couldn't vent at kids anymore. Thankfully, with her and Joe living in Jersey— they'd sold their house in Franklin Lakes and now had a condo in Fort Lee—I didn't have to see her very often. I felt sorry for Joe, though. He was a sweet guy, and he'd had to put up with Stella's bullshit for, Jesus Christ, forty-two years. I wasn't surprised he had high blood pressure, but as Stella's spouse I didn't know how he'd avoided having a massive heart attack or stroke.

"I'm so glad I made it here on time," I said to everyone. "I had a work meeting that ran a little late."

"What happened to your blouse?" Of course, Stella had to notice it.

"Blouse?" I pretended to be momentarily confused. "Oh, it's nothing. I tripped hailing a cab and had a little fall."

"You okay?" Now Michael seemed genuinely concerned.

"Yeah, totally. It was nothing. I'm fine, really."

I didn't feel like telling them about seeing Colin and the car hitting me. I was probably still in shock and a little embarrassed. Also, I knew, especially with Stella here, it would just lead to a lot of questioning and drama, and I didn't want to have to deal with all that.

"I'm so excited about tonight," I said, changing the subject. "How was Harrison? Was he nervous?"

"No, he seemed very calm actually when we got here," Joe said. "I told him, I hope you haven't been smoking anything."

"Stop." Stella nudged Joe with an elbow.

"What?" Joe held up his hands like he was under arrest. "It was a joke."

"There are kids here."

"What, you think these kids don't smoke pot? They got dispensaries on every other block these days."

"We should probably go in," I said. "Is Carson in yet?"

Carson was my youngest son; he'd recently turned fourteen.

"Yes, he went in already with his friends," Stella said. "I'm excited too. I can't wait to hear Harrison sing. I love his voice so much."

Well, at least there was one thing Stella and I agreed on.

Stella and Joe went in ahead of Michael and me. I could tell Michael was still upset—maybe about my lateness, or maybe it was just because he didn't really want to be here. He'd been against the kids acting and wanted them to play sports instead.

"What's wrong?" I asked.

"I know you tripped," he said, "but if you were running late, you could've texted."

He was right—I could've, okay, *should've* texted from the cab. I'd noticed he'd texted me a couple of times, asking where I was, but I was so jolted from my accident and shocked over spotting Colin, that it hadn't occurred to me to text back.

"Oh, sorry, I didn't have a chance to," I said. A voice in me said, *Let it go, Vanessa*, but as usual I ignored my own wise advice and said, "Why? You think I *wanted* to be late?"

"But you said you'd be here by seven the latest," he said, "and you had the tickets so we couldn't go in."

Now I was getting seriously upset.

Stage whispering, really stage-*yelling*, I said, "You know that's ridiculous, they would've let you in without tickets. This isn't Lincoln Center."

"I didn't know which seats we had, and I had no idea when you were getting here."

"How many times do you want me to apologize? And it's funny that you're upset about me being late when I have to practically drag you to come to these shows."

"That isn't the point. You should've texted."

He looked away. Great, now we were both angry. I hoped my friends weren't noticing.

An acting student—Staci's son Zachary—handed us programs that I'd helped design, then, as we joined Michael's parents at our seats, I smiled and waved at them and mouthed hellos to several of my friends—Isabella, Suji, Kathleen.

Then Justin Reedy's dad, Andrew, came over and said, "Congratulations."

Andrew was a sweet, nerdy American history professor at Hunter College. He was a widower—his wife had died from ovarian cancer a few years ago—and recently his son Justin—who was starring as Evan Hansen tonight—had started dating Harrison.

"You too," I said, happy to have a break from arguing with Michael. "Did you see the kids backstage?"

"Yes, and they seemed more excited than nervous."

"Aw, that's great, I know they'll kick ass. I wanted to get here earlier to wish him luck before the show. It's so frustrating."

He squinted, looking at my torn blouse. "Are you okay? What happened?"

"Oh, it was no big deal. Just a little fall, that's all."

"A *fall*?"

"It was nothing."

I wasn't sure he believed me, then he said, "A few of us are going out for drinks later, if you guys want to join."

"Oh, that sounds like fun," I said. "I'd love that, but Michael's family's here from Jersey."

"No worries, another time. Congrats again."

"You too, Andrew."

As I settled into my seat, I could tell that Michael was still annoyed with me. I almost said something to him about how his shitty attitude was taking away from Harrison's big night, but then the lights dimmed; my excitement took over and I wasn't going to let Michael, or anything else, distract me.

When I was a kid, my father had taught me how to whistle through my fingers, and I still kicked ass at it. When the show began, I unleashed a shrieking whistle so loud it overwhelmed everyone else in the audience. I could tell

Michael was making a face—he hated it when I whistled like that, saying it was going to make him deaf—but I tried my best to ignore him.

As Harrison appeared on stage for the first time, I couldn't whistle again because I was filming with my phone camera, but I screamed "Woohoo! Yeah! Go, Harrison, go!" and then yelled some more later on in the show when he began singing, "Sincerely, Me." He totally killed it—it might've been his best performance ever, better than when he'd played Doody in *Grease* last year and sang "Those Magic Changes," though that had been amazing too. Harrison had worked so hard on this role—I'd been staying up late with him, running lines—and it was great to see him thrive.

Harrison exited and I cheered again, letting out my loudest "woohoo" yet. Michael was clapping, but not nearly as enthusiastically as me. He didn't like musical theater, and he'd been opposed to the kids' interest in acting. He wanted them to be athletes and couldn't accept that they didn't even like sports.

I filmed the entire rest of the number, so I could post it online later. With the camera app still open, I swiped back to the photo of Colin in the taxi. It was still hard to believe that I actually had a photo, a *new photo*, of Colin on my phone.

Michael leaned as close to my ear as he could, then whispered in an aggravated tone, "Do you have to do that now?"

I was discreet; no one else could even tell that I had my phone out. Besides, it was ridiculous for Michael to complain about it when he was always sending "important" work texts or emails when we were at movies and plays. I knew he was right, though—I shouldn't be looking at my phone during the show, so I turned off the display.

At intermission, when I tried to stand, I realized my hip had stiffened.

"You sure you're okay?" Michael asked.

"Oh, I'm fine," I said. "Wasn't Harrison amazing?"

"Yeah," Michael said, but he didn't sound like he meant it.

Smiling at my friend Stephanie, who was heading up the aisle, I mouthed, *One sec.*

In the hallway outside the theater, I caught up with her, then Cheryl and Suji joined us. Cheryl asked me about my torn blouse, and I rattled off the lie about falling, sounding convincingly nonchalant, and then I changed the subject quickly, saying, "The kids were incredible, weren't they?"

We continued talking about the show. Although I participated in the conversation, I was distracted, not as engaged as I usually was. My hip didn't hurt as much when I was standing, but my shoulder hurt more now. I was aware of Michael and his parents, maybe twenty feet away, engaged in conversation. Although they weren't looking in my direction, I knew they were talking about me. Right now, Stella was probably saying, "What's wrong with her?" and Michael was saying, "I honestly have no idea, Ma," and now Joe was chiming in with, "Okay, just leave her alone, it's none of our business," and now Stella and Joe were arguing with each other; that's why Michael was shaking his head now.

"What's that?" I realized Suji had asked me a question.

"I said are you coming out with us later?"

After the opening nights of shows, I usually joined my friends at a restaurant or wine bar nearby.

"Oh, I'd love to, but I don't think I can tonight. Michael's parents are here and we have plans."

"It's so nice they're here to support Harrison," Suji said.

"Excuse me," I said, smiling, and headed toward the bathroom.

I just wanted to get away from people for a few minutes. Although I didn't have to go, I went into the stall and locked it.

On my phone, I looked at the screenshot of Colin and the cab again. When I zoomed in, I could see one side of Colin's face. While I was certain it was him, I couldn't deny that I'd made mistakes before. I'd mentioned Colin in therapy sessions over the years, and one ex-therapist pointed out how sometimes a person could want something so bad that the mind fills in the blanks.

Looking at the photo again, I thought, *No, this time was different. This time it was definitely him.*

He'd been dressed like he was going out for the evening—maybe to meet someone, or to a work meeting, or to an event. When we were engaged, he'd been attending medical school at Mount Sinai, studying to be a neurosurgeon. Did he finish school? Was he working as a neurosurgeon now? I knew he wasn't working at a local hospital, or *any* hospital, or his name would have come up in one of the countless Google searches I'd done over the years. Had he changed his name? Left the country? Maybe he was just in the city on vacation or for business. Was there some neurosurgeon convention going on this weekend?

I did a quick search—nope, no neurosurgeon conventions—then noticed something in the photo that I hadn't seen earlier. I'd been so absorbed in staring at Colin that I hadn't focused on the other details. On the side of the cab, extremely visible, was the driver's medallion number: 917043. There had to be a way to track down a driver by a medallion number. If I could, maybe I could figure out where he had dropped off Colin, and then maybe I could find Colin.

The chimes, signifying the end of intermission, snapped me out of my thoughts. I put my phone away and exited the stall. Kathleen was at the sink washing up. She saw me in the mirror in front of her and smiled.

"Hey, Vanessa," she said. "I thought you went back in already. The kids are so amazing tonight, aren't they?"

Kathleen's daughter Emma was playing Zoe in the show. I wasn't really in the mood to chat but, figuring it would look odd if I just left the bathroom right after leaving a stall, I washed up next to her.

"Yeah," I said, rinsing my hands in the warm water. "They work so hard. It's always so rewarding to see it all come together."

While drying her hands with a paper towel, Kathleen said, "So where did you fall?"

"Oh, just, um, around the corner, when I was getting out of a cab."

"I'm so sorry. You're lucky a bike didn't hit you. The way they ride on those e-bikes is crazy. One almost killed me the other day, going in the wrong direction on First Avenue. You're really lucky."

"Yeah, I guess I am."

We returned to the theater just as the lights dimmed. When I sat next to Michael, he gave me an irritated look that I knew meant, *Where have you been*? I could've acted annoyed too, but I was feeling upbeat, still buzzed from spotting the medallion number of that cabbie, and I smiled at him and held his hand and even squeezed it a little. He squeezed mine too.

The rest of the show was fantastic, and Harrison was

amazing in "For Forever." I shot some great video of him, including the entire finale and, after the show, when he got called out for a curtain call and bowed in an exaggerated way, hamming it up for the audience.

"Woohoo!" I screamed. "Wooooohoooo!"

Next to me, Michael was clapping enthusiastically and grinning and I could tell how proud he was of Harrison even if he couldn't admit it.

In the lobby, I waited with Michael, Stella, and Joe until Harrison came out. We all hugged him and congratulated him.

"Did you like my last song?" he asked.

"Yes," I gushed. "It was perfect. They were *all* perfect."

"Are you sure? Because Thalia changed my key in rehearsal yesterday and I barely had time to practice."

Thalia Clark was the director and ran the whole program.

"Whatever you did was fantastic," I said. "We're so proud of you."

"Can I go with my friends for pizza?"

"Yes, just make sure you text us, please, and let us know where you are."

As Harrison continued to accept congratulations from our family and others, I took Michael aside.

"Harrison's going out with his friends, so he'll miss dinner with your family."

"It's okay," Michael said, "I already told them he probably wouldn't make it. They understand."

"I'm actually in some serious pain here. Do you mind if I miss dinner too? I just want to take some Advil and get into bed."

"From your fall?" He seemed genuinely concerned. "I

thought you were okay?"

"I thought so too. I'm sure it'll be fine, but sitting for another two hours is probably a bad idea."

I knew Michael so well; I could tell that now he felt guilty about all the tension between us earlier and wanted to make up for it.

"Do you want us to go home with you?"

"No, I want you all to have a great time out. I'll bring all the flowers home, so Harrison doesn't have to carry them around."

I went backstage to tell Harrison I was going home and he gave me all the bouquets of flowers he'd received—six of them. Several minutes later, outside the church, I exchanged goodbyes with Joe and Stella.

"Have a safe trip back," I said.

"Thanks," Joe said.

"Hope you feel better," Stella said.

Her tone was loaded with sarcasm; obviously she didn't believe my explanation for missing dinner. Honestly, I didn't give a shit what she thought; I just made sure that I continued to appear appropriately in pain so Michael would continue to be understanding.

I kissed Michael on the lips, then whispered in his ear, "Sorry for before."

"Yeah, me too," he said.

THREE

DURING THE RIDE home in a Lyft, I saw that Suji, Kathleen, and other moms had tagged me in the videos and photos they'd posted. On TikTok and Instagram, I posted my own videos, including the one of Harrison singing briefly in "Disappear" with the caption: **Harrison and the whole cast were amazing tonight!!!** I picked out a few of the best photos of Harrison that I'd taken during the show, including his curtain call, and a few of the after-show photos. After I cropped and filtered them, I made a collage and then posted it on Facebook and Instagram, tagging friends and family. Making collages was my "thing," and my friends always expected to see my collages after our kids' performances, or after our get-togethers and parties. I printed many of my favorite collages and framed them and hung them around our apartment.

At my building, on Fifty-Second Street, I walked through the courtyard, pleased to see that my collage had already gotten eleven likes and three shares.

"Hi," I said, as I passed Raymond, the evening doorman.

We'd been living in the building for fourteen years and Raymond had been working there the entire time. He was more like a family friend than a doorman.

"How was Harrison's show?" he asked.

"Awesome," I said. "He really kicked ass up there."

"He was nervous, but I knew he'd do great. Goodnight, Mrs. Rizzo."

"Thanks, you too, Raymond."

I didn't like putting tasks off—I needed to cross things off my to-do list—so when I entered my apartment, I popped two Advils, then got right to work unwrapping all the flowers, disposing of the plastic and paper, and trimming the stems over the kitchen sink. Then I organized the flowers in several vases and placed a vase on the counter in the kitchen, a vase on the dining room table, a vase in Michael's and my bedroom, and the biggest, fullest vase on the desk in Harrison and Carson's room, so Harrison could see the flowers when he got home.

After I cleaned the stems from the sink and scrubbed the counter spotless, I remembered that I needed to eat, so I had some leftover salad from last night. As a teenager, and occasionally as an adult, I'd had issues with anorexia, so I was always monitoring my eating habits. At my latest checkup, my GP told me I was too thin and I'd been forcing myself to get my 1,500 calories a day even when I wasn't hungry.

Sparkle, our Siamese cat, entered and meowed harshly. We'd named Sparkle sarcastically. Even as a kitten he was the opposite of sparkly—brooding, whiny, even a little mean—but we still loved him.

"Don't worry, I won't let you starve to death either," I said.

Sparkle continued to glare at me with his blue eyes, meowing as loud as the most annoying alarm clock. After I filled his bowl with Meow Mix, he went back to his usual self, acting like I suddenly didn't exist.

Wanting to check the next thing off my mental list, I went to the dining room, where I'd left my laptop, and answered some work emails. My business—Get Organized with Vanessa!—had been growing rapidly lately. When I'd started it several years ago, I never dreamed it would get to this point. Initially, I'd helped some friends find more efficient ways to use their closet and drawer spaces; I wasn't even charging people. Then Renee, a friend on the PTA with me at the kids' school, Birch Wathen Lenox, insisted on paying me to organize her daughter's closet. From there, things gradually snowballed. I got steady clients by word of mouth, and by clients posting pics of the spaces and rooms I'd organized on social media. Last year, I'd made almost forty thousand dollars and this year I was on track to make over sixty and was considering hiring an assistant. While making money and growing my business felt nice, helping people gain more control over their lives felt even better. Living with clutter and disorganization in small spaces was a major cause of stress and anxiety, especially in Manhattan. I'd gotten many thank-you letters from clients, telling me how much my work had helped them, which always felt extremely gratifying. I'd changed my company's motto a few times, but my current one was: "Uncluttered Apartment, Uncluttered Life."

Usually, once or twice a day, I created a TikTok video—pointing at fun, catchy captions—to promote my business. My kids teased me for being a "TikTok mom," but I didn't care; I enjoyed coming up with new, creative ideas for videos.

I hadn't created a TikTok today, but I didn't feel like doing any more work right now.

I went into the bedroom and undressed. My bruises looked worse than I'd expected—black and blue with some dark green too and still oozing. I realized that if the car hadn't braked, my injuries would've been much worse, but I was so preoccupied with excitement over seeing Colin, and what this meant, that I wasn't concerned as I probably should have been about my injuries.

I spritzed some infused lavender essential oil into the tub and then took a relaxing shower. Feeling refreshed and rejuvenated, I put on panties and a long, comfy pink T-shirt that read: *Warning: I Might Break Out into Showtunes.* Then, after I moisturized my face and dressed and bandaged my wounds, I lay in bed and said, "Alexa, play Jason Mraz."

As "I Won't Give Up" began, on my phone I looked at the photo of Colin in the cab again. He really did look good—still had all his hair, and those perfect rounded cheekbones. He was half-British, half-Zimbabwean, and had a beautiful bronze skin tone. Expanding the photo with my thumb and forefinger, I focused on his right eye. While I couldn't actually *see* his eye in the photo, it was easy to fill it in from memory—that stunning, almost surreal shade of hazel—and then it was easy to imagine both eyes, then his entire face. Although I was only looking at a sliver of Colin, it was incredible how I could see all of him so clearly in my mind.

But it wasn't enough; I needed more.

In the cloud, I had a file: Colin Photos. I used to look at them often, too often, but I hadn't opened the file lately— maybe in about a year. I knew it wouldn't accomplish anything, I should just watch that true crime show I'd been streaming, and fall asleep in front of the TV—that would be the smarter thing to do—but it was too late; the file was already open and my pulse was already pounding. I'd never tried coke, but this was probably what doing a line felt like—or maybe this was *more* intense. My latest psychiatrist, Dr. Stone, had once suggested that I might even be a love addict. Without telling Michael or anyone, I'd attended several Sex and Love Addict Anonymous meetings at a community center downtown. I never spoke at a meeting, but I identified with the stories people told about getting obsessive after breakups and finding it hard to let go and move on. But I didn't think I was an actual addict because, for me, the problem was isolated. I'd had other relationships that had ended, and I'd never felt addicted to another ex the way I felt addicted to Colin. If it was true that I was a love addict, I was only a love addict for Colin.

The pictures were a mix of posed shots of Colin, selfies he'd sent me, selfies we'd taken together, and shots of us out with my friends. He didn't have any friends or family in New York, as he'd come here from London to attend medical school. As I scrolled through the photos, the movie of our time together played in my head—from meeting him randomly at a midtown bar one evening when I was out with friends, to getting engaged in Tulum, and of course all the great sex. I'd never had that kind of physical connection with anyone else, including Michael. Whenever I saw Colin, I wanted to rip his clothes off and attack his body, and I knew he felt the same about me. As always, when I looked at the pictures of Colin, I focused on his hazel eyes, and this sent me back to exactly how I'd felt whenever he looked at me—from across a room, or when he was on top of me in bed.

Then I looked at the photo that had always had the biggest effect on me, the last photo I'd ever taken of him. I'd snapped it on Shelter Island the morning he disappeared. He was outside the house we'd rented—smiling with those amazing dimples, his arms crossed in front of his chest. I'd stared at the picture so many times over the years. I'd analyzed it from every possible angle, looking for clues. For example, did his crossed arms indicate that he was holding something in, hiding something, some big secret? Whenever I looked at this photo, I wished I could go back in time and grab him and tie him down and prevent whatever had happened to him from happening.

As usual, looking at this "final picture" of him ignited memories of that awful day. I must've replayed these events thousands of times. Each time they seemed extremely vivid, like I was actually *there* again, but sometimes I wasn't sure if I was embellishing some of the details. I'd once seen a story on *60 Minutes* about how people's memories can change over time and how sometimes you're not remembering the actual memory, but a memory of the memory, or something like that. Anyway, the memory started playing again.

I was in a lounge chair in the backyard, reading a book I'd taken out of the Shelter Island Library—*Harm Done* by Ruth Rendell—when he appeared in the doorway. He was wearing a turquoise bathing suit, a clean white crewneck T-shirt with Ray-Bans latched over the neckline, and beige flip-flops. The late-day sun was shining directly on him—his skin glowing and his eyes sparkling. I remembered how happy, hopeful, and in-love I felt. We'd been planning our life together—a destination wedding in Costa Rica, a house in upper Westchester, romantic vacations, kids and grandkids. Our future seemed like a perfect dream.

"I'm gonna head for a swim," he announced.

"Oh?" I said, slightly surprised. Remnants of a hurricane had passed the night before and there were warnings about riptides. "You sure that's a good idea?"

"I'll be careful." He grinned.

I wasn't seriously concerned—he was a strong swimmer, had been on the swim team at Cambridge. He was adventurous, but he was also pragmatic. If the conditions looked at all dangerous, I knew he'd stay close to the shore.

"Where do you want to go for dinner tonight?" I asked. "Should I make a rez at that seafood place we passed in town?"

"Hmm, I was thinking it could be nice if I cooked tonight. How about I make my famous paella?"

Colin was a great cook, much better than me.

"That sounds like a great idea. With the shellfish out here I'm sure it'll be amazing."

"We can go to that store near the docks and get the fish and we can find saffron somewhere, maybe at the gourmet place. I'll make some ice-cold sangria too. We can eat outside, should be a great sunset tonight."

"Sounds perfect. Have a great swim."

"Thanks."

He came over and kissed me, then I watched him head back toward the house. At the entrance, he looked back at me one last time and smiled again, then the door shut and he was gone.

One detail that had always nagged at me—I wasn't sure if he'd actually looked back at me again at the door the way I remembered it, but I was sure about his words. I'd replayed those words so many times, searching for hidden meaning, anything I might've missed, even in his tone, but I could never detect any clue or warning sign.

When he didn't come back after an hour, I started to get concerned, but I wasn't panicking. I didn't think anything had *happened* to him, but it had gotten to the point where it seemed extremely unusual that he'd been gone for so long. He knew the stores would close soon and it would take time to make paella, so why would he hang out at the beach after his swim? It wasn't like Colin to be inconsiderate or unreliable. After another hour passed and he still hadn't returned, I began catastrophizing—about the rip current warning and horrific stories I'd heard about swimmers getting sucked out miles into the ocean. I even thought about the possibility of a shark attack as there had been recent sightings and beach closures all along the Long Island coast. I tried to calm down, telling myself that Colin was a great swimmer and that there had to be some explanation for this. Maybe he'd been relaxing on the beach after his swim and fell asleep.

I hurried to the beach, but I didn't see him anywhere. *What the fuck? Where the hell was he?* As the beach was officially closed for swimming, there was no lifeguard, and no one was in the water. I walked along the beach, screaming, "Colin! Colin!" over and over, even though my voice was overwhelmed by the crashing waves. I asked several people who were hanging out on the beach if they had seen Colin and described what he looked like. A teenage girl thought she saw a guy who "kinda looked like that" a couple of hours earlier, but no one else recalled seeing him.

After the sun set and he'd been missing for about two and a half hours, I called the police. A couple of officers showed up and, shining flashlights, they began looking for him along the beach. I knew they were just wasting time because I'd already checked most of the beach and he obviously wasn't there. Later, I'd wonder if the police had wasted valuable time by not notifying the Coast Guard right away. What if Colin was out there somewhere in the ocean, clinging to something, barely staying alive and we'd had a chance to save him?

At some point, in the middle of the night, the Coast Guard began searching and in the morning Colin's belongings were discovered on the beach—his T-shirt, sunglasses, flip-flops, wallet, keys, and the navy towel. Some reporters from nearby Long Island newspapers arrived on the beach, as well as locals who'd heard the news about a missing man. They were all strangers—we were just renters and had never even been to Shelter Island before—and I was upset when people tried to comfort me. I didn't need comfort because I knew that Colin was okay. I had no idea what had happened to him, none of this made any sense to me, but I knew he was too strong to die in a rip current, and he wouldn't have risked swimming in dangerous conditions anyway, especially after I'd warned him to be careful. He was a smart, sensible, responsible guy, not some thoughtless risktaker.

The main investigator for the Coast Guard, Ray Parkins—an older guy with thin gray hair and heavy bags under his eyes—believed that a strong current was the most likely explanation.

"It really doesn't matter how strong a swimmer Colin was. This ocean isn't messing around. If a current got him, an Olympic swimmer wouldn't have been able to make his way back."

Thinking, *Thanks for mansplaining rip currents,* I said, "I know he's out there somewhere. Just fucking find him."

The Coast Guard continued searching near the shoreline and, as conditions improved slightly, they were able to look further out. As time passed, the odds that they would find him alive were increasingly slim, but I refused to accept this. I kept insisting that he was alive and that I was positive he wouldn't have done something stupid.

"There aren't any large rocks like that in this area," Parkins said.

"Well, he could've hit his head on something," I said. "Maybe he made it back to shore and he can't find his way back."

While Parkins agreed that nothing could be ruled out, he didn't seem to take this idea very seriously. He told me that local authorities had already been alerted to the situation and if Colin was wandering around someone probably would have found him by now. Although I was desperate to find any viable, hopeful explanation, I agreed with Parkins' assessment. Shelter Island wasn't very big, about six or seven square miles. The most common way to leave it was by ferry and no workers on the ferry could recall seeing a man fitting Colin's description. There wasn't much surveillance video in the area around the ferry ports on Shelter Island or on the mainland in Greenport, but the video that they had didn't show Colin.

Two days passed and I continued to refuse to accept that Colin wasn't coming back. I hadn't slept at all since he disappeared and, although I was exhausted and worn out, there was no way I was going to waste time sleeping. I had to find him—there was no alternative. I don't know how many times I walked along the shoreline, even miles from where Colin had disappeared, screaming his name. It was pointless, of course. If he were alive, he couldn't be anywhere within earshot. He couldn't still be alive in the water, even clinging to something, after all this time. Still, I kept calling out his name until my voice went hoarse, but I continued trying to yell for him anyway, refusing to give up.

After day three and day four of the search, Parkins held a press conference, announcing that the Coast Guard was calling off their search, that Colin was "presumed dead" and that the Suffolk County Police Department would be taking over the case. I couldn't believe this was happening. My mother and my friends tried to convince me that I had to "let go" and "get on with my life," but I thought this was insane. How could they give up when Colin was out there?

Kevin LaMont, a detective for the Suffolk County Police Department, took over the investigation. He was a young guy, maybe thirty, and I had no idea how he'd become a homicide detective or why he'd been put in charge of a case that was getting so much media attention. At the press conference where Parkins announced that LaMont was taking over there were about twenty reporters, including local TV news reporters and reporters from the major New York City newspapers.

LaMont contacted me and came over to meet me at the lobby of the hotel I'd checked into near the beach, walking distance from where Colin had disappeared. In the hotel lobby, LaMont didn't take off his Aviators as he explained to me that this wasn't a homicide investigation; they were still treating it as a missing person's case, but going by the questions he asked me I wasn't sure I believed this. He wanted to know if Colin had any enemies or had been in conflict with anyone lately.

"No," I said. "Everyone loved Colin, he was the nicest guy."

When he brought up the possibility that Colin might've committed suicide, I thought this was even more ludicrous.

Colin was happy, optimistic, one of the most mentally sound people I'd ever met and had shown no signs of depression. He talked about his feelings, didn't take life too seriously, and was excited about the future, about *our* future. He was looking forward to passing his exams and starting his career as a neurosurgeon. He was also excited about planning our wedding and honeymoon and having kids and grandkids. Even if he were struggling with issues that I didn't know about, ending his life wouldn't have been an option—not because of himself, but because of me. He wouldn't do something that he knew would devastate me. He loved life and *our* life way too much to just walk away from it.

Then the nightmare got worse.

A reporter for the *New York Post* discovered my father had been in the Gambino crime family and had been "rubbed out"—a total lie—and he wrote an article trying to connect this "fact" to Colin's disappearance. The whole thing was ludicrous. Yes, my father had had some very, very, *very* low-level organized crime connections. When he was in his twenties, he'd worked briefly for a bookmaker in Bensonhurst who'd had connections to the Gambino family, but he'd never been a "made man" like the article claimed. Also, his death had absolutely nothing to do with the mob; he'd died in a car accident on the New Jersey Turnpike.

A worse article, this one in The *National Enquirer*, was published with the headline: "Mobster's Daughter Suspect in Murder of Fiancé." Although it was the sleazy *Enquirer*, the article still got a lot of attention online with people making horrible assumptions and crazy false claims about me, including one about how I'd gotten jealous of Colin and "another woman" and had used one of my father's old "mob friends" to have Colin killed. My close friends claimed they believed me, though I could tell there was underlying distrust.

Finally, the police investigation ended, though without any closure. They called Colin's disappearance "an apparent drowning." Maybe if his body had been found, it would have been easier to let go. I could've grieved and gone on with my life. But without proof that he was dead my fantasies of him returning persisted. I kept telling myself that he had to be out there somewhere, that he couldn't have just drowned. I couldn't accept the idea that I'd never see him again. Every time I got a text, or a phone call, or even an email, I thought, *Please let it be from Colin.* I convinced myself that he'd hit his head on a rock and developed amnesia and imagined him coming home and us resuming our lives, as if nothing had happened. We could continue planning everything we had discussed—our wedding, our honeymoon, looking to buy an apartment, and having kids.

I'd been raised Catholic and I'd been praying for Colin every day since he'd disappeared, but when it set in that he wasn't coming back, I lost faith in God and didn't see the point of religion anymore, or praying for anything ever again. I fell into a deep depression to the point where I could barely get out of bed. I'd already been too thin, but I became *dangerously* thin. I moved back to my mother's house in Staten Island, into my old room. My mother was distracted by a new boyfriend—a guy named Phil, whom she would end up marrying and divorcing—and couldn't give me the attention that I needed. One day when she was out shopping, I OD'd on Ambien. She discovered me unconscious, barely alive. Later, at Staten Island University Hospital, I claimed the overdose was accidental, though it was hard to explain how I had "accidentally" taken almost an entire bottle of my mother's pills. On the advice of my psychiatrist, I was sent to an inpatient mental health facility in the Bronx. A couple of months later, when I got out, instead of moving home—the doctors were worried that home life would be "too triggering" for me—I moved in with a couple of friends from college in an apartment in Normandie Court, AKA Dormandie Court on the Upper East Side. I got a job as an administrative assistant for the CEO of a hedge fund where I put my organizing skills to work. I found that when I was organizing other people's lives, it made *me* feel organized, in control. I still had bad days when I was haunted by memories of Colin, especially the day he disappeared, but at least I wasn't suicidal.

I didn't socialize much, which was very unusual for me, but I felt more comfortable alone than when I was around other people. My roommates tried to get me to go out to bars and clubs, but I spent most of my free time alone in my room reading true crime books and watching true crime on TV. I wasn't interested in another relationship, and I thought I'd spend the rest of my life alone.

Late one evening, I was shopping at Gristedes, when a guy approached me and said, "Do I know you?"

I smiled politely, but in my mind, I was rolling my eyes at the extremely obvious pick-up line.

I mumbled something like, "Don't think so," and tried to walk away.

He approached me again in the next aisle and said, "Do you live in the hood?"

I took my first good look at him. He was actually kind of cute—tall, broad shoulders, a nice smile—but even if I were in a trying-to-meet-guys mood, he wasn't my type. He had a conservative vibe, in a gray suit and his hair parted to the side and slicked back, and I was into edgier, stylish men like Colin.

He seemed harmless, though, so I said, "Yep, live in the hood."

"I live downtown," he said. "I was just meeting up with some college buddies."

"Cool."

He'd positioned himself in a way that I couldn't easily get by him. He asked me some more awkward questions and I basically answered them. He seemed more nervous and awkward than creepy. I actually thought there was something familiar and endearing about him, and he got funnier as he became more comfortable chatting with me. I liked him, but I didn't know if I was actually *interested* in him or if, after everything I'd been through, I was just enjoying the attention. When he asked me for my number I gave it to him, but I doubted I'd actually go on a date with him.

"By the way, I'm Michael. I didn't get your name."

I didn't see the harm in telling him.

"Vanessa."

He called me the next day and left a voicemail, telling me how great it was to meet me and asking if I wanted to get a coffee sometime. I didn't respond. A couple of days later he called again and I felt bad, so I picked up. I planned to say that it was nice meeting him, but I'm not looking to date right now, but surprisingly I had a good time chatting with him. He made me laugh—it seemed like I hadn't laughed since Colin had died—and I liked that we were both third generation Italian-Americans.

So when he asked me out for coffee again I said, "Why not? What the hell?"

I had doubts—I told one of my roommates that "I dunno, he's not really my type"—but after everything I'd been through I wanted to get out of my rut, so I decided to give him a chance. I thought I'd go on one date and that's it, but then we went out again, then again, and eventually became exclusive. My feelings about him didn't really change. There wasn't really a romantic spark, and the sex was just okay, but he was a solid, successful guy, the type of guy I *should* like, and after going through so much, I could finally envision a life without Colin.

After several months of dating, Michael asked me to marry him. My friends were happy for me and my mother was thrilled that I was marrying "a fancy Italian lawyer." Michael, who'd recently graduated from Rutgers Law School, was working as an estate attorney for a firm in Manhattan. We had a beautiful wedding at Tavern on the Green, then the boys were born and they became my main focus. I loved being a mom and Michael was a great provider. But our "lack of spark issues" continued. There was almost no romance in our marriage. We didn't have date nights or go on vacations without the kids and sex was always predictable, mechanical. I almost always faked orgasms. I never told him this because I would never hurt him in this way, but I just wasn't attracted to him. It had nothing to do with his looks or his personality—it just was what it was. He was a friend, companion, a partner. We made big financial decisions well together and, aside from conflicts about raising kids, we got along well; most of the time, anyway.

Sometimes I didn't know if we'd last long term, or if we'd decide to get divorced when the kids went away to college. But I'd never seriously thought about leaving him. It was hard to know where Michael's head was at. He was introverted, secretive, hard to read. There were times I'd suspected he was cheating on me, but I'd never considered cheating on him. Not that I didn't have opportunities. Occasionally ex-boyfriends from high school and college reached out on social media—usually when they were going through divorces—and random men hit on me, but the only other guy I'd actually fantasized about was Colin. When Michael and I were having sex, I couldn't get into it at all without a vivid Colin fantasy. I used to feel bad about it, like I was being deceitful, but when I got turned on it turned Michael on, so by fantasizing about Colin I was actually doing Michael a favor. Well, this is what I told myself anyway.

I knew that my Colin fantasies weren't normal, that I was still obsessed with him and it wasn't healthy. Despite my involvement—okay, *over*involvement—with my kids, I couldn't get Colin out of my head. Sometimes I thought I saw him—in crowds, or even in the background of live events on TV. Once, watching the Grammys with friends, I shouted out, "Colin!" The sightings were far less frequent than they'd been during the first few weeks after he disappeared, but the fantasies of him returning someday had never fully waned. For years, I'd been having a recurring dream—I'm on the beach screaming for Colin the way I'd been screaming that night, and then he comes out of the ocean—in his turquoise bathing suit. Weirdly, he isn't wet at all, and the moon is big and bright, and I run to him; it takes a long time to get there, but when I finally do, we hug in the moonlight and he promises he'll never, ever leave me again.

JASON MRAZ WAS singing "I'm Yours" and my pillow was soaked with tears. I hadn't cried this much in years, since the height of my grieving about Colin, when everything seemed dark and hopeless. Since then, I'd had relatives and friends pass away, but nothing had upset me as much as losing Colin did, maybe because of the way I'd lost him—so suddenly, with so many unanswered questions. My last chance to see him again was today, at Columbus Circle. Now it didn't matter if he was alive or dead, because he was gone from my life, as if a current had sucked him out into the ocean all over again.

While I felt ridiculous for crying over a guy who'd ghosted me before ghosting was even a thing, it was still impossible for me to hate him. I'd never loved a man like I'd loved Colin, and I needed to know what happened to him that day and why he abandoned me and our future. Maybe I didn't need closure anymore, but I wanted answers.

I was looking at the last photo I'd taken of him in Manhattan, before our weekend on Shelter Island. I remembered that moment so well—that morning, we'd had our usual amazing sex, and my body was still shaking. Now it was afternoon, and he was in a clean white button-down, with the sleeves neatly folded, leaning back casually against the tall brick wall, grinning, with his arms crossed in front of his broad chest. The photo reinforced that I wasn't making any of this up. The man I'd seen today was, without a doubt, Colin—his body had barely changed. I zoomed in on the photo, focusing on his face and his hazel eyes. I stared so intensely that my eyes were stinging, and I had to blink, but I didn't look away. I knew I should stop looking at the photo, that this wasn't doing me any good, but I did what I used to do on those darkest days after he disappeared—and continued to scroll through old photos of him, focusing on his eyes, telling myself that the answers were in his eyes, that if I stared into them long enough, all of the mysteries would be solved.

FOUR

"CARSON, YOU FORGOT your lunch."

With the front door open, I was leaning into the hall, dangling the plastic bag with the turkey sandwich I'd prepared and a KIND bar. Carson was by the elevators.

"Sorry, Ma," he said, dashing over to grab the bag from me, and then he sprinted back, just in time to get on.

It was just past eight thirty. Carson had hockey practice this morning at Chelsea Piers. Hockey was all Michael's idea, not Carson's. Carson didn't like hockey or any sports really. He was a musical theater kid, like his brother, but Michael had been practically forcing hockey on Carson since he was about five years old—sending him to after-school hockey programs, taking him to Rangers games. Although Michael always denied it vehemently, it was obvious he believed hockey would prevent him from ending up with two gay sons. I thought Michael's position was ridiculous, and incredibly insulting to Carson *and* Harrison. It was one of the major issues we'd been discussing in couples counseling.

"Have fun!" I called out to Carson as the elevator doors

closed.

Michael and Harrison were still asleep. Harrison had returned home from Justin's place late last night after Michael and Carson returned from dinner.

In the kitchen, I made a second cup of hazelnut in the Keurig. I'd already showered and put on jeans and the nice silk blouse I'd gotten at a boutique on Madison Avenue last month. I'd lost a couple of pounds since then, but the blouse fit nicely, looked better than I expected. I put on a little makeup—eyeliner, blush, lipstick, then went out to our balcony to record my daily TikTok.

I spent a few minutes making sure my hair looked just right, then I set up my camera and started recording:

"Hey, everybody, Vanessa here from Get Organized with Vanessa. Summer is almost here, and you know what that means—it's time to get organized! Are there any procrastinators out there? Anyone feeling like they want to put off a project because it's too overwhelming, or too complicated, or too *whatever*? Do you ever feel so overwhelmed by a project that you keep procrastinating, figuring you'll get to it eventually? Well, don't worry, you're not alone! I feel the same way sometimes and you know what I do? I just dive in and do it. Sounds simple, I know, but the only way to get a project done is to dive in and get started. You know the feeling you get when you accomplish something? Something challenging that you've been putting off for a long time? Well, imagine having that amazing feeling right now—use it as your motivation. You'll feel amazing, I promise!"

Not my best video, but it was far from my worst, and I'd done it in one take—not bad. Sitting in the leather armchair in the living room, I quickly did some editing, adding captions like "STOP PROCRASTINATING" and "EMBRACE THE

CHALLENGE" in one of the fun squiggly "signature fonts" I liked to use. As soon as I posted it, I got a good response—lots of likes and comments in the first few minutes, a great sign.

I answered a few work emails, including sending a follow-up to Angie Ferguson, whom I'd met with on the west side yesterday. I wrote that it was lovely meeting her and discussing her project and that I'd follow up with a full proposal by Monday. It felt good, taking my own advice about not procrastinating and getting some work out of the way.

On purpose, I hadn't tried to track down Colin's taxi yet. Before I fell asleep last night, I'd figured there was nothing I could do in the middle of the night anyway, but I also didn't want to start searching, fearing it might only lead to disappointment. What if the medallion number didn't lead to anything? I didn't have a plan B. I also hadn't felt this much hope about anything in a long time, and I wanted to savor it.

I searched online and found a site to locate taxi drivers by their medallion numbers. I entered the number for Colin's taxi. Rather than a driver's name, the name of a taxi company had come up—TaxiFleet Management LLC. The company probably owned or managed numerous taxis. There was a phone number with a 718 area code, so the company was probably in Brooklyn or Queens. I was imagining meeting Colin later today, looking into his hazel eyes again and kissing him slowly and passionately. It was a fantasy I'd had maybe thousands of times since he died—or was presumed dead—but it had never felt like this. This felt real, like we were actually *there*, like we were actually—

"Morning."

I hadn't heard Michael enter the room or approach behind me. Instinctively, I swiped away the Safari app and tapped the Instagram app.

"Hey, good morning."

His gaze darted briefly toward my phone; maybe he'd noticed me switch apps, like I was trying to conceal something.

"Everything okay?" he asked.

"Yeah, I was just responding to comments on the videos I posted from last night. Everyone thinks Harrison was amazing and did such a great job."

"Yeah, people really seemed to like it."

"All of that practice paid off, and he really loved working with Thalia. I hope they have a chance to work together again. It really makes a difference who the director is, and Thalia really likes Harrison and I think that's so important too."

Without responding, Michael headed into the kitchen. I returned to Safari, to the page with the phone number for TaxiFleet Management and screenshotted it. Then I found the company's address—in Sunnyside, Queens—and screenshotted the page. Then, back on Instagram, I liked or loved the comments people had made on my videos and the collage from the show last night and I occasionally responded to the comments with short comments, like "Thanks so much!" or "You're so awesome!" or just heart emojis.

Michael reentered, holding a mug of coffee.

"So…are we good?"

Responding to a comment from Kerry Fong, an old friend from elementary school on Staten Island, with three heart emojis, I said to Michael, "Good? Why wouldn't we be good?"

I knew he meant the tension between us last night, but also "good" in general.

"Yeah, I just couldn't go to dinner last night, if that's what you mean."

"Just making sure," he said.

"Why? Did your mother say something?"

"No, it's not that."

"Because she probably thought I was lying about falling to get out of dinner. Maybe I should send her pics of my bruises to prove it."

"She believes you fell, Vanessa. I'm talking about us. Is there something we need to discuss?"

"No, I told you what happened. It has nothing to do with us."

"Come on, Vanessa, I'm just trying to be proactive here. That's what Donna told us to do, right? Discuss things when they come up, not let them simmer."

Donna was our therapist in couples counseling. We'd started seeing her about nine months ago. We talked about the usual problems—not enough sex, not enough communication, not enough closeness. I didn't think we were making much progress, but at least it gave us something to do together on Monday evenings. In a way, the sessions had become our date night.

"Well, in this case I seriously have nothing to discuss," I said. "Nothing's *simmering* on my end. We're also not supposed to overanalyze each other's language, remember? That's what Donna said. So maybe it's better to wait till Monday to talk about this, at the appointment."

"That's totally fine. Like I said, I'm just trying to check in, make sure everything's okay. But if you're telling me things are fine on your end, that's all I need to know."

"How about bagels for breakfast?" I was standing.

"Sounds like a plan," Michael said, "or I can make omelets."

"We only have a couple of eggs—I have to do a FreshDirect order later. It's no big deal, I'll run out. It'll be nice to have a special breakfast for Harrison when he wakes up, and he loves bagels. Do you want lox spread?"

Michael said whatever I wanted to pick up was fine with him. I hurried out of the apartment, telling him I'd see him soon.

In the elevator, on my phone, I opened the screenshot I'd taken and, as I was exiting the building through the revolving doors, leading to the large courtyard, I called TaxiFleet.

I listened to several rings, beginning to fear that it was a bad number that would never connect me to the company, or the driver of the cab Colin had gotten into, or Colin himself.

Then a woman answered.

"Taxi." She had a Slavic accent.

"Hey!" I sounded like I'd just connected with a beloved relative. "I'm so happy I got through. My name is Vanessa Rizzo."

"*What?*"

I realized I was either speaking too fast, or not loud enough. So louder and slower, I said, "My name is Vanessa Rizzo. I need to contact the driver of a taxi I was in yesterday."

I hadn't planned to lie when I made the call, but it felt like the right decision. If I said I wanted to contact the driver of a cab I wasn't in, would she really agree to help?

"What happened? You lost something?"

"Yes, actually. A bracelet. I lost a bracelet."

"I'll give you the number of lost and found. Got a pen?"

"Oh, can you please give me the driver's name and number? I'd like to contact him directly."

"We don't give that information."

"*Please.*" I was trying to sound as desperate and upset as I possibly could; I was practically crying. "You don't understand. I lost my grandmother's bracelet in that cab, and I already called lost and found and they don't have it. Please, I'm begging you, I just need to talk to the driver. Maybe he found it or saw someone who took it."

Patti Glazer, a neighbor whose son Ben was friends with Carson, had left the building and was passing by. She must've overheard some of my pleading because she was squinting in a concerned way. I smiled at her as if saying, *Don't worry, it's fine,* and she continued toward the street.

The woman at TaxiFleet was silent. I didn't know what I'd do if she refused to give me the information. Maybe I'd have to go to Brooklyn or Queens and beg in person.

Finally, she said, "I lost my mother's necklace once, on a train; she never forgave me. I know how you feel. Okay, one time only. Got a pen?"

I didn't but I tapped the number into my notes app.

"Do you have his name too?"

"Singh. Mr. Singh with an H, but you didn't get it from me."

"Thank you. You're a lifesaver."

"Hope you find the bracelet." She ended the call.

As I walked toward First Avenue, I called Singh but reached an automated voicemail. I left my number but figured I'd try again later.

At Tal Bagels, I was waiting in line to order when my phone vibrated with Singh's number displaying.

"Hi," I said excitedly. "Thank you for calling me back so quickly."

"This Vanessa?"

"Yes, I—"

"What do you want?"

"Well, I…This is going to sound a little, well, unusual, but yesterday at around a little before seven—you picked up a man near Columbus Circle. Do you remember that?"

"How'd you get my phone number?"

"Um, wasn't easy. Took some detective work. I saw the medallion number on the side of the cab and I—"

"What do you want? C'mon, c'mon."

"I just want to know if you remember by any chance where you dropped that man off."

"How am I supposed to remember some guy?"

"He was tall, in his forties, close cropped afro, black leather jacket."

"Look, I can't talk now, okay?"

"Please, Mr. Singh. Can you just tell me where you dropped him off? He's a relative, my cousin, and his mother's dying and I—"

"Your cousin's dying?"

"No, my mother. I mean, *his* mother. Please, can you just help me?"

Maybe my desperation was finally getting through because he said, "Yesterday?"

"Yes. Yesterday. Columbus Circle."

"I came back from LaGuardia. I think I remember. Midtown."

"Where in midtown?"

"I went to the thirties. East, okay?"

"Where in the thirties?"

"I dunno, okay? Thirty-seventh, -eighth? I dunno, okay?"

"Do you know where he went?"

"No, okay? Look, I gotta go."

"Do you know if he went into a building or—"

"No, I don't know nothing. Bye, okay? Bye."

He ended the call.

There were mainly office buildings on Park Avenue near Thirty-seventh Street, but there were also hotels. What if he was staying at a hotel, but only for a day? He could be checking out this morning. If I didn't return home with the bagels, it could cause more drama with Michael, but how did I know this wasn't my only, and maybe last chance, to see Colin again, and find out what the hell was going on?

I left the line, hailed a cab and said to the driver, "Thirty-seventh and Park."

As we headed downtown, I tapped out a text to Michael:

Ugh, got a call from my new client, Angie Ferguson on the west side. Her son doesn't like my design and I need to adjust. Will pick up bagels on way home before Harrison gets up. Sorry!

I got a notification that Michael had read my text, but he didn't respond to it. He was probably pissed off at me and thought I wasn't bringing the bagels home to be passive-aggressive, but I'd deal with him later.

As the cab cut over to Park Avenue and then wound through the Helmsley Building, I was imagining going into the lobby of a hotel, asking to see Colin, and Colin appearing. What would it feel like to actually see him again, from up close? It would be beyond surreal. What would I say to him? I would be excited and happy and angry all at once. I had no idea how I'd react, or how he'd react, what possible explanation he could have for what had happened.

Only when the cab dropped me at the corner of Park and Thirty-seventh did I realize how bleak my prospects actually were. There were mainly office buildings and larger residential buildings—most of the hotels were further downtown. I walked downtown to Twenty-Eighth along the west side of Park, then I crossed and went uptown along the east side. I glanced into mainly vestibules, hoping to spot Colin, though I quickly realized this was ridiculous. What was I thinking coming down here? I'd spotted him getting into that cab about fifteen hours ago. Even if Singh was remembering correctly about where he'd dropped him, that didn't mean that he was staying in the area, or living in the area, or had stayed in the area for any significant amount of time. He could've met someone, gone out to dinner, or did practically *anything*, but there was no reason to believe he was still around here. Contacting the taxi company and Singh had been a total waste of time.

Since I was down here anyway, I went into a few of the doorman buildings, asking at the concierge desks if Colin Grant lived here. They all said no. I went to the Kitano Hotel—no Colin Grant. I walked downtown again, past Thirty-fourth, where there were several large hotels. The Mondrian seemed like a "Colin type place"—well, at least the Colin I'd known. He grew up in Europe and came to the United States to go to medical school at Mount Sinai. He was smart, edgy, and stylish. The hotel had a trendy, Euro vibe with techno music playing. A thin guy with a man bun came out from the back.

"Good morning, can I help you?"

"Hey, yeah," I said, "I'm looking for a friend of mine who might be staying at the hotel. Colin Grant."

Looking at the screen, the guy said, "Sorry, we have no guest by that name."

"I must've made a mistake. Thank you."

I tried two more nearby hotels, then the letdown fully hit. Since spotting Colin yesterday evening and especially since talking to Singh, I'd been in a hyped-up, semi-delusional state. Despite the horrible odds, on some level I truly believed that I'd somehow find Colin again, that it was only a matter of time. But now reality was setting in.

Wandering east, toward First Avenue, I told myself that things probably weren't as hopeless as they seemed. I knew that I had the tendency to look at things in a distorted way, especially during an intense, emotional situation. When I was in what one of my shrinks had called a "mind storm," I had difficulty putting things in perspective, or fully under-standing my behavior or reactions. After time passed and things settled, I could usually see situations more clearly.

But I just hoped that I was right, that the storm would pass and that I wasn't about to spiral.

FIVE

I ENTERED MY apartment and saw Michael and Harrison sitting at the table, having scrambled eggs and toast. I'd been so caught up in my thoughts that I'd completely forgotten to go back and get the bagels.

"Oh, great, you picked up stuff for breakfast," I said. "I was hoping you did. Sorry, I got so caught up."

"Hi, Mom," Harrison said.

"Morning, sweetie."

"Your pics are getting lots of likes." Harrison was looking at his phone.

"Not surprised one bit," I said. "You were so amazing last night."

Michael, focused on eating, hadn't looked at me since I walked in.

"So how did the design adjustment go?"

This comment was loaded. He was obviously making a dig about me forgetting the bagels, but he was also belittling my career. Although I'd been kicking ass lately, I knew he still didn't take my work seriously as a business. He used to tell me things like, "It's a nice hobby, but you should think about getting a real job." He hadn't made a comment like this lately, but his overall attitude about my work hadn't changed, and he knew how much this infuriated me.

Glaring back at him, I said, "It went well, thanks."

"Yeah, I bet it did."

"What? You don't believe me?"

"Of course I believe you." He still wasn't looking at me. "Why wouldn't I believe you?"

"Maybe because you won't look at me, and because your attitude's disgusting."

"*My* attitude's disgusting?"

While Harrison was seemingly ignoring us, I knew he was listening and was probably getting upset. He was a sensitive kid and had always had a hard time when there was tension between Michael and me. Sometimes he would withdraw; sometimes he'd act out in other ways.

"Well, you two enjoy breakfast," I said, forcing myself to sound cheery. I went over and kissed Harrison on top of his head and then said, "So proud of you. Love you."

"Love you too," he said, returning to scrolling.

After breakfast, Harrison said he was going out to meet some friends.

"We'll see you later," I said. "I can't wait to see you crush it again tonight."

In the kitchen, I checked my Instagram, responding to comments on my posts from last night. In the dining room, Michael called out that he was going to "catch up on some work," and then I heard him head to the bedroom where he had a mini home office set up in a corner, with a small desk and a laptop, and I heard the door close.

I was still feeling anxious about the Colin situation, and

the tension with Michael wasn't helping. Cleaning and organizing usually helped to relax me, made me feel more in control. So, I straightened up a little around the apartment, cleaning the coffee table with Windex, and aligning the remotes just the way I liked them, then I worked on a project I'd been meaning to get to—reorganizing the kitchen cabinet below the sink. I took out all of the large pots and saucepans, scrubbed the cabinet until it was spotless, and then replaced the pots and pans in a better, more functional way, with the pots we rarely moved far in the back. Unfortunately, organizing didn't do the trick—I was still feeling very stressed. A barre class would've helped, but I didn't think that exercising was a great idea when I still had pain and stiffness from the car hitting me yesterday. I did my next favorite stress-reducing activity—I plopped myself on the couch and watched a true crime show on Netflix.

I'd already seen a few episodes in this series, about a mother who killed her four children and her husband during a camping trip in Vermont. As I expected, the violent, gruesome, disturbing show helped to distract me and made me feel like my own problems were a little more manageable.

After two episodes, I went into the bedroom. Michael was still at work on his laptop, tapping on the keyboard, and didn't hear me enter. As I approached behind him, he turned, startled, as if I'd sneaked up on him.

"Who'd you think it was?" I asked, smiling.

"Sorry, I just didn't hear you come in."

"Busy?" I gazed past him, toward the screen where some legal document was displayed.

He minimized the screen—maybe just out of habit—then said, "I was just, um, finishing up some work. I'm doing an estate plan for a new client, and it's a pretty complicated one."

"Oh, I can let you finish."

"No, I'm pretty much done actually. So…do you want to talk?"

"I thought we agreed to wait till counseling."

"I want to talk now."

"Well, there's really nothing to talk about on my end, but I can tell you're annoyed with me for some reason."

He gave me a look that said, *Come on.*

"I'm not an idiot, Vanessa. I know something's going on."

I backed up a little, crossing my arms in front of my chest. "And what exactly do you think is going on?"

"I don't know, why don't you tell me?"

"I told you, I have no—"

"Come on, we both know things have been tense lately. Then, last night, the way you rushed home."

"I wasn't feeling well. You know I fell. I still have a bad bruise on my hip. Wanna see?"

I unsnapped my jeans as he said, "I don't need to see the bruise, but what about today? The bruise didn't stop you from going wherever you were going when you said you were getting bagels."

"Last night I was shaken up, I feel a little better today. I told you, I went to Angie Ferguson's."

"Come on, I know you weren't at Angie Ferguson's. Are you going to tell me where you really were?"

I stared at him, then said, "How do you know I wasn't there?"

"How do you think I know?"

"I don't know, why don't you tell me?"

"All right. I went into your contacts on your laptop. I called her and asked her if you were there and she said you weren't."

"You went into my *contacts*?"

"Yes."

I couldn't believe this.

"Oh my God, you didn't really reach out to her, did you?"

I could tell he had.

"How could you do that, Michael? Do you realize how embarrassing that is for me? She's my client. What if I started contacting *your* clients?"

"I don't like being in the dark. I want to know what's going on."

"What did you say to her?"

"What diff—"

"She's a client. I know you don't give a shit about my business but…I want to know what you said."

"I told her I couldn't reach you and wanted to make sure you were okay."

"Wow. And you don't think there's anything wrong with that?"

"Not when you're acting shady."

"*I'm* acting shady? How exactly is not bringing home bagels shady? You had no right to go into my contacts."

"So, I guess the rules that apply to me don't apply to you?"

Of course, I knew exactly what Michael was alluding to. A few months ago, he was working on his laptop in the dining room, and I noticed that he had his Messenger app opened and he was DMing with Jennifer Sears, an ex-girlfriend, and the chat included several heart emojis. When he realized I was behind him, he immediately closed the chat, which made the whole thing seem even more suspicious. When I asked him why he was sending her heart emojis, he said that her sister just had another baby and he was congratulating her.

"That's different," I said. "I didn't go into your personal files, I just happened to notice something that seemed suspicious, so I—"

"Seemed suspicious," he said. "Exactly."

"What did I do that was so suspicious? I forgot to pick up bagels."

"Okay, so where did you go?"

"I was just taking a long walk. For real."

"A long walk with your bad hip?"

"It's only a bruise. I can still walk."

"Where did you walk to?"

"Nowhere. Just around the neighborhood."

"The neighborhood." He still seemed incredulous. "Come on, Vanessa, just be honest, tell me what's going on, I know things haven't been great with us, we haven't been getting along. Did you meet someone? Is it what's-his-name? That guy with the glasses you're always talking to at Harrison's shows?"

"*Andrew*? Justin's father? That's crazy."

"Is it? Come on, it's obvious he's into you. Did you tell him we're having trouble? We're in counseling? Because when you tell a guy you're in counseling, he sees an opening and he thinks he can work his way in."

I *had* told Andrew, in passing, that I was in counseling, but I said, "Stop it, that's crazy. You really think I have something going on with Harrison's boyfriend's father?"

"Why not? He's divorced, right? You have a lot in common—both theater lovers." He said this like it was something repulsive.

"Well, the answer is no," I said. "*I'm* not a cheater."

I was purposely implying that if anyone was cheating in this marriage, it was him. He looked at me, like he was trying to read my mind, then said, "I know you too well, Vanessa. Maybe it's not that Andrew guy, but I know when something's wrong, I know when your anxiety starts acting up, when…" He cut himself off, as if he was having a revelation. "This isn't about what I think it's about, is it?"

We both knew he was referring to Colin. I wasn't sure how to respond.

Finally, I said, "What if it is?"

"Seriously?" He looked exasperated, like he was back in the middle of a crisis. "I thought you'd moved past all that."

"See? This is why I didn't want to talk about this with you, because I knew you'd judge me like you always do."

"Then it really does have to do with Colin?"

I turned away, shaking my head. Finally, I turned back and said, "Yes. Yes, it's about Colin, all right? So, the fuck what? I hate that I have to, that I have to…" I was searching for the right word, then went with "…*tiptoe* around everything with you. Why can't I just tell you everything that's going on and why can't that just be okay?"

I knew I wasn't being entirely accurate in describing how I felt, but we'd had similar conversations so many times I knew he got the gist.

"Jesus Christ, Vanessa. So where do you think you saw him this time? In a crowd, I'm sure. That's what it usually is. You spot a random face in a crowd and tell yourself that it must be Colin, that he must still be alive, even though you *know* he's not."

I hated his tone, like he was talking to a crazy person.

"Ugh, why do you have to get like this? So fucking condescending?"

"I just can't believe that this is what this is about—another Colin sighting. So last night, when you left the theater early, it had to do with you thinking you saw *Colin*?"

"I didn't think I saw him. This time I actually saw him."

His look said, *Please*.

"Well, whether you believe it or not, it's true."

Talking fast, I explained how I'd spotted Colin yesterday and managed to take video of the cab he'd gotten into. I also told him that I got hit by a car, that I didn't trip.

"Are you serious with this? *A car* hit you?"

"Yes. Why? You think I'm making that up too? I was distracted, trying to get Colin's attention, and a car slammed into me."

"Well, thank God you weren't seriously hurt. But why didn't you tell me?"

Because I knew you'd act like this.

"What was the point of telling you? So you could judge me? Make me feel like a crazy person?"

"You should get checked out. We should go to the ER."

"It's okay. Thanks, I'm fine, if it was anything serious, I'd know by now. It could've been worse, and I'm sorry I wasn't honest with you about it right away, I really am. I just didn't want to get into a whole *thing*, having to explain to your parents and everyone what had happened. I wanted the night to be about Harrison."

He seemed confused. "Wait, so what does all of this have to do with where you were today?"

"Well, because I was out…trying to find Colin."

"Trying to find Colin." He repeated back, like it was a complicated concept that he needed to process. "I thought you saw him, or you *thought* you saw him, getting into a cab?"

"I *saw* him."

"But you didn't speak to him, right?"

"No, I yelled his name, but I don't think he heard me."

"So then how were you looking for him today? *Where* were you looking?"

I explained how I contacted the taxi company and then tried to find Colin this morning. As I spoke, Michael seemed to become increasingly uncomfortable.

"Look, okay," I said, "I know I've gotten a little obsessed about all this, okay? I'm aware of that. But I'm fine. Really, I am."

"A *little* obsessed?"

"Awareness is a good sign though, isn't it? Those other times I wasn't aware and that's what made it worse. That's why this time is different. That's why I'm not concerned about having a setback. This time it's real, I actually saw Colin. He's actually alive, in New York, and he might *still* be in New York."

Michael was glaring at me, with no effect, like I was a misbehaving child.

"You know I really don't appreciate this," I said. "You call my client to check up on me, and now accuse me of having an affair, and then you act like *I'm* the one who owes you some kind of apology? I told you what happened and now I just have to figure out where he is, and why he's back, and what happened nineteen years ago."

"There's nothing to figure out, Vanessa, because you didn't see him today, and you didn't see him those other times either. Colin's been dead for a long time. I thought you accepted that. I thought you promised you were past that, that this would never happen again."

It was true, I *had* promised this, more than once.

"I *was* past it," I said, "but then yesterday happened."

"Nothing happened yesterday. Vanessa, please, don't do this again." Now he had a sad, hurt expression. "Don't put me through this, don't put the kids through this. It's too much."

"You want proof? Okay, I'll show you proof."

On my phone, I showed him the image of Colin from the video I'd taken.

"What's that supposed to be?" Michael was glancing at the phone, obviously not looking closely.

"Just look," I said. "*Look.*"

"What am I looking at?"

"*Colin.* That's him in the back of the cab. And that's how I got the medallion number of the cab he got into."

Michael squinted at the phone. "*That's* Colin?"

Michael had seen photos of Colin, so he knew what he looked like. Well, at least how he looked about twenty years ago.

"Yes, I know it's a little blurry, but that's definitely—"

"A *little* blurry? Come on, Vanessa. It's impossible to tell who it is, I can barely tell that it's a man and not a woman."

"That's ridiculous. It's a clear shot; you can see him clearly. Look at the jawline…and the hair. Besides, I *saw* him. I know what I saw."

"Okay…you can put the phone down now."

He sounded like he was telling a suicidal person to drop a gun.

"Stop talking to me that way."

"What way?"

"Like…like there's something wrong with me. I saw Colin, he's alive. I always knew there was a chance he was alive, so it's not totally shocking. I get why you're concerned, because you think I'm going to get obsessed again, but that's not happening—that *won't* happen."

"You called a cab company. Then went looking for him today."

"So? Why shouldn't I look for him? I don't see what's so unusual about that. Am I supposed to just forget I saw him?"

"You'll never get answers, Vanessa. Sometimes you have to just let go."

He sounded sincere, like a therapist counseling a patient, but there was something so disingenuous about it.

"Why can't you be supportive, instead of so fucking cynical? This time is different than all those other times, okay? Don't you get it? This time I have a photo. This time I have *evidence*."

"You have to stop, Vanessa—for the boys."

I knew why he was playing "the boys" card, because he knew that bringing up the boys always got to me. I knew he was trying to manipulate me to get what he wanted, but it worked anyway. My children always trumped everything.

"It doesn't matter," I said. "Whether I saw him or not, I'm not going to find him. All I know is the cab he got into, but he might not even be in the city anymore, he might be on a different continent."

"So you'll let it go?" Michael asked.

"I don't have any choice," I said. "I mean, if I somehow found him of course I wouldn't let it go. I'd want to talk to him, just to find out what happened, why he did what he did, so I wouldn't have to go through life not knowing. Why isn't that normal? Why can't you understand that?"

"I think you should reach out to Dr. Stone," Michael said. "Just for a check in."

I hadn't seen Stone in a couple of years. I still had some

Klonopin but hadn't taken any lately.

"Why would I do that? There's nothing wrong with me."

"I think it would be a good idea, just to report what happened."

"I don't need to see a psychiatrist to try to convince me that I didn't see what I know I saw, especially when I have proof of what I saw."

"Well, maybe you should just trust me. Maybe I have some perspective that you don't right now. I'm more removed from the situation. I can see what you can't."

"I can see just fine, thanks. *I* know I'm fine."

"I'm not saying you aren't." He was raising his voice. "I'm just saying, why not have a couple of sessions with him, just to check in? You used to rave about him, say he was the best psychiatrist you ever had."

I let out an exaggerated annoyed breath, then marched away, into the kitchen. I poured a glass of diet iced tea and drank it, standing, leaning against the sink, staring at the cabinets. I didn't look at Michael when he entered.

"Sorry, I think that came out harsher than I meant it," Michael said. "Obviously do whatever you think is best. If you don't want to see Stone, don't see him. It's just a suggestion, that's all."

I still hated his tone, but I didn't want to get into an argument about the way he was speaking to me. That's how things always escalated with us, when we went from talking about *something* to talking about nothing.

"Don't worry, I have it under control," I said. "This isn't like other times—that I can promise you. I have coping strategies now. If I feel myself slipping, like I can't handle things, yes, I'll go see Dr. Stone, okay? But that's not going to be necessary. I'll just let it go, forget I even saw Colin. Just from talking about it I feel like I'm getting it out of my system."

Michael came over and kissed me on the forehead and said, "I know you'll be okay. You're incredibly strong and I love you."

I hated how condescending he sounded, like he was the authority on strength, and I should feel flattered because he'd declared me strong.

Well, the flattery wasn't working.

"Love you too," I said.

I watched him walk away, then I glanced at my phone, which was still displaying the photo of the cab and Colin inside it.

Fuck forgetting—Colin was alive, and I was going to find him.

SIX

CARSON'S BODY ODOR was stinking up the entire apartment.

"Oh my god." I had my T-shirt pulled up over my mouth and nose. "Get yourself in the shower right this instant, before I have to fumigate you."

"But I'm starving, Ma."

"I don't care, let's go, right now." I held him by the hand, dragging him toward the bathroom. "You're in puberty now, you have to wear deodorant *and* antiperspirant."

"That's disgusting."

"No, *you're* disgusting, but you won't be as soon as you shower." I shoved him into the bathroom, then shut the door. "And wash your hair too!"

Michael came out of the bedroom in jeans and a gray button-down.

"What's going on?"

"Can't you *smell* what's going on?"

He winced, knowing the familiar stench all too well. "Jesus."

"Sorry, Dad!" Carson yelled from the bathroom.

"You're ready to go already?" I said to Michael. "We don't have to be at the theater for another couple of hours."

"I know, Rob just texted. He wants to meet for a beer, so I thought I'd swing to the west side for a quick one, then meet you later at the show."

Rob Heller was a friend of Michael's, his old roommate at Cornell.

"Oh, that's fine," I said. "I want to get there earlier anyway and help out tonight if I can."

"Sounds awesome," Michael said. "See you later."

He kissed me quickly on the lips, then put on his loafers near the door and left.

Of course, Carson took forever in the shower. His showers were getting longer and longer lately—it wasn't exactly a mystery why—but it was annoying when we were in a rush to go somewhere.

I gave him another five minutes, then I banged on the door and said, "Come on, we have to get going."

"Ok, one minute, Ma!"

Ten minutes later he came out.

"When we're in a hurry it's not fair to take your time in there," I said.

"What's the big rush? The show doesn't start till seven-thirty."

"I know, but I want to get there early to help out. Suji's bringing Jack and Kathleen is coming with Aiden."

Excited because now he knew a few of his friends would be there, Carson was dressed and ready to go within a few minutes.

Hailing a cab on First Avenue, I flashed back to yesterday evening—seeing Colin, screaming his name while trying to chase down his taxi, the car hitting me. When I sat in the cab, I took deep breaths, trying to center myself.

"Where to?"

I was aware that the driver had already asked me this at least once.

"Sorry. Seventy-fifth and Third, please."

Is it possible I was in Singh's taxi?

Although I knew the odds of this happening were nearly impossible, so were the odds of seeing my supposedly dead ex-fiancé and *that* had happened. My pulse was throbbing as I checked the photo adjacent to the partition—of course it wasn't Singh.

I took deep breaths, trying to calm myself. I definitely had anxiety symptoms, and I'd probably need more than my "coping strategies" to get through it. In the past, getting on meds sooner rather than later always turned out to be a good idea.

"You okay, Ma?"

Carson was looking over at me with a concerned expression.

"Yes, yes…I'm totally fine."

"You were breathing funny."

"I said I'm fine."

When Carson got reinvolved in whatever he was doing on his phone, I looked at mine, at the photo of Colin. I didn't know if what Michael had said last night was having an effect on me, or if I was just doubting myself in general, but now the photo seemed blurred—more blurred than yesterday somehow—and it was hard to make out any specific details of his face. *Was it Colin?* It could be him, yes, but it also could be somebody else. I reminded myself that when I'd seen him getting into the cab I was certain it was him, but when I looked at the photo yesterday, I was also positive it was him, so if I was uncertain about the photo now, how could I be certain about what I saw, or *thought* I saw?

"What's that?"

Carson was trying to glance over at my phone. I immediately shut the display.

"Nothing," I said, distracted by my thoughts.

"Why'd you take a picture of a taxi?"

"How about you mind your own business or do you want me to look through *your* phone. Is that what you want?"

His eyes widened with panic. "Okay, I just asked a question. Sorry."

As the cab continued uptown, I stared out the window, through my hazy reflection. My eyes were tearing a little, blurring my vision even more. My pulse was still racing, and I worried I'd have a full-blown panic attack. Without turning toward Carson, I reached over and put my hand over his and squeezed a little.

"No, I'm sorry, sweetie. I didn't mean to snap."

"It's okay, Ma."

It wasn't okay. Irritability was another symptom I had to watch out for.

Maybe Michael had been right—maybe I did need to make that appointment with Dr. Stone as soon as possible.

I WAS GLAD I got to the theater early. Hanging out with Isabella, Francine, and Staci—chatting about the kids, schools, theater, was a welcome injection of normalcy into my day. I helped Charles, the stage manager, organize the props, and it was nice to hear raves about Harrison. Then Thalia, the director, joined us.

"I really think he's getting better and better," she said. "You can see his confidence growing, not just with his singing, but with his acting too. I mean, just in the past year alone he's played Doody and Connor. Talk about range! And for a kid his age it's really extraordinary."

"Thank you," I said. "It means so much to me to hear you say that, coming from you, especially because I know how hard he works and how dedicated he is."

"Just putting this out there," Thalia said, "but Harrison has told me he'd love to audition for film, TV and even Broadway opportunities. Of course there are no guarantees, but if you feel it's right for him it's something you should explore. I have some contacts with managers in the city. Again, no guarantees, but I think he definitely has the talent."

"Wow, it's so flattering to hear you say that," I said. "It's something I'm going to have to discuss with Michael and Harrison, though."

"I understand." She was looking beyond me. "And speaking of the man himself…"

I turned, expecting to see Michael, but Harrison had just arrived, along with several of his friends and cast members. I saw a flash of paranoia and concern—no doubt he was wondering what I was talking to Thalia about. Like a typical teenager, he didn't like it when his mother got into his business, and I tried to be respectful of his space. Although he loved going to the theater with me, he didn't like it as much when I got involved with his productions, especially on performance days.

"What's up?" he asked me.

"What's up is I'm leaving." I gave him a quick hug. "Break a leg, sweetie."

I returned to the lobby where Carson was hanging out with his friends.

"Hey, Ma, can I go for pizza?"

"Of course you can, sweetie." I gave him a twenty-dollar bill. "Text me if you go anywhere else and be back here by seven-fifteen, seven-twenty the latest."

He ran out to catch up with his friends who'd already left.

Someone tapped me on the shoulder. Again, I expected Michael, but it was Andrew Reedy.

"Hey, didn't mean to startle you," he said.

"No, hey, how are you?"

"Not too bad, not too bad. Isabella, Suji and a few others and I are heading around the corner for a drink, if you'd like to join."

"Actually, a drink sounds perfect. I'd *love* that."

The women were waiting out front, and the five of us went around the corner to Orsay on Seventy-fifth and Lexington. It was one of the "go-to places" for the parents and their families to head to before and after productions.

As I sat down, I saw Colin at the bar. Well, *thought* I did. On a second glance, I realized the guy barely resembled Colin. This guy was overweight and maybe twenty years younger. Aside from their hair, they barely looked alike.

"Everything all right?"

I didn't know if Andrew had caught me staring toward the bar or was just being perceptive.

"Oh yeah, fine." I was still recovering from the adrenaline rush. "But now I *really* need that drink."

I ordered a Prosecco. The conversation, as usual, was lively. I loved this group. Everyone was down-to-earth and easy to talk to and a few of them, including Andrew, had grown up in the city, which always made me feel more connected.

When my drink came, I gulped half of it in one long, steady sip. We were talking about the usual subjects—schools and theater. Isabella and Kathleen were raving about the recent revival of *Sweeney Todd*, and I chimed in that it was "on my list." When Suji replied to a text from someone, everyone looked at their phones too. I didn't have any messages, but while I had my phone out, I tapped on the photo of Colin in the cab. I didn't care what Michael thought—the photo was clear, and it was definitely him. Maybe the other times I'd imagined seeing Colin, but this time I had proof, and I was staring at the proof right now.

"You sure everything's okay?"

Andrew was glancing over at me again.

"Oh, sorry." I put my phone away. "Just a work email."

"How's your business coming along?"

"Really well, thanks for asking. Yeah, actually I've been getting more work than I can handle lately."

"I should hire you. Justin could use some serious organizing. His ADHD can get pretty bad. I try to help him, but it gets overwhelming sometimes with work and other obligations."

"I totally get that. Everyone needs help organizing their lives, including me."

I laughed at myself.

Smiling, Andrew said, "So, tell me—where does an organizer go to get organizational help?"

"Nowhere," I said. "We're on our own."

Remembering how Michael had accused me of having an affair with Andrew, I thought, *Where had* that *come from?* It was so unlike Michael to get paranoid or jealous. He'd never been suspicious about me with Andrew or *any* guy before, even when we'd just started dating.

"Michael coming to the show tonight?"

"What? Yes." It was a little jarring that Andrew had brought up Michael at the same moment I was thinking about him. "Oh, yes, he is. He'll come a little later."

"It's great how supportive you both are of Harrison."

"Yeah, I guess so," I said.

"Well, that's how it seems."

"Yeah, but you know how it is with Michael and all his issues."

Andrew knew I was referring to Harrison's sexuality, and how Harrison was dating Justin.

"Oh, I thought that wasn't a big deal anymore."

"Nope, still an issue, and now he's also accusing me of cheating on him, that was fun."

"I'm sorry to hear that."

"It is what it is." I finished my Prosecco. Feeling like I was revealing way too much and wanting to change the subject, I said, "So how's it going with Laura?" referring to a woman he'd brought to one of Encore's previous productions.

"Laurie, you mean."

"Right, Laurie."

"We're not seeing each other anymore."

"Oh no, that's too bad, she seemed really nice."

"I thought so too, until she ghosted me."

"Seriously? That's awful."

"Eh, it's okay. I have thick skin, but it's rough out there these days. People used to take dating seriously, now on the apps everyone's so disposable...Sorry, I don't mean to be such a downer. I just never expected to be a single dad doing online dating in my forties, but here I am."

Suji interrupted: "Sorry, are you talking about *dating*?"

"Well, *not* dating per se," Andrew said.

"Because I met a woman at a party the other night who'd be perfect for you. She's a friend of a close friend and she's getting divorced. She's a professor somewhere in the city, I think Pace or another college in the city, so you have that in common. She loves theater too. Very, very sophisticated."

"Wow, she sounds amazing," I said.

"They all *sound* amazing," Andrew said, "until you start hearing about their stalker ex-boyfriends and personality disorders."

"I can get you her number from my friend," Suji said. "What do you have to lose?"

"I appreciate it," Andrew said, "but I'm really not looking to meet any new people right now."

"Well, if you change your mind, let me know."

"I definitely will."

Later, back at the theater, many more people had arrived as showtime was only a few minutes away. Carson and his friends returned from the pizza place a few minutes before curtain time, but Michael still hadn't arrived. It wasn't like him to be late for one of Harrison's shows—in fact, that had never happened. Being passive-aggressive against me was one thing, but did he really have to take it out on Harrison too?

I left Michael's ticket with Cara at the door and sat in my seat. The lights were about to dim soon so I silenced my phone. I checked my texts, but there was nothing new from Michael. While I had my phone out, I glanced at the photo of Colin—was it him or not? Now, somehow, I wasn't sure. What if, like Michael had said, I hadn't seen Colin; I'd just imagined it, like those other times? I felt foolish for how I'd acted last night and this morning, but I tried to look on the bright side—at least I hadn't sunk into a full-blown depression over it. Maybe this was progress.

The show began. During the first number, I cheered and yelled "Woohoo!" when Harrison came on stage briefly. I took some videos and pics, but then put my phone down, wanting to just enjoy the show. Ah, this was exactly what I needed tonight. There was no better mood changer than theater, no better way to let yourself get carried away to a happier place and minimize all your problems. It always made me wish that I lived in a world where I could sing a song and instantly feel better.

A few minutes later, Michael rushed in and mouthed "Sorry" as he sat next to me. While I was upset he was late, I mouthed "It's okay," just to end the tension.

During intermission, Michael said he needed to go outside "to make a work call." It wasn't unusual for him to make work calls on weekends, but he was usually specific about who he was calling; he wasn't so mysterious.

I chatted with Andrew, Suji and some other friends and we all agreed that the show was much tighter tonight as opposed to last night. About a minute before the intermission ended Michael returned from outside, seeming distracted.

"Everything okay?" I asked.

"What?" he said. "Oh, yeah, sorry, yeah, everything's fine. Just that thing I was working on earlier. It's one of those hands-on clients—everything's urgent, everything can't wait till tomorrow."

Something seemed off, but maybe it was just leftover tension from our discussion earlier.

I couldn't wait to escape into the second act. I didn't think there was any way to top the first act, but it somehow managed to. In "Disappear" and "Good for You," Harrison absolutely killed it, and I captured great video of his biggest moments. Michael also seemed to enjoy the show. As tense as things had been lately, I was still glad that Michael and I were here together.

After the show, outside the side entrance to the church, on Seventy-Sixth Street, Michael, Carson and I waited for Harrison. We were all on our phones—I was posting a video on my socials, Carson was watching YouTube videos, and Michael was texting or emailing. Then Harrison came out.

"You were so amazing," I said, hugging him.

It was a fun cab ride back home, with all of us discussing our favorite moments from the show, and I read out loud some of the amazing comments my video was already getting from family and friends.

Later, the kids were in their bedroom, and I was in bed, on my phone, posting photos of Harrison, and commenting on video and photos that other parents had taken. Michael had just showered.

"How's the reaction?" he asked.

"Great," I said. "People really love it."

"I got to admit, you were right, and I was wrong."

I glanced up from my phone. He was standing at the foot of the bed, a bath towel around his waist.

"Wrong about what? Me and Andrew?"

"That too, but I mean *everything*. I realize how ridiculous I was now, with all that pressuring Harrison and Carson to play sports. It's obvious theater's Harrison thing, and I know I have to accept who he is too."

"Wow." I had to take a moment to let this sink in, then I

said. "This is a huge shift, and it's about time and I'm thrilled. But where exactly is this coming from? I mean, why now?"

"I guess I just realize I've been wrong, and I see how happy Harrison is now, and, well, I want things to stay that way. I've also done some, you know, *soul searching* lately. I decided that life's too short to have tension with your family. Harrison really has loads of talent. I mean, I know I'm his father, but I see him out there killing it, and his singing, even his dancing, is better than all those other kids. I'd like to say he gets it from me, but I know it all comes from his mom."

"That's very sweet," I said. "Thank you for saying all of that but wow it's…it's a lot and, well, I think you should talk to Harrison about all this. I'm sure he'd love to hear what you have to say."

"Oh, we already had a talk about it. It went well."

"You and Harrison *spoke*?" I was surprised. "When?"

"Earlier today, when you were out looking for Colin."

"How come you didn't tell me? How come *nobody* told me?"

"Well, it was a father-son conversation. I wanted to respect his privacy, I guess, but—"

"Well, it couldn't have been *so* private. I mean, you're telling me now."

"I'm not trying to upset you, Vanessa. I thought you'd be happy that I—"

"I *am* happy, of course I'm happy, but if you want to make Harrison extra happy, and you really support his dreams, I was talking with Thalia, and she thinks Harrison should start auditioning for—"

"Let's go for it," Michael said.

"You serious?"

"Hell yeah. I mean, as long as it doesn't affect his grades, and he has to study for the SATs and has college applications and visits coming up, but I think he can handle it now, and he's old enough to go to auditions on his own if he wants to, so I say let's go for it, and if he needs any help coordinating anything I'll help any way I can."

"Wow, this is so exciting." I put my phone on the night table and sat up. "Thalia has mentioned some managers before, one I actually met one time at a lunch, this woman Greta. She seemed really great."

"*That* I can definitely help out with," Michael said. "I know a few entertainment attorneys who probably have manager contacts."

"Really? Wow, that would be wonderful."

As we were talking, the towel around his waist had loosened a little.

"I also want to apologize for what I said about you seeing Colin," he said. "That was wrong."

He entwined his hand in mine and squeezed a little, but I didn't squeeze back.

"No, you were probably right about all of that," I said. "I must have made a mistake and didn't see him, just like those other times. I feel silly now for believing I saw him and how carried away I got."

"No, it was my fault." He was caressing the inside of my wrist now. "I shouldn't have judged you for it and said some of the things I said. I know how hard it's been for you. Forgive me?"

I still didn't understand where this huge shift was coming from, but I wasn't going to question it. If it took a Colin sighting and a little drama last night to help jolt Michael into fixing his relationship with Harrison and bring our whole family closer, then I didn't regret any of it.

As we fell back onto our sides facing each other, his towel fell off completely. Kissing me, his clammy hand moved up under my baggy T-shirt, over my left breast. It felt awkward, like a stranger's hand, and I jerked back a little. When was the last time we'd had sex? Three months ago? Four months ago? Longer? Our sex life had been declining for years, and it was hard to feel attracted to him when we weren't getting along. Although he didn't try to initiate nearly as much as he used to, when he did, I usually told him that I was "too tired" or "not in the mood" or invented other excuses.

"Everything okay?" he asked.

"Yeah, your hand just feels a little cold."

"Oh, sorry." He rubbed his hands together, then put a hand over my breast again. "Better?"

"Yeah," I said, although it still felt cold.

I tried my best to get into it. We always got along a lot better when we were having regular sex and I wanted to get back to that. As we continued to kiss, I rubbed his muscular shoulders. He'd been going to the Equinox near his office a lot lately and he'd gotten in much better shape. For years, he'd had a dad bod or had been about twenty-five pounds overweight, depending on how you wanted to look at it. Now he had an actual six-pack, but the change in his body type was another reason why I felt like I was with someone else, a stranger.

"You look so fuckin' sexy," he said.

I didn't feel sexy—at least not right now, in bed with this stranger—but I said, "So do you."

He pushed me on to my back. As he went down on me, I was trying to focus on how good it felt, only it didn't feel good. He was pressing too hard with his tongue, and I hated how he was squeezing my thighs, like he was feeling around for fat. Then I couldn't focus on the pleasure anymore: I could only focus on my thighs.

Abruptly, I turned away onto my side.

"What's wrong?"

"My bruise," I lied.

"Oh, shit, sorry. Was I pressing on it?"

"A little bit."

"Sorry, baby."

Seriously?

Colin used to call me baby, but he could pull it off with his British accent. Michael's "baby" sounded fake, forced.

Michael continued with his stiff tongue, but I couldn't focus, so I shifted away again and said, "Your turn."

"You sure? I can keep going if you—"

"Positive."

As I went down on him, he moaned in his usual way, with an occasional "Oh, yeah" or "Oh, shit," or "Oh, fuck yeah."

I was making fake sexy sounds—*mmm, mmm hmmm, mmm*—like I was enjoying the jaw pain and the smell of his clammy balls. I guess I used to actually enjoy it, but now I was distracted, and felt very unsexy, and my TMJ was acting up a little too, and I just wanted him to come already so we could go to sleep.

To distract myself, I imagined Colin, his face glowing in the sun the last time I saw him. I was looking into his hazel eyes, and he was looking back at me, like he would never say goodbye. Now I was *actually* getting excited, and my sexy sounds weren't fake anymore, because in my head it was Colin I was going down on, not Michael.

"Oh, yeah, like that, baby, like that," Michael said. "Don't stop. Oh yeah, yeah, yeah."

I didn't want to hear Michael, though, I wanted to hear *Colin*, and I wanted to feel *Colin*. So, I climbed on top of Michael, imagining that he was Colin, and that it was *Colin's* hands squeezing my ass and *Colin* saying, "Fuck, baby, I love it." It was painful at first, but as I saw Colin clearer, it stopped hurting, and actually felt good, even great, because I was on top of *Colin*, feeling *Colin's* sweaty chest, looking into *Colin's* eyes, and *Colin's* moaning overlapping with mine as we came hard and loud together.

Catching his breath, lying next to me, Michael said, "Wow, that was fuckin' awesome, baby," but I heard Colin's voice, and smelled Colin, and it was Colin spooning me from behind, and I was speaking to Colin when I replied, "Yes. Yes, it was."

SEVEN

"I'M HEADING FOR a run."

I had just entered the living room and saw Michael kneeling near the front door in shorts and a hoodie, putting on his running sneakers.

"Oh, nice," I said. "It looks like great running weather today."

To my phone, I said, "Hey Siri, what's the weather today?"

Siri said, "*Looks like it will be sunny today*," and I said, "Yeah, it's gonna be a nice one."

Michael came over and kissed me.

"Last night was great," he said. "We should do that more often."

Thinking about Colin's gorgeous face, I said, "Yeah, we definitely should."

"See you in a bit," Michael said. "Text me if you want me to pick up anything."

"I think we're fine," I said. "I'm expecting a FreshDirect order this morning."

"Cool."

Michael left.

I made a cup of Pumpkin Spice in the Keurig, then I did some work, ordering containers and baskets for a client I had an appointment with next week, and did some research on the latest shelving options for another client. When the kids woke up, I made chocolate pancakes. I had a little piece of one myself, though I was trying to avoid carbs in the morning. We talked more about the show last night and Harrison's performance.

"Oh, so I had a chat with Thalia," I said.

"I know," Harrison said, in a tone that ensured I knew he was peeved about it. "What were you saying about me?"

"Actually, *she* was saying that she thinks it's time for you to go on auditions."

"Yeah," he said sullenly, "but Dad's against it so what difference does it make?"

"Not true. We had a talk last night and he's open to it."

Harrison brightened. "Seriously?"

"*If* it doesn't take time away from your SAT prep and your other classes."

"It won't, don't worry. Wow, this is awesome."

We went on, discussing possible managers that Thalia had suggested in the past. It was great to see Harrison so excited. I wanted to ask him how he felt after the "big talk" that he and Michael had had, but I didn't want to do it with Carson right there. I always made an extra effort to respect my kids' boundaries.

"Can we go sneaker shopping today?" Carson asked.

"Sneakers? You already have at least five pairs."

"None of them fit."

"None of them? Or is there some new trendy style you want?"

"Okay, *maybe* there's a new one."

"I need to go shopping too," Harrison said with a sly smile. "I have nothing to wear for my auditions, and I have to look good if you want me to get a part, right?"

"Fine, I guess I could do a little shopping too," I said.

We planned to head out to the Shops at Hudson Yards.

After breakfast, the weekly FreshDirect order arrived. As the kids helped me put the groceries away, Carson said, "Where's Dad?"

I could tell that Carson was eager to talk to him about auditioning and manager possibilities.

"That's a good question," I said, glancing at the clock on the stove. He'd been gone for about two hours, and he usually returned from his runs in about forty-five minutes. He could've stopped somewhere to do some shopping or something, but he still should've been back by now.

"Where did he go?" Harrison asked.

"For a run," I said. "Carson, just put the cereal away and then let's get ready to go."

After I changed into jeans and a sweatshirt with the pink, all-caps logo from *Waitress*, I checked my phone—no texts, missed calls, or voicemails from Michael. We had the kids on Find My iPhone but not each other, which was why Michael hadn't been able to track me when I went looking for Colin yesterday.

I tapped out a text: **Where are you?**

Then I decided this sounded too bitchy, and I was trying to improve my marriage, not cause unnecessary tension.

So instead, I texted: **Taking the boys shopping**

That was much better—more casual, yet not addressing that he'd been gone for an unusual amount of time or making a big deal about it. Maybe he'd stopped for coffee and lost track of time. Or maybe he'd gotten another important work call.

In the cab to the west side, I checked my texts. Michael hadn't responded and mine had turned green—maybe his phone was off, or he was out of range, though was anyone ever out of range in Manhattan? He had to have service, unless he was stuck on a subway, but why would he be on a subway? And his phone couldn't have died because he had charged it overnight, like he always did. This meant his phone was off or in airplane mode, which ruled out getting distracted at a coffee bar. Was it possible he was still, on some level, resentful that I'd gone out searching for Colin yesterday, so he was doing this on purpose, passive-aggressively, to make a point? This seemed crazy, but I couldn't think of any other logical reason why my texts had turned green.

"Did Dad text back yet?" Harrison asked.

I realized I was squeezing my phone so hard my hand hurt. "No. Not yet."

"Why would Dad go running for so long?"

"I'm sure there's some explanation."

"My texts are green," Carson said.

"Mine too," Harrison said.

"Maybe he forgot to charge his phone," I said. "Or maybe his phone isn't working and shut off. He was due for an upgrade."

I knew that both these explanations were farfetched, especially as, come to think of it, I remembered seeing his phone plugged in on the dresser in the bedroom last night.

"I'm gonna call him," Harrison said. He called, then said, "Voicemail picked up right away. He probably has his phone off."

"Dad never has his phone off," Carson said.

"Okay, that's enough," I said. "When we get home, I'm sure he'll be home. Let's just forget about it, okay? You too go ahead and do your shopping. Harrison, pick out some nice clothes for your brother."

"Can't wait, this is gonna be so much fun."

Sometimes Harrison's gayness wasn't so apparent. Other times, like when he talked about fashion and decorating, or sang Taylor Swift songs, it was impossible to miss. For years, Michael had been in denial, occasionally making idiotic comments like, "You never know, maybe it's just a phase." He usually didn't like it when Harrison and Carson went shopping together, maybe because he was afraid Harrison's gayness would "rub off" on Carson. That's why Michael's shift last night had been so unexpected. What had caused him to suddenly change his views when he'd always been so resistant? And was there a connection between our discussion and him going off the grid?

I also remembered that "work call" he'd made between acts last night. What if *he* was having an affair? Maybe that's why he'd accused me of having an affair with Andrew, because he was cheating on me. Isn't that what cheaters do, accuse the other person of doing what *they're* guilty of?

Okay, just calm down, stop it with the overanalyzing and catastrophizing. Things are never as bad as you think.

As the kids shopped, I went outside, near the Vessel, and texted Michael: **So when are you coming home? Is there an ETA?**

To hell with not sounding bitchy: I was officially upset.

When the text turned green, I wondered if I'd been in denial, or just naïve.

Michael's shift last night had seemed odd; maybe because it *was* odd. Maybe accepting Harrison's sexuality and having sex with me was to make me believe that things were normal, to hide the fact that he'd been having an affair—with his ex, Jennifer, or someone else. He was worried that I was catching on and that if we *didn't* have sex, like happily married people, I'd get suspicious and find out the truth. In retrospect, lately he'd had a lot of late nights at work, hushed phone calls, and he'd been acting distracted and aloof. An image flashed in my brain—Michael fucking Jennifer. She was on top with her fake tits, bouncing on him as hard as she could.

Nausea hit; I felt like I could throw up.

I bought a small bottle of water and guzzled it down. It helped a little, but not much.

Maybe Jennifer wasn't the only one. Aren't most cheaters serial cheaters? Maybe he was having *multiple* affairs. At his last office Christmas party, I noticed that he took an oddly flirty tone when we said hello to Nikki, an attractive, smiley paralegal in her mid-twenties. Instead of a simple "Hey," he said, "Heyyyyy." Incredibly brazen since I was standing right there, probably giving her the evil eye. Then, during cocktails, I noticed that he kept looking over at her and a few times she smiled at him a little. I tried to make light of it, saying, "Seems like you have a fan," and he said, "Oh, Nikki? Yeah, she's fun, isn't she?" I'd never heard Michael use that word to describe someone—*fun*. It stuck out at the time, but I let it go, telling myself that I was probably making a big deal about nothing.

But was I?

If Nikki was flirting with Michael so openly in front of me, how did she act when his ball-and-chain wasn't around? It wouldn't be like Michael to have a work affair, and risk his career, but wasn't that the nature of affairs? No one *wants* to ruin their life. People get carried away, act in a way they don't normally act. I could see Michael taking a dumb risk, just for the thrill of it, and then having to cover it up. He was a lawyer after all—he knew how to strategize and get away with things.

Harrison texted me that they were still shopping, so I killed time, looking at shoes, but I couldn't really focus. Later, when I met my kids, Carson was holding a bag from Twenty Four New York with his new sneakers, and Harrison had bags from Banana Republic, Levi's, Coach and Athleta.

"I thought you guys were here for sneakers."

"We are," Harrison said, "but I have *nothing* to wear this summer, and I got some amazing shorts and these shirts I *had to* have. I still had birthday money from Grandma and Grandpa to spend, so it's all cool."

"I was kidding," I said. "I can't wait to see what you got."

"Did Dad text back yet?" Harrison asked.

"No, not yet," I said.

"My messages are still green," Carson said, looking at his phone.

"Why isn't he texting back?" Harrison asked. "Do you think something happened to him?"

"Stop it," I said. "It's only a few hours and he's probably home anyway, charging his phone. Want to get something to eat?"

"No, let's head back," Harrison said.

"I wanna go too," Carson said.

I'd had enough with cabs, so we took a Lyft. During the ride, the kids were anxious, continuing to check their phones. I was trying to stay calm, but I was anxious too. While I was angry at Michael, I also wanted to be wrong about everything. I wanted to get back to the apartment, and for Michael to be home, and for there to be some real explanation for where he'd been. I wanted Michael and I to continue with counseling and work on our problems, and get past this weird, bumpy period in our marriage, and get back to the way we were a few years ago, when things weren't perfect, but they were pretty good. I'd take pretty good. At least I'd trusted Michael and he'd trusted me. I wanted to get back to that at least.

When I opened the door, Harrison rushed in, saying, "Dad? Dad?"

But Michael wasn't home and there was no sign that he'd come home. His running sneakers weren't by the door and nothing in the apartment had been disturbed.

Okay, now something was officially wrong.

"He's not home, he's not home." Carson was shaking, starting to cry.

I hugged him, saying, "It's going to be fine, I promise. There's nothing to worry about."

I sounded convincingly calm. I didn't care about how I felt anymore; I only cared about my boys and I didn't want them to be frightened.

"Then…then where is he?"

"If I had to bet, I'd say he's at his office," I said.

"But before you said he'd be home."

"But now I've had more time to think about it. He's been extremely busy at work lately, so it makes sense that he'd go into the office to get some stuff done."

"When he told you he was going running?" Harrison said. "No, that doesn't make any sense at all."

"Maybe he told me and I forgot," I said. "Sometimes he works out during the day at the Equinox near his office. He keeps changes of clothes at the office, so yes it does make sense."

While I actually didn't believe that any of this could be true, it had enough logic in it to at least subdue Carson's crying fit.

Not letting it go, Harrison said, "But I called his office, and nobody picked up."

"Well, no one's going to be there to pick up on a Sunday," I said, "but that doesn't mean he isn't working. He's probably engrossed in a project, you know how he gets when he gets focused on something. He's like a horse with blinders." Changing the subject, I said, "Carson, don't you have that science quiz tomorrow?"

"Yeah," he said, "but I'm ready for it."

"That's what you said before the last one and you got a seventy-two. Go to your room and study." Then I said to Harrison, "And you have an essay due next week, don't you?"

"Not till Friday."

"Well, at least start outlining it so you don't fall behind. You have the show tonight, so you don't have much time today."

When the kids went to their room, I glanced at my phone—at the still-green text messages. It was one thing to hurt me, but how could he put the kids through this?

All day I hadn't allowed myself to seriously consider this possibility—had something *happened* to Michael? Is it possible a car hit him, or had he been in some other accident? Maybe the police or hospital didn't know how to reach me.

In my bedroom, with the door locked, I closed my eyes and took a series of deep breaths. I was trying to steady myself, but I kept thinking about when Colin didn't come back from swimming, after sunset, when the panic began to set in, the panic that had never fully subsided.

Stop! This isn't then; this is now. This is different.

Deciding that I had to be calm, pragmatic, strong, if not for my own well-being, then for my boys', I called the most likely hospitals—NYU, Bellevue and Mount Sinai. It took a while to get the right people on the phone, but none had any record of Michael Rizzo. I felt ridiculous for checking, as ridiculous as I'd felt yesterday when I was looking for Colin in random hotels. I had to stop letting my imagination take over; this tendency had never led to anything positive in my life. I'd probably jumped to a conclusion about him having an affair too. That was one possibility, but it wasn't the only possibility.

The boys were so upset, they said they couldn't focus on their schoolwork. I had no idea how Harrison was going to perform tonight.

Teary again, Carson asked, "Can't you call the police, Ma?"

Hugging him, I said, "Look, I think in situations like this it's important to stay logical. The police won't do anything because he hasn't been gone for very long, which means that, in just about all situations like this, it turns out the person is fine, and I'm sure that's what's going to happen in this situation."

"What if he's dead?" Harrison asked.

"Stop it," I said. "He's not dead."

"You don't know that. He could be."

"Why can't we call the police?" Carson asked.

"Okay, that's enough of this," I said. "I don't want any more talking about Dad at all. He'll be home soon and there'll be an explanation and that's final."

Carson turned and marched away down the hallway to his room.

"Maybe I'll call the police myself," Harrison said.

"Don't do that. Your brother's scared already, that'll just make things worse."

"Fine, then maybe I'll go looking for him."

"Where are you going to look?"

"The park, I guess. That's where he usually goes running, right? I can go to the park before I go to the theater later. I can find him there."

"How're you going to find him there? Are you going to walk around calling out his name?"

"Maybe I will. So what?"

"If he was in the park, don't you think he would've called us?"

"Maybe he got injured. Maybe he's unconscious. Maybe his phone broke or fell in the water and that's why he isn't calling."

It terrified me, at times like this, when I noticed my own behavior in Harrison. It made me fear that maybe his love of theater wasn't the only trait he'd inherited from me. Like me, he could get anxious, obsessive; he had trouble letting go. He'd had issues with anxiety and executive functioning since he was a kid, and he took Adderall.

At times, I felt he was getting too obsessive, losing control. He needed support and understanding, so I went over and hugged him.

"It's okay," I said. "It's going to be okay, I promise."

"It's not okay," he said. "I have to find him. I have to find him right now."

"There's nothing you can do," I said. "Do you understand that? You can't control every situation. Sometimes you just have to let go. Relax."

"But I can find him," he said. "If I go to the park, I know I can find him."

"There's nothing you can do," I said. "There's nothing any of us can do but wait for him to come home."

I continued to hug him. For a long time, maybe two minutes, neither of us said anything. Then I let go and he seemed better.

"You're right, Ma. I'll try not to worry so much."

"It's okay," I said, "and you don't have to act in your show tonight if you don't want to. Thalia will understand and your understudy can play the role."

"No, I have to be there," Harrison said. "Jacob doesn't even know the whole role; he kept messing up in rehearsals. Besides, if what you're saying is true, and Dad's okay, and there's just some weird explanation for all of this, then I know he'll be at the show. I *know* he wouldn't miss my show."

I had to agree with Harrison. Disappearing for most of the day for whatever reason was one thing, but it was hard to imagine Michael blowing off one of the kids' shows without explanation, unless something awful had happened.

"It's up to you," I said. "But if you're there, you know I'll be there."

For the rest of the afternoon, the kids managed to focus on their schoolwork, and I got some work done as well, ordering stackable storage bins and organizer drawers and turntables from The Container Store for a job I was set to start next week. I managed not to think about Michael very much, or wonder where he was, by telling myself that he was going to show up at the theater tonight. He'd come directly from his office, from some client meeting that he'd forgotten to tell me about, and with an explanation for why he hadn't received our messages. Maybe his phone had broken, or malfunctioned.

When the kids and I arrived at the theater at around six-thirty, we were all so confident that Michael would be there waiting for us, that it felt almost shocking that he wasn't.

"I thought you said he was gonna be here," Carson said, with his voice cracking, like he was about to start crying again.

Already I realized that coming to the show tonight, acting like nothing was wrong, was a huge mistake. I hadn't even considered what I'd do, or how I'd manage the kids' reactions, if Michael didn't show up.

"He'll come," I said. "Remember last night he arrived last minute, just when the show was starting? He'll probably do that again."

I wished I could believe this.

Harrison was supposed to be backstage, but he kept coming out to check if Michael had shown up and I had to keep telling him he wasn't here yet. Carson hung out with me as I tried to have normal conversations with my friends while I kept looking at my phone, at the green texts. It didn't seem to make any sense to send another text when he hadn't responded to this one yet, but I figured it was worth a shot.

I tapped out: **I really hope you have an explanation for this I can't believe you'd do this to the boys. Please be okay!!**

I sent the text, then saw it turn green.

During the moments before the play started, Carson and I kept looking back toward the doors to the theater. It seemed like there wouldn't be any latecomers, then the door opened—but it was Andrew Reedy who entered. We made eye contact for a second or two, smiling at each other, and then he took a seat in the back center area.

The show began. When Harrison entered for his first scene, I recognized a completely different vibe than the other performances. He was off-key, especially on his high notes, and I could see the anxiety coming through in his facial expressions. I felt so awful for him, and I was angry at myself for letting him perform tonight—I should've insisted he stay home.

As the show continued, his performance got even worse. A few times he messed up lyrics—so unlike him. I had trouble focusing myself, as I was thinking about Harrison and Michael. Next to me, Carson seemed agitated and upset; occasionally, I squeezed his hand and whispered, "Don't worry" or "He's okay, I promise." I didn't bother filming as I knew *this* was a night we were all going to want to forget.

At intermission, I couldn't get away, outside, fast enough. Carson came with me. I looked at my phone, at the green texts, muttering, "What the fucking fuck, Michael?"

"Can't we call the police now?" Carson asked.

I didn't know what to do. I felt totally helpless, out of control. It was a familiar feeling, and then it hit why; it amazed me that I didn't realize it sooner because the connection was so obvious. Colin disappeared nineteen years ago and Michael disappeared today—*it was happening again.* The circumstances were different, but the feeling was the same—the denial, followed by the shock, then the realization that he was *gone*, that he wasn't coming home.

"This can't be happening. Not again. It's not possible."

I didn't mean to say this out loud, especially for Carson to hear.

"Sorry." I was mortified. "I was just, um, talking to myself."

"*Again*?" Carson was a smart, perceptive kid—he didn't let things slide. "What do you mean *again*?"

"Nothing," I said, "except I still believe he's coming here or he'll be home later."

"I'm really scared, Mommy."

The "mommy" got to me. He hadn't called me mommy in ages.

"I'm scared too, sweetie." I hugged him. "But it's okay to be scared sometimes."

"I don't want to go back in there," he said.

I dreaded the thought of having to sit through the entire second act, but I didn't see what choice we had if Harrison wanted to continue.

"I know," I said.

When we returned to the lobby Harrison was there. He didn't even have to ask us if Michael had shown up; our expressions showed that he hadn't.

"Fuck," Harrison said, loud enough that several people nearby looked over.

"Hey, watch that language in here," I said. "And if you don't want to go out for the second act you don't—"

"Of course I'm doing the second act," he said. "You can't stop me."

"Who said anything about stopping you?"

Harrison stomped away, heading backstage.

Carson said he had to use the bathroom, and I said I'd wait for him in the lobby.

As I glanced at the green texts again, I heard from behind me, "Everything all right?"

I turned and saw Andrew. He looked and sounded concerned.

"Actually, everything is definitely not all right," I said.

I told him how Michael had gone running this morning and hadn't returned.

"Wow, are you serious?" He seemed very worried. "So how long has he been gone?"

I gave him the details, and he made appropriate comments like, "Maybe he lost his phone," "Maybe his phone broke," and "Did you try calling him at work?" I knew he was just trying to help, but I should've known that if I went to a guy for emotional support, I'd get problem solving. What did he expect me to say, *Gee, try him at work, why didn't I think of that*?

I was polite, though, and told him I appreciated his help—which I did. It felt nice to have someone to talk to at least.

"No worries," he said. "Let me know if there's anything I can do."

Carson returned from the bathroom, and we retook our seats. The second act was just as difficult to watch as the first. Harrison messed up another line and his singing was still off. For one scene, he missed his cue and was several seconds late coming on stage and the whole audience noticed; I even heard a few "Awws." Almost nothing makes a mom feel more awful and helpless than watching her child fail. I wished I could go up there and rescue him the way I did when he was four years old and inadvertently bumped into a wasp's nest outside my friend Carrie's house in Woodstock and I pulled him out of the way in the nick of time. But tonight, I just had to sit there and watch.

Finally, mercifully, the show ended.

Harrison was the first cast member out and said, "He's not here, is he?"

I shook my head.

"Mom, you have to call the police," Harrison said. "*Please.*"

Kathleen overheard and was glancing over with a concerned expression. Great, she was the biggest gossip in our moms' group, so now within minutes everyone would be talking about this, trying to guess what was going on.

"We'll discuss on the way home," I said. "Let's go."

The boys and I got into a cab on Lexington. They were extremely upset, both crying, and there was nothing I could do to console them. I knew any reassurances would fall flat after I'd been so wrong about Michael showing up at the theater. Now it was hard to find any reason to be optimistic.

"Let's see if he's home," I said. "If he's not home, I'll call the police, okay?"

We didn't speak until we entered our building's lobby and Harrison asked our doorman, Raymond: "Did my Dad come home?"

"I didn't see him, no."

"Fuck," Harrison said.

"Something wrong?" Raymond asked. "What's going on?"

"You two go upstairs and wait in the apartment," I said to the boys.

"Are you calling the police?" Carson asked.

"Yes, yes, I'm calling the police. Go on, go up."

The boys got on the elevator.

To Raymond, I explained quickly that Michael had gone running this morning and I hadn't heard from him since.

"Jesus," Raymond said. "Hope he's okay. I'll pray for him."

I went back outside, through the revolving doors, and

stood in the courtyard in front of the building. As I tapped 9-1-1 into the phone, I flashed back to nineteen years ago, to the last time I called 9-1-1. I was on the beach on Shelter Island, my voice hoarse from shouting Colin's name, and I heard the same words from the operator that I heard right now.

Oh my God, this is really happening again. I'm really living through this nightmare again.

"Nine-one-one. What's your emergency?"

EIGHT

"My..." I couldn't believe what I was about to say. "My...my..."

"Ma'am?"

"My husband's missing. He's fucking missing."

"Okay, ma'am, just stay calm. Can I have your name please, ma'am?"

"Can you stop with the ma'am shit? My name's Vanessa. Vanessa Rizzo."

"And who's the missing person?"

"I told you. My husband."

"His name, ma'am."

"Stop calling me fucking ma'am."

"Sorry, miss. What's your husband's name?"

"Michael. Michael Rizzo."

"How long has he been missing?"

She didn't sound particularly alarmed. I knew she was just doing her job and probably got calls like this all the time and was trained to stay calm and robotic. Still, her chill attitude made me feel like she thought I was a crazy person who was panicking, getting hysterical for no reason.

"Since early this morning," I said, doing my best to remain patient.

"So less than twenty-four hours."

"Yes, but he's been gone all day, and something is definitely wrong."

"Does he have a cell phone?"

Did she really think I hadn't tried to contact him?

"Yes, he's not answering his phone or texts, and he's not receiving texts apparently. They all turned green."

"Could he have gone somewhere? Where he's not getting service?"

Imagining Michael naked, on top of Jennifer Sears, thrusting into her, saying, "Come for me, baby," then making that ugly face he always made right before he orgasmed—squeezing his eyes shut, biting on his lower lip— I said, "It's possible, but I don't think he'd scare our kids like this. I have two boys. They're very worried right now."

"I understand, ma'am…miss. Where are you calling from?"

"From outside my apartment building."

"And where's that?"

"Fifty-Second between Sutton and First."

"There's not much I can do right now, miss. It's best if you go into your local precinct and explain the situation. Do you know where your local precinct is?"

"Can't you start searching for him? Can't you send a detective here or something?"

"Not at this time, miss. I suggest you file a report at your local precinct and they can take steps from there."

"Why can't you just find my fucking husband?" I realized that getting belligerent with the operator wasn't going to help the situation. I'd often told my kids, "*If you want somebody to help you, be nice,*" but sometimes it was hard to take my own advice. "Sorry, I didn't mean to take it out on you—I'm just under a lot of stress right now. Can't you put out an APB or whatever you do in these situations?"

I knew exactly how the protocol went, unfortunately. With Colin, they searched for his body immediately, but they didn't declare him officially missing until twenty-four hours had passed.

"If you go to your local precinct you can talk to a detective here. That's the best I can do. Do you know how to contact your precinct?"

"Yeah, thanks."

I went back to my apartment and told my extremely anxious boys that I had to go to the precinct. I knew it would be a waste of time telling them not to wait up for me to return because I knew they would.

I pulled Harrison aside and whispered: "I need you to be strong for your brother, okay? Can you do that?"

Harrison nodded.

"Thank you." I rushed out of the apartment.

The ten-minute cab ride from my apartment to the Six-ty-Seventh Street precinct happened in a blur and felt like only a few minutes. I should've been thinking about Michael and my poor boys, but it was impossible to repress flash-backs of when I had my first conversations with that detective and Coast Guard investigator on Shelter Island.

Oh, God, am I gonna have to go through all of that again too?

I kept replaying random snippets: *What time did you last see Colin?...What was he wearing?...Was he acting odd in any way?...What was your relationship like with Colin?...Had you and Colin been getting along lately?*

I'd been to this precinct once before—Michael's wallet had once gotten picked on the subway and I came with him to report it. It was in a pre-war building that reminded me of my elementary on Staten Island, maybe because it had the same pale, vomit-green paint that many of the city's municipal buildings had. Aside from technology, it didn't seem like much about the building had changed in the past fifty, or even a hundred years.

Off to the left, there was an old wooden desk. A gray-haired man in plain clothes was seated, talking to a female uniformed officer who was standing next to him. They were laughing about something.

"I'm telling you, that's why I never go up there," the officer said.

"Hey, I don't blame you. Why would ya?"

They continued to laugh, then the man saw me standing there and he suddenly had a serious expression.

"Can I help you?"

"Um, yes," I said. "I called nine-one-one."

The female officer looked me up and down a little, then walked away.

The man said: "No worries. I'm Officer Briscoe, do you want to take a seat?" He seemed like a nice man, appropriately concerned.

"Okay, but I came here to talk to a detective," I said. "On nine-one-one, I was told if I came here I could talk to a detective. That's why I'm here, to talk to a detective."

I was nervous and aware that I was rambling.

"Sorry," I said, sitting down, "this has just been a very difficult day for me. It's hard for me to believe I'm even here. I think I'm in shock actually."

He offered me water, but I told him it was okay. Then he asked me similar questions that the operator had and I answered them as calmly and patiently as I could. He continued to seem like he genuinely cared and wanted to help.

"We're gonna get to the bottom of this," he said. "I've been working here twenty-six years and these situations almost always have happy endings. That said, we're not gonna waste any time, either."

Briscoe excused himself and went to the back. I took out my phone, noticed the texts with Michael were still green.

I texted Harrison: **No word.**

Almost immediately he responded: 😠 **What did police say????**

Before I could reply, a man said, "Ms. Rizzo?"

Briscoe had returned along with a tall black guy with a shaved head.

"Yes," I said to him.

"Detective Randle, follow me."

No "How are you" or even "Hello"?

I followed him to a desk in the back of the precinct. As I sat across from him, I noticed a family photo hanging on the wall to the left—him with his wife and two sons.

"I understand you're here about your missing husband?"

"Yes, that's right."

I explained the situation. I still felt anxious, like I was rambling, but I managed to get all the information out.

"As you probably know," Randle said, "we can't officially report him as missing until tomorrow morning, but I'll alert officers in the area, including Central Park right away, just in case somebody saw something, okay?"

"I appreciate that," I said, "but this is really highly unusual. Michael has never done anything like this before, otherwise I wouldn't be here."

"I understand," Randle said, though I wasn't convinced he believed me. Everyone who reported a missing person probably told him how unusual the behavior was, and how the person has never done anything like this before. "Have you contacted any of his friends or coworkers yet?"

"No, I've been hoping he'd just come home. He usually doesn't work on Sundays—especially when he leaves to go jogging. And he doesn't have a lot of friends, in New York anyway. Well, that's not true, he has some college friends."

I thought about Rob, whom he'd had drinks with just yesterday. I didn't see how Rob could possibly relate to Michael not coming home after a run this morning, but it probably made sense for me to contact him in case Michael had mentioned something to him. I didn't have Rob's phone number or email, but I could probably figure out how to reach him.

"It may be a good idea to contact some people just in case." Randle handed me a card. "If we find out anything on our end, we'll let you know. Do we have your contact info?"

I gave him my phone number and address, then he walked me to the front of the precinct. Briscoe was standing, chatting with the female officer. They were both laughing again.

"I'll be in touch," Randle said.

He turned and walked away without saying goodbye or anything nice or reassuring. He'd done nothing to disprove that my first impression was correct.

Outside I checked my phone and saw about ten texts from Harrison—most were just question marks, but there were others like: **what's going on????** and **Why won't you**

fucking answer me?!?!?!

I called him and said, "There's no news."

"Why wouldn't you text me back?"

"I was talking to a detective."

"Are they looking for him?"

"Yes, they're looking. How's Carson?"

"They won't find him, Ma."

"Stop. You don't know that."

"He's dead, Ma. You know it and I know it. He's dead."

WHEN I GOT home the boys were crying, so hard they couldn't speak. I tried, but there was nothing I could do or say to console them, especially when I was losing hope myself. Finally, at around one a.m., I convinced them to at least get into bed.

Harrison was sitting up, with his back against the headboard, holding his phone out in front of him. Carson was sitting at the foot of Harrison's bed.

"Come on, you have to get some rest," I said. "You have school tomorrow, and Harrison you have a midterm next week and you still have that *Great Gatsby* paper to finish."

Looking perplexed, Harrison asked, "Are you serious? How're we supposed to sleep? How're we supposed to go to school when we're going to have a funeral to plan?"

Carson bawled hysterically.

"Can you just stop it, right now?" I said to Harrison. "You're upsetting your brother and we all need rest."

"I don't want Daddy to die," Carson said.

"Your father isn't dead."

"How do you know?"

"Because I just do, that's why."

"You don't even believe in God. You wouldn't even let Dad take us to church."

It was true that Michael wanted to raise the kids Catholic, but that I'd given up on religion after Colin vanished, and Michael had eventually acquiesced. That said, it wasn't like he was super religious himself. It was Stella who was hellbent on Catholicism. Michael didn't care as much about religion as he did about not rocking the boat with his mother.

"The lights are going out and both of you are going to sleep. If either of you get out of bed again, I'm going to be very upset, and I don't think you want to upset me more than I already am tonight."

I shut the door. I didn't know if they'd get to sleep tonight, but I knew they'd try especially after I'd pulled the guilt card.

Standing in the dark bedroom, I looked outside, past the rooftops, up toward the Manhattan sky which had its usual pale-orange nighttime hue. I wished I still believed in God. Praying at least used to make me feel proactive, like I was doing something. Closing my eyes, I whispered, "Father God, in this time of uncertainty and longing, I entrust my missing loved one into your loving hands…" Then, as I recalled saying the same prayer, nineteen years ago, on the dark beach on Shelter Island, I muttered, "Fuck it" and started to undress.

Getting ready for bed felt strange without Michael at home. I'd put on a strong front for the boys, but it was getting harder to stay optimistic, to stop imagining the worst.

"Alexa, play spa music."

As "Watermark" began, I went into the master bedroom and opened the medicine chest and took out the bottle of Klonopin. I had eleven pills left. Because of my past, Dr.

Stone was careful about the meds he prescribed. I didn't have any refills but was allowed to take a pill on an as-needed basis, and I needed one now.

A few minutes later, I got into bed. I checked my phone, telling myself that if the texts to Michael had gone through, this would be a sign from God that I'd been wrong about His nonexistence and that Michael was okay. It was very deflating to see that the texts were still green.

I went to Michael's Facebook page. He rarely posted anything himself, so most of the posts were from the kids' shows and family photos. The most recent post was the video that I'd taken on Friday night, of Harrison bringing down the house with "Disappear," which seemed beyond ironic now. It was hard to believe that it had only been a little over forty-eight hours ago. It seemed like weeks had passed since that happy night.

Viewing Michael's friends list, I went to Rob Heller's page. Though Rob and I weren't connected as friends, I was still able to send him a message on Messenger. I wasn't certain he'd see the message as a lot of people didn't even check their DMs from their friends, but it was worth a shot.

Hi Rob.

Not sure if you'll see this. Sorry to write you here, but did you happen to hear from Michael today, or did he mention any plans he might have? We're trying to locate him. If you've heard anything, please let me know. And PLEASE don't share this publicly, I don't want to make a big deal about this right now or panic people, especially my children.

Thank you very much!!

Vanessa

I added my cell number, then sent the message.

I'd hoped the spa music would help relax me, but it was making me feel like I was at a funeral.

"Alexa, turn this shit off."

She didn't obey.

"Alexa, off!"

The room was quiet—well, as quiet as a room in Manhattan could get. You could always hear a honking horn, a distant siren, or someone screaming if you focused hard enough. I couldn't tell if the Klonopin was kicking in or not. With just the nightlight on, I lay on my back and repeated the mantra a meditation instructor had one suggested for me—*I listen to my body*. It made me feel calmer, then I worried that I'd put the chain on the front door and if Michael came home, he wouldn't be able to get in. I went and checked, but the door was in fact unchained.

Back in bed, I tried to focus on my stupid mantra until I finally fell asleep.

WAKING FROM A nightmare, I expect to see Michael next to me. Whenever we had nightmares, we told each other about them right away. Although our marriage had big problems, we did the little things well. It took a few more seconds for reality to refocus fully, to remember that Michael was missing, and then my nightmare didn't seem as important anymore.

I didn't know how long I'd been asleep, but some early morning light was leaking through the blinds. I glanced at the clock—4:02 am. Well, at least I'd gotten a few hours.

I didn't think the Klonopin had helped much—I probably needed another pill—but thanks to anxiety and adrenaline, I had plenty of energy. I prepared a cup of

French roast anyway, mainly out of habit. As I sipped it, I checked my phone, but there was still no word about Michael, and nothing from Detective Randle or Rob. It was so early, so I didn't necessarily expect anyone to get in touch with me, though it would've been relieving to get some sort of hopeful news. Instead, it was nearly twenty-four hours since Michael had been gone, at which point he'd officially become a missing person.

I was trying to remain optimistic, but this was getting increasingly challenging.

At around six a.m., I was pacing in the living room when Carson entered, clutching "muffin," a little stuffed bear that I hadn't seen him with in years. Carson's eyes were bloodshot, with deep bags underneath them. When I told him nothing had changed since last night he started sobbing. I held him, crying with him, flashing back to the first time I'd cried over Colin, when it had finally set in that he wasn't coming home—denial turning into grief—but this time it would be worse, because this time it wasn't just about me. I knew how to deal with grief—the Colin experience had forced me to develop coping mechanisms, like my organizing business, and managing my kids' lives, and I knew that even in a worst-case scenario, I could get through it. But for the boys, a tragic outcome would be devastating. Harrison was just coming into his own—with his acting and getting more comfortable with his sexuality. I had no idea with how he'd deal with this kind of stress. A couple of years ago, he'd had issues with drinking and vaping; what if he turned to harder drugs this time? Or, if not now, when he was on his own, in college? As for Carson, I had no idea how he'd cope. Michael was his absolute hero, and he was such a sensitive kid; I could easily imagine him having drug issues too, or, at the very least, developing issues with anxiety and depression.

"Do you want something to eat?" I said. "Come on, you must be starving."

"All I want is Daddy."

"I want Daddy too, but we have to eat. How about some cereal? Come on, I'll pour you a bowl of shredded wheat."

I had stopped buying sugar cereals after my nutritionist friend, Amy, told me that a high sugar diet could contribute to Harrison's anxiety issues.

Carson sat at the dining table with the cereal in front of him, but wouldn't touch it. He had his phone out and I could see him tapping out a message. I knew he was writing to Michael again.

"You have to stop that," I said.

"Why?"

"Because it's not doing any good."

"Maybe the other texts didn't go through. Maybe this one will."

I was going to take his phone away, but I stopped myself, knowing that it wouldn't do any good. I didn't see how I could send the kids to school today. While distraction would be good, I knew they'd just be on their phones all day and would be too distraught to focus.

When Harrison came out of the bedroom, looking ex-hausted as well, I told both boys that they didn't have to go to school today. They didn't seem happy or relieved about it, or have any reaction at all.

"Did the police find Dad's body yet?" Harrison asked.

"I can't, I just can't." Exasperated, I headed into the kitchen.

"Well, did they or didn't they?" Harrison called out from behind me. When I was in the kitchen, he added, "Guess that means they didn't!"

My phone played a few bars of Justin Timberlake's "Can't Stop the Feeling!"—my current ringtone. It was a number I didn't recognize.

"Hello," I asked anxiously, expecting to hear Michael say, *Don't worry, I'm okay, the craziest thing happened…*

"Hi, Vanessa, it's Rob."

"Oh, hi," I said, feeling the letdown. "Thanks for getting back to me."

"Sure thing." His voice sounded hoarse, crackly, like he'd just gotten up. "Sorry, I know it's super early, but I wanted to check in. So what's going on?"

"Well, hopefully nothing serious, but it *is* extremely concerning unfortunately."

I told him about how we hadn't heard from Michael since he went on a run yesterday.

"Holy shit. Jesus."

"I know," I said, "but hopefully there's some logical explanation. I just wanted to know if, maybe, I don't know, he mentioned something to you, like maybe he told you about a meeting I didn't know about, or just any reason why you think he might've done this, I mean not gotten in touch with any of us. It's just so unusual."

I didn't want to come out and just *ask* about what I'd been suspecting about Michael and Jennifer, or Michael and someone else, but if Michael *was* having another affair it seemed logical that he would've told his buddy Rob about it. But would Rob be honest with me or stick to a "bro code"?

"I hear ya," Rob said, "but why do you think he would've mentioned something to me? I mean, I haven't even talked to him much in months."

This actually made me tremble. This was an issue that

had come up for me many times in therapy. When somebody violated my trust, or lied to me, I always had a visceral reaction.

I took a couple of deep breaths, steadying myself, then said, "He told me he met you for a drink on Saturday."

"He *said* that?"

"Yes, he fucking said that."

"Look, I'm sorry, Vanessa, I'm really confused about what's going on here. I told you I haven't even spoken to Michael lately, I swear on my life."

I was still having trouble absorbing this. So if Michael had totally lied to my face about meeting Rob, what else had he lied to me about? Had my hunch about Jennifer Sears been right? Was he fucking his ex-girlfriend while going to marriage counseling with me? Or did he get involved with someone else, like that little, flirty, curly-haired Nikki from his office? *Or* was he serial cheater? Did I need to get an AIDS test?

"Are you still there?" Rob asked.

"Yeah, yeah, I'm fuckin' here."

After Rob asked a couple of unhelpful questions—"Did you call the police?" "Did they find out anything yet?"—I thanked him for getting back to me and told him I'd let him know as soon as I heard something.

When I ended the call, Harrison—whom I didn't realize had been behind me, listening in—asked anxiously, "Who was that?"

"No one," I said. "No one helpful anyway."

"Are you gonna tell Grandma and Grandpa that Dad's dead?"

"He's not dead, he's missing. There's a big difference."

"Whatever," Harrison said. "What about Grandma and

Grandpa?"

"No, but I guess I have to tell them."

"Of course you have to tell them." He swiped on his phone, to turn on the screen. "Or I'll tell them myself."

"Don't you dare. You haven't texted them or called them yet, have you? Have you?"

"No, but—"

"Then don't. You know they're both going to be hysterical. I'll call them and tell them, only if it's necessary."

"What if Dad went to their house?"

"He didn't go there."

"You don't know that."

"Why would he go to his parents without telling us? Why would he miss your show? Think about it. That doesn't make any sense."

He held up his phone. "If you don't call them now, I will."

"Fine. You're probably right, they should know. I'll call them right now, okay?"

I called Joe's cell. Joe was going to be hysterical too, but it would be better to tell him and let him tell Stella than to tell Stella directly.

"Hello," he said.

I already recognized anxiety in his tone, probably because I almost never called him, and he was already wondering if I was calling with bad news.

"Hi, it's Vanessa." I was trying to not sound panicked, but I knew I was failing. My voice was shaking as if the temperature in the apartment had suddenly dropped to zero degrees. "Is Michael at your house, or have you heard from him by any chance?"

"No, why?"

Here we go.

"Well, I don't want to upset you or anything but…well, we…we're not exactly sure where he is."

From behind me, Harrison blurted out, "Dad's missing, and he's probably—"

Before he could say, "Dead," I put a hand over his mouth and mouthed, *Shut your mouth.*

"Missing?" Joe said. "*Missing*? What the hell are you talking about *missing*?"

Now in the background, I heard Stella saying, "What's going on? Who's missing?"

After that, hell ensued. It was even worse than I'd imagined—Joe and Stella were screaming at each other *and* at me. Harrison and Carson were screaming at me too, and I was screaming at everyone.

Several minutes later, I was sitting on the couch, alone, holding my cell phone, feeling numb, and I wasn't sure exactly how I got there. All I remembered about the rest of the call was Joe saying that he and Stella were on their way to Manhattan. I could hear the kids in the kitchen, still screaming at each other and crying.

I was vacillating between wanting Michael to come back and for him to be okay, to feeling incredible resentment for what he'd done to us. Even if Michael came right now with some explanation for where he'd been, how could he explain flat-out lying to me on Saturday? Why would I ever trust him again? What did he think we were going to do, just pick up where we left off, like nothing had happened? I didn't see how we could ever recover from this.

Carson was still sitting at the dining table, looking at his phone, with a soggy bowl of cereal in front of him.

"Where's Harrison?" I asked.

"He went into the bathroom, he was bleeding."

"*What?*"

Alarmed, I rushed down the hallway, then turned the handle on the bathroom door. It was locked. I heard water running.

Banging on the door, I probably sounded crazed, shouting, "Harrison! Harrison, open the door right now! I said—"

Harrison came out, holding a wash towel over his mouth. I realized what had happened. When I'd put my hand over his mouth to shush him, I must have pressed harder than I'd realized. His lower teeth must've cut into his gums.

"Oh, no, baby, I'm so sorry. I didn't mean to hurt you. I didn't know what I was doing. Are you okay? Let me see it."

He removed the washcloth, and I saw the cut on his lower lip, oozing blood.

"Oh, fuck, I'm sorry. I'm so sorry."

"It's okay."

"Come on, let's put the ice pack on it."

"It's fine."

"It's not fine."

I dragged him into the dining room, then made him sit on a chair with his head tilted back, holding the icepack over his face. He wasn't hurt badly, but I felt awful for hurting him at all.

"I'm really sorry, sweetie. I was just so afraid you were going to scare Grandma and Grandpa and I'm under so much stress right now."

With the icepack muffling his words, he said, "It's no big deal."

The bleeding stopped. He said he didn't feel like eating. I poured him a bowl of cereal anyway, then I tried to distract the boys with small talk about theater, school, and plans for the summer—they were both planning to attend the Performing Arts Camp at French Woods in upstate New York. It was hard to keep their attention, though, and they eventually returned to their room.

I was in the kitchen, loading the dishwasher, when the phone started Timberlake-ing again. I had to change that fucking tone.

This time it was Detective Randle, asking, "Has your husband returned?"

"I was hoping you were calling with news."

He explained that they had no leads.

"Unfortunately, as you know, we're going to have to declare your husband as officially missing. This will allow us to utilize not only all of our resources to try to locate him, but we can also alert law enforcement in surrounding areas. I'm sorry it's come to this, but this step often leads to a positive resolution."

As Randle spoke, I experienced another wave of déjà vu. Randle had the same annoying matter-of-fact tone that Detective LaMont on Long Island had after Colin disappeared. Was I going to have go through this *again*? It took nineteen years for Colin to return. Was Michael going to be gone for nineteen years too, or was he gone for good?

"Ms. Rizzo, are you still there?"

"Yes…Yes, I'm here."

"I'm going to need some recent photos of your husband, the best ones you have. Can you get those to me right away?"

"Yes, of course."

"I'm also going to need your husband's height, weight, what he was wearing last, and whatever other information you think will help us."

"I'll text it to you."

"Is your husband's passport at home?"

"I don't know. I can check."

"Do that."

"Can you describe Colin Grant to me?" LaMont asked.

"He's six-two, two hundred pounds, very lean and strong, the body of a survivor."

"Ms. Rizzo, are you still there?"

"Yes, I'm sorry," I said to Randle. "Of course, Detective. I'll tell you whatever you need to know. I'll tell you…everything."

NINE

"CHECK IT OUT, Dad's on Citizen, Dad's on Citizen."

Carson was holding his phone in front of my face, showing me the Citizen app that reported local 911 activity. I glanced at the headline: MISSING UPPER EAST SIDE MAN, with our address below it.

"Oh, my God, they have our *address*?" I said. "That's *public*?"

"Yeah, they sometimes post the address. Wow, I can't believe he's really on Citizen. It's like we're famous."

Then I read the text below the headline—the report of a missing man, forty-five years old, last seen on Sunday morning at approximately 8:25 a.m. He was wearing a gray hoodie and light blue running shorts and was probably headed toward Central Park.

Shit, now that Michael was officially missing the news would start to spread quickly. When Colin was declared missing, local reporters showed up at our rental house on Shelter Island within an hour, followed by reporters from local TV stations, media from New York City, and some national media too. But nowadays, the internet, and especially social media, was much bigger, and the news would spread much faster. Hopefully, the attention would have a positive effect. Maybe there would be tips—maybe someone saw Michael jogging, or knew what had happened, or even where he was. From all the true crime shows that I'd seen, I knew every new clue would get analyzed and reanalyzed by internet sleuths, sometimes giving law enforcement access to information that would've taken days, or even weeks, to discover otherwise. When Colin disappeared, reporters harassed me for weeks, trying to dig into my personal life, searching for information and evidence that didn't exist. I didn't care so much about how this would affect me, but I was worried about the boys. They were under too much stress already, and the last thing they needed was to be in the middle of a media frenzy.

I glanced outside of one of the living room windows, where I could look down at the front of the building on Fifty-Second Street. No news trucks, but that could, and probably would, change very soon.

The intercom buzzed, the doorman announcing a visitor. Detective Randle hadn't said he was coming by, but maybe he'd forgotten to mention it.

Carson was about to speak into the intercom when I said, "Let me," and he moved out of the way.

"Hi, it's Vanessa."

"Your parents are coming up," said Carlos, one of our daytime doormen.

I knew he meant Michael's parents, but I didn't know how the hell they'd gotten here so fast from New Jersey. Either they'd sped here or I'd lost track of time—probably some combination.

The doorbell rang several times in quick succession and there was banging too.

When I opened it, Joe and Stella pushed their way inside. Stella was wearing no makeup and a beige cropped jacket over her nightgown, and Joe was in sweatpants and a New York Giants jersey with MANNING 10 on the back.

"He's not here," Stella said. "My boy isn't here?"

"No," I said.

"Then where is he? What the hell happened to him?"

"We don't know."

"She doesn't know," Stella said to Joe. "She says she doesn't know."

Carson went over and hugged Stella. Harrison was off to the side, watching, holding a wad of partially reddened paper towel over his lower lip.

"Don't worry, we'll get to the bottom of it," Joe said.

"I'm gonna have a heart attack," Stella wailed. "Where is he? Where's my boy?"

Her face was pink and there was a thick vertical vein on her forehead.

"Maybe you should sit, Stell," Joe said.

"Sit, no she *wants* me to sit. I'm not sitting. Where is he? Did you call hospitals? Did you call the police?"

"Dad's on Citizen," Carson said, showing Stella the open app on his phone.

"What's Citizen?" Stella asked. "What's he talking about?"

I explained how I'd filed a missing person's report, which was now public information.

"My boy, my poor boy. What could've—" Then Stella noticed Harrison with the bloodied paper towel. "And what happened to *him*?"

"Nothing," I said. "Just an accident?"

"What kind of accident?"

"Mom put her hand over my face a little too hard."

"Hand over his face?" Stella glared at me.

"Unintentionally," I said.

Stella rushed up to me and shoved me so hard I almost lost my balance.

"You did that to my grandson? You *hit* him?"

"Of course I didn't hit him."

"She didn't hit me, Grandma."

"Sure you didn't hit him. His lip is bleeding all by itself. I knew you were a nightmare, I've *always* known. I didn't want Michael to marry you—with your Mafia father and your disappearing fiancé, I knew you were trouble."

"If you push me one more time—"

"You'll what? Slap me in the face too? Or maybe you'll try to kill me!"

"Hey," Joe said to Stella, "can you stop this please, huh? We're here to find Michael, let's focus on that, okay?"

I didn't know how long I could last with Stella here. Usually, I let her nastiness slide because she was my kids' grandmother, but this situation was going to test my patience. I knew she was under incredible stress, but I wasn't going to just let myself be the target of her venting.

"I agree with Joe," I said, "but unfortunately I don't know what any of us can do at this point."

"We can find him, that's what we can do," Stella said. "Unless you already know where he is." She turned to Joe. "Does she know where he is?"

"Of course I don't know where he is," I said. "I understand you're upset, but if you keep attacking me in front of my children you're gonna have to leave this apartment."

"Listen to her threats." Stella looked at Joe. "Are you listening to this?"

"He's probably with a friend," Joe said. "Like when he was in college and got drunk and slept on his friends' couches. Can you give me a list of numbers? I'll start making calls."

Michael wasn't a drinker and there was zero chance that he had passed out drunk on a friend's couch, especially early on a Sunday morning when he was going jogging, but if exploring this theory was going to make Joe feel like he had some control over the situation, then God bless him.

"Well, I spoke to one of his friends," I said, "the most likely one, but that person couldn't help. If you want to try some work contacts, you can, but at this point I don't see how that's possible. He wouldn't be at work for twenty-four hours."

"Okay, then where would he be?" Stella asked me. "Do *you* know where he is?"

Again, I was thinking about Jennifer Sears, Nikki, or some other random bimbo he might've hooked up with, but I didn't want to start talking about Michael's possible affairs in front of the boys.

"I have no idea," I said.

"She's lying. I know she's lying. She's a criminal, just like her father."

I couldn't hold back any longer.

"Fuck you! Just fuck the hell out of you, you dried up old biddy!"

I rarely totally lost it, so rare that it got everyone's attention. The apartment was suddenly silent. Joe and Stella looked stunned, but the boys appeared flat-out shocked. That said, I didn't regret lashing out—it was a long time coming.

If the boys weren't home, I would've screamed louder and said much worse things.

Then Stella said to Joe, "See? What did I tell you? Look at that temper. She can't control herself."

"Boys," I said ultra calmly. "Can you please go to your room?"

The kids didn't budge. Why would they? They were theater kids; they loved drama.

"This is all because of *you*," Stella raged. "He was unhappy with *you*."

"All right, Stell," Joe said.

But the mother-in-law from hell wouldn't let up. "It's the truth! The other night you wouldn't come to dinner with us, acting so rude. Michael was so upset about it. He took me aside and said he didn't know what's going on with you lately, you've been acting crazy, and I know my son—I saw how hurt he was, how much *you* hurt him. If something happened to him, it's *your* fault." Stella had moved so close to me I could smell her awful halitosis; seriously, my cat had better breath. She continued, "You've been a horrible wife to him. He probably felt so trapped, just wanted to get away from you, like he had no other options."

"Yeah?" I screamed back at her. "So, what exactly are you implying? Are you saying that because I didn't go to dinner the other night, because I wasn't feeling well, this sent Michael into some kind of deep depression that led to him what, jumping off a fuckin' bridge?"

Glaring back at me, Stella said, "If that's what happened, I swear to God, I'll kill you. I'll strangle you. I'll—"

"Okay, that's enough." Joe separated us with his arms, like a referee trying to untangle a couple of boxers. "Yelling at each other isn't going to bring Michael back, is it? We have to start doing things, being proactive."

The boys were still watching, slack jawed. I felt bad for losing control in front of them; the last thing I wanted to do was cause them more stress.

"Sorry," I said. "This is an emotional time, but your grandfather's totally right." To Joe I added, "I'll give you his work number. I gave it to the police too, but it couldn't hurt to make calls ourselves. Talk to Russell, his partner. Maybe I'm wrong. Maybe someone does know something."

Stella didn't apologize—the word "sorry" wasn't in her vocabulary—but I could tell she regretted crossing a line too, acting so inappropriately in front of her grandchildren.

"Come, Carson. Come, Harrison. Give your grandma a hug. Your grandma needs hugs."

As they embraced, Joe and I went into the living room. I gave him Michael's work contact information, and he went into the nook in the corner, sitting on the leather chair, and made calls. On Michael's Facebook page, I went through his friends list and tried to identify all of his closest contacts—some people who'd been to our wedding whom I hadn't seen since, and some I'd heard him mention but had never met. I sent the same message to each of them:

> **Hello,**
>
> **This is Michael's wife. If you happen to have heard from Michael in the past day or two, can you please let me know?**
>
> **Many thanks,**
>
> **Vanessa Rizzo**

I thought it was best to keep the message as simple and as impersonal as possible. I doubted it would lead to anything, and writing to them, out of the blue, was weird enough.

Jamie Nieves, who went to college with Michael at Cornell, wrote back right away: **No, haven't heard. Everything okay I hope?**

Another friend of Michael's, Gary Walsh, whom he grew up with, also replied quickly: **No, sorry!! Hope all well. Please let me know if I can help!!**

Dan, a friend of his from law school, replied: **No, I haven't, but let me know if I can do anything to help.**

I replied to each of them: **Thanks!**

More replies would probably dribble in, but so far I'd avoided reaching out to the most obvious possibility: Jennifer Sears. Her profile was easy to find in Michael's friends list on Facebook. I wasn't sure why I didn't try her first—maybe the possibility that Michael had been having an affair seemed too real and I was in denial?—but now as I looked at her latest profile photo, a selfie with that wide, gummy smile, wavy red hair, and blood-red lipstick. Of course, she was wearing a tight low-cut top with bulging cleavage. When I saw her relationship status—"Single"—I couldn't help muttering to myself, "Should be 'husband stealer.'"

"Who's she?"

I hadn't heard Joe come up behind me.

"Oh, just an old friend of Michael's."

He squinted at the screen. "Jennifer Sears." He remained perplexed. "Don't think I've heard that name."

"Michael dated her before me."

More silence, then, "Oh, Jenny, that's right. I'm not sure if we ever met her or not. She's kinda cute though, huh?"

I gave Joe a look.

"Sorry, I didn't mean it like *that*."

"Did you find out anything?"

Looking at a sheet from a notepad where he'd scribbled some notes, he said, "Spoke to Helena Boxer, one of his partners. She said she hadn't spoken to Michael since Friday. I haven't been able to reach his other partner, Russell. I just spoke to another attorney, Brian…"

"Gottlieb," I said.

"Right, Gottlieb. He hadn't heard anything either and he said he'd been emailing Michael because Michael missed a meeting this morning.

"Shit." It was so unlike Michael to miss any appointment, especially a work meeting, or even to change plans at the last minute. He often said to me, "I do what I say I'm gonna do," and it was true.

"Gottlieb and Boxer both said I should talk to a woman he's friendly with in the office, Nikki." Joe must've noticed a change in my expression because he said, "What? You *know* her?"

"No, don't know, but she's definitely friendly with Michael."

I left it at that.

"You think she might know something?"

"I don't know, but I think it's definitely worth looking into."

"Okay, she wasn't in the office today, but Gottlieb suggested I try back."

"Wait, not in the office? Are you serious?"

"Yeah, that's what he just said."

"Well, that's coincidental, Michael and her both not showing up to work on the same day."

"I guess so, but there are a lot of reasons why people miss work."

He went back to the corner, to the leather chair, to make the call.

Meanwhile, I returned to Jennifer's Facebook. I scrolled by her other photos—of course she was wearing tight tops in most of the photos, showing off her fake boobs. I don't know why Joe thought she was cute—could men see beyond a woman's tits? Maybe she was more toned than me, but I was much prettier. Most of the photos were of her with friends at restaurants, bars, Hamptons and rooftop parties, where she was holding drinks, laughing in an exaggerated way as if she wanted everyone to know how laidback she was. It was easy to imagine her and Michael reconnecting, especially if Michael confided in her about how unhappy he was in our marriage and how I was such a controlling shrew. I'd always known that Michael wished I had been more fun, more of a party girl. He liked to drink—after work, at parties, on vacation—and one was usually my limit.

Now I was more convinced than ever that Michael was having an affair—with Jennifer, maybe with Nikki, maybe with someone else. Maybe Michael was on Ashley Madison, or one of those cheating sites. He once told me a story about a friend of his from high school who lived in LA now who routinely had affairs with women he'd met online. Maybe the friend had convinced Michael to give it a try, especially if Michael was complaining about how he was unhappily married and wasn't making any progress in couples counseling.

This scenario seemed real. Too real.

I tapped a message to Jennifer:

Michael's WIFE here. I don't know exactly what's going on with you and MY HUSBAND, but if you have an idea where he is I suggest you contact me immediately. FYI

I'm notifying the police about you and him as well.

I clicked send. If I'd waited before sending the message, I probably would've toned it down. After all, the main objective was for Jennifer to help us find Michael, so sending her a threatening note probably wasn't the best idea.

I figured she'd ignore the note, or maybe consult with her friends or even a lawyer before she got back to me, but surprisingly she responded almost immediately:

Dear Vanessa,

I have no idea what this about or where Michael is, but I really don't appreciate being threatened by you.

I hope all is well with both of you.

Sincerely, Jennifer

"Dear Vanessa"—was she fucking serious? Unless that was sarcasm, though, in a way, that would have made it even more fucked up. The whole tone of the message was infuriating—seeming not to care that I was basically accusing her of fucking my husband. "I hope all is well with both of you," implying that, what, she thought I was mentally ill? I wondered what she *knew* about me, about my past. Did she know that I'd been questioned by the police after Colin disappeared and that I'd been a murder suspect? Did Michael tell her about my struggles with mental illness? Had Michael been complaining to her about me throughout our marriage, trying to get her to feel sorry for him?

I knew I was just making up stories in my head, but I was getting angrier. I didn't believe for one second that she had "no idea" where Michael was. She might've responded immediately because she thought it would look suspicious if she'd ignored me. Besides, if she was lying naked in bed at her apartment, or in a hotel room, and Michael was in her bathroom showering, would she have replied to me any differently? Naturally, she'd deny everything and make it out like I was crazy for being so suspicious.

Joe was in the corner making phone calls, and the boys had gone to their room with Stella. I'm glad that at least she was keeping them occupied. I was feeling queasy—a combination of everything I'd been going through and not having eaten anything since yesterday. I went into the kitchen and had a granola bar and made myself a cup of French Roast with the Keurig.

I wanted to stay optimistic that Michael would return soon, but I also knew I had to stay realistic and prepare for the very real possibility that there wouldn't be a happy ending. After Colin disappeared, I'd gotten obsessed with missing persons' cases. I read about every case I could, maybe—as Dr. Stone would point out later—because I was looking to have a sense of control over a situation that was uncontrollable. I knew all the statistics and the likely outcomes as time went by, and they weren't good. After twenty-four hours, and especially after forty-eight hours, the odds of a missing person returning decreased drastically as leads dried up and memories faded. Already the odds weren't in Michael's favor. Of course, this didn't necessarily mean that he couldn't come home at any second. There had been cases where people returned weeks or months later, and Colin had reappeared after nineteen years.

Still, as each minute passed, I knew that the likelihood of a happy ending was dwindling. I imagined the police showing up, informing me that Michael was dead, and total chaos ensuing.

We found his body in his lover's apartment. It appears as

if they had an argument and she murdered him. I'm very sorry for your loss, Mrs. Rizzo.

No, somehow it was hard for me to make this scenario seem real. Anything was possible, but was it actually likely that a woman he'd been involved with had murdered him, or even hurt him to the extent where he'd become incapacitated and couldn't contact us? Yes, things like that happened all the time in true crime shows, and sometimes the most normal, most benign-seeming people turned out to be vicious killers. Still, this seemed like a giant leap as Michael was so level-headed and rational; it was hard to imagine him getting into a crazy situation with a psychotic woman.

This all begged the question—if a woman or an affair he was having wasn't related to his disappearance, then where the hell was he?

Maybe two things could be true at once—he was having an affair, *and* he was in an accident. What if, instead of running in Central Park, he went running along the East River? He sometimes ran up along the promenade near Gracie Mansion. He'd started taking blood pressure medication a couple of years ago. He didn't have a serious heart issue, but he could've had an episode, or a reaction to the meds, and got dizzy. He could've stopped to rest and then fell over the railing into the river. It was possible, if it happened quickly enough, that no one had witnessed this, and there were probably cases where people had fallen into the river and their bodies had sunk or drifted out to New York Harbor or wherever.

Now, the river theory seemed more likely than a lover killing him, but neither seemed great. If Michael was never found, or even if—God forbid—he really had been killed, I'd be devastated, but I doubted it would affect me the way losing Colin had. I didn't think I'd sink into a deep depression and need drugs and years of therapy before I could stabilize. I was older now, could handle my emotions better. I'd been through this before, mourning Colin, so I'd know what to expect, and it wouldn't seem quite as crushing. I'd also get over it quicker because I'd never loved Michael the way I'd loved Colin.

All marriages had problems, but there had always been more distance in ours, compared to other couples I knew. It was so different from how my relationship with Colin had been. Colin and I had never had any major conflicts; we'd never even had an argument—well, one that I could remember. We were always in synch, whether we were travelling or hanging out in the city, and our physical connection was off the charts—sex with him was by far the best sex of my life. I couldn't get enough of his body; I wanted him all the time. We didn't keep secrets from each other and the idea of him having affairs never would've even occurred to me.

If Michael was dead, we would all be devastated, but at least financially we'd be okay. A few years ago, Michael had upped his life insurance from two million to four. I could pay off our mortgage and, with our savings factored in too, I'd never worry about money again. The kids already had college savings plans so their financial futures wouldn't be an issue. I could continue to build my business, help Harrison with his acting career, and, with a little luck, I could reconnect with Colin. Now that I knew that Colin was out there somewhere, all I had to do was find him. I could post about him online or hire a P.I. to help find him. Once we were together, it would be magical, like we'd always imagined it would be before our fantasies were abruptly interrupted. He would explain what had happened nineteen years ago and, whatever the explanation was, unlike how I felt about Michael, I knew I'd be able to forgive Colin. We'd have the destination wedding in Costa Rica, only inviting a few close friends, and my boys, of course. It would take some time for the boys to adjust, but eventually they'd fall in love with Colin the way I had, and I knew he'd make a great stepfather. I would sell our apartment, and we'd get a bigger place, a three-bedroom so the kids could have their own rooms, or we could use the additional room for another child. Getting pregnant at forty-three years old would be difficult, but not impossible. I had a client, Emily, who'd had twins at forty-six with in vitro. Maybe, with a little more luck, Colin and I could have twins, a boy and a girl—we'd always wanted one of each. Maybe it wasn't too late for all our fantasies to come true. For so long, it had seemed like our dreams were dead, sucked away in a rip current, but now they were alive again, because Colin was alive, and nothing seemed impossible.

TEN

"SORRY, WHAT WAS that?"

Joe had come up behind me.

"I said I couldn't get through to the other partner, but I just talked to her."

By "her" I knew he meant Nikki.

"Oh, okay, very cool. What did she say?"

Now that I'd begun to move on—even if only in my fantasies—the woman Michael might, or might not, have been having an affair with didn't seem nearly as important to me as she had just a little while ago.

Before Joe could continue, Stella burst into the living room to join us.

"What did who say?" she asked. "What're you talking about? Did they find Michael?"

"This woman Michael works with," Joe said.

"Nikki? Who's she?"

"A woman Michael works with. A paralegal or something."

"What about her? She found Michael?"

"Nobody found Michael." Joe, aggravated, was raising his voice. "Jesus Christ, can you get that hearing aid already? She said she talked to him on Saturday. They were working on some will together."

"That makes sense," I said. "I mean, I know he was working on a will. What else did she say?"

"She doesn't know where he is," Joe said, "but she sounded very upset."

"I'm sure," I said.

"What're you sure about?" Stella asked. "What does that mean?"

I had to hand it to Stella—she was a royal pain in the ass, but she was also incredibly perceptive. Nothing slipped by her.

First, I pushed open the swinging door and peeked down the hallway to make sure the boys were still in their room, then I let the door close and returned to Joe and Stella and said, "Well, I'll be completely honest with both of you. I have no idea if this relates to anything or not, but I believe Michael was having an affair, or multiple affairs."

Glaring, as if in disbelief, Stella said, "Oh, really." Then she said to Joe, "D'you hear this?"

Joe said to me, "So you think he and this Nikki were—"

"I don't know anything," I said, "but I think we have to at least consider the possibility that that's what's going on here, that Michael met someone else, and maybe, hopefully, he's with that person right now."

I was thinking about Colin, his hazel eyes glowing as he smiled at me. I knew how inappropriate this was, timing-wise, and I forced the image out of my mind.

"Michael cheating?" Stella said. "Isn't that interesting?"

"Okay, Stella," Joe said.

Ignoring him, she continued to me, "Michael was telling us just the other night about you and that professor at Harrison's play."

Stella wasn't raising her voice, but it was loud naturally, and I was worried the boys could overhear her.

"Hey," I said, "can you *please*?"

"So you don't deny it?"

"Of course I deny it. That man is a friend of mine, that's all. Why? What did Michael tell you about him, about us?"

"He didn't say it in so many words, but it was obvious what he meant. He didn't like the way you were flirting with him, he thought it was disrespectful."

"He used that word? Disrespectful?"

"He used worse words than that."

"Please keep your voice down," I stage-whispered. "I don't want the boys overhearing this bullshit."

"It's better they hear the truth from me, than lies from you."

"I'm not cheating on Michael, and I don't know if Michael's been cheating on me. Like both of you, I'm just digging for an explanation, *any* explanation for where Michael can be."

"Well, I know my son a lot better than you do," Stella said, "and he's not a cheater. If anyone's a cheater, I'm looking at her."

Before I could respond with a zinger of my own, Joe said, "Okay, that's enough, Stella."

Stella glared at him. "You're defending her?"

"We don't know everything that's going on with Michael," Joe said. "I mean, everybody has secrets."

Now Stella gave her husband an accusing look. "Sorry, that's right, I forgot who I'm talking to."

Michael had told me stories about Joe's philandering years ago and how he and Stella had almost gotten divorced when Michael was a kid. It seemed like there had been either a recent incident, or Stella was still resentful about the past.

"Believe me, I hope I'm wrong about Michael," I said. "I'm just giving you the facts."

"Facts!" Stella turned back toward me. "The *fact* is, *you're* the cheater. *You're* the one from that crazy, troubled Staten Island family."

I couldn't listen to any more of this. I left the living room and went into the kitchen. I checked my phone, looking at the green messages to Michael.

While the green was frustrating, it wasn't as frightening as yesterday. Maybe a sense of inevitability, of acceptance, was setting in.

Pacing, squeezing my phone, I was upset about Stella, but I couldn't totally blame her. She was terrified because her son was missing, as I would be if one of my boys had disappeared. She was lashing out at me and Joe because there was no other way for her to express her anger and pain. But, while I would never admit this to Stella, she wasn't entirely wrong about me. She was a stubborn, difficult woman with a nasty edge, but she was extremely perceptive too. She'd picked up on something about, maybe just a vibe or a change in my mannerisms, but she knew something was off. She falsely assumed I was having an actual affair, but Colin had always been "the other man" in my marriage with Michael. I thought I'd gotten past my attachment to Colin, but since seeing him on Friday, that had changed. Stella had no way of knowing about any of this, of course, but I know she still *knew.*

I heard Harrison and Carson, mingling near the front

door. I went over and saw that they had their hoodies on, about to leave.

"Where do you think you're going?" I asked.

Harrison wasn't looking at me when he said, "What difference does it make?"

"You can't just leave."

"And you can't just keep us locked in here all day."

Stella, naturally needing to get involved in any conflict, came over and said, "They're right. Let them leave."

I knew Stella was just being her usual oppositional self and didn't actually think they should leave or care one way or another. She just wanted to express a strong opinion to usurp me, to get some conflict going. Her M.O. was to force me to take the bait and double down on my own stance, so I could come off as the controlling monster and she could be the kind, rational grandma. She'd been pulling crap like this for years when she was around me and the kids. I could take her in small doses, but too much Stella was always a nightmare. I wanted to cut her some slack this time though, reminding myself that she was just grieving about Michael and this had nothing to do with me.

"You're staying," I said to the boys. "It's important for our family to be together right now and I don't want you walking around alone now, while we're all so upset."

"C'mon, Ma," Carson said. "We just want to get some pizza, we're starving."

"We have food here," I said, "and I'll order in pizza, Chinese, whatever you want."

"Actually, we want to go to Central Park to look for Dad," Harrison said.

"He's not in the park."

"Maybe they didn't look in the right places," Harrison

said. "I know where Dad goes running, in the Ramble. He could be there. Maybe he fell and broke his ankle or something. Maybe he can't move. Maybe he's unconscious."

"That's extremely unlikely," I said, "but the police are looking everywhere for him now and I'm sure they're looking in the Ramble too. There'll be news soon, hopefully good news."

"*Hopefully*? Why *hopefully*?"

"Harrison, please—"

"Yesterday you promised me he'd come home, now it's hopefully. Why is it hopefully now?"

"Because I *am* hopeful."

"Why only hopeful. What did you find out? What do you know?"

Joe came in from the living room, saying, "What's happening now?"

"Vanessa won't let the kids out," Stella said, "and she's upsetting them."

Carson was crying again. Harrison angrily took off his hoodie, threw it against the door, and marched to his room. Carson followed him.

With flared nostrils Stella said to me, "Instead of ordering Chinese food, you should be finding that detective and finding out what the hell is going on. Why haven't you heard anything? Are they really trying to find him? Maybe if it's not a little kid missing, they don't even try."

I didn't want to get into it again with Stella, so I walked away. Of course I had no place to actually *go*. Our apartment was two bedrooms, approximately 1400 square feet—not too shabby for Manhattan, but with five tense people in it, it felt like a tiny studio.

Back in the living room, I gazed out the windows beyond

the balcony. Still no sign of any news trucks. Stella could be right about her theory that the police might not exactly be working as hard as they could to find Michael, a forty-five-year-old man. It wasn't exactly like they were going to put out an Amber Alert for him. Grown men and women probably disappeared every day in New York and the media couldn't cover every story. When Colin vanished it had been much different because Shelter Island is a small community, and he was a young med student who presumably disappeared swimming in the ocean, which was much more newsworthy and dramatic than a middle-aged man disappearing in Manhattan.

It looked like another beautiful day—sunny with a 9/11-like deep blue sky. I didn't blame the boys for wanting to go out, to get away from all this tension in the apartment. It was hard to feel trapped and claustrophobic anywhere, but it was even harder in a big city, with so many possibilities. Gazing toward the midtown skyscrapers, I wondered where Colin was right now. I had a feeling, a very strong feeling, that at this moment he was looking out a window—maybe at the hotel he was staying at—thinking about me. He was fantasizing about spending a day with me in the city, like the average, amazing days we used to have together. We used to love walking anywhere together, like on that trip to Paris and London, or when we went hiking all those weekends in the Catskills and Berkshires. But our favorite, by far, was walking around New York. Sometimes we walked around downtown in the Village, or along the Hudson, or in Fort Tryon Park in Washington Heights. We always picked up food along the way, and ate as we walked, or sometimes picnicked in the park. I remember always laughing and stopping to make out like teenagers.

Colin reappearing and Michael disappearing had to be fate. Colin and I had always told each other that we were soulmates, that we were meant to be together, and maybe God was trying to tell me that He knows, and that He was listening. Yes, that must be it. Colin and Michael had never been in my life at the same time, maybe because there wasn't room for both of them. In order for Colin to return, Michael had to leave. This wasn't a tragedy; this was destiny.

"Well, did you call the detective or not?"

Stella's grating voice jolted me out of my fantasy. It felt horrible to realize I was back in this jail-cell apartment.

"Calling right now," I said, trying to remember how it felt with that mist against my face, and Colin squeezing my hand, with our whole lives ahead of us.

NOT SURPRISINGLY, DETECTIVE Randle had no new information. If there had been a break in the case, or anything substantial had come up, he would have called.

"We're actively searching for leads," he said. "These things take time."

I knew he was saying this to try to be optimistic and reassuring. He seemed sincere and I did believe he was trying to find Michael, but I still felt like he was holding back with me, like I was a child who couldn't handle bad news or "the truth," like he needed to soften things for me.

"I totally understand," I said. "I appreciate all your help."

Stella and Joe were overhearing the conversation. When I ended the call, I glanced at them and said, "Nothing."

"They're not doing anything," Stella said. "See? I told you."

"I think he wants to find him," I said.

"What do you know?" she said.

It was a challenge to take this nastiness without reacting to it, but I somehow managed to stay calm.

"I'm ordering Chinese," I said. "If you'd like me to order something for you two lemme know."

"I don't have an appetite," Stella said. "I'll never have an appetite again until they find Michael."

Stella, crying, walked away.

Joe whispered to me, "Get her chicken chow fun. I'll take a shrimp with lobster sauce."

When the food arrived, I made the kids come out of their room. Carson, Joe and I ate a little bit, but Harrison refused, and Stella wouldn't even come to the table. Stella continued to sob, complaining how the cops weren't doing enough to find "my baby boy." My claustrophobia was getting worse. I felt like if I stayed in the apartment for much longer, I wouldn't be able to breathe.

"Come on, kids," I announced, "let's take a walk."

"I thought you wanted to keep them locked up in here," Stella said.

Of course I'd never said that, but I didn't want to get into it with her. I said, "It's a nice day and some air will do us some good."

I suggested that Stella and Joe stay at the apartment in case Michael came home. They agreed that this was a good idea; I was glad as I needed a break from all the tension.

It was good to get outside in the sun; even breathing in high-AQI city air was refreshing. The boys still wanted to go to the park, and I agreed. I still didn't think it would lead to anything, but if it distracted them for a while, made them feel like they were being proactive, it was worth it. As we walked west, then uptown on Fifth, the boys kept checking their phones for a possible text from Michael, and I checked a few times too. In the park, we went to the Ramble, the hilly, woodsy area between the lake and Great Lawn.

I'd been to this area a few months ago, but now the leaves on the trees were blocking visibility to the buildings surrounding the park. With the rocks and rushing streams, it really did seem more like the country than the middle of Manhattan. We'd gone on family walks in this area many times, and sometimes the boys went running with Michael, so they knew exactly what paths he normally took. I reminded them that we didn't even know for sure that Michael had gone running in the park, that he could've gone along the river, or in the streets. Of course, I didn't want to tell the boys that there was a chance that he didn't go running at all, that he could've gone to meet a lover who'd subsequently murdered him, or he'd fallen in the river and drowned.

"On Sunday mornings, he always went running in the park," Harrison said. "I know that's where he went."

We walked along the various paths, as well as through the tunnels and up the stone steps between the rocks. The boys were taking photos on their phones of "evidence" they thought they'd discovered, like footprints and a discarded Evian bottle because Michael liked to drink Evian. I let them continue to play detective until we started retracing our steps.

"I think it's time to head back," I said.

"No, we can't, not yet," Harrison said. "We have to find more evidence."

He had a tone in his voice, obsessive and intense, and I knew the stress of this situation was triggering him.

"We've done as much as we can do," I said. "Let's go

home now, like we agreed we would."

"No, we're staying."

"Did you remember to take your Adderall today?"

"Look, over there, what's that?"

"Where?" Carson asked.

The boys rushed over toward a large rock where there were streaks of what looked like blood but could've been soda or coffee. They were both frantically taking photos with their phones.

"The police need to see this," Harrison said. "I was right, he could've hit his head and now he's wandering around the city unconscious."

"Maybe the cops can check the DNA," Carson said.

"They *have to* check it," Harrison said. "They also have to start searching the city for people with head injuries, one of them could be Dad."

This was getting out of control. Harrison's anxiety was affecting Carson now—the way it often did—and now they were both riled up. As a parent, it was hard to watch your kids act out with negative behavior that reminds you of your own, especially when you remember how much pain it caused you.

"We really have to go now," I said to Harrison. "Please."

I knew pulling the guilt card would get to Harrison; he was very empathetic and always knew when he'd pushed me too far.

"Okay, c'mon, Carson. Mom's right, let's get back."

I mouthed, *Thank you.*

The walk home was mostly quiet. I was absorbed with worries about Michael, mainly concerned with how it would affect the boys, but also fantasizing about our new life with Colin. As a teenager, when I first began showing serious signs of depression, my first therapist had told me: "You always have to remember, life goes by in waves, and bad times never last forever." Throughout the years I'd always thought about this when I was going through a dark period. I told myself that if I just got through the rough patch, better times would come. It was usually hard to do this, though, especially without medication, but this time I was confident I could get through it. I just had to focus on what I could control, stay strong for my kids, and eventually the veil would lift and, when it did, Colin would be there waiting for me, waiting for *us*. It was so clear—the vision of Colin, Harrison, Carson and me arriving at the Shubert Theater on West Forty-fourth Street for the latest hot musical. We were all dressed up, laughing, with all the bleakness in the past, and the future exciting and full of possibilities.

We continued east, to First Avenue. Waiting to cross at Sixty-third, I noticed a black SUV passing by in front of us. I was almost certain that I'd seen the same SUV on Fifth Avenue when we were leaving the park. It could have been a coincidence, though, or maybe the driver was driving around, searching for a parking spot, not easy in Manhattan these days with all the CitiBike docks and outdoor dining setups.

Later, the boys were walking a little ahead of me. As they turned onto Fifty-Second Street, they stopped and Harrison said to Carson, "Oh, shit."

I couldn't see what they saw, but I braced myself, taking a deep breath and letting it out slowly, reminding myself: *Life goes by in waves.*

Then I turned the corner and stopped alongside them, looking at the news trucks—at least four of them—and about twenty people congregated in front of the building. There was no doubt there was some major news about the case. Was Michael dead? Had his body been found in the East River after all? I tried to brace myself. If he was dead, the next several days were going to be a total shit show, but there would be lightness ahead. There would always be lightness ahead.

"It must be about Dad," Harrison said.

"Is he dead?" Carson said. "Does this mean he's dead?"

Every mother wants to protect their children from pain, but there was no way I could protect them from this, maybe the worst day of their lives. I held their hands, squeezing tightly, and we continued ahead.

There was a camera crew from Spectrum News, but thankfully they weren't filming. I just wanted to get inside, get the kids safely into the apartment, and then I'd deal with whatever was going on.

"Ms. Rizzo."

I glanced to my right and saw Detective Randle approaching, with a solemn expression. I felt the way families of service people must feel when uniformed officers arrive at their front door.

"Is my dad dead?" Carson asked. "Is he dead or not?"

"No, he's not," Randle said. "We have nothing to report yet on that front."

"Then what's going on out here?" Harrison asked.

Randle looked at me. "Can we talk somewhere in private?"

"Sure," I said, completely confused myself. Then I spotted the camera guy about to start filming us and I shouted, "Don't film my children!"

This got the attention of reporters and a woman with short blonde hair held out her iPhone in front of my face—I assumed it was filming—and asked, "Have you heard anything from your husband today?" Then some guy from behind me asked, "What do you think happened to your husband, Vanessa?"

Instinctively, I yanked the boys by their arms and, as reporters shouted questions behind us, I pulled them into our building's lobby.

"Both of you, go up to Grandma and Grandpa right now."

"But we want to know what's going on," Harrison said.

"I'll let you know as soon as I know. I don't want you two on TV."

I saw Randle approaching.

"We have information," Harrison said to him. "We think we found my father's blood in Central Park."

Holding his phone up for Randle to see, Carson said, "See? We took pics and everything."

"Let me talk to the detective alone now," I said to the boys. "Upstairs, right now."

Shaking their heads, the kids got on an elevator. I waited till the doors closed, then I said to Randle:

"Sorry, my kids have wild imaginations sometimes. I'm fairly certain that they did *not* find any blood, at least not my husband's blood. But can you please tell me what the hell all this fuss is about?"

There was something different about Randle. He didn't seem as empathetic as yesterday. Unless I was totally imagining it, he seemed to be trying to analyze or judge me.

"There's been a development," he said.

"I thought you said there's no news, that his body wasn't found or—"

"I said his body hasn't been found, yes, that's true, but I

didn't say there wasn't news." Still looking like he was studying me, trying to see into me, he added, "Is there someplace we can go or not, Ms. Rizzo?"

ELEVEN

THERE WAS NO way that I was inviting a police detective up to our apartment. I didn't want the kids, or even Stella and Joe, listening in. I figured that if I got this news first, and if it was disturbing, at least I could figure out how to deliver it to my family.

"Sure, I guess we could sit on the couch over there."

The couches in the lobby were adjacent to the window, right where all of the reporters and other onlookers were gathered. I recognized a few of my neighbors from the building out there.

"Actually," I added, "that's not very private either."

Tony, our doorman who'd just started his afternoon shift, overheard us and said, "You can go to the lounge in the back."

"Oh, really? Great idea, Tony. Thank you, that's so nice."

Tony led us into the lounge, which was mainly a "dressing room" where the doormen put on their uniforms. It was undecorated, nothing on the walls. Strewn on a chair in the corner were the clothes Tony must've worn to work: jeans, a hooded blue-and-orange Knicks sweatshirt, Nikes.

Randle sat at the desk. Of course it wasn't *his* desk, but I felt like he did this to exert his authority.

"I assume that you aren't aware of the conversations that have been taking place online," Randle said.

"No, I… I mean, I was online earlier, but I didn't see anything unusual, and like the boys said we were just in Central Park. I wanted to get them out of the apartment, get them some air. I needed air too, to be honest."

I knew I was rambling. Why wouldn't I be? I was stressed and Randle's attitude, which made this feel like an interrogation, wasn't fucking helping.

"I see," Randle said. "Well, I guess then I'm giving you a heads up. Some news about you came out, not from us—from a reporter at The *New York Post*."

"*What*?" I was shocked. "What about? What's going on?"

"How about you tell me about you and Colin Grant?"

I had to take a few moments to absorb this; it felt so out of context. Why was Randle asking me about Colin?

"Colin?" I decided to play dumb, like the classic negotiation tactic—thou who speaks first loses. "You mean my ex-fiancé, Colin? Why would I say anything about him to you? He has nothing to do with Michael."

Randle was studying me again.

"You didn't answer my question."

"I think I did."

"So, you're telling me you don't think it's relevant that your fiancé disappeared years ago and now your husband disappeared? You think it's just a coincidence?"

"Yes, I do actually…Wait, is that what the *Post* reporter is posting about? About the coincidence of this? Okay, yeah, so what, it's a coincidence. You think I'm unaware of that?

That's not newsworthy and it certainly doesn't deserve having news cameras pointed at my kids' faces after we return from the park after what's been an extremely stressful, traumatic day for them, and for me too."

"Slow down," Randle said. "Take a couple of breaths, okay?"

He sounded so fucking condescending I wanted to smack him.

"I'm fine, thank you, and I really need to be with my kids right now."

"I'll only be a few more minutes. I hear what you're saying, but I happen to think it *is* relevant. I also happen to think it's relevant that you were a suspect in your fiancé's disappearance."

"A suspect? Oh please, come on, that's ridiculous. I was never a *suspect*."

This wasn't true—technically I *had* been a suspect.

"I've looked into the case, and I know you were questioned multiple times by—"

"Yes, I was questioned. Of course I was questioned. A lot of people were questioned."

"You were also a person of interest."

"For five minutes, and then I was no longer a person of interest. The last time I saw Colin was when he left to go swimming."

"And the last time you saw your husband is when he left to go running."

I stared at Randle, then said, "Seriously? Is that what this is all about? My fiancé disappeared swimming in the Atlantic Ocean. There was a search for him, a media frenzy, and yes there was speculation about *everything*—every possible scenario. Actually, this makes sense now, because the *Post* ran some of the most ridiculous, most sensational stories. I bet that same reporter who was covering the story came out of the woodwork—Hoffman. Was it Hoffman who wrote the story?"

"Yes, actually it was Hoffman. Bob Hoffman."

"Oh, God, that guy was making up nonsense—pure nonsense—and I was never, never an actual suspect. The *Enquirer* said I was a suspect; do you believe *that* too?"

"I'm just wondering why you didn't make me aware—"

"Aware of what? There's nothing to be aware of."

"Look, Ms. Rizzo. I just want to hear, from you—what happened with you and Colin Grant, okay?"

"Why? What do you think happened exactly? You think I killed Colin nineteen years ago, and now I killed my husband? You think I'm a psychopath? Why don't you talk to my friends? Why don't you talk to people who know me, and you'll see how insane this all is."

"I'm just asking for transparency, Ms. Rizzo. I don't like feeling like I'm one step behind social media."

"Okay, you want transparency? I'll give you fucking transparency…I actually spotted Colin on the street the other day. How's that?"

Randle's eyebrows lifted. "*Spotted* him?"

"Yes, getting into a cab at Columbus Circle on Friday. It was a fleeting thing, and we didn't speak at all, unfortunately, but it was definitely him. He's alive, okay? Nothing even happened to him. Now you see how ridiculous this all is?"

"So, you're saying you think he's alive?"

I couldn't tell if this was an earnest question, if he thought I was nuts, or some combination.

"Yes. He's alive."

"Okay, so how's that possible? What, you think he ran

away, faked his death?"

"Maybe. Or maybe he had amnesia, but he definitely didn't die. I've always suspected this, but I never had proof until now. Wait, I'll show you."

On my phone, I swiped to the screenshot of Colin getting into the cab, then held up my phone for Randle to see.

"What am I looking at?"

"That's Colin."

"It is?"

"Yes."

"Where?"

"In the back of the cab."

"I can't make that person out."

"It's *him*. And I saw him before I took the photo. *Clearly*."

Okay, maybe I was exaggerating a little about *clearly*, but I wanted to get my point across.

"Did you tell anyone about this?"

"Just Michael."

"You didn't tell the police?"

"Why would I tell the police? What would you have done? I didn't think you'd exactly start a search for somebody who's been missing for nineteen years. But my point is this should end any ridiculous talk online about this having anything to do with Colin, since as you can see, Colin's alive, and I'm praying that Michael is alive too."

"The photo's extremely hard to make out."

"It's him. I'm telling you. It's him."

He took a deep breath—for dramatic effect obviously—then said, "How was your relationship with your husband lately?"

"Excuse me?"

"Were things good? Was there tension between you two? I mean, you'd mentioned you thought he might've been having an affair."

"Things were normal. Nothing out of the ordinary."

"Then why did you suspect—"

"He was cheating on me? Because that's what men do—they lie and they cheat and they have secrets. Do you want Jennifer Sears' contact info? I'm not saying she's definitely involved but I'm willing to bet she knows *something*. Also, there's another woman Nikki at his office, I know Michael has flirted with her—maybe she knows something. Or there could be another woman I don't know about."

"You can give me the info, sure, but even if your husband was having an affair, I don't see why you think that has something to do with where he is right now. I mean, what do you think, one of these women *abducted* him?"

"I have no idea. Am I the cop or you? My husband was acting…weird …secretive. Like having hushed phone conversations, hiding his laptop when I came by. I don't know if it's related or not, I'm just telling you what I know."

"What was this about your kids finding blood on rocks?"

"Oh, we were in the Ramble in Central Park earlier, but I think that was just the kids' imagination. I think they're panicked, scared, like we all are. But on the way home from the park I saw a black SUV following us."

"Following you?"

"Yes…I mean I saw it twice, several blocks apart, on Fifth Ave, then on First."

"How do you know it was following you? I mean, why is that so unusual?"

"It's not *so* unusual, but it's something I noticed so I wanted to bring it to your—"

"How do you know it was even the same SUV?"

"Well, *it looked* the same. It was black with tinted windows and—"

"Let's just try to focus on facts, okay, Ms. Rizzo? Time is not our friend right now."

Hating his tone again, I said, "Okay. Fine. Gotcha."

A few minutes later, as I walked back through the lobby toward the elevators, I glanced outside through the large windows, seeing that the number of people outside had increased; there was officially a crowd there now. I spotted news trucks from WPIX and FOX that must've just arrived.

I texted Randle, with links to Jennifer Sears' Facebook page and Nikki Fox's LinkedIn. Then, riding the elevator up, I went online on my phone. I did a search for "Vanessa Rizzo," to see what all this ridiculousness was about. I expected to see a few posts and I felt a sharp jolt in my chest when I saw that my name was "trending in New York City." Then I swiped up and saw that there were dozens of posts about me, most quoting or referring to the *New York Post* story entitled *Manhattan Woman's Lover Vanishes...Again.* I couldn't believe what I was seeing. *Vanishes*? Michael had been missing for about thirty hours, that was hardly *vanishing*, and this reporter, Alex Diaz, had dug up details about Colin's disappearance from Bob Hoffman's nineteen-year-old article, lamely trying to make the case that the incidents were related. It was sensational, irresponsible, and inflammatory and if it kept up, I was going to have to think about a lawsuit. Maybe I could even ask one of Michael's partners for a referral.

On the fourteenth floor, I got off, continuing to swipe through the posts. I didn't read any of them fully, but I got the gist by comments like "I bet she killed him," "Ooo this is gonna be a good one!" and "Bitch look crazy" with a photo of me cut-and-pasted from my LinkedIn. I did not look crazy in that photo, thank you very much. It was actually one of my best pics from a shoot I did for my business last year, at a photography studio in midtown. I was in a cute flowy boho dress with my hair recently cut and colored, looking back over my shoulder and smiling at the camera. I wasn't hurt—I couldn't give a shit about what some random stranger thought about me—but I was trying to figure out what, if anything, I could do to fight back about this. I knew responding to any of the posts was a bad idea, it would only make me seem defensive or, worse, like I had something I needed to defend. Should I consult with a lawyer? Should I sue the *New York Post*, or Alex Diaz?

I went back to the beginning of the search results, seeing that there had been several new posts in just the past minute about me. The *Post* story had been released while I was in the park with my boys. It was incredible how fast this had gone viral and I feared for what was coming next. I'd seen enough true crime shows to know that once the online mob started spreading distorted stories, the internet sleuths got involved, and then things would really get out of control. People I knew were going to read this crap, if they hadn't already read it, but I was most concerned about the boys. I didn't want them to hear about any of this crap, especially without hearing about it from me first. They knew about Colin—well, the basics anyway. They knew we were engaged, that he'd disappeared swimming, that his body was never discovered, and that he was presumed dead. But as far as I knew they had never seen any of the articles from the past, about how I was questioned, *routinely* questioned by the police. I had to prepare them for this current viral craziness before they found out about it themselves.

After a few breaths to collect myself, I continued along the hallway to my apartment. I was rehearsing in my head what I was going to say to the boys—*It's all ridiculous lies...We can't pay any attention to it... We have to stay focused, strong, resilient*—and then I opened the door and faced Stella in the vestibule. She was aiming her index finger at my face.

"Murderer! Murderer!"

Joe came from the living room and stood alongside her. By the way he was glaring at me, I could tell he shared her sentiment.

All I could think about was my boys. I tried to get by, but Stella stepped in front of me, standing in my way.

"Oh no you don't," she said. "If you think I'm letting you anywhere near my grandchildren you're crazy. Acting like you're searching for Michael while you know very well what happened to him."

"Oh, stop it," I said. "This is insanity. Pure insanity."

Harrison and Carson left the kitchen and lingered behind Joe and Stella.

"So I guess everyone saw some of the same bullshit online that I just saw," I said. "It's clickbait. Some desperate *New York Post* reporter is trying to get attention. What happened to ex-fiancé years ago has nothing to do with what happened to Michael. Zero, zilch, *nada*."

"Ah ha, h*appened to Michael.*" Stella was looking around for support. "You heard her say, *happened*, right? How does she know something *happened* to him? Why would she say that if she doesn't know *something*?"

"Stop it." I was looking at the boys. "You know I didn't mean it like that. That's ridiculous."

"She's a serial killer," Stella said to Joe. "Michael got married to a serial killer, and she killed him, just like she killed that other guy."

I'd had enough.

"That's it, I want you out of my apartment. You too, Joe. Out of here, both of you! Stay in the city, stay at a hotel, do whatever you want. I just want to be alone with my children right now."

"Over my dead body," Stella said. "We're not going anywhere without our grandchildren. We'll get custody too. You're not gonna kill any more of my children!"

I *saw myself* grabbing Stella by the arm, forcibly pulling her into the hallway, then dragging Joe into the hallway too, and slamming the door. I might've actually *done* it if Harrison didn't say:

"I agree with mom," Harrison said. "Mom wouldn't hurt Dad, that's stupid. All that stuff online is stupid."

"Yeah, I think it's stupid too," Carson said. "So stupid."

"What do you expect them to say," Stella said, "you're their mother. But that doesn't mean we're leaving them here."

"We're not going anywhere," Harrison said.

"Yes, you are," Stella said. "Pack suitcases, both of you."

The boys came over and stood alongside me, to make it clear whose side they were on. As it registered for Stella that she wasn't going to win this argument, she began to sob. Joe came over and held her, as the boys and I just watched.

Finally, after a couple of minutes, I said, "Look, I know how upset you are. But I swear to you, on the boys' lives, that I had nothing to do with this. The things you said were extremely hurtful and I deserve an apology."

Of course, she didn't say sorry, or acknowledge what I

said, or even look at me. Joe wouldn't make eye contact with me either. Stella's attitude wasn't surprising because we'd always butted heads, but Joe seeming to turn on me was pretty surprising.

"C'mon, Stella," Joe said, "let's go."

Stella said something to Joe that I couldn't make out, but I assumed she was agreeing to leave because he was leading her toward the front door. Then she turned back and said, "Wait" and she came over to me. I thought she was going to slap me and I was bracing myself, readying to avoid her hand if she tried. Instead, she leaned in close and whispered into my left ear, "You better be telling me the fucking truth, because if you hurt my Michael, I swear to God, I'll kill you. You have my word."

When Joe and Stella left, I sighed, feeling like clamps that had been pressing against my chest were suddenly released and I could breathe freely again. I could tell the boys were relieved too.

"Wow, Grandma's a hot mess," Carson said.

Harrison and I both laughed. Although none of us were in the mood to laugh, it felt great to have something to bond over, even if it was only for a moment.

I sat on the couch, between the boys, holding them. Sometimes we watched TV this way. I glanced at the armchair across from us and imagined Colin there, holding our baby girl as she drank from the bottle he was offering her.

"What's that?"

I knew Harrison had asked me something, but I didn't know what.

"I said is that detective going to check out that blood on the rock?"

"Oh, yes, I told him about that."

"What else did he say?"

"He didn't have any new information." I was looking at the empty chair.

"So do you admit he's gone?"

I was walking along the dark beach, screaming his name at the ocean.

"Ma, are you even listening to me?"

"No, I don't admit it. He's alive. There'll be an investigation. He's alive."

I went out to the balcony. It was shady this time of day, the sunshine mostly blocked by buildings. I hoped I wasn't about to descend again. If I did, I wasn't sure I could get through it.

After a while, I returned to the apartment. The boys were absorbed with their phones. I sat across from them, but I didn't need a phone to distract me; my thoughts were distracting enough.

Then I glanced at the clock beyond the chair, at the small clock on the armoire, and saw it was five-forty. Shit, it was Monday—Michael and I had our marriage counseling appointment in twenty minutes, and I'd forgotten to cancel it. I got up, with my phone out, and was about to call Donna, our marriage counselor, when I had another idea. "Actually, I have to go somewhere."

The boys popped up.

"Can we go too?" Carson asked.

"No, you two stay here, in case Dad comes home, you can let me know. But stay off the Internet, especially social media. Promise?"

I knew I was wasting my breath. Telling teenagers not to do something was pretty much the same as telling them to do it.

"Where're you going?" Harrison asked.

I was at the closet adjacent to the front door, taking out my thin suede jacket.

"Someplace where I think your dad might be."

"Where?" Harrison asked excitedly. "Why can't we come?"

"Because I said so." I opened the door. "I don't think I'll be very long. Don't let anyone in, especially not any reporters, and text me if you hear anything."

I shut the door. Harrison reopened it, asking me to tell him what was going on, but I kept refusing to answer and got on an elevator.

I didn't want to exit through the front of the building and deal with the reporters and neighbors, so I went down to the basement and exited through the garage in the back of the building. The strategy worked, as there was no one there. At the corner, I hailed a cab to Fifty-seventh Street.

Donna's office was on the nineteenth floor of a beautiful high rise. As I walked through the large tree-filled atrium toward the elevators, I knew it wasn't rational, yet I was certain that if Michael was alive and okay, he would show up here. Maybe he had some big secret—an affair he was having or something else—and he wanted to tell me about it in therapy. As he revealed it, I'd listen calmly, but inside I'd be seething. Then, when it was my turn to speak, I would matter-of-factly inform him that his behavior was beyond disrespectful, it was disgusting, and our marriage was officially over. It would be good to have closure with Donna present, though, as she could advise us on how to deliver the news to the kids and maybe refer us to a mediator.

When I was buzzed into the office, I was so convinced that Michael would be in the waiting room that I was surprised to see that the room was empty, and now the idea that Michael would just show up here, without contacting me, seemed like pure fantasy. What the hell had I been thinking? Sometimes it seemed like I could talk myself into literally *anything*.

I sat in one of the chairs as Lionel Richie's "Say You, Say Me" played from the little speaker in the corner. Donna always played 80s light FM in her waiting area. Michael and I always joked about it after our sessions. Once I said to Michael, "I don't know if she's helping our marriage, but soon I'll know every Barry Manilow song by heart."

Several minutes before six, the door to Donna's office opened and the couple who usually had the appointment before us—the skinny, jerky-looking gray-haired guy who always had the same sarcastic, half-smile, and the curly-haired woman who seemed to hate his guts—exited and passed by, as usual, without making any eye contact with me, acting like I wasn't even there. At six exactly, Donna poked her head out of the office and asked, "Is your husband here yet?"

I'd been wondering whether Donna was aware of any of the online buzz about me and Michael, but going by her question I assumed she had no clue.

"No, I actually just came to see if he was here."

"No, he isn't. Would you like to continue waiting?"

"I should probably just go."

"You can come inside if you'd like to talk."

I considered it, then said, "Okay."

In her office, she sat at her desk, with the big window and downtown skyline behind her, and I sat on the brown leather couch across from it. Donna was about sixty with wavy blonde hair, always very stylishly dressed with perfect makeup. I could tell she'd gotten some work done, especially around her eyes, but she didn't look overdone like so many women I knew. She had a slight Long Island accent, which I liked because it made her seem more down to earth. She wore what looked like a two carat Princess cut engagement ring, but like any good therapist, she rarely mentioned anything about her personal life. For all I knew, she was in a miserable marriage and just wore that big engagement ring for show.

"What's going on?" Donna asked, squinting, obviously concerned.

Looking at my lap, I was thinking about how Colin often asked me, *What's going on?* He was always attuned to my emotions in a way Michael never could be.

"It's okay, there's no rush," Donna said.

We sat in silence for at least a minute. I felt awkward so I took a tissue from the box of the Kleenex and dabbed my dry eyes just to do something.

Then I said, "It's weird being here alone."

"I understand. I'm sure it is."

After a few more moments of silence, I told her what had been going on, including my run-ins with my mother-in-law. I didn't tell her about the *Post* story and the social media frenzy, figuring it was too much to explain all at once. Donna seemed calm, rational about the whole thing, but I knew she had to be this way as a therapist. Even if she was thinking, *Oh my God, he's been missing all day, he must be dead*, she couldn't come out and *say* it.

"I'm sure you're all extremely worried, as well you should be. How are you coping?"

Thinking about my fantasy of Colin returning, of him watching TV on the couch with Harrison, Carson and me, I said, "Okay, I guess. I mean, as well I could be doing under the circumstances. But I guess I'm not sure if…"

As my voice trailed off, Donna waited patiently without interrupting.

Then I said, "I guess I'm just not sure why I came here. I mean, I thought there was a chance that Michael might show up. That's what I *told* myself anyway, but did I actually *believe* this? I don't know? I think I was just psyching myself up. Michael sometimes tells me that I'm 'too optimistic.'"

"I've heard him say that."

"He could be right, but the worst part was when I didn't see Michael here, I wasn't sad about it. Disappointed, yes. Upset, I guess, yeah. But sad? No, I wasn't sad. What's wrong with me? Am I a terrible person? I mean, why wasn't I crying hysterically when I didn't see Michael waiting here? I mean, if I seriously believed he'd be here, shouldn't I be incredibly disappointed that he isn't?"

I was aware that I was rambling, probably not making much sense. I wished I hadn't come here. I could be searching for Michael, or spending time with the kids.

"Would you like to hear my theory?"

Donna was looking at me intently with her perfectly made-up face. She must've spent an hour to get her eyelashes like that and the lip liner looked like a makeup artist had applied it.

"Yes, please. Trust me, I need all the help I can get."

"Well, I think you just answered your own question. This is an emotional time for you. Maybe you didn't come here to see if Michael was here, but you came here because there are things you wanted to discuss. Maybe you needed the session."

"You mean I wanted to talk about my marriage?"

"Or talk about yourself. In some of our previous sessions, you've talked about trauma you experienced in your past. I'm sure this is bringing out some unpleasant feelings and memories for you. Perhaps you're not aware of it."

"So you think this has to do with my childhood? My father leaving?"

"Maybe, though I'm mainly thinking about your past relationships—well, one in particular. You've talked about your abandonment issues after your fiancé disappeared."

Was it possible I was wrong, that Donna *did* know about how Colin and I were trending? Or was she just making a perceptive observation based on information I'd given her in the past?

"You think it has to do with Colin?"

"What do you think?"

I let her continue:

"You've talked about how when Colin disappeared it affected all of your relationships, including your relationship with Michael. How hard it was for you to move on and let go of your anger, shock, and disappointment. Has this situation triggered any memories of Colin?"

"Actually, it has. I mean, Colin disappeared in the ocean and Michael went jogging, but I'm definitely aware of the similarity of the situations and you're right, it does remind me of how I felt when Colin disappeared. I felt very powerless, very out of control, and I feel the same way now. I feel like I want answers, and I want things to be a certain way, but I don't know how to make it happen…I don't know if this makes any sense."

Donna uncrossed her legs, then recrossed them again, and said, "It makes a lot of sense actually. I think you'd like to control this situation with Michael too. You want instant answers, you want him to come home right away and for all to be well, but that's not in your control right now. I think it's hard for you to not feel in control. Given the work you do, I imagine it's especially difficult for you at times when there's disorder in your life, when there's disarray. Your whole job is about control, precision, putting things in their perfect places, and now you're in a situation where you can't do that."

"Yes, that's all true."

"I think you have to cut yourself some slack, Vanessa. You feel anger toward people for leaving you. For you, it feels like abandonment, betrayal. So now, with this happening, I'm not surprised that you're feeling anger toward Michael for, on some primal level, deserting you, but I also think you have to be kind to yourself right now. You can't expect everything to be perfect like when you're organizing a closet for a client. You're in a difficult, incredibly stressful situation and you have to expect that it's going to stir up your past, and you have to expect to continue to have the resentment toward Michael that you've been experiencing lately. Allowing yourself to have these feelings doesn't mean that you don't love him, or care about him, or want him to return safely. You also don't have to feel like you need to magically feel differently about him and your marriage just because your family is going through this situation. In other words, if you want to continue to feel resentment toward him, go ahead and experience that resentment. It's always better to feel your emotions, rather than hide from them."

We spent the rest of the session discussing my resentment toward Michael. I told her about how sex had been awkward lately, and how he'd accused me of having an affair with Andrew. I told her that I suspected that he was having an affair. She didn't come out and say she agreed with me—as our marriage counselor she couldn't do that—but she hinted that she thought it was at least a possibility, saying "Michael often seems like he's withholding emotionally" and that he's "certainly protective of his personal life."

Ironically, without Michael here, I felt like this was the most productive marriage counseling session I'd had. When Michael was here, we spent forty-five minutes bickering, getting defensive, and we never seemed to accomplish anything. Thanks to Donna, I wouldn't feel guilty about fantasizing about Colin anymore. I had to allow myself to feel however I needed to feel, without attaching any shame to my emotions.

Leaving, I said, "I'm so glad I came here today. Really, you've been a lifesaver. You have no idea."

"I'm glad I could help," she said. "Please feel free to call me anytime and when there's news about Michael, can you please let me know? I have a feeling everything is going to be okay."

"Me too," I said, though I didn't really believe it. Too much time had gone by. The chance for a happy ending seemed remote.

It was a nice evening—warm, with a slight breeze. I walked along Fifty-Seventh, then downtown on Second Avenue. Because of the nice weather, most of the restaurants and bars were busy for a Monday night. Passing a tapas place that Michael and I had gone to many times, I imagined going there with Colin. Sometimes it was so painful having to listen to Michael go on and on about his work, or his political opinions, or whatever else he felt like droning on about. Colin and I used to have actual *conversations*. He listened to me, and I listened to him.

I wanted that kind of connection again. I deserved it. With Michael, for eighteen years I'd been settling for a relationship that wasn't working, that had never worked. I wanted passion, I wanted to feel something again. The kids were older now, they could handle their parents getting divorced, and they'd be better off with happy parents. Even Michael would be happier. He could meet someone he was truly in love with, and Colin and I could model a loving relationship.

On my block, I saw that the group in front of the building was still there and might've gotten larger. I was going to turn to re-enter the building the way I'd left it, through the garage around the corner, but I decided that I had to stop avoiding. Confronting was a much better strategy.

With confidence, I walked right up to the reporters.

"Hi, I'm Vanessa Rizzo, and I'd like to make a statement."

The reporters assembled around me, including a bearded reporter from Spectrum News, and another guy aiming an over-the-shoulder camera. I recognized some familiar faces from my building, but no one I knew personally. I waited a few moments, collecting my thoughts, then began.

TWELVE

"I'LL KEEP THIS very brief. My family and I are obviously extremely worried and concerned about my husband, Michael, and are praying for him to return home safely as soon as possible. We're asking everyone to please respect our privacy right now at this extremely difficult time." Then I stared at the camera. "Michael, if you're listening to this, please come home. We all miss you so much."

As I turned away and headed into the building, through the revolving doors, reporters shouted questions. I heard most of them mentioning "Colin," but they were all screaming over each other and I couldn't make out what they were saying.

Although the circumstances were awful, I couldn't deny that it had felt a little exciting to be on TV. I'd been so involved with organizing the kids' lives that I hadn't been focusing enough on myself lately, on what makes me happy. When I was growing up, I wanted to be an actress. My mother took me to Broadway shows, and I took acting lessons and starred or co-starred in most of my high school productions. I went to auditions after school and even got roles in a couple of local commercials. It would be fun to audition again and, hey, I still had my SAG card. Maybe I should audition for commercials again, or try to get a role in an Off-Off Broadway play, or even join a community theater.

When I entered my apartment, the boys were waiting in the foyer.

"Did you find Dad?" Harrison asked.

I hated having to deliver more disappointing news.

"No, but they'll find him soon. I know they will. And I just made a statement for the news."

"Why does he need to hear a message from you?" Harrison asked. "If he wanted to come home, he'd just come home."

He had a point. I couldn't really imagine any scenario where Michael would see my plea for him to return on TV and think, *Gee, that's a good idea, I'll come home. Why didn't I think of that on my own?*

But, wanting to remain upbeat for my boys, I said, "We don't know what's going on, so we can't make any assumptions about anything, okay? It's possible somebody else will hear the message, somebody who knows or saw something or who can help locate him."

"What about the rock?" Carson asked. "Did the cops check out the rock?"

I was hoping they'd decided to forget about the rock.

"I don't know anything about that, but I'm feeling more hopeful in general."

"Hopeful?" Harrison looked at me like he was the parent and I was the disappointing child. "What the fuck do we have to be hopeful about?"

"Hey, watch that language."

"Dad is missing, he's probably dead. Somebody killed him in the park. I'm sick of pretending like things are going to be better, like there's something to hope for, because there fucking isn't."

"Hey, I found it!" Carson had been busy on his phone. "Mom's on TV."

"Already?" I said.

"It's on Citizen. Somebody was filming on their camera while you were being filmed."

Looking over Carson's shoulder, I watched myself on the app on his phone. The video was shot by somebody who was to my right while I was talking to the Spectrum reporter.

"This is great," I said. "Well, let's hope Dad is watching."

"He's not watching," Harrison said. "You know he's not watching. You know he's—"

"Okay, that's enough from both of you," I said. "I want you to stop and be positive. You hear me? Be fuckin' positive."

"Look, there's another one," Carson said.

He played another video of me on the Citizen app, this one taken from a head-on angle, from someone who was standing behind the TV cameras. I hoped Michael was somehow seeing this and then it occurred to me—there was probably a better chance that Colin was seeing it. Assuming he was still in New York, he was probably aware that his name, along with mine, was getting buzz online. He had to be at least curious about me and my situation and want to see what I had to say, or even if I'd mention him, so he'd look for any information about me online, especially a video I'd just posted. Why wouldn't he? It made perfect sense.

When the video ended with me walking away toward the building, I said to Carson, "Play it again."

"But I just—"

"Just do it."

As I re-watched, I wished I'd given Colin some kind of message to let him know that I'd seen him the other day, slipped in some sort of inside reference. While I knew I was being ridiculous, that the point was to locate Michael, not Colin, I still felt like I'd allowed another chance to connect with Colin slip away.

Then Harrison slammed the door to his room so hard the big mahogany mirror on the hallway wall rattled and the noise jolted me from my thoughts.

"Jesus," I said.

Sparkle scampered by Carson and me and hid under the love seat as we watched Spectrum News.

After the sports and weather came the major stories at the top of the hour—a fire in the Bronx that had killed a family of eight and two firefighters, and a story about a stabbing late last night near Penn Station—then the anchorman said, "And now the latest on the disappearance of Manhattan attorney, Michael Rizzo." The broadcast cut to a bearded reporter—the one I'd approached outside—who gave the basic facts about the case, before the feed of me, giving my pleas for Michael to return, came on. I felt lucky that Michael's disappearance was getting so much media attention, much more than Colin's had gotten at first. But Colin was mixed race and Michael was an affluent white man in Manhattan. Despite how woke the media claimed to be these days, it was obvious that not much had changed.

"You're famous now, Ma," Carson said.

"Let's just hope Dad is watching. That's the important thing."

And Colin too, I thought.

"Do you really think Dad was watching?"

"I really hope so."

"Where do you think he is? What do you think he's doing?"

"I'm afraid I don't have those answers, sweetie. I wish I did."

Carson was squinting at his phone. Whatever he was looking at seemed to be upsetting him.

"What is it?"

His expression didn't change.

"*What*?" I asked.

I glanced over and saw he was swiping through posts.

"Didn't I tell you and your brother not to read that shit anymore?"

"They're saying a lot of bad stuff, Ma."

"Of course they are, that's why I didn't want you to go on there. Put your phone away."

"They're talking about that guy you were engaged to once…Colin Grant."

Fuck. I'd thought they'd stop with that, or at least let up, after I made the statement, but I should've known better. Once an online wave starts it's almost impossible to stop it.

"Colin is ancient history and it's all nonsense," I said. "Just a bunch of idiots who have nothing better to do with their time than lie and attack people, just so they can feel better about themselves."

"One guy said you hired a hit man to kill him and Dad."

"Just stop, okay? I said stop it! I don't want you reading any more of that bullshit, do you understand me?"

I was so angry I was shaking.

"Why not?" Carson said. "I want to know what's going on."

"That's exactly why you shouldn't read it."

Now he was tapping on his phone.

Grabbing his arm by the wrist, I said, "I said that's enough. Put your phone away, right now."

"But would they lie for no reason?"

With my other hand, I tried to grab his phone, but he yanked it just out of my reach.

"Look at me, Carson. I said look at me."

He wouldn't so I let go of his wrist and grabbed his shoulders and shifted him so he couldn't avoid eye contact.

"I'm your mother, and don't you ever, *ever* disrespect me like this. Do you understand me?"

"You're hurting me."

He was being melodramatic; I wasn't *hurting* him. I was barely squeezing, but I loosened my grip anyway.

"You know I love your father," I said, "and you know he loves me."

"Yeah, okay," he said, but not like he meant it.

He was massaging his wrist, pretending he needed to relieve the pain.

"I'm devastated by all of this. I want your father back more than anything. You know that, right?"

"Yeah." Again, he sounded unconvinced.

"See? This is what happens when stories go viral. I see it happen all the time on those true crime shows I watch. Whenever a husband disappears people start blaming the wife, and when the wife disappears, they always blame the husband. It's just the obvious, knee-jerk thing to do, and they're never right of course. Imagine what celebrities and athletes have to go through every day, with people making up ridiculous rumors about them online. Everyone's trying to be crazier and more sensational than the next person, everyone's trying to win the internet."

"But you and Dad do fight a lot."

"No we don't. Well, not any more than any other married couple, and what does that have to do with anything?"

"We heard you fighting with Dad Saturday night. It was the last time we heard Dad's voice."

His lower lip was trembling, like it always did when he was trying not to cry. He'd been doing this since he was an infant and it always got a reaction from me, made me feel guilty for hurting him if his pain had nothing to do with me.

"That wasn't a fight," I said. "It was a *discussion*."

"It sounded like a fight."

"I love your father, okay? Just because we had a loud *discussion* the other night, doesn't mean we don't love each other. You know that, right?"

My phone vibrated, displaying "Stella." I let voicemail answer.

Carson had started to cry.

Holding him, my guilt kicking in, I said, "It's okay, sweetie, it's okay. I'm sorry I got so upset. It's just stress. I'm under so much stress."

Then Harrison came out of his room, holding his phone, saying to me, "Grandma wants to speak to you."

"Tell her there's no news."

Into the phone, he said, "She said there's no news."

Then to me: "She still wants to talk to you."

"Well, I can't talk now."

I rubbed Carson's back while he sobbed.

Into the phone, Harrison said, "She said she can't talk right now... I don't know...okay." Then he said to me, "She says if you don't pick up she's coming over here."

"Tell her I'll call her back."

"But—"

"Just fuckin' tell her, Harrison!"

Harrison went into the kitchen, so I couldn't hear the rest of the conversation. I continued to console Carson.

"Come on, how about some dinner?"

"I'm not hungry."

"I'm not either, but we have to eat. Come on."

Harrison came out of the kitchen and said, "Grandma said if you don't call her back in five minutes she's coming over to get us."

"You're not going anywhere, *and* you're both going to school tomorrow."

"We are?"

Carson stopped crying to listen to me.

"Yes, we're all going to go about our lives. We can't spend every second staring at the TV and our phones, waiting for news. We have to be able to function."

I left the kids and went into the kitchen to prepare a late, makeshift dinner. While the chicken nuggets were microwaving and I was stir frying some frozen veggies I called Stella.

"Do you know where my son is?" Her voice was hoarse, probably from crying and screaming all day.

"Are you serious? Is that why you—"

"If you hurt him, I'll kill you! I swear I'll kill you! I'll kill you! I'll kill you! I'll—"

In the background, Joe was shouting, "Hang up! Just hang—" and the call cut off.

I cocked my arm, ready to throw my phone against the wall, but I didn't. Instead, as I stirred the veggies, I muttered to myself, "Michael, you son of a bitch, where are you?"

I didn't believe he was dead. I didn't think I was in denial either. My gut was screaming that he was alive, and I couldn't help hating him for what he was doing to us. Was he angry at me and acting out in an incredibly immature, dramatic way? Is that why he ran away with another woman? Were they at some resort in the Caribbean, maybe that all-inclusive one in Jamaica where we'd gone a couple of times before the kids were born. That would be *so* Michael, passive-aggressively taking his new woman to the same place we'd gone to. He'd probably requested the same room, the same bed. They were probably in bed right now, fucking each other's brains out.

Although the kitchen counter looked spotless, I sprayed it with Windex and scrubbed it as hard as I could, then I wiped down all of the cabinets, and cleaned the stove, feeling like I was scrubbing Michael out of our lives.

"Come on, boys, we're having dinner!"

Several minutes later, I insisted that we all sit at the dining room table and then I brought out the food I'd prepared, as well as the leftover Chinese from lunch. I forced myself to take a few bites. Carson kept stabbing a nugget with his fork while Harrison just stared ahead.

"Doesn't this bother you?" Harrison asked.

"We have to eat," I said.

"I mean sitting here with Dad's seat empty."

"Oh, sorry." I stood. "I'll move the chair."

"No, don't touch it."

I remained standing. "Okay, so what do you want me to do?"

"Do whatever you want," he said. "I told you I'm not hungry." Then he left the table and went to his room.

Carson put down his fork and joined his brother.

The apartment was suddenly silent except for distant city

sounds—honking, an ambulance's siren. Staring at Michael's empty chair, I imagined him sitting there, smirking, enjoying this chaos.

I muttered, "Fuck you," then I got up and looked outside, down toward the street.

A couple of additional news trucks were there now—what the hell? I'd thought after I made that statement and they had their quote from me they'd disperse.

My phone was vibrating.

Glancing at the display, I was surprised to see: **William**

My *brother*? I hadn't heard from him in ages, maybe four or five years. He lived in Atlanta—well, last time I heard. We didn't have any big falling out, but he was nine years older than me and we'd never had much in common. He worked at a tech company and was some kind of computer programmer. As a kid I resented that he was safely away in college at Ithaca when my father's drinking was out of control and he was verbally, and sometimes physically, abusing my mother. I had to try to stand up for my mom— which was hard when my father was drunk and raging—and I had to handle everything on my own. As adults, William and I had drifted even further apart. This was partly my doing. After Colin disappeared, when I was going through the worst of my anxiety and depression, I'd checked out for a while, distancing myself from most of my relatives and friends. I think the last time William and I had spoken was when he'd called to tell me that my uncle Frank had died. Who'd died now?

I hesitated long enough that my voicemail picked up. I waited till I could access the message, then listened:

"Hey, um, Vanessa, it's me, um, Will. Heard the news. Just, um, checking in. Sorry to hear about Michael, but can you, uh, do me a favor and try to leave my name out of it? I mean, if they're digging up Dad's mob connections and all that I don't want people at my job to find out about it, you know? I mean, with the way people are getting cancelled these days and everything. Anyway, sorry again and talk soon. Bye."

So typical. He didn't call because he actually cared about me or Michael; he was only calling because he was worried about himself. Selfish prick. But how had he "heard the news" in Georgia? Did someone tell him? A friend from the city?

My phone vibrated again—this time my mother calling from Phoenix, where she'd moved about ten years ago after divorcing her second husband Phil, and I knew another boyfriend had recently died from pancreatic cancer. I decided not to pick up as I wasn't in the mood to talk to her right now. My mom and I spoke on the phone occasionally, so it wasn't totally unusual that she was contacting me, but my mother and brother contacting me on the same day? That *never* happened. The news about Michael must be spreading—not just in New York, all over.

What were they saying about me now? I was afraid to know but, bracing myself, I went online on my phone.

There were many more posts than before—hundreds of new ones since the last time I checked. I swiped through some of them, quickly getting the gist:

She did it #VanessaRizzo

Mafia Queen Bitch did it!!! #VanessaRizzo

Did the cops arrest Vanessa Rizzo yet? What's taking em so long?

Vanessa Rizzo ex and her husband gone? Pa-leeeeze

There were memes too like:

A gif of a guy sprinting then tumbling down an escalator with the text: **Vanessa Rizzo when the cops come**

And:

A woman winking sarcastically with: **I'm not a man killer, I swear! #VanessaRizzo**

I swiped faster, skipping some, and going further down. A post from just six minutes ago already had 72 likes and 30 reposts.

Somebody gonna have to make this Vanessa Rizzo shit into a podcast

Netflix series coming soon! #VanessaRizzo

A few posts included a twelve second segment of the footage of me talking to reporters in front of the building:

Bitch lyin!!! #VanessaRizzo

There was a screenshot from video of me with upturned lips with the caption:

Look, she thinks it's funny smh #VanessaRizzo #killer #serialkiller #mankiller

I'd only searched for posts that included my name. There had to be more, a lot more; how viral was this going to get? Were people going to recognize me on the street? Was I going to have to wear disguises? What about my kids? Were they going to get dragged into this too?

I couldn't take this anymore. Again, I wanted to fling my phone and this time I didn't stop myself. Fortunately, it bounced off the couch onto the rug.

When Colin disappeared, the culture was different—online mobs weren't lurking, constantly ready to pounce on a new target. Nowadays, it didn't matter whether or not a story was true; the internet mob made assumptions, rushed to judgment, assumed guilt. I knew because I'd often been in those mobs. There were many times when I couldn't resist chiming in about stories in the news, offering an opinion, even after I'd only read the headline, or someone else's post about it, and I didn't have any actual facts.

That all said, I still blamed Michael for all of this. If he hadn't abandoned me, abandoned *us*, none of this would have happened.

My mom called again and this time I picked up.

Before she said anything, I said, "Don't worry, I'm sure everything's going to be okay."

I was trying to diffuse her panic, but she didn't sound calm. "Yes, a friend sent me something about you, so I just wanted to make sure everything's okay."

"Thanks, Ma. Well, things definitely aren't okay, but I'm hoping they will be soon."

I explained what had happened, how Michael went for a run on Sunday morning and didn't return.

"Hmm," she said. "That's so unusual."

When I was growing up, my mother and I were very close. We spent a lot of time together, cooking, shopping, and seeing lots of Broadway shows. When she had all the problems with my dad, I was there for her, but I'd always resented that she wasn't there for me after Colin disappeared, and I think part of the reason I took those sleeping pills was to try to get her attention. At least this was what a couple of therapists had suggested. It was also upsetting that my mother didn't seem to fully believe my version of what happened on Shelter Island; how could a mother not fiercely defend her child? If one of my kids—God forbid—suffered through a tragedy I would be there for him no matter what. And now I could hear that doubt about me in my mother's tone again—*That's so unusual*—like she suspected I was lying.

I straightened up the apartment. Usually housework relaxed me, or at least centered me, but not this time.

"Where the fuck are you?" I said to myself.

Sparkle sashayed into the room.

"Not you."

The cat came over anyway and brushed his head against my leg.

Later, lying in bed, I kept ruminating—resenting Michael, and missing Colin. I realized I wasn't being irrational. What Colin had done was just as hurtful as what Michael had done, but I couldn't see it that way. Maybe it was because what Michael had done seemed much fresher and I hadn't had a chance to fully process it yet, but if Michael returned home with some lame excuse, claiming the whole thing had been some "big misunderstanding," I didn't see how I'd ever be able to forgive him. Running away from your fiancé was terrible, but running away from your family was unforgivable.

I had my phone's ringer on with the volume turned up, just in case Michael tried to contact me, but the periodic notification pings kept going off from friends and acquaintances. Oddly, one of my close friends, Jenny, whom I'd known since Harrison and her son had gone to the same preschool, texted me around midnight: **Are you okay?** A couple of old work acquaintances texted, then Andrew Reedy reached out with: **I just heard about what's going on from Justin. Please let me know if there's anything I can do**. How come my other close friends like Kathleen, Staci, Isabella, or any of my longtime clients hadn't reached out to support me? Lying alone in bed when your husband is missing can fuel paranoia, and I hoped I was just paranoid in imagining that my friends and family, including my mother, had joined the online mob and turned on me, like Michael's parents already had. If your friends and family won't stick by you in a crisis, who's left?

At around two in the morning, I finally silenced my phone so I could get some rest. I needed something to sleep so I took a Klonopin. I didn't think that was enough, given how much stress I was under, so I took an Ambien too. I continued to stir for a long time, though, continuing to imagine worst-case scenarios.

THIRTEEN

I DIDN'T KNOW if I'd slept at all, but I must've, for longer than I'd realized, because morning light was shining through the blinds. Maybe some of those scenarios had been actual nightmares.

I checked my phone just to see if Randle had reached out with any news. He hadn't. There weren't any more texts or calls from friends either, just a missed call from Joe.

The boys were in their room, getting ready for school. When they came out, I had breakfast waiting for them. They didn't want to eat, but I insisted, in my I'm-not-fucking-around tone that usually got through to them, and they sat at the table and slowly picked at their scrambled eggs and pancakes and sipped their orange juice. When they were leaving, I hugged them goodbye, telling them how much I loved them, and promising to let them know as soon as I heard anything about their father. They were both solemn and subdued.

"Exit through the garage," I said. "Don't talk to anyone. If reporters try to talk to you, just ignore them."

With the kids gone, and just Sparkle and me left, the apartment seemed emptier and bleaker. I tried to fantasize about Colin returning, which usually got me out of my funks, but it didn't help at all. Colin probably wasn't watching me on TV, and I probably hadn't even seen him on the street. It had all been magical thinking, delusion, and maybe it was a huge red flag. Maybe I was having a major setback and hadn't realized or accepted it yet. Maybe, without intervention, I'd wind up in that dark, horrific place again if I wasn't there already.

I cried a little, then forced myself to stop.

I logged on to check work emails and saw that I'd lost another major client—Rebecca, whose entire apartment I'd organized, as well as her summer house upstate in Beacon. I was supposed to start a new project for her in Manhattan next week. I read several lines of the email, getting the gist that I'd been fired, and then shut the laptop, too upset to continue reading.

Is this what was going to happen now? Was everyone who I thought had my back going to turn on me? Was I going to lose everything?

I went out to the balcony. It occurred to me that I could jump now, end it all. I wasn't seriously thinking about doing this, but given my past, it was still very disturbing that this thought had even crossed my mind.

I shut and locked the terrace door and took a Klonopin.

My phone pinged, another text from Andrew:

Hey, give me a call if you can :)

Andrew and I had always been friendly, but we weren't actually *friends*. Outside of theater events, I didn't really know him very well at all. Still, it was kind of him to keep reaching out when no one else seemed to care.

I texted back:

It's been rough thanks Yeah definitely will

Right now I didn't feel like talking to anyone, though. Why the hell wasn't that Klonopin working? I usually felt improvement within about a half hour or so. Maybe I needed to up the dose or switch to another medication. Being cooped up, feeling like a prisoner in my own apartment, definitely wasn't helping. I needed air, I needed to breathe, but I knew going outside, dealing with that mob, would only heighten my anxiety.

I spent the rest of the morning and the afternoon in my apartment. When the kids returned from school, I told them there was no news. They seemed as depressed as me and went into their room and shut the door. I took another Klonopin—it didn't help much—then I got a call from Detective Randle.

With dread, I said, "Hello."

Then he said, "We may have a break in the case."

The news was so unexpected it took a few seconds for me to comprehend it, then I said, "Wow, that's amazing. Is it about Michael? Did you find him? Is he okay?"

"Yes and no."

"*What*?" My pulse was so intense I was shaking. "What does that mean? Did you find him or not? Tell me what's going on."

"We didn't find him, but we might've located him. It's better that we talk in person."

"Why? I don't under—"

"Are you at home? Can I come to you? Or it might be best if you come over to the precinct if possible."

Why wouldn't he just tell me? What was so complicated that he couldn't tell me over the phone? I didn't want to argue about it with him, though, since the kids were right in the other room.

"I'll be there as soon as I can," I said.

I didn't want Randle to come over to my apartment building again, not with all those reporters outside.

The kids were still in their room and hadn't eaves-dropped on the conversation. Good, I didn't have to mention anything about it—I didn't see the point in raising their hopes, maybe for no reason. I told them I was heading out to "do a little shopping" and would be back soon.

MY STRATEGY OF exiting my building through the parking garage backfired. Several people—three women and a man, all in their twenties—were waiting for me in the garage. I didn't get a professional reporter vibe from any of them. They seemed like bloggers, internet sleuths, or maybe just social media influencers. One of the men—prematurely balding yet with a thick beard—was holding up his phone, filming me while a woman with big, glaring eyes shouted, "There she fucking is!"

I couldn't go back into the building—bypassing the crowd in front of the building would be much harder—so getting past them seemed to be the best option.

They were shouting questions:

"What do you think happened to your husband?"

"Did you kill him?"

"What did you do with the bodies?"

I wanted to scream at them to leave me and my family the hell alone, but I ignored them, avoiding eye contact, as I rushed up the ramp to the street level. They were walking alongside me, continuing to shout questions about Michael and Colin. I had no idea what they thought they were achieving by this. Even if I was a killer, did they think I'd confess into their phone cams? I'd managed to escape justice for nineteen years, but now I was going to spill my guts to some overaggressive vloggers? On the sidewalk, several people spotted us and rushed over, shouting their own questions and holding up phones. Approaching First Avenue, I already had my hand up to hail a cab. When I got to the curb, the bearded guy was still holding up his phone, filming me.

I gave him the finger.

He laughed, then said, "Crazy skeleton bitch."

I could take a lot of shit, but body shaming always triggered me. I turned and grabbed his phone. Then, in the next instant, I stepped into the gutter and dropped the phone into the sewer grating.

"The fuck you doin'?"

Wishing I could throw him into the sewer with his phone, I gave him the finger again. Then a cab pulled up to the curb and I got in.

As the cab pulled away, I saw the guy, squatting over the drain. I was happy about what I'd done, though I knew I'd just given the internet mob some great new material. People had filmed me snatching that phone and flipping the guy off, and if the guy had been filming live there would be a great POV video of me throwing his phone down that drain. He could easily delete the "crazy skeleton bitch" comment to make my actions look totally unprovoked.

Trying to stay positive, I reminded myself that Randle might have a break in the case, and that soon this nightmare might end—Michael would be okay and, no matter what happened with our marriage, the boys would be okay too, and we'd go on with our lives.

I entered the 19th Precinct. There wasn't an officer at the front desk this time, but when I entered, I saw Randle at his desk. He was talking on his cell, but he motioned for me to sit, so I did.

His office space needed serious organizing. There were piles of papers and folders strewn around the desk, as well as takeout containers and a couple of Diet Pepsi cans. I couldn't help myself, and I took the empty cans and plastic containers and put them in recycling.

Watching me do it, Randle said into the phone, "She's here now…Yeah, will do… Thanks, Tom."

I didn't know who Tom was, but I assumed he was another detective.

"Thanks for straightening up."

"Sorry, it's what I do for a living."

"You're a cleaner?"

"An organizer."

"Yeah? What do you organize?"

"People's spaces, people's lives."

"Interesting."

He gave me a weird look, like he was trying to see through me or discover a clue.

"Will you please tell me what's going on? What's the news? Did you find Michael or not?"

"As you know, since this officially became a missing person's investigation, we've been going all-out trying to locate your husband. You can rest assured, we have the best detectives in the NYPD working on this case."

Was he seriously going to give me a preamble, trying to pump up his ego while he kept me in suspense? What did he want me to think: *Wow, you're such an amazing detective,*

I'm so lucky you're working on this case?

"I really appreciate everything you're doing," I said, trying to hide my sarcasm, but I'm sure a little—okay, a lot—leaked through.

He gave me a displeased look, then said, "We've been looking into ATM, credit card records, and where applicable, security footage, and we discovered something very interesting." He was tapping on his phone. "Your husband used his Chase debit card on Saturday at six oh eight at Starbucks on Chambers and West Broadway."

Saturday was the day that Michael had told me he was meeting Rob, which I already knew was a lie. But what was he doing at a Starbucks in Tribeca?

"Why was he there?" I asked. "Was he with a woman?"

"Actually, we know exactly who he was with. We have video. This is a screenshot."

He rotated the phone so I could see the display.

"Do you recognize this man?"

I stared at the photo—trying to process what this meant, but I couldn't. It was too baffling, too overwhelming, too insane.

"Ms. Rizzo, are you okay?"

I continued to stare, not saying anything, because I couldn't organize my thoughts into words that would've made any sense. My lips were trembling; my whole body was shaking.

"I said, are you all right, Ms. Rizzo?"

I took another few seconds to collect myself, then said, "That's…that's him."

"That's who?"

"My ex-fiancé. That's Colin Grant."

FOURTEEN

THIS HAD TO be some sort of setup, or trick. How could this be *real*? How could Michael and Colin be there… *together*?

"Lemme make sure I'm getting this straight," Randle said. "You're saying you're sure that your husband was with your ex-fiancé, the one who's supposedly been dead for twenty years?"

I blinked a few times and Randle and his messy desk were still here, and *I* was still here. I wasn't hallucinating; this was actually happening.

"Nineteen," I said. "He's been gone for nineteen years."

I was still staring at the screen, at Michael and Colin, realizing what this meant—I was vindicated. All those times I doubted myself, when I thought I was insane, I wasn't, because here was proof—apparently *definitive proof* that Colin was alive. Or at least he was alive when this was taken.

"This was Saturday?" I asked. "Are you sure it was Saturday?"

"Yes, I'm sure it was Saturday. It's from surveillance video at that Starbucks. Can you tell me what the hell's going on here?"

Michael, I realized, was in the gray Calvin Klein button-down and faded jeans that he'd been wearing on Saturday. The man he was with was definitely Colin. He looked exactly like he had when I'd spotted him on Columbus Circle, with his close-cropped, receding afro. Flung over the back of his chair was a black leather jacket, the *same* leather jacket I'd seen him in.

"I really…I really have no idea."

"So you're telling me you had no idea that your husband and Colin Grant know each other?"

"No idea. I swear. This is totally fuckin' surreal to me. I still can't believe what I'm seeing. When was this taken?"

"I told you, on—"

"I mean what time?"

"From approximately six to six forty-five p.m."

Why did Michael lie to me? And if Michael knew Colin, how *long* had he been lying to me?

I felt dizzy.

"Are you okay, Ms. Rizzo? Do you want some water or—?"

"How did you get this footage?"

"We got a tip, someone saw someone fitting your husband's description, so we checked the surveillance video. We had to confirm it was him, which we did earlier today. We've also been checking video from around the area to see if they arrived or left together, but we didn't know who the other man was. Are you positive that's—"

"Yes, it's Colin, it's fucking Colin."

"I need you to be one hundred percent sure because—"

"I'm a million percent sure. That's the man I was engaged to. Of course it's Colin. I told you I saw him the other day, getting into the cab. I showed you that photo, the screenshot."

"Can you send that to me?"

"That's it? You don't apologize? You just want me to send it to you?"

"Yes, and do you have any other photos of Colin?"

"From nineteen years ago. Otherwise, the one I showed you is the only one."

"Why do you think your husband was meeting with him?"

"I have no idea. If I knew what was going on, why wouldn't I tell you?"

He looked at me like he was asking himself the same question, then he said, "Do you think Colin Grant could have something to do with your husband's disappearance?"

"I don't know. I know as much as you do, but you have to go public with this. Put it online. Tell people that Colin is alive so they could stop spreading crazy rumors about me."

"Let's focus on finding your husband and bringing him home safely, okay?"

"That *will* help bring him home safely."

"So you *do* think Colin might be involved?"

"I have no idea. I guess he might, otherwise all of this seems incredibly coincidental, doesn't it? Colin showing up out of nowhere and then my husband disappearing out of nowhere? Yes, it seems like there must be some connection, but I have no idea what that connection could be."

"So, if that's Colin Grant in the video, why do you think your husband and Colin were together? I mean even if you had to take a wild guess?"

"It *is* Colin, and I honestly have no fucking clue."

My heart rate was accelerating. I could hear my psychiatrist's voice in my head: *Anxiety is the flipside of anger.* I was anxious because I was actually furious—furious at Michael for lying to me, maybe for years. Worse, I couldn't express my anger because Michael wasn't here, because he was fucking missing.

"I don't know. But they must've recently met."

"What would they meet about?"

"I have no idea, okay?"

"I know this is extremely stressful for you. Are you sure you don't want some water?"

Was my anger that obvious? That wasn't good. I'd definitely need another Klonopin, or maybe some Xanax. I had a bottle of Xanax that Dr. Stone had prescribed about five years ago. I knew that I had five pills left because I'd counted them recently.

"No thanks," I said, "but why wouldn't Michael *tell* me? When I told him I thought I saw Colin on Friday he made me feel like I was an idiot, or that I was crazy, like the other times."

"Whoa, back up. *Other* times?"

I told Randle about the times throughout the years that I thought I'd seen Colin, and how Michael had always pooh poohed it.

"Was my husband gaslighting me for years? Is that what's been going on?"

Randle was talking, but I wasn't listening. In my head, I was replaying snippets of dozens of conversations I'd had with Michael over the years, when Colin's name had come up. I'd never had any indication that he knew Colin—none at all. Yes, Michael could be secretive, but this was crazy. It was like two periods of my life that had nothing to do with one another had suddenly collided.

Interrupting whatever Randle was saying, I said, "I mean they can't know each other…There has to be some explanation."

"But you just ID'd Colin—"

"I know, so what? I don't know, maybe…maybe that picture was Photoshopped, or the video was edited. Or *something*."

"The video came directly from the security company at Starbucks. We have no reason to believe it was altered in any way."

"Can I see the video? Not just an image from it, the actual video."

Randle tapped on his laptop then rotated it so I could see the screen. The video was pretty clear for surveillance footage. It was taken from some distance away, from across the room, but there was no doubt that it was Michael and Colin. Michael was doing most of the talking, doing a lot of hand gesturing like he usually did when he was trying to make a point or going on about something. Colin seemed to be mainly listening.

"Any thoughts?" Randle asked.

I didn't respond.

"Come on, you must have a theory."

I was silent for several more seconds, then I said, "Okay, just spitballing here, but you want a theory—here's a theory. Maybe, I don't know, Colin came to New York because of me, to look for me. Maybe he saw me the day I saw him, or in retrospect realized he saw me, and he tracked me down, found out where I lived. Maybe, when he showed up, Michael confronted him and told him to stay away from me. I don't know why Michael wouldn't tell me about this, but maybe he was trying to protect me. He knew that 'Colin sightings' had caused a lot of, well, *issues* for me over the years, so maybe he was trying to prevent that from happening again. Maybe Colin didn't want to leave me alone, so Michael arranged to meet him to discuss it. Maybe that's what's going on in the video. This would also explain why Michael lied to me about meeting his friend Rob on Saturday night."

"He lied about meeting his friend?"

I explained, then Randle, seeming somewhat interested, said, "So let's say this is all true. What do you think happened on Sunday morning?"

"Well, maybe they met again, had some kind of altercation or… No, I'm sorry, that doesn't make any sense at all. I know them both too well. Well, at least I know my *husband* well and he's not a violent man, and Colin—well, the Colin I used to know—wasn't violent either. I can't imagine either one of them getting into a fight, let alone fighting each other."

Randle started to say something, but I interrupted, "Or, okay, maybe they went somewhere together. Sunday morning, I mean. That would make more sense than them fighting. Maybe they're still together right now. Whatever's going on, it's obviously something I don't know about and there has to be a reason why they're keeping it a secret. They have to be watching the news or going online, they have to know what they're doing to me and my boys, and there has to be a reason for it. Sorry, what were you going to say?"

"I just want to make sure you've been totally up front with me. You've had no further contact with Colin Grant, other than seeing him on the street…on Friday was it? Is that correct?"

"Correct, though I wouldn't call what happened on

Friday *contact*. I saw him getting into a cab, that's it."

"And you're telling me you haven't seen him again since?"

"If I saw him, I would've told you. Why wouldn't I?"

"I'm not saying you wouldn't, I'm just—"

"I'm telling you I have no idea why Colin was with my husband, and I have no idea why Colin is back in New York, alive and well."

"Something funny, Ms. Rizzo?"

"No, why?"

"You were smiling."

"I was?" I realized I might have been smirking a little. "I guess I'm just happy about the video. It gives me hope that Michael might be alive, and yes I'm excited to see Colin too. It makes me feel…vindicated, if that makes sense."

"I get that," Randle said. "I mean, to an extent. Seems like you should be angry at Colin, no? I mean, if this is who you say it is, and he ran away from you, or whatever he did, why would that make you happy?"

"I'm not *happy*, but yes, I'm happy that he's alive. Can you imagine what it's like to have someone you're madly in love with just disappear from your life with no explanation? Wouldn't you want answers? Yes, I want to know what happened. Did he run away? Did he meet someone else? But why disappear? What did I miss? What am I *still* missing?"

Twisting his thick wedding band, Randle said, "Well, one thing's for sure—you didn't know Colin *or* your husband as well as you think you did. *If* it turns out Colin faked his death years ago, that's obviously a very sick, twisted thing to do. I also don't think you know your husband as well as you think you do. I mean, you didn't know he had a connection to Colin, and it's clear now that he did."

"So what's your point, detective? That I'm a bad judge of character? That I'm attracted to liars? What exactly?"

He stopped twisting his ring and leaned over the table a little.

"My point is I need your help, Ms. Rizzo. I know this is hard, I'm sure this is a lot for you to absorb all at once, but if I'm going to find your husband I'll need you to be one hundred percent transparent. Those stats you might've heard, about every second a person is missing the odds decrease of finding them alive—they're unfortunately true. The clock is ticking. If we don't find your husband soon, time might run out."

"What about his ex-girlfriend, Jennifer Sears? Did you look into her yet?"

"That woman you mentioned, the ex-girlfriend? Yes, and we have no reason to believe she's involved. We talked to the other woman from his office, Nikki Fox? That also led to nothing. She had an alibi *and* we have no reason she and your husband were involved romantically. Did he mention anyone else lately? Maybe someone he met online?"

"No, but I guess these days you never know who somebody's talking to online, right? I mean I never thought Michael had secrets, or was capable of keeping a big secret, or living any kind of double life...well, until five minutes ago. I guess there could be things I don't know about him. I mean, if he kept Colin secret, he could've been lying to me about practically anything."

"I've talked to the partners at his firm. They gave me some names, but it hasn't led to anything, at least not yet. Can you think of anything else? Any recent conversation with Michael that seemed unusual in any way?"

"If there was, I would've told you already."

"Maybe you forgot, you've been under a lot of stress. Was there anything that he mentioned that's related to Colin, or could be related to him?"

"No, nothing, except the conversation we had after I saw Colin on the street."

"How did he react to that?"

"I told him exactly what I told you, how I saw Colin getting into the cab, and of course he didn't believe me. He told me it was just like those other times when I thought I saw Colin, that I was imagining it, making it up, but now I'm wondering—how long was he fucking with me? For all these years, making me think something was wrong with me, that I was sick because I couldn't let go of Colin, and the whole time he knew Colin was alive? Why did he do that to me? Why did he put me through that kind of hell?"

"It's possible that he didn't know," Randle said. "That he and Colin met recently, or even on Saturday for the first time. I mean, isn't that possible? Even likely?"

"I guess so, but he still made me crazy for telling him I saw Colin getting into the cab and he knew *that* was true."

"Why do you think your husband would lie to you?"

"I have no idea. I honestly don't. But it's making me think everything, everything I thought was real. My entire marriage feels like a lie."

Randle let out a breath, shaking his head, then said, "Let's take this one step at a time, okay?"

"Please stop talking to me like that."

"Like what?"

"With that tone."

"What tone is that?"

"Like I'm hysterical or crazy."

"All right, how's this tone? Is this tone okay?"

It wasn't, but I said, "Go ahead."

"You told me the last time you saw your husband was Sunday morning at a little before eight-thirty. What did you do after he left?"

"What did *I* do?"

"Maybe there's something you forgot to tell me, something you didn't think was significant, but actually is."

"I was with my children, shopping at Hudson Yards, but if you're thinking about talking to them too, you're out of your mind, I'm not involving them in any of this. They've been traumatized enough."

"Did you make any phone calls on Sunday?"

"Except trying to reach Michael? No, I don't think so."

"Texts?"

"Probably, for my business."

"You have a business?"

"I told you, I'm a professional organizer."

"Oh, that's right. You go into an office for that?"

"No, I…Why do you care? What does this have to do with finding Michael?"

"We looked at the surveillance video in your building. I know you didn't leave after your husband left, but I haven't seen your phone records."

"My phone records? Seriously?"

"If you contacted somebody now's the time to tell me."

"This is crazy. Who would I contact?"

"I don't know. Maybe a friend, acquaintance, somebody you're involved with?"

"*Involved* with? Are you seriously asking me if—"

"Yes, I am."

"That's ridiculous."

"Is it?"

"Yes it is."

"What's the nature of your relationship with Andrew Reedy?"

I couldn't believe this.

"*Andrew*? How do you even know about *Andrew*?"

"Your mother-in-law told me that you husband suspected you were involved with him."

Michael really told Stella about his theory about Andrew and me? And in our counseling sessions he'd complained to Donna that *I* created drama?

"I can't believe he told his mother that. It was nothing. Andrew and I are friends. Not even friends, acquaintances. Michael just got jealous, maybe because he had a lot to hide himself."

"Maybe."

"Wait, what's going on here? You seriously think *Andrew* has something to do with Michael disappearing?"

"If your husband thought you were involved with someone, yes it could create motive for a confrontation, or at least a meeting."

"That's ridiculous."

"I'm just trying to get a full picture of what's—"

"Instead of listening to my mother-in-law's bullshit, you should be looking for Colin. It makes more sense that *he* has something to with this, or even that he's with Michael right now. I mean, you have actual video of them together, you have evidence, and you're asking me about *Andrew*?"

"We also have video of your husband jogging toward Central Park on Sunday morning."

I stared at him. "Wait, what?" I couldn't believe he hadn't told me about this yet. Was he just making this up, trying to get a reaction from me? "What video? What're you talking about?"

"Security footage in the area, piecemealed together."

"How long have you had this?"

"Since yesterday."

"Un-fucking-believable."

"We had to confirm—"

"Lemme see it."

"Can you please keep your voice down, Ms. Rizzo?"

"No, I won't keep my fucking voice down. I want to see that video. Now!"

"You're going to have to calm down, all right?"

I wanted to say fuck you, but I said, "I don't have to be calm, I'll be however I want to be. If you have video, if you're not making this up, I want to fucking see it."

"I don't have access to it at the moment, but we know your husband crossed Second Avenue, and was near Third on Sixty-First, and then on Lexington and Sixty-Second, and there's nothing after that."

"What do you mean, nothing? What're you saying?"

"We believe one possibility is that somewhere within this area he got in a car—maybe under his own volition, maybe not."

"Why do you *believe* this?"

"We don't know anything for sure, but we canvassed the buildings in the area and talked to doormen and other potential witnesses. It's possible he went somewhere else and cameras didn't pick up, or that he got into a car or another type of vehicle, or that he was taken somewhere."

"Okay, so what's your theory now? You think Andrew Reedy, a history professor at Hunter College and theater geek, kidnapped Michael, why? He's secretly madly in love with me? Or is he just mad? Seriously, is this all you got?"

"I never said that I think this Andrew guy is or isn't involved."

"You literally asked me if I'm having an affair with him."

"I'm just exploring all possibilities."

"You know what I think? I think this is all a waste of time, that's what I think." I was raising my voice again, but I didn't care. "Put the video of Colin and Michael online. Maybe somebody'll recognize Colin. If you find Colin, maybe you can find Michael."

"We'll decide when or when not to release the video."

"Just do it."

"Believe it or not, I know how to do my job, Ms. Rizzo."

"Really? Actually, I'm not sure you do."

He gazed at me for a few seconds with a half-smile, like he was thinking something that he didn't want to say out loud, then said, "Do you still see a psychiatrist, Ms. Rizzo?"

"How is that any of your business? And how do you even know I ever went to psychiatrists. Who…Wait, did Michael's mother tell you about that too?"

"It was mentioned in an old article in the *Post*, after Colin Grant went missing. It said you had some kind of breakdown and stayed at a treatment center. That isn't true?"

"This is what you call doing your job? Following conspiracy theories online?"

"Is it true or not?"

"Yes, years ago I was treated at a mental health facility. So what?"

"Have you been on any medication lately? Antidepressants? Antianxiety meds? Antipsychotics? Anti anything else?"

Thinking about the Klonopin and Ambien I'd taken, I said, "Are you serious?"

"Meds have side effects, can make you drowsy, forget things. I dunno, maybe you had a conversation with somebody on Sunday morning and forgot about it?"

Getting up, I said, "I've had enough of this bullshit. I'm not talking to you again without a lawyer."

"Why do you need a lawyer?"

"Because you're trying to bully me and belittle me and I think it's disgusting."

"Am I? Or am I just trying to find your husband?"

"*And* I went to that treatment center after Colin disappeared, because I was at the lowest point in my life and I needed help because I was extremely depressed. How dare you try to shame me for my mental health issues."

"All I said—"

"You're married, aren't you, Detective?"

"*What*?"

"Can you imagine your wife just disappearing one day? Can you imagine what that would feel like? Now imagine it happening twice. Can you do that? I don't think you can. Because doing that requires empathy, *something* you obviously don't have."

He might've said something else, but I was already marching away, thinking, *Mic drop*, as I exited onto Sixty-Seventh Street.

FIFTEEN

WALKING DOWNTOWN ON Third Avenue, I said into my phone: "Hi, Hannah, this is Vanessa Rizzo."

Long silence. That was weird—Hannah, the receptionist at Michael's office, was usually chatty with me. Why wasn't she at least saying hi, asking how I was doing?

"Can I please speak with Russell?"

"Hold on."

Was I imagining it, or did she sound cold, distant, like I was a stranger—or worse, a *telemarketer*?

Maybe a minute passed, then she returned and said, "Sorry he's in a meeting right now, can I take a message?"

Nope, not imagining it.

"Why won't you put him on?"

"I told you he's—"

"Why are you acting this way?"

"What way?"

"Like I'm a freakin' stranger. This is urgent. It has to do with Michael, a *partner* at your firm, who is missing and might've been kidnapped."

A pause—I thought I heard her let out a deep breath—then she said, "I'm sorry, but Russell can't speak right now. If you'd like to leave a message I'll make sure he gets it."

"What's with the tone? I need to speak to him right now. Put me through." I was aware that I was raising my voice and people passing by were looking over at me, but I didn't care. "My husband's missing, okay? I need legal help from his firm, so tell Russell to get off the phone right now."

After an even longer pause than before, Hannah said, "I can take a message, but I can't—"

I ended the call, muttering, "God fuckin' damn it."

Then I saw that I'd gotten another missed call from Andrew while I was with Randle. Ugh, had Randle already spoken to Andrew?

Continuing along Third Avenue, I called Andrew back.

"Hey, Vanessa, I heard about what's going on. I'm so, so sorry. How're you holding up?"

It was nice to get support from *someone.*

"Thanks, I appreciate that. Pretty awful actually."

"I'll bet. I heard about what's going on, on TV."

"Oh, so the police haven't contacted you yet?"

"Me? Why would the police contact *me?*"

I stopped at the corner of Sixty-Sixth and Third as I noticed a black SUV facing me across the street, waiting for the light to turn. It looked like the same SUV I'd seen walking home from the park with my kids. Maybe a reporter was driving it or one of those internet sleuths. With its lightly tinted windows and glare from the sun, I couldn't see the driver.

"Vanessa? Are you still there?…Vanessa?"

"Yeah, yeah. I'm here."

"What's this about the police?"

"Nothing. I was just at the station, talking to a detective. It's ridiculous, but I wanted to give you a heads up."

"Where are you now?"

"Um…Third Avenue."

I realized my hand holding my phone was trembling.

"Third and where?"

"Like Sixty-sixth."

"You're not far from my place. Why don't you just swing by? We can have some tea or something strong. You shouldn't be alone right now."

He was right. I shouldn't be alone. Not when I was feeling like this.

"That's very sweet, Andrew, but I think I have to talk to a lawyer now and for some reason Michael's partner, whom I've known for years, won't take my fucking calls…Sorry, I didn't mean to snap, it's just—"

"Just come by. I might be able to help out with your lawyer situation too. My brother's a litigator, knows criminal defense people. You could at least consult with him if you want to."

I looked back and saw that the black SUV had turned and now was double parked, about twenty yards behind me. I still couldn't make out the driver through the tint, but I wasn't imagining this—the SUV was following me. Could it have something to do with Michael's disappearance? Or Colin's reappearance?

I'd stopped walking and was about to open the camera app on my phone, but the driver must have seen me because the SUV suddenly accelerated past me.

"Vanessa? You still there?"

"Yeah, yeah, I'm here, I'm here. What's your address?"

HARRISON HAD TOLD me how nice Andrew's building was—
he'd been there with Justin—but I didn't expect it to be *this*
nice. It was the most elegant building on a block of elegant,
upscale, pre-war buildings on Sixty-Fourth between Madison
and Park. I didn't know much about Andrew's background,
but as a professor at a city university he couldn't have been
making huge money. Maybe he came from money, or his ex-
wife had been wealthy, and he'd gotten a big settlement.

His doorman announced me, then I rode the elegant, old
elevator—it even had a red velvet fold-out seat—to the
eleventh floor. Andrew was waiting at the end of the hallway,
at the open door to his apartment.

"Hey there."

He was dressed how he usually dressed—casual, preppy,
professorial—in a light-blue checked button-down tucked
into nice-fitting jeans and dark brown Mephistos.

He came toward me and hugged me and said, "I'm so
glad you came. Come in, come in."

His apartment was amazing—tall ceilings with gorgeous
crown molding, hardwood floors, a beautiful crystal
chandelier in the large foyer leading to a bright, airy living
room. It was tastefully decorated—minimal but warm. I
recognized at least two pieces from Restoration Hardware.

"Wow, I love what you've done with it," I said. "Have
you lived here long?"

"Yes and no," he said. "I moved in here with my parents
when I was six years old actually. Went to school in the
neighborhood—P.S. 6, then Hunter. My parents passed the
apartment along to me after I got divorced. They're in South
Carolina now."

"It's two bedrooms?"

"Three actually. I'd give you the tour, but I want to hear

what's going on."

"No, it's okay, I'd love to take the tour. I could use the distraction honestly."

The living room and dining room were huge and he had my dream kitchen, with all new appliances, including a stainless-steel Masterpiece oven and a refrigerator with a French door bottom freezer that I've always wanted, but would never fit in our kitchen. Best of all, there was no clutter—not even any magazines, newspapers, or mail out anywhere.

"I'm so impressed how neat everything is."

"Hold on, you haven't seen Justin's room yet."

I followed him down the hallway. He showed me the bathroom, at least twice the size of mine, fully renovated in marble, with tasteful brass fixtures. His bedroom was huge, spotless, and very well decorated.

"Love the wrought-iron bed," I said. "I've always wanted one, but Michael has this weird phobia about getting his head stuck between the bars of the headboard."

"Ha, well I guess there are worse phobias."

"Are there really?"

We laughed.

Andrew had been right—Justin did need organizational help for his room, though actually it was immaculate compared to Harrison and Carson's.

"Okay, I get it," I said. "Well, I'm happy to make some suggestions."

"Wow, we'd both really appreciate that."

Then he showed me a third bedroom that he was using as a home office.

As we headed back toward the kitchen, he continued telling me about his family's move to Manhattan from

Queens, as, feeling a rush of dizziness, I flashed back to Detective Randle showing me the footage of Michael and Colin, and spotting the SUV that might've been following me.

"Hey, are you okay?" he asked.

"Yeah, fine, but can I just get something to drink?"

"I have juice, wine, or I can make you something stronger if you—"

"Just water's fine."

While he got me the water, I looked at my phone, hoping for a miracle text from Michael, but there was nothing. I texted Carson and Harrison: **Be home soon**, as Andrew returned with a glass of water.

"Here you go."

Andrew handed me the water and sat next to me.

"Thanks for inviting me over," I said. "It's nice to see a friendly face."

"I'm glad you came. So what happened at the police station? Any news about Michael? Something hopeful?"

"Unfortunately, no," I said. "I guess Detective Randle still hasn't contacted you?"

"I'm sorry, why do you think a detective would contact me? What do I have to do with anything? Do they think I was a witness to something or—"

"I'll take that as a no."

He looked at me seriously. "What's going on, Vanessa?"

"Well, I just got some, well, extremely weird news. Michael was spotted with Colin on Saturday, the day before he disappeared."

"Colin?"

"Yeah, remember I mentioned my ex-fiancé?"

"But that must've been a long time ago. Why would—"

"I guess you haven't seen what they're saying about me online."

"I saw a couple of news stories, but I'm not on social media."

"Oh, that's right, you don't even have an Insta. I guess that's why you weren't worried about inviting a potential killer over to your apartment. Now it all makes sense."

"Potential killer? I'm sorry I really don't understand any of this."

Talking fast, I told him about my engagement to Colin, how Colin had disappeared years ago, how I'd spotted him on Friday night, and how Randle had shown me the video of Michael and Colin together.

"Why were they together?"

"I have no idea; it makes no sense. As far as I knew they didn't know each other. Now it's making me question everything, my entire marriage, the past twenty years of my life. It all seems like one huge lie."

"But what does this have to do with me? And I still don't understand why a detective would want to talk to me about anything?"

"I'm dreading telling you this."

"Well, now you *have to* tell me. Seriously, what's going on, Vanessa?"

"All right, whatever, I guess it doesn't make a difference now." I paused, then said, "Well, the other night Michael asked me if anything was going on with me and you?"

"With *us*?"

"Yeah, and I told him it was ridiculous, and I don't think he seriously believed it. Now that I know about this big secret he was keeping, he was probably just trying to make up something, you know, as distraction. He must've told his mother about it and his mother told Detective Randle. His mother's been impossible, a total nightmare, but I'm sorry your name came up. It's really embarrassing actually."

"Stop it, Vanessa. I want to be here for you. I want to help."

"I appreciate that, Andrew. Actually, you're the only friend who's even talked to me. No one else has called, even texted."

"Well, I'm here for you."

He rested his open hand on my thigh for a moment or two, then moved it away.

"Thank you," I said, "that means a lot. It seems like everyone's been turning against me the past couple of days—my in-laws, my friends, my clients—well, *ex*-clients—that detective, even my own kids. Well, not Carson so much, but Harrison. I can't get angry at them though—I know they're just scared and confused and miss their father. I've watched so many true crime shows, now I feel like I'm *living* in one—*is she crazy or isn't she*? When I'm watching, I always feel so removed, so judgmental, asking myself how could those people get into those horrible situations, happy I'm not like them, you know? But now I see I am like them, *anyone* can be like them, *anyone*'s life can turn into a nightmare."

"I hear you," Andrew said. "Maybe there's something you don't know. Some other explanation for all this."

"You mean an explanation other than Michael is a total fucking liar? I mean, just the other night, before he disappeared, he was *still* lying to me, acting like I was crazy for thinking I saw Colin when he knew Colin was alive. You know what he said to me? 'You'll never get answers, Vanessa. Sometimes you have to just let go.' Can you believe that shit? Lying to my face when he knew Colin was alive, he was even having meetings with him. Now I have no idea how long they've known each other, if it's days or years."

"Jesus, I'm sorry." His hand was on my thigh again.

"He's been acting weird for a while now—working late, taking emergency phone calls where he leaves the apartment so I can't overhear what he's saying. I thought maybe he's having an affair with his ex or someone from his office, but after I saw that video of him and Colin I don't know what to think anymore. Sorry, I didn't mean to come here to vent and ruin your afternoon. This is probably the last thing you needed today."

"Do you want me to put you in touch with my brother, just to consult? He's a really good guy, very knowledgeable."

"It's okay, I'm sure Michael's firm will help me, but I do appreciate the offer. It's very kind of you, really."

"I just feel awful that you're going through all this. If you and your kids need someplace to stay, you can all crash here."

"That's nice of you to offer, but I wouldn't want to impose."

"It wouldn't be imposing at all. You shouldn't be alone right now, Vanessa." He had started to massage my leg, kneading the inside of my thigh with his fingertips.

"What're you doing?"

"What?" He seemed confused.

"With your hand."

"Come on, I know how unhappy you and Michael have been, and I know you feel a connection with me. Why don't we just admit it?"

I couldn't believe this was happening. I was so shocked that I didn't swat his hand away or try to move.

"Come on, Andrew, stop," I said, trying to play it off as a

joke, even though there was nothing funny about this.

"I know you're feeling what I'm feeling. When we had drinks on Saturday there was a moment when I knew you felt it too."

I had no idea what he was talking about. *A moment? The fuck?*

I shoved his hand away and got up.

He stood too and grabbed my left wrist.

"It's okay, Vanessa, you don't have to be afraid."

Then he pressed his face against mine and his tongue was worming into my mouth. I bit down on it.

"Ow, fuck. Jesus Christ!"

"You think I'm fuckin' afraid of you?" Freeing myself, I hurried toward the front door.

"Come on, Vanessa, don't be like that."

As I fumbled with the locks he came up behind me and tried to grab me again. I turned fast and slapped him across the face, then kneed him in the balls.

As he keeled over, groaning, I managed to open the door. I rushed out of the apartment and pressed the button for the elevator.

Leaning out of his apartment, Andrew said, "Vanessa, come back! Vanessa! Let's talk about this!"

I didn't want to wait, so I took the stairs down to the lobby and out to the street.

SIXTEEN

WELL, SO MUCH for a relaxing visit with a *friend*. Apparently, I really didn't have any friends anymore, and I couldn't trust anyone—especially a man.

As I walked down Park Avenue, I kept looking around for the SUV. I didn't see it anywhere, but that didn't mean it wasn't following me. I hated feeling this way—like a passenger, a victim. I felt like things were happening to me, that I wasn't in control of anything. My brain was spiraling, grabbing any story that fit.

Crossing Sixty-Third Street, I realized I was only a couple of blocks from the area where Michael was apparently last seen. I could've headed east instead of going downtown. Was it an accident that I was here? Fate? Or did I come here unconsciously, for a reason? Maybe there was something the police had missed, or something that Michael had dropped. While I knew that this was mostly ridiculous, I still felt like I had to go there.

On the corner of Sixty-First and Park, I stopped. I imagined Michael running here on Sunday morning, on his usual route to the park. Now the idea that he had left me and the boys, ran away, seemed completely ridiculous. If he wanted to run away with Jennifer or another woman, why would he do it in such a crazy, dramatic way? Why not just ask me for a divorce, or move out? We were already in counseling—I would've been upset if he'd announced he wanted to end our marriage, but I wouldn't have been shocked. It could have been like any other Manhattan divorce. No, he didn't leave us—I was certain of it. Something happened to him and it had to have something to do with Colin. He met Colin for coffee on Saturday, then disappeared on Sunday. And there was no connection? It had to be related; I just had to figure out how.

I kept looking around for the black SUV. It was almost dark now and car headlights made it hard to ID specific cars. Maybe it was still following, maybe for a block or so away, and I just couldn't see it. Or maybe I'd imagined that it was following me. I hadn't gotten the license plate, so maybe I'd seen a different black SUV. While the cars looked identical, it wasn't an unusual model, so I could've jumped to the wrong conclusion—it wouldn't have been the first time. Though was that true anymore? All the times over the years when I thought I'd imagined seeing Colin, he might've actually been there. If I'd been wrong about Colin did that mean I was right about the SUV? Paranoia and an active imagination were a lethal combination; I wasn't sure what was real, what wasn't, and it seemed like the confusion would go on forever.

While I was convinced that something awful had happened to Michael—he was injured or dead—I was also aware of how I wasn't as upset about this as I should've been. I was too angry at him—for gaslighting me, maybe for years. Telling me that I was crazy for thinking I'd spotted Colin all those times, that I had to "let go," including just the other night, saying that I should see Dr. Stone again, when he not only knew Colin was alive, but had actually met with him. There was no possible excuse for any of this, none, and no way I could ever forgive him.

"Yeah, I'll let go all right," I said to myself.

I rushed east along Sixty-First Street, practically jogging. On Lexington, near Bloomingdale's, I thought I saw the SUV up ahead and ran faster to try to get a view of the driver, but when I got closer I realized it was actually a van. But that didn't mean the SUV wasn't still following me. Maybe the driver was a reporter, or just a member of the internet mob, trying to fuck with my head. Maybe somebody was in the van live streaming video of me. Maybe they'd been streaming the video for hours and people were commenting about how paranoid I was acting, and how "obvious" it was that I had killed Michael and Colin, and that my behavior was "proof" of how crazy I was. I needed the police to release that video of Colin and Michael together—not only for someone to possibly identify Colin, but also to show people that they were alive, or at least alive as of last Saturday.

My phone pinged—a text. I stopped running but was still gasping. Shit, I hadn't made my kids dinner—they were probably starving. But it wasn't Harrison or Carson; it was from a number I didn't recognize, with the 617 area code. Normally I didn't answer unfamiliar calls, because they were usually spammy, but I hoped it was Michael calling, or someone calling to tell me that Michael had been found, that he was alive and well and this nightmare was over.

"Hello?"

"Vanessa?"

It was a woman; she sounded young.

"Yes," I said hopefully. "This is Vanessa."

"You deserve to die too, bitch! Fucking husband killer, fucking—"

I ended the call and had to resist an urge to smash my phone against the sidewalk. How the hell did she get my cell number? Did someone give it to her?

I was running again, just wanting to get home. Maybe Michael would be there, and the boys would be excited talking to him and hugging him. I wouldn't forgive him, but at least the nightmare would be over—I could start to heal. While this fantasy seemed improbable, it gave me hope and made me run a little faster.

On my block, there were still news trucks and people in front of my building, but this didn't mean that Michael was still here. Maybe the media was here to cover the story of Michael's return, and they were waiting to get a statement from him, and from me. I didn't want to talk to any reporters now, for any reason. I went around the block, to the back of the building, expecting a confrontation.

No one was there, though—just Jimmy, the parking attendant, who was talking to another guy and didn't notice me passing by. I entered the building, then took the elevator up to my floor. As the elevator approached, I thought I smelled chicken nuggets. Michael never cooked dinner, but he sometimes microwaved nuggets for the boys when I wasn't home.

The elevator doors opened and I raced to the apartment door, ready to see Michael and the kids, ready to get my life back.

"Hi!" I shouted, then it took a few seconds to register that the lights were out and apparently no one was home.

No one? Where were my boys?

"Carson! Harrison!"

I flicked on the light and raced around the apartment. Not in the living room, or their room, or my room—definitely not home. What the fuck?

Neither Harrison nor Carson had responded to any of my texts. What the fuck? They were usually glued to their phones.

I texted Harrison and Carson: **WHERE THE HELL ARE YOU?????!!!!!!**

Then I called Harrison; it went straight to voice mail, and a call to Carson went to voice mail as well. Okay, now I was officially panicking. I imagined their phones, in the gutter somewhere, near wherever they'd been abducted. This was it—my biggest nightmare was happening.

I texted Harrison again: **You have to text me immediately! Are you in the park looking for dad WHERE THE FUCK ARE YOU????!!!**

I told myself, *Stay calm, just stay calm*, but I knew this was impossible. I needed fucking Xanax.

I thought about the SUV, the phone messages, the online mob, the horrible things people were saying to me, and how people kept disappearing from my life—Colin, Michael, now my children. Where were Colin and Michael? Were they playing some sick game trying to torture me? Were they both psychopaths? I thought I knew them so well, but I apparently didn't have a great track record, reading people.

My phone was vibrating—Andrew calling. I could still feel his hand on my thigh, tickling me with his disgusting fingertips.

"Leave me alone!" I shouted as I sent the call to voicemail.

I heard a noise coming from the boys' room. Were they

in their room, tied up in their closet? I hadn't checked the closet. I ran swinging the door open, right into Sparkle. He meowed and keeled over onto his back.

"Shit, sorry!" I shouted.

I rubbed his back and he made it up onto his feet on his own.

"I'm so so sorry, sweetie," I said. "I'm so, so sorry."

The pissed-off cat glared at me, then scampered away under the bunkbed.

I was shaking, grinding my jaw, but I was too distraught to cry. I hadn't felt this way in a long time. The darkness was creeping in, and I knew how quickly it could overwhelm me.

I checked my phone—no messages or missed calls.

"Fuck, what the hell?"

I cocked my arm, ready to fling my phone across the room, but held back.

Trying to calm myself with deep breaths, I returned to the living room. I tried Randle but, of course, got his voice mail. It was like everybody had disappeared, abandoned me. Well, except for a creepy single dad.

Walking through my apartment, out to the hallway, I left a message for Randle: "It's me—Vanessa. Now my children are gone, can you find my fucking children? Fucking do *something*!"

Somehow, I wound up in my building's lobby—I barely remembered leaving my apartment—screaming at Tony about my missing children. He explained that he hadn't seen my kids, but that he'd taken a break earlier, and Constantine, one of the building's maintenance people, had been filling in. I asked him to call Constantine, but Constantine wasn't answering his phone.

"Keep trying him!" I screamed. "I'm begging you!"

Outside, several reporters noticed the fuss in the lobby. I exited and said, "Please, has anyone seen my boys? They're fourteen and sixteen and they're not answering their phones."

Now TV cameras and phone cameras were aimed at me. A couple of reporters said they hadn't seen my kids, but most of them were just shouting questions over each other. The ones I made out were:

"Have you heard from your husband today?"

"Where's your husband?"

"Did you kill your husband?"

"Were you questioned again by the police, Vanessa?"

I couldn't take it anymore. I leaned in toward one guy who was aiming a phone: "You're disgusting, get that shit out of my face!" Then I said to the whole crowd, "All of you are pathetic and I hope you all go to hell!"

I knew I'd regret this later—more viral footage of me acting unhinged—but right now I didn't give a shit about anything except finding my boys.

Looking directly at one of the news cameras I pleaded, "If anyone has seen my children, please, *please* contact the police immediately." Then I dashed back into the building and screamed at Tony who had his cell phone to his ear, "What? What is it?"

"Nothing," he said. "I can't reach him."

"Fuck, fuck, fuck!" I shouted as I flashed back to the beach on Shelter Island, screaming *Colin!* repeatedly in the darkness.

As I rode the elevator to 14, I was saying, "Not my children, not my children. Please, God, not my children."

God, what a joke.

I wished I still believed in God. At least I'd have someone

to blame, to curse out. I'd never felt so alone.

I glanced at my phone—still no callback from Randle. Back in my apartment, I was going to call him again, then I thought, *What's the point?* I knew he wouldn't help. When had the police *ever* helped? They couldn't find Colin, they couldn't find Michael, even though they had video, and now I expected them to find my kids? He'd probably just give me more of that "they have to be missing for twenty-four hours" bullshit.

My phone vibrated—a text from a 914 area code:

Husband killers go to fucking hellll, bitch !!!!

I blocked the number and deleted the message, but maybe this was a mistake.

How did I know if one of those online nuts was responsible for all of this? Maybe there was something else going on? What if some psycho had been out to get me for years, someone I don't know about? Was it something that happened in college, or when I was growing up on Staten Island? Or maybe those tabloids years ago were right, and it was related to my father and the mob. Maybe he'd been more involved than I knew, and an old enemy was getting revenge on my father by destroying his daughter's life. Maybe this mob guy had kidnapped Colin and kept him hostage for years, then Colin escaped, so he kidnapped Michael and my kids. Maybe that person was driving the black SUV, and maybe my kids were inside it. Maybe instead of running away from that SUV, I should've run toward it, broken in, attacked whoever was driving and saved my children.

I knew this was crazy, but *was* it crazy? Or was *I* crazy?

I had to stay centered, stick to the facts—Colin was alive, and Michael and my kids were missing, and someone was following me around the city. It seemed logical that whoever was in the SUV was responsible for everything else. I could believe one or two coincidences, but not three.

"Where are my fucking children?"

Oh, fuck, it was happening again—I was losing control, falling into that dark hole again, but I couldn't let that happen, not now. My children needed me. I was their only hope. Without me, they wouldn't have a chance.

From the bathroom medicine chest, I took out the Xanax. I let two pills dissolve under my tongue to get into my system faster. Two was more than a normal dose but, what the hell, I needed help, *a lot* of help as fast as possible. I couldn't risk feeling overwhelmed and doing nothing. I had to stay focused, in control.

My phone rang again—Stella or Joe calling from their landline.

I answered, screaming, "Have you heard from the kids? Do you know where the fuck they are?"

"Ma." It was Harrison.

"Oh my God! Thank God, Harrison, thank God you're okay. What happened? Did a man from Staten Island take you?"

"Man from Staten Island? What're you talking about?"

I was aware of how ridiculous I sounded. That was a good sign at least. If you're aware you're crazy then you can't actually be crazy, right?

"Never mind, are you at Grandma's? Is Carson there too?"

"Yeah, we're both here."

More relief, then I said, "Thank God, thank God, thank God, I can't tell you how happy I am right now." I realized I was out of breath; as I took a few seconds the relief morphed into anger. "Wait, how did you get to New Jersey? Did *she* take you away? How come your Find My iPhones aren't working?"

"Grandma and Grandpa picked us up. Grandma made us turn off our locations."

"She *what?*" *That bitch.* "She had no right, *no right* to do that. Put Grandma on the phone right now. She kidnapped my children, and terrified me like this? I said put her on the phone right this—"

"She didn't kidnap us, Ma. We left on our own. We *told* her to come get us."

I had to let this sink in. "Told her? What do you mean, *told her?*"

"We *wanted* to go with them."

"Why? I need you here, both of you, and you need to be with your mother. And what about school? Did you forget about school?"

"Grandma said Grandpa can drive us to school from New Jersey."

"Harrison, just come home. Call a Lyft and come home."

"People are saying a lot of weird stuff about you online, Ma."

"You know that's all ridiculous. You know it's all lies."

A few seconds passed.

"Harrison? You still there? Harrison, are you—"

"I better get back to the dinner table."

"You know none of that is true, Harrison. You know it's lies."

"Then why's it on the news now?"

I didn't know what he meant. "What's on the news?"

"It's online, it's everywhere. They're saying you're a person of interest now."

"They're saying *what?*"

"I said they're—"

"*Who's* saying that?"

"The police."

I put Harrison on speaker as I checked online on my phone. It wasn't difficult to find—a quick search of "Top" results for my name displayed several links from news sites, including FOX and the *Post*, all with the same quote that "Police have labeled Vanessa Rizzo as a person of interest in her husband's disappearance."

"Son of a bitch," I said. "I just met with that fucking detective and he didn't say anything about this. Then I noticed that the tweets about me being a 'person of interest' were from about twenty minutes ago. "Oh my God, this is insane. It has to be a mistake, a reporter making it up. How can I be a person of interest when they have that video?"

"What video?" Harrison asked.

I told him about what Detective Randle had shown me.

"So what?" Harrison said. "That was the day *before* Dad disappeared."

"No, don't you get it? Your father was with *Colin*. That means something is going on that none of us understand, and it also means that Dad could be alive, with Colin, or that Colin knows what's going on."

"There's nothing about any video online, Ma."

"What, you think I'm lying to you? You think I'm crazy? The police haven't released the video yet because…because…because I have no idea why they haven't released it, okay, but I'm sure they're doing that now. They're both alive, which means I obviously don't have anything to do with anything."

"Wait, it's only *you* saying it's Colin and Dad in the video?"

"They probably have to ID the people officially or whatever. But it *was* them, Harrison. I can recognize my own husband and my own ex-fiancé for god's sake."

"Just like the other times you thought you saw Colin? Dad's told me about all the times you thought you saw him, but it turned out you didn't. Even when I was a baby it happened. But now you expect me to believe this time is different?"

"This time *is* different."

"What about you and Justin's dad? Grandma said you and him—"

"Nothing is going on with us, thank God."

I could feel Andrew's fingernails again.

"So you're saying Grandma is lying?"

"Yes, she's lying."

"Justin said you were at his apartment before with his dad. Is that a lie too?"

"No, I was there, because I thought he was a friend, but he isn't a friend. He's actually the opposite; he's a horrible person."

"So now Justin's dad is a horrible person too? I thought you liked him. You're always talking to him, laughing."

"He just did something horrible to me, Harrison."

"Justin's dad? The *college professor*? You really expect me to believe that?"

"What does his profession have to do with it? But don't tell Justin. I might have to involve the police at some point."

"The *police*? With Justin's father? What the fuck, Ma?"

"He could've…" I almost said "raped me" but I didn't want to cause drama and upset Harrison, so I went with, "It could've been worse. Much, much worse."

Again, there was silence.

"Harrison? You still there?"

"Yeah, I'm here, I'm here."

"I'm telling you the truth about everything, Harrison. You need to believe me."

More silence then he said, "I want to believe you, Ma, but what if what they're saying online is true? Maybe you're crazy, you make things up. Maybe you killed that guy Colin—"

"Stop it."

"—and maybe you killed Dad too—"

"I said shut up, Harrison! Just shut the hell up!" I didn't mean to scream as loud as I did. "Sorry, I didn't mean to yell, I'm just very upset right now obviously and—"

"Sorry, Ma." Harrison's voice was cracking up; I could tell he was about to cry. "I can't anymore…I just…I just can't."

"Harrison, sweetie. It's okay. I'm your mother here. I'm here, sweetie, I'm here."

"I gotta go."

"Listen to me, Harrison, just listen to me. You have to come home now. You have to—"

"Grandma told me not to call you. I guess she was right."

"Your grandmother's an idiot. I'm your mother, your fucking mother and …Harrison?…Harrison, are you still there? Harr…Shit, goddammit."

I ended the call and tried him back right away, but it went right to voicemail. I cocked my arm, ready to throw my phone again, but stopped myself.

I was shaking and could barely breathe. The apartment and the city had never been this silent.

This isn't me.

Things were getting worse, the drugs weren't working,

and I was starting to spiral. How was this happening *again*? Just when everything was going well in my life a man, a significant other, had to disappear and ruin everything. After years of hard work, my business had been starting to take off, I was excited about Harrison's acting career, and Michael and I were making progress in couples counseling. The future had seemed bright, until I spotted Colin getting into that taxi, and now I'd lost everything, including my family, and I had no reason to—

"Stop it," I said. "Just fucking stop it, Vanessa."

Maybe things weren't as bad as they seemed; they were *never* as bad as they seemed. It was always my perspective that got skewed, especially during dark periods. When I was in this state it was impossible to tell reality from fantasy. Or maybe I just thought I had trouble telling fantasy from reality. Maybe I'd never imagined seeing Colin any of those times—maybe he'd actually been there. Or, if I did have the tendency to slip into some kind of delusional state, did it really matter? I mean, nothing was permanent, right? Eventually my perspective would change, and everything wouldn't seem as bleak and hopeless as it did right now. *You have to let life happen,* Dr. Stone had once told me. In the meantime, I had to stay grounded and logical, focus on what I knew was *true*. Michael and Colin were alive, or at least they had been alive as of Saturday. When the police found them, and found out what was going on, the online chatter would die down, and my kids would come back. All I wanted was to clear my name and have a normal, happy life with my children. Nothing else mattered.

I considered calling Harrison back and insisting that he come home, but I decided to let it be for now. Maybe, in the end, it was actually a good thing that my kids were with Joe and Stella. When I was getting harassing phone calls, there was a mob in front of the building, and an SUV was following me around the city, it was probably safer for them to be in New Jersey than with me in Manhattan.

Then I did something I probably shouldn't have done—I went online.

I knew social media could be toxic, but I had to find out why I was a "person of interest." Was there new information? Had the police made a statement, maybe in the last couple of minutes?

I thought I'd see a few new comments about me, but it felt surreal to see "Vanessa Rizzo" trending.

Trending?

"What the fuck?"

Jesus, a verified news account had quote-tweeted the video snippet of me grabbing that guy's iPhone and dropping it in the sewer grating—without the "skeleton bitch" comment that had incited it—and the retweet count was exploding. I looked like an absolute madwoman. There was also already video of me, screaming at reporters outside my building.

The posts about me—well, the ones I *saw*—were horrible. Like:

Vanessa Rizzo is a monster
I feel sorry for her kids
Karen strikes again!!!

And a closeup of just my eyes with the comment:

Killers always got crazy ass eyes smh

Even Janet Crider, a City Council Member in Manhattan, posted: **Let's hope justice is swift**

Then I checked news stories, and saw a brief one from NBC Online, just six minutes ago, stating that the police had "officially designated Vanessa Rizzo as a person of interest in the disappearance of her husband, Manhattan attorney, Michael Rizzo."

I felt the way I did in school, in seventh grade, when I was bullied every day by a group of girls who'd made my life hell.

Without giving it any thought, I responded:

Actually I saw a video of my husband and my ex fiancé today. When I'm vindicated I expect a FULL apology, especially from elected officials. I AM NOT CRAZY and I AM NOT A KILLER

Maybe I wasn't actually fighting back, but posting this—*and* tagging Janet Crider—made me feel a little better anyway, like at least I was doing *something*, and I was happy to see the rapidly increasing likes and retweets.

Then my phone vibrated: Detective Randle finally getting the fuck back to me.

I answered, saying, "What the hell is going on with this fuckin' case? Why am I a person of interest?"

"Hey, calm down, let's calm it down, okay?"

Let's calm it down? Fucking seriously?

But I didn't want to waste any time calling him out, so I just said, "What's going on? Is there any news?"

"I thought *you* had news. I saw your missed calls."

"Why am I a person of interest, and why haven't you released the video yet? People need to know that Colin is alive, that I'm not making all this shit up."

"I'll take that as a no."

"Do you know what it's like for me now because of you? My family and friends are deserting me, people online are saying horrible things, my business might be ruined…Oh, and I think someone's stalking me."

"Stalking you? Who's stalking you?"

"The SUV that's been following me around the city."

"What SUV?"

"I told you, I saw it following me and the kids from the park."

"Oh, right. Do you have any plate or model?"

"No, I don't, but why didn't you get back to me sooner? Why don't you try to actually find my husband instead of pinning shit on me?"

"Did you see the driver of this SUV?"

"No, but I can describe it. It's a black SUV—one of the big ones."

"That's very specific."

Sarcastic prick.

"I'm not an expert, all right? Maybe it's a Highlander. The windows are tinted, and it was far away and…The answer's no, I couldn't see anyone inside."

"Did you get a plate?"

"No, I did not. Don't you think I'd tell you that if I did?"

"Well, if you see it again, get the plate."

"That's it? You're not going to do *anything*?"

"What do you want us to do? There are a lot of big black SUVs in New York City, Ms. Rizzo. Maybe a thousand, maybe ten thousand. What do you want me to do, check out every one of them? You think that'll be a better use of my time?"

"You don't believe me, do you? You think I'm making it up?"

"No, I definitely believe you've *seen* an SUV." I imagined him rolling his eyes. "Do you have any idea who's driving it?"

"Of course I don't. What kind of question is that? Oh, wait, I forgot, I'm a person of interest now, so I can't be trusted about anything. Maybe I'm crazy too, right?"

I heard a notification ping on my phone and saw that I'd received Facebook message from Jennifer Sears, Michael's ex-girlfriend. She was probably angry at me for having the police contact her.

"Are you still there?" Randle asked.

"Yeah, yeah I'm here."

I switched the call to "speaker" and opened the Facebook Messenger app where Jennifer had written:

I think I have some important information to share with you. Are you there?

Important information?

"Was there anything else about the SUV?" Randle asked, sounding frustrated. "Decals, dents, bumper sticker, anything?"

"It seemed new, or new*ish*," I said, typing: **Yes I'm here.**

Ellipses appeared as Jennifer typed.

"Well, obviously if you see this new black SUV again, contact me immediately or call nine-one-one."

The subtle sarcasm was infuriating, but I ignored it and said, "Why do you think someone's following me? Do you think it's Colin? Did you find anything else out?"

"Nothing specific, no. And we haven't been able to identify the other person in the video yet, nor do we know if the video is relevant to your husband's disappearance."

Jennifer was still typing.

I said, "Not relevant? Are you kidding me? And you don't need to ID the video, I'm telling you, it's Colin, Colin Grant. I've never been surer of anything in my life."

Jennifer's message arrived:

It has to do with Michael. Can you meet me right now? I live in Greenpoint, maybe meet in the middle? Pret A Manger on 17th, upstairs in the back. But PLEASE don't tell the police

you're coming. I'll explain everything I promise!!!

I had already tapped out and now sent:

Do you know where Michael is?

She answered almost immediately:

No

I realized Randle had asked me something and I said, "Sorry, what was that?"

"I said I hope for your sake that you're being up front with me. If not, you're definitely going to need that lawyer you said you're gonna get."

Jennifer responded:

No I don't But I have information that can help you I'm leaving now. See you soon!

She went offline and I said to Randle, "I am. I swear to you."

He said, "Yeah," then ended the call.

SEVENTEEN

A HOODIE, DARK sunglasses, and a medical mask weren't exactly a master disguise, but it was better than nothing. I took the elevator down to the lobby, then lingered in the mailroom for a couple of minutes, sifting through my mail and checking my phone. When two young couples exited the elevator and headed out of the building, I rushed up behind them like I was part of their group. I walked right by a group of reporters and a Spectrum News truck and continued toward First Avenue.

On First, I walked fast, heading downtown along the dark avenue, looking around constantly, making sure no one was following; I was especially on the lookout for the black SUV. I didn't see anything suspicious, but did that really mean anything? In New York, someone was always watching; if you couldn't see them, that didn't mean they weren't there. I pulled up my mask to conceal as much of my face as possible, then I spotted a free cab waiting at a red light.

I got in the back and said to the driver, "Union Square,

Seventeenth Street, one seven."

As the cab cut over to Second Avenue, I kept looking around, out the window. I didn't see the SUV, but I still didn't feel safe. How did I know whoever was following me hadn't switched cars? Shit, I wished I'd taken more Xanax. Two pills had never been enough when I was under extreme stress, and the effect wore off quickly. I couldn't tell if it was starting to work or was already wearing off.

At Pret A Manger, I bought a coffee, then went upstairs. There were several people—a homeless guy was spread out across two chairs, a couple of giggly girls in their early twenties, and a guy in the corner across from me with longish salt-and-pepper hair and glasses, typing away on his laptop. No one seemed to notice me as I sat at a table near the bathroom.

I checked my phone to see if Randle had called or texted an update—of course he hadn't. It was also upsetting that none of my friends were checking up on me, at least to see if I was doing okay. There were only two texts from Andrew:

Hey! Can we please meet and talk?

And:

I'm so sorry, Vanessa, but I swear you got the wrong idea! I can explain!

Muttering, "Fuck you," I deleted both.

I already wondered if coming down here was a mistake, if I was just wasting valuable time. I could be looking for Michael or Colin—if I found one of them it might lead to the other. How did I know Jennifer had any actual information? How could I even trust her? Maybe she was lying to me to get revenge for accusing her of having an affair with Michael and having the police contact her? For all I knew, she was the one who'd been harassing me with the texts and the calls or was following me in the SUV.

I was angry again about the Xanax, wishing I'd brought a couple of pills with me just in case, as I saw her, coming up the stairs. I'd expected her to look fake, like she did in her filtered photos online, but she actually looked very pretty and down to earth. Although she was five years older than me and barely wearing makeup, she looked pretty, even in the coffee bar's unforgiving fluorescent light. She was in jeans and a black leather biker jacket that she unzipped but didn't take off. And, yeah, her boob job was annoyingly good.

She recognized me right away, but seemed nervous, glancing at the other people before coming over and joining me.

"Thanks for coming," she said.

"No worries," I said. "Thank you."

Already this was awkward. I'd told the police to check on her as a possible suspect in my husband's disappearance, and now I was a suspect myself, or at least a "person of interest," and we were both trying to be cordial.

She leaned in and in a low, urgent voice said, "Did any-one follow you? Did you see anything suspicious?"

I didn't know why she was so paranoid, but it felt sort of comforting; at least I wasn't the only one.

"No, I was careful."

"Are you sure?"

"Sure as I can be, but how did you know someone's been following me?"

"So you *were* followed?"

"No, not now, but earlier. Well, the last couple of days, since Michael disappeared, yes, I think someone's been following me, but can you tell me what's going on?"

"Shit, this was a bad idea." She was about to stand. "I should probably go."

"No, don't, please." I quieted my voice, almost whispering: "No one followed me here, I swear. It's okay. Please…don't leave. Do you want a coffee or something? It's on me."

"No, I can't drink coffee this late, I'll be up all night. God knows how the Italians do it."

"I'm Italian. Well, Italian-American."

"That explains it."

We smiled.

"I know how weird this must all seem to you," she said, "messaging you like that on Facebook. But thank you for trusting me enough to come here. Also, I want you to know that I had absolutely nothing to do with Michael disappearing. I'm not angry at you for asking the police to talk to me, but I just wanted you to hear this from me directly."

Now that I was sitting across from her and she looked so harmless, it seemed ridiculous that I'd had Randle talk to her. I wondered if she knew that I was a person of interest now, though.

"Thank you for understanding," I said.

Leaning over the table to get a little closer to me, she said in a hushed voice, "I can't imagine what you've been going through lately. I'm so sorry about Michael. Have you heard anything new? Do you know if he's okay?"

"I have no idea. I was hoping you know something or have some idea where he is."

"No, like I messaged you before, I have no idea, but I think I have some, well, important information for you." She glanced at the giggly girls who still seemed oblivious to us, then said, "First of all, Michael and I have not had any kind of relationship, I mean *any* since before you two met. I hope you believe me about that. The last thing I want you to think is that I'm some kind of homewrecker."

Now that I knew how Michael had been lying to me about Colin and God knows what else, it seemed crazy to even care whether he was cheating or not, with an ex, or with *anyone*. My attitude all along should have been—*You want him? Take him, he's all yours.*

"Excuse me if this sounds rude," I said, "but why are we here? This has all been extremely stressful, obviously, so do you have something specific to tell me or not?"

"You're not recording this, are you?"

"*Recording*? Why would I—"

"You have to swear to me you aren't. And my name can't be associated with any of this, okay? No more police. Believe me, I have enough stress in my life right now."

I held up my phone for her to see. "Look—I'm not recording. Nothing in my purse or pockets, I swear. Please, just tell me if you know anything or not. My children are terrified right now."

"The short answer is I might know something." She looked around again, maybe to make sure no one was eavesdropping, then said, "When you told me Michael was missing I had a feeling who might be involved, but I wasn't sure, I thought I was just being paranoid actually. But then I read online that you saw your ex-fiancé, that he's alive, and then I knew what it was about, or could be about."

"Sorry," I said, "but I still have no idea what you're talking about. How do you know *anything* about Colin? And if you know anything, why didn't you tell the police when they contacted you?"

"I told you, no police. The police can't know about any

of this, especially if my name's involved."

"Fine, I promise, no police, no police." I didn't know if I should be giving her this reassurance or not, but I just wanted to hear what she had to say.

Still whispering she said, "The first thing you need to know is his name's not Colin, or at least that's the name he used when I knew him. He went by Adam then. Adam Taylor."

"*What*?" I was trying to process this, but I still didn't understand what she meant. "Excuse me?"

"I know, it's a lot. Believe me, I wish I could've told you sooner. There were times I wanted to reach out, but it was complicated."

"Complicated? I don't under…What the fuck?"

"I'm talking about years ago, when I heard what happened on Long Island. I wanted to reach out then, but I was afraid to get involved. I'm still afraid, but better late than never, right?"

Still trying to absorb it all, I said, "When you say Long Island, you mean when Colin disappeared?"

"Did Michael ever tell you anything about our breakup?"

I shook my head.

"I don't know what he told you about our relationship, but we dated for about two years and were practically living together. I had an apartment—actually, not far from here, in Gramercy Park—and he stayed with me most of the time. We had some problems, but nothing that seemed super major, but then Adam became, well, a major issue in our relationship."

"How did Michael and Colin even know each other?"

"You mean Adam," Jennifer said. "I never got all the details, but Michael said they were old friends. That they'd met at a youth hostel in Amsterdam when he was on a study abroad program, backpacking in Europe."

"I know Michael studied abroad his junior year, but he's never mentioned anyone named Adam."

"Somehow that doesn't surprise me." Jennifer rolled her eyes a little. "I didn't know Adam very well. I only met him a few times—out at bars and I think at a party once. I always thought there was something *off* about him, something that, I don't know, *concerned* me. Sorry, I know you were engaged to him and loved him, but this was just the vibe I got. I also thought something seemed off about his relationship with Michael."

"What seemed off about it?"

"Mainly like how secretive they were. Michael kept me at a distance from Adam, never gave me any details about him, like where he lived and what he did for a living. I pushed him about it once and Michael said Adam worked on Wall Street, but something still seemed off. We had other issues in our relationship. Michael was busy, didn't have time for us. He was just out of law school, working long hours, so it was a problem when he started spending the free time that he did have with Adam, and I wanted to get serious, maybe start a family, and his head wasn't there yet, or at least that's what he kept telling me."

"So you guys broke up?"

"Yes. I mean, honestly, maybe I just used Adam as an excuse. You know how sometimes you want to give the other person a reason? You don't want to just *leave?* So I broke up, a clean split. About a year went by, then I heard about you in the news, your fiancé disappearing on Long Island. I was shocked when I saw a picture of him in the paper, I think the *Daily News,* because instead of a picture of the guy they said it was, Colin, it was a picture of Adam, so I knew one of the names wasn't his real name, or maybe they were both fake. Also, the articles said that Colin was in med school, which surprised me. What happened to Wall Street?"

"How do you know you weren't making a mistake about all of this? Maybe Colin and this Adam just looked similar."

"I'm good with faces, I don't make mistakes like that, but I wanted to make sure, so I did a little research, looking for information about Adam Taylor and guess what I found?"

"What?"

"Nothing. Now if a guy works on Wall Street there would have to be something about him, right? So it was pretty clear that Michael had lied to me."

"Why would he lie?"

"I don't know, but it confirmed for me that *something* weird was going on. Of course, like I said, Michael and I weren't in touch at all at that time, we had a clean break, and I didn't feel like contacting him out of the blue. I thought he'd think I was using it as an excuse to get back in touch with him, you know, the way everyone contacted their exes after nine-eleven, just to make sure they were doing okay? So I didn't contact him. Fast forward to like ten years later. Life happened—I moved to Brooklyn, met my future ex-husband, tried to have kids, went through fertility treatments…well, that's a whole other story. Finally, I joined Facebook and did the usual connecting with people. Michael came up as a suggestion, I guess because we had a couple of mutual friends. I wasn't going to friend him because, well, because I thought it would be awkward, but then I saw his status was married and clicked on your profile and you looked so familiar, and I didn't know why. Then it hit me, and I did some Googling to confirm it and I saw that you were her—

the woman who had been engaged to Adam—well, to Adam going under that other name, Colin. Now I was angry. I felt—what's the word?—betrayed, I felt very betrayed, but I didn't know exactly why I felt this way, if this makes any sense. I mean Michael hadn't done anything to me directly, but I still felt like he'd been deceitful. So I friended Michael. He seemed happy to hear from me and we started chatting online, DMing. I mentioned that years ago I'd seen that his wife had been engaged to a guy who'd disappeared, who she'd been accused of killing, and that the guy looked exactly like Adam. I remembered that there was a long pause before he wrote back and I remember thinking that this was very telling, like he was trying to come up with a good explanation, or a lie, then he finally wrote that I had to be making a mistake, that his friend Adam was alive and had moved back to London. I knew this was a total lie. Yes, it was possible that Colin and Adam were two different people who looked incredibly similar, but it didn't make any sense that you had been engaged to the man who drowned and then married Michael, who had been the drowning victim's friend, unless you knew Michael before you knew Adam, but then why didn't Michael mention this to me?"

"I didn't know Michael before I knew Adam."

"See, I knew it!"

"Go on." My fists were clenched, my fingernails digging into my palms.

"Well, I didn't understand why Michael was lying to me," Jennifer continued. "I knew there had to be more to it, but it was awkward to get into, in Messenger. I wrote something like, 'It's so weird that you married the woman whose fiancé looked so much like Adam,' and he responded with something lame like, 'Ha,' like he wanted me to think that he thought I was joking so I'd stop digging about it. Then he said he had to go and we said goodbye. A couple of weeks later, I got my first breast cancer diagnosis, and my life, well, went to hell. Stage three. My marriage was already rocky and my husband couldn't deal with my diagnosis and bailed. Can you believe he ended our marriage with a fucking text message two days after I got my breast cancer news? Fucking prick. I posted on Facebook about what I was going through and Michael sent me some very sweet messages. You probably saw one of my responses."

"Yeah, the one with heart emojis."

"Oh my God, I know how that must've looked—your husband's ex-girlfriend sending him heart emojis, but I swear, it wasn't like that at all. I just needed support—from anyone—and I had no one at that point. Actually, Michael offered to take me to my first chemo treatment, and I stupidly said yes. I regretted it afterwards, I really did. In the moment, I wasn't thinking about you, and your feelings, whether you were cool with it or not. I was just incredibly vulnerable at the time, and I couldn't—"

"It's not your fault, it's mine," I said. "I had no idea about your cancer."

Jennifer's eyes were glassy, and I could tell she was doing her best to hold it together.

"I guess I just don't know why Michael was so secretive about you, why he didn't just tell me," I said. "I mean if he said his ex-girlfriend has cancer and he wanted to support her, I would've totally understood. I've gone on breast cancer marches for my friends; I donate to St. Jude's every year."

"I have a theory about that." Jennifer said. "Maybe Michael was worried that if you and I somehow got in touch we'd start comparing notes about you and Adam, and about

Michael and Adam. So maybe Michael wanted to keep distance between us."

I nodded as this made sense. Then I said, "So if Michael and Colin, or Adam, or whatever his name is, they knew each other, that means it wasn't a coincidence when I met Michael. I mean, they must have arranged it somehow. But how? I mean—"

I was feeling panicky again. I definitely needed more Xanax or more *something*.

"How did you and Michael meet?"

"At a supermarket in the city." I closed my eyes tightly then opened them. "It seemed random, but I guess it's possible that it wasn't."

"It definitely wasn't a coincidence," Jennifer said. "Adam must've told Michael about you and *wanted* you two to meet for some reason."

"Why would they do that?"

"I have no idea. Sorry, I don't know if this is helping, but I thought you'd want to know."

"No, I definitely want to know, thank you. But why are you telling me all of this now? I mean, instead of when I first contacted you?"

"When you messaged me yesterday, I panicked. It brought back all the weirdness about Michael and Adam, and I just didn't want to get involved in any of it again. I've been trying to find peace in my life, you know? I go to yoga retreats; I became a reiki master last year. But when I saw online that you saw Adam again I felt like I had to tell you what I know. I guess, in the back of my mind, I always suspected that Michael and Adam were involved in something, something that Michael was trying to protect me from, if this makes any sense. I don't want to get involved in anything, but I wanted you to know, in case it has something to do with why Michael disappeared."

"So you think that Colin had something to do with Michael disappearing?"

"*Adam*. But I don't know if Adam is still alive. I just—"

She must've seen something in my expression.

"What is it?" she asked. "You know something about Adam?"

"I saw them together."

"Saw who together?"

I didn't have to answer this. She got it.

She looked around nervously, then whispered, "You *what*? I thought you had no idea where Michael is."

"I don't."

I told her about the video Randle had shown me.

"Are you fucking serious?" Now it was Jennifer who looked like she needed some meds. "I knew I shouldn't have come here."

The girls were still yapping away and the homeless guy hadn't stirred, but the guy on his laptop glanced over. I stared back at him until he started typing again.

Then I said to Jennifer, in a very low voice, "No, I'm glad you contacted me. This could be important info."

"You can't tell the police that we spoke. I don't want Adam to know about me, that I was involved in any way. There was something off about him, he's a dangerous person."

"But how do you—"

"I'm telling you, this is bad. Very bad."

"What is?"

"That Adam's back. It must mean I was right, that he does have something to do with Michael disappearing. See? I knew it couldn't be a coincidence."

"But I still don't get it. Why would he want to do something to Michael? I mean, in the video I saw they were chatting, having coffee. They looked like they were friends."

"I'm telling you there was always something weird about their relationship. And what about that SUV that you said has been following you since Michael disappeared?"

"What about it?"

"It has to be related too, I mean to Adam. Adam's probably in that SUV. Could you see who's in it?"

"No, but why would Colin, I mean *Adam*, be following me around in an SUV?"

"I don't know, and I really don't want to know."

She was about to get up and I held her arm, not hard, and said, "Please, I need your help. I don't think you know this, but I'm a person of interest now in Michael's disappearance."

"You are?"

"It's ridiculous of course. I obviously have nothing to do with it."

"Let go of my arm please."

"It's because I was accused last time when Colin, Adam, whatever the hell his name is, disappeared. You'd think seeing that Colin's alive in that video would've convinced the police that I have nothing to do with what happened to Michael, but the police are trying to build a case against me, but if you just spoke to Detective Randle and—"

"I said let go."

"Please, Jennifer, I need your help."

She yanked her arm free. Now everyone around us, including the homeless guy, was looking over.

"Sorry," she said, and left, heading down the stairs as fast as she could.

I considered going after her, but I'd already caused enough of a scene; I was lucky one of these people hadn't filmed this and created another viral TikTok.

Trying to act nonchalant, like nothing out of the ordinary had just happened, I finished my coffee in several sips, then headed down and exited. I was jaywalking across Broadway when a car stopped short, inches in front of me. Great, that was all I needed—to get hit by a car again, just when my hip was starting to feel better.

Across the street, in Union Square, I had to take a break. As people rushed by me in practically every direction, I bent over with my hands on my knees. I still hadn't fully accepted that my marriage was based on a huge lie—Michael and I hadn't met randomly; Colin/Adam had *arranged* for us to meet. If Michael had lied to me about this, what else had he lied to me about? Was anything real? While I had no reason to believe that Jennifer had been lying about anything, I wanted to believe that she was. I told myself that I knew nothing about her or about her background. For all I knew she had worse paranoia than I did and had made up or exaggerated everything she'd told me, including that Colin/Adam was a "dangerous person" who might've had something to do with Michael's disappearance. The Adam identity might not have existed at all. He might've just been Colin—the kind, attentive, charming guy I'd fallen in love with. I had no idea why Jennifer would lie to this extent, but it was possible that she was crazy and obsessed with Michael and wanted to hurt me any way she could.

While I didn't really believe any of this, it made me feel better about myself, and I needed something to help me keep going. I was a person of interest in my husband's disappearance, and for all that I knew I was going to be arrested soon. I had to use whatever time I had left to clear my name, and I couldn't waste time feeling sorry for myself.

I walked away, slowly at first, then faster and faster, zigzagging, avoiding people, as I descended to the busy subway station.

EIGHTEEN

I TOOK THE 6 train to Thirty-third Street, then walked over a few blocks to the townhouse on East Thirty-second where Russell Moss, one of Michael's law partners, lived with his wife Grace. I had been to their place once before, for a New Year's Eve party a few years ago. Ground floor lights were on, but that didn't mean anyone was home. It was almost nine-thirty; Russell could still be at the office. On some nights, Michael worked until ten or later.

I rang the bell. No one answered, so I rang again, then again. I thought I heard movement inside.

I noticed the security camera off to the right and looked directly at it and waved and mouthed *Please, open the door.* He or Grace would definitely recognize me.

I rang a couple more times and was thinking about giving up when I heard locks unlocking, then the door opened, but with the chain on, and Russell was there.

"Hi, it's me, Vanessa. Vanessa Rizzo."

"You have to leave, Vanessa. I can't help you."

"Why not? What's going on?"

"I'm sorry, I can't—"

"You have to. Is it because of what's in the news, because I'm a person of interest? You know that's ridiculous. I have nothing to do with what happened to Michael, but I might know who—"

"I told you, I can't help you."

He tried to close the door, but I stuck my foot partway in and blocked it.

"Look, I don't understand what's going on. Michael's a partner at your firm. Why won't you even talk to me?"

"Move your foot."

"You've invited me to your house as a guest, your wife wanted to hire me to organize your closets and office. If you wanted to hire me, why won't you let me in? How could you treat me this way? How could you turn on me the way strangers are?"

"Okay, okay, fine," he said. "I'll let you in, but you're gonna have to move your foot so I can close the door and take the chain off."

I stopped blocking the door. He shut it, then undid the chain and let me in.

Grace, Russell's wife, was standing beyond Russell, near the bottom of the stairwell.

"Hi, Grace, how are you?"

Grace and I had a friendly relationship since Michael began working at the firm years ago. Like me, she had a theater background and had done some acting here and there when she was younger, and last time I'd seen her at the firm's holiday party we'd had a great conversation about Broadway. We even talked about getting tickets to go to see something together some time, though this plan had never materialized—probably my fault; I'd gotten too caught up in work and the kids' schedules.

"Okay, thanks." She sounded oddly awkward and was avoiding eye contact.

Russell nodded at her, as if saying, *It's okay, I got this*, then he said to me, "Come on, let's go into my office."

I followed him and he shut the door behind us. It was a big office, with a beautiful antique mahogany desk and a wall of tasteful floor-to-ceiling bookshelves, but he wasn't using the space efficiently at all. He had papers stacked on the desk and the bookshelves were disorganized with books stacked haphazardly without a consistent theme. He needed better storage solutions too, as there were piles of papers and file folders on his desk, and on the floor in front of the bookshelves.

"Have a seat," he said, gesturing toward the leather couch.

Remaining standing, I said, "What the hell's going on? Is it because you guys have been reading that bullshit online? Because I'm a person of interest?"

"No, we don't think you're guilty of anything."

"Then what's with not taking my calls before or keeping the chain on the door?"

"Want a drink? I have a great Blue Label."

I'd never been a big drinker and hadn't drunk at all in the past several years, but if I ever had a reason to start drinking again it was now.

"I'm a Red Label gal," I said, deadpan. Then I said, "Kidding. Sure. Why not?"

As he poured glasses for us, he said, "Look, I'm sorry about what happened at the door, but try to see things from my perspective. I'm sort of between a rock and a hard place here."

"Why is that?"

"Loyalty," he said. "I try to be honest with everyone, no exceptions, but especially in my profession this is easier said than done sometimes."

He handed me a glass. I sat on the couch with it. He waited a few seconds, then sat in the chair across from me.

"You have to let it sit on your tongue before you swallow," he said. "Cheers." He raised his glass.

"Cheers," I muttered. Then I took a sip, wincing a little. "So who're you trying to be loyal to?"

"Michael," he said. "Look, I don't know where he is, and I hope to God he's okay, but last week he gave me a sort of heads up that something might happen."

"A heads up? Are you serious?"

"It was unusual to say the least. He came into my office and told me that something might happen this week and that if it does I shouldn't have any contact with you."

"That's insane. What does that even mean?"

"I didn't know, and I still don't know. He wouldn't elaborate. As you know, Michael could be a private person, which is, frankly, a problem when it comes to our practice. He has clients I've never met, or he doesn't even tell me about, so I wasn't incredibly alarmed. That said, I didn't think he'd disappear, or that there would be a police investigation. I wanted to keep my word to him, if this was possible, that's why I was avoiding you. But to be honest, I don't even know if what Michael was telling me about is even related to him disappearing. The whole thing is so bizarre."

Now I *needed* the drink. I took a longer sip without wincing then said, "It seems like it has to be related. It's too coincidental—him giving you a heads up, warning you that something might happen, and then disappearing."

"I agree, but I also think, knowing Michael, there was a reason he didn't want me to be in contact with you, but I can't figure out what it could be. Do you have any ideas?"

"He was afraid you'd tell me something," I said. "Like you said, Michael's good with secrets, but maybe not as good as he thinks."

"What do you mean?"

"Did he mention anything about Colin Grant to you? Or Adam Taylor?"

Russell pursed his lips, thinking, then said, "No, those names don't ring a bell. Why? Who are they?"

"They're apparently the same person. My ex-fiancé."

"Oh, the one I heard about in the news, who went missing years ago."

"Exactly."

"But isn't he missing? Presumed dead?"

"He was until a few days ago."

I told Russell about how I'd seen Colin getting into the taxi on Friday evening and how Detective Randle had shown me footage of Michael and Colin in a Starbucks on Saturday.

"This is getting even more bizarre," Russell said. "Did you know Michael was in touch with him?"

"No, I did not. Did you?"

"I just told you, Michael never mentioned anyone named Colin or Adam to me. What do you think their connection is?"

"I was hoping you could help me figure that out."

"I wish I could, but I know nothing about this."

"Are you sure there isn't anything? A weird phone call you overheard? *Anything*?"

Russell was shaking his head. "It's very possible Michael could've been hiding something, with his secretiveness and all, but I can't think of anything unusual. He missed a monthly meeting last week—it didn't ring any alarm bells, but he's normally steady, shows up for everything."

"Anything else? Did he seem, I don't know, scared?"

"No, that's the thing. Even when he told me about this vague thing that might be happening soon, he didn't seem particularly worried. He was matter of fact, pragmatic."

"Did he mention meeting with anyone? Anything that seemed unusual?"

"No. Over the past couple of weeks, it was just his usual client meetings. There was one with Roger Pratt, one of our oldest clients. I think they had a lunch at Smith & Wollensky. What else? He had a meeting with Bonnie Morris, another old client, I think that was early last week, and, oh, he had a meeting with a new estate client. But other than that, I can't—"

"New estate client? Who's that?"

"I don't know his last name, but his first name was Ken, no Kevin, that's right?"

"You met him?"

"Briefly. Actually, it was a few blocks from the office. They were coming out of a restaurant, Gallagher's on Fifty-second near Broadway. Michael loves steakhouses."

"Did Kevin have a British accent?"

"I didn't speak to him, just a quick hi. Later Michael told me he was a referral from another client." Russell squinted. "Why *British*?"

On my phone, I went to my file of "Colin Photos," and opened the last one I'd taken of him before he disappeared, smiling, orange sunshine illuminating his face.

"Hold on, didn't think I'd be doing any reading."

Russell got up and started looking around for his glasses.

It was frustrating; if I'd organized this room he'd know where everything was.

"Whoop, here we go." He found them on the shelf of the bookcase, then he came back over to me and glanced at my phone that I was holding up for him to see. "When was that taken?"

"Nineteen years ago."

"Interesting."

"What's interesting?"

"That's him. I mean he's older now, but that's definitely the same guy. How did you—" He shifted the glasses toward the tip of his nose and looked over them at me. "Wait, that's *Colin*? But Michael called him Kevin?"

"I guess Jennifer was right." I didn't mean to say this out loud.

"Who was right?"

"Michael's ex-girlfriend. Long story, but she also thought Colin had a different identity years ago when she was…"

Nausea hit—booze on an empty stomach or maybe a side effect of the Xanax. I had to take a breath.

"Are you okay?"

"Yeah, fine. I…I guess I just drank too fast."

"Why is this guy using fake identities? And what does it have to do with Michael disappearing, or going somewhere, or whatever happened to him?"

I coughed a little then said, "I have no idea."

"I'll get you some water."

"No, it's okay, really. So you're saying that Colin or Adam or whatever the fuck his name really is, was a new estate client of Michael's?"

"That was the implication, yes. I didn't speak to him, or we barely spoke. I might've said hello. Actually, Michael did seem a little surprised to see me there."

"Why would Colin need an estate attorney?"

"The usual reasons, I suppose—to make a will or redo a will. But I can't even confirm he's an actual *client*. I didn't have any conversation with Michael about it."

"Wait." I had an idea. "Gallagher's must have security cameras, inside and out. Did you see him leaving Gallagher's before or after he gave you the heads up that something might happen?"

"Before. Definitely before."

"Well then, this seems like it definitely could be related to Colin, especially as he knew you'd seen them. He was probably concerned about you making the connection and then telling me about it. I should give all this information to the police, something might be useful."

"Whoa, let's slow down for just a second now." Russell sat back down across from me. "I think we have to think this all through. Let's not forget what Michael told me, about not wanting me to be in contact with you. You may have been right, that he didn't want you to find out he was in touch with this Colin, Adam guy, but he might have had a good reason for this."

Remembering what Jennifer had told me about Adam, I said, "You could be right about that. So?"

"So, it seems obvious that if Michael wanted to tell me what was going on, he would've, but he kept it from me too, perhaps because he was concerned about getting the firm mixed up in this, you see what I'm getting at?"

"Yes, I can see it exactly. You're more concerned about the firm than giving the cops information that might lead to finding Michael alive."

"We don't have any facts right now, we don't know if

he's even in danger. But if this becomes criminal, *everything* becomes discoverable. It drags the firm into it. Michael understood that."

"Unbelievable. All I want is to find Michael and get him home safely, and that's all you should be concerned about too."

With his reading glasses still resting on the brim of his nose, Russell started pacing in front of me. Shaking his head, seeming very agitated, he said, "This was probably a mistake."

"What was?"

"Meeting with you at all. I shouldn't have let you in. If Michael knew that something was going to happen—and it seems likely he did—there had to be a very good reason why he wanted to keep you out of it. Michael's a logical guy, a planner. I think we have to figure out what we're dealing with here, because Michael certainly knew."

"Sorry if this is such an inconvenience for you, but I'm a person of interest now; I might even get arrested. Do you think Michael anticipated *that* would happen? Well, I don't."

Russell had stopped pacing. He removed his glasses and said, "Look, I'm very sorry this is happening to you, Vanessa, I really am, and I wish there was something I could do, but I have to respect Michael's wishes."

"Well, there is something you can do. A reference to a good criminal attorney would help."

"Sorry, but I can't do that."

"Excuse me?" I was so pissed off my eyes were pulsing. "What do you mean you can't—"

"If Michael wanted me to help you find a lawyer he would've. But he told me not to have any contact with you at all, and I gave him my word."

"Russell, can you *please*—"

"I'm sorry the answer's no."

I glared at him, wanting to lash out. But then I said, "Fine, whatever," and went back through the house, toward the front door. I saw that Grace was standing where he was before, in the foyer.

I was going to pass by without saying anything, but then she said, "Vanessa," and I stopped.

"Elana Krauss," she said. "Excellent criminal defense. Her practice is under her own name. Tell her I referred you. We're old college friends from Barnard."

"Thank you," I said. "That's extremely kind of you, you don't know how much I appreciate this. If I can ever help you in any way, I will. If you ever need help organizing anything in your house, or organizing your time, or even if you ever need to talk or—"

"It's okay, no repayment necessary, and I'm sorry for Russell's attitude. I know how stubborn he can be sometimes, but he's loyal to a fault and he means well. Just tell me one thing. You have nothing to do with Michael's disappearance, right? You *are* innocent?"

"Of course I'm innocent."

"I believe you, but it's still nice to hear you say it."

I thanked her again, then let myself out.

It had started to rain. I didn't have an umbrella, but I wanted to walk and I didn't care about getting wet. I went east to First Avenue and uptown past NYU Hospital. As I walked in the rain, I called Elana Krauss but got her voicemail. I was going to leave a message, then decided to just try again later from home.

Maybe the Xanax was finally kicking in. Although my situation hadn't gotten any less stressful—my husband was still missing and I was still a person of interest—I was *feeling* less stressed. I even felt a little relaxed, way more relaxed than I should've felt. I had a warm, hopeful feeling that was related to Jennifer and Grace. It seemed like every man in my life had deserted me, used me, or flat-out lied to me. I needed to make it a goal to spend less time obsessing over disappointing men.

I passed a small park where the block got darker, more concealed by overhanging tree branches. If I hadn't been so distracted by my happy thoughts about sisterhood, I might have noticed the SUV sooner, but I didn't turn around until I heard tires screech as a car came to a stop alongside me. In order to do this, the SUV had to block the bike lane. A moment later, the back door swung open and a man in a black ski mask rushed out and grabbed me.

NINETEEN

I SHOULDN'T HAVE had a chance. The guy was tall and probably weighed at least two hundred pounds. But when he grabbed me, I was still thinking about the horrible men in my life and how there was no way in hell that I was going to let this guy hurt me too.

"You messed with the wrong girl, asshole."

With strength I didn't know I had, I managed to shove him away and he slammed back against the SUV, his head smacking the metal. He groaned and seemed dazed. Then a guy on a CitiBike had stopped short near us. He was in a suit, had a Wall Street vibe. The guy who'd tried to grab me looked over at the cyclist through the slits in his ski mask, then he jumped back into the SUV and it pulled away as he was slamming the door shut.

"Hey, you okay?" The cyclist was next to me now. He had thinning gray hair, was in his fifties.

The SUV sped away, crossing the next traffic light.

Fuck, the license plate.

"Shit. Damn it."

"Did you know that guy?" the cyclist asked.

"What? No, I…Never mind."

He had his phone out and he looked like he was tapping in a number.

"What're you doing?"

"Calling the cops."

I knew Randle wouldn't help, especially without a license plate number, and I didn't want to waste time filling out a report with disinterested cops.

"No," I said, "please don't."

"Sure?"

"Positive. I'm okay and it's okay. Thank you."

I walked away uptown. My pulse was pounding; so much for the Xanax calming me. I was sweating as I kept looking around for the SUV. I was still angry at myself for not getting the license plate number. It was dark, but if I'd been more alert, I could've gotten it.

Walking faster now, across the street from the United Nations, I wondered what would have happened if I hadn't pushed the guy away. I'd be in the SUV now, or maybe I'd be dead, like maybe Michael was dead. Is *this* what happened to Michael? Had the same people in the SUV kidnapped him? Yes, *people*, because there had to be at least two—the driver and the guy who had abducted me. It seemed like it had to be related to Michael since the SUV hadn't started following me until after Michael had disappeared. But who were these people? What did they want? The guy who'd grabbed me was about the same height as Colin, or Adam, or Kevin or whoever the fuck he was. I remembered how Jennifer had thought that "Adam" had to be in the SUV. But if he was, that wouldn't explain why he might have been involved in abducting Michael, and why he might've tried to abduct me.

I was feeling the panic coming on again, the darkness closing in. No, I couldn't let it happen again—not now. I started running, as fast as I could, as if I could outrun my bleak, depressing thoughts. The rain was heavier, steadier, but I was barely aware of it. I was just thinking about how I wanted to get away.

I was exhausted, out of breath. There was a slight hill on this part of First Avenue, but it felt like I was running up a mountain. It was like I was in one of those recurring anxiety dreams I sometimes had, where I was running, trying to get to an appointment or to take an exam, but I felt like I was on a treadmill. In those dreams, I never got where I needed to get to, and I always woke up, feeling angry and frustrated. But I eventually arrived at East Fifty-Second Street and slowed to a jog, then a brisk walk. There was the biggest group of people in front of my building so far. There had to be at least fifty people there, and more cameras and news trucks than before too. This raised my anxiety and panic a couple of notches. I knew they were here because I was now a person of interest in the disappearances of two people. This was going to be the type of story that the tabloids, like the *Post* and the *News*, wouldn't be able to get enough of. They'd sensationalize it, make me out to look as unstable as possible, just so they could sell more newspapers and get more clicks. They were ready to bombard me with questions, aim cameras at me, and especially in the state I was in now I couldn't deal with any of that. Besides, there was no way I was saying anything to anyone before consulting with my lawyer.

Before they spotted me, I doubled back and went around the corner to the parking garage. Word about how I'd been exiting and entering the building must have been getting around because now there were about fifteen or twenty people in the back, including one TV cameraperson. When they saw me coming, it seemed like everyone had their phone cams aimed at me and the questions started, everyone shouting over one another. I could barely make out what anyone was saying, but I heard, "Did you do it, Vanessa?" and "Why did you do it, Vanessa?" and "Where have you been, Vanessa?" I thought about trying to get back to the front of the building where at least there was a doorman, but I didn't think I could get there now without everyone chasing me, and probably catching up with me, so I decided to just go for it.

Walking quickly, avoiding eye contact, I headed toward the garage entrance. People rushed alongside me, following me like I was some celebrity, which I guess I was at this point. If Michael was never found, there might be a true crime series about *me* someday—The Vanessa Rizzo story, about the woman who was accused of killing her fiancé and husband; is she innocent or guilty? If I was arrested and the prosecutor was out to get me, I could even go to jail, get sentenced to two life sentences. That would make the true crime series even better.

I was scanning my keycard to enter the building through the garage door when someone grabbed my shoulder. After what had happened with the guy from the SUV I was hypersensitive and wheeled around and snapped:

"Get your stupid hand off me, you disgusting fucking piece of shit."

Then I managed to make it into my building and close the door without anyone following me, but I knew within a minute the video of me screaming like a maniac would be online, going viral.

Riding the elevator up, I prayed to a God I didn't believe in for a miracle—for Michael to be safe at home. After everything I knew, I knew my marriage would be over, but I'd be happy to get my life back.

Sometimes when I wanted something to happen badly, I tried *creative visualization*. It had never worked, but at least it gave me something to do, made me feel a little more in control, and I needed some control right now. I imagined Michael, the way he usually looked at night—scruffy, in his boxers, standing in the kitchen with the fridge door open, eating slices of salami or cheese or whatever he could get his hands on. I opened the door, but of course he wasn't home because of course creative visualization was bullshit. My apartment looked exactly like I'd left it and Sparkle strutted over to me, meowing loudly.

"I'll feed you, I'll feed you. Just let mommy get settled." Then when he meowed even louder, I said in a sterner tone, "I said let mommy get settled, do you understand me?"

I locked and chained the door, then went into my bedroom and changed into sweats and my baggy black sweatshirt with the slogan: *Can't Talk Right Now I'm Listening to Kinky Boots*. It felt good to be back home, in my safe, doorman building, talking to my cat, and ironically, I was happy now that Joe and Stella had snatched the kids and taken them to Jersey. I had my issues with Stella, but I knew that she and Joe loved my kids, and I trusted that they'd keep them safe.

Sparkle was still meowing loudly, demandingly.

"Okay, okay."

The hungry cat followed me into the kitchen where I poured some Meow Mix into his bowl, quieting him immediately. I glanced at my phone and saw I'd gotten a voicemail from Andrew. I was glad I'd gotten away from him, but I was angry at myself for not trying to scratch his eyes out.

I deleted the message, then texted my boys in our group chat:

Checking in? Is all well?!

Within ten seconds, Harrison and Carson responded almost simultaneously. Carson responded "yes" and Harrison check-marked my text. Knowing my kids were safe made me feel a little calmer, but the relief only lasted for a few seconds—if that—and then anxiety and dread took over again. What if the SUV went to New Jersey? What if they were after my kids now? I tapped out another text—**make sure grandma and grandpa lock all the doors tonight**—but then I decided the text would only alarm them and it didn't matter anyway because Joe and Stella lived in a gated complex with twenty-four-hour security.

Instead, I wrote **I love you goodnight** and added three heart emojis.

Pacing from the kitchen to the vestibule and back, I called Detective Randle. Of course I got his voicemail—*Did this guy ever answer his fuckin' phone?* I was going to hang up and try later, but I couldn't hold back:

"It's me, Vanessa Rizzo, your *person of interest.* Anyway, I just saw that SUV again, I almost got abducted. No, I didn't get the license plate, but are you even seriously *looking* for the SUV? A guy named Adam—maybe using the name Kevin—might be in it. Oh, yeah these are Colin Grant's other names, aliases, whatever. The people in the SUV probably kidnapped Michael. What are you doing except trying to find more bullshit about me? Are you even looking for my husband? I fucking doubt it. Call me back."

Venting had felt good, though I knew that leaving a message where I sounded unhinged didn't exactly help my cause. Randle probably thought that I was crazy, that I'd invented the SUV. He didn't give a shit about the truth. He was just looking for more circumstantial evidence to use against me, and I'd just given it to him.

I went into the living room and said, "Alexa, turn on the lights," and the overhead light and the floor lamps came on. Normally I'd chill, work on my social media, or watch more of my true crime show, but since I felt like I was starring in my own real life true crime show, this was the last thing I needed. I took two more Xanax. There was only one pill left so, fuck it, I took it too, then I looked at my phone. Andrew had texted me again—*Can we please talk?*—and I shouted "No, we can't!" and I called the lawyer, Elana Krauss, while pacing around my apartment. Her voicemail answered and, not wanting to get into all the details without explaining the situation directly, I left a brief message, saying that Grace had suggested I contact her regarding a "difficult situation" I was in, and asked her to please call me back as soon as she could.

In my bedroom, I went on my phone, avoiding social media—I didn't feel like reading more nasty posts about me. I did searches for "Michael Rizzo and Colin Grant" and "Michael Rizzo and Adam Taylor" and "Michael Rizzo and Kevin." I couldn't find anything, but what did that mean? The name changing was obviously going on for a reason. What was my ex-fiancé's actual name? Was Jennifer right—was he "dangerous?" Had he kidnapped Michael and had he just tried to kidnap me? What had Michael been meeting with him about at that restaurant in midtown and at that Starbucks in Tribeca? Why and how had Michael gotten involved in this craziness?

It was still hard for me to accept that Michael had lied to me, to his family, for years. He'd always been such a solid, middle-of-the-road guy. He invested conservatively, drove conservatively, had sex conservatively. He was the opposite of a risktaker. When we went on trips with the kids, *I* always went on the rollercoasters, or went ziplining, while he waited behind. I could see him having an affair if he was horny and bored, but to maintain a secret relationship with my ex-fiancé and to lie to my face for years required a lot of emotional energy. Despite being a horrible thing to do to me, it was just so out of character for him. How had this happened? I'd always been a perceptive person, always telling my friends how I was "great at reading people." Was he just more manipulative and twisted than I'd ever imagined, or was it my fault for being too absorbed with my kids, organizing their lives, and organizing everyone else's lives, that I'd been oblivious to what had been happening right in front of me? Were there obvious signs that I'd ignored? I'd always thought I knew my husband better than anyone, but apparently, I didn't know him at all.

My heart was beating so hard I was shaking; it was hard to get a full breath. Either the Xanax hadn't hit my system yet or I hadn't taken enough, because I couldn't calm down at all. All I had left was Klonopin and some Codeine I'd saved after Michael's dental surgery last year. I knew combining Xanax and Klonopin was a bad idea, so I went with Codeine, downing a couple pills.

As usual, Sparkle jumped onto the bed to take his usual lap around me, but I guess I had too much nervous energy because he only stayed for a few seconds before leaping away.

"Alexa, play spa music."

"Watermark" didn't help at all this time, as I couldn't

stop stirring and ruminating about what Michael had done to me, and to his family. Now my head was pounding, like I was getting a migraine. Maybe adding painkillers to the mix had been a bad idea, but it was too late now unless I made myself throw up, but I hadn't done that in years and I didn't want to start *that* habit again. I realized I was starving and had barely eaten anything today. This always happened when I was under extreme stress—I forgot to eat.

When I got up, I felt dizzy. I tried to grab something to steady myself—why did it feel like the night table wasn't where it was supposed to be? Then my legs buckled and I was falling and, shit, my head hit something.

I was on the floor—what the hell was I doing on the floor? I wasn't sure if any time had gone by or not. I felt much dizzier than I had before and nauseous too. I was thinking about the Codeine. I wasn't sure how much I'd taken in the past several hours, but it was probably too much. I also knew it wasn't an accident. I'd known exactly what I was doing, but now it didn't feel like I'd done it— someone else had done it. I couldn't have possibly made those decisions—why would I? I always thought about my kids first and there was no way I'd do this to them. They needed their mother; what would they do without me? Somebody else must've done this to me, someone who was controlling me, trying to hurt me, trying to hurt my family.

My mouth was dry, I needed water, but when I tried to get up I couldn't. I felt dizzier and weak too, and why was there blood on my hands? Shit, had I hit my head worse than I realized? Was I actually *dying*? I couldn't die, not now, not *here*. What if my kids found my body? Why did someone do this to me? I wanted to scream, but I couldn't get my mouth to work. I felt myself slipping, weakening, and I thought or said, "Don't let go," but I couldn't stop myself, and then I was walking, but it was hard to get anywhere because my feet felt like they were in sand. Wait, they *were* in sand, because I was walking along a beach at night. I was screaming "Colin! Colin!" into the darkness, but it didn't feel like *me*. I felt like I was just a passenger, watching it all happen, with no control over any of it.

TWENTY

"VANESSA. VANESSA, CAN you hear me?"

The familiar voice sounded so comforting. Could it really be…

"Colin. You came back. Thank God."

I was relieved yet not surprised. Of course he came back, why wouldn't he have? He'd only gone for a short swim and he was a great swimmer, on his team at Cambridge.

"Yes. Yes, it's really me, Vanessa."

"I was so worried about you. I think you fell and hit your head, though it doesn't look serious."

"Here, have some water."

I sipped it even though I wanted to gulp all of it, then I said, "Let's go back to the house. You must be starving. Is it too late for paella? Maybe we can save it till tomorrow."

"Come, drink more."

I took another sip as my eyes opened. He looked older now—lines on his forehead, specks of gray in his hair. He wasn't in the turquoise bathing suit he'd worn to go swimming. Instead, he was in a black leather jacket, kneeling next to me, and pressing something cold against my head.

"Where did you get that jacket? Did you go home and change? I've just been…waiting for you."

"It's okay, Vanessa. You're going to be okay."

And how come we weren't on the beach anymore? We were in a room…a familiar room. It looked like my…

"Where…are…"

"You'll be fine. If you have a concussion, it's a minor one. The bleeding's stopped. Were you taking drugs? Prescription? Something else?"

His voice was reassuring. Made sense—he was a doctor after all—but why were we here, in *my* apartment? I remembered stumbling, hitting my head, but why…

"You need more water. Drink more water."

But were we really here? Was I actually looking into his hazel eyes again, or was I inventing this, dreaming it, or having some kind of hallucination? It wouldn't have been the first time.

He was holding empty bottles of Codeine and Xanax. "Is this what you took?"

The voice sounded like his voice—same refined British accent—but that didn't prove anything.

"Vanessa, I asked you if this is what you—"

"Yeah…yeah…and some other stuff."

"What other stuff?"

"Some…some Klonopin…I think."

"You *think*? How many do you think?"

"I'm not…I don't…"

Then it all came back—seeing Colin on Columbus Circle, Michael disappearing, Detective Randle, the mobs of reporters, my in-laws, Andrew's smarmy hand on my leg, Jennifer Sears, the masked man from the SUV trying to abduct me, the pills, hitting my head…

"Oh my God, it's really *you*. You're really *here*."

"Yes, I'm here, and I think you might've OD'd. Do you remember exactly what you took?"

This wasn't a fantasy, which also meant that this wasn't the Colin I'd fallen in love with. This was asshole Colin who'd disappeared from my life, who'd made me a murder suspect, who'd driven me crazy, and who might've kidnapped my husband and tried to kidnap me…and now he was in my apartment? In my *bedroom*?

"Vanessa, I asked you if you can remember what pills you took. I found the bottles in the kitchen."

He was in *my* kitchen, looking through *my* cabinets? Somehow this seemed like the biggest violation of all.

Holding out the water again, "Come on, you need to hydrate. Drink, Vanessa. Can you drink please?"

Maybe he'd drugged the water, trying to kill me, but I wasn't going to let that happen. I wanted to see my kids grow up. They needed me.

"Just take one sip."

In a self-defense class I took in college I remembered the instructor explaining how you should always go for an assailant's eyes—"index finger and middle finger straight in"—so I lunged at Colin's face. My fingers didn't get in too deep, but it was enough to startle him and make him groan. I swiped the glass out of his hand, and it smashed onto the floor.

"Jesus, Vanessa, what're you—"

I punched his forehead as hard as I could. I'd probably hurt my hand more than I hurt him, but at least I managed to knock him off balance. I still felt dazed myself, like I might pass out, but I had to get away now—this could be my only chance.

I grabbed my phone from the night table and dashed out of the bedroom, holding the walls to balance myself. I made it to the foyer, to the intercom. I lifted the receiver to call my doorman.

"Wait." Colin had grabbed me from behind. "Just hear me out, just hear me out, okay?"

"Get the fuck away from me!"

He grabbed my upper arm. I flashed back to Andrew's hand on my thigh and bit down hard on Colin's wrist. Well, I tried to, but my teeth clanked against his watch—a silver Rolex. I groaned.

"C'mon, stop it, Vanessa. You'll hurt yourself."

I started to yell for help, but his hand muffled my mouth instantly. He grabbed me again, much firmer than before. He was much stronger than me. There was no way for me to get free, at least not now.

He pried the phone from my hand as he said, "If you don't behave, I'll have to tie you up and gag you and I don't want to do that. I'll leave long before anyone arrives here, and you'll never see me again, which means that Michael will likely die, and you might die as well. Do you understand me, Vanessa?"

Behave? Fuck off.

I nodded. My teeth hurt from biting the Rolex and his hand pressing on them wasn't helping.

"Are you sure?" he said. "Because I'm serious about everything I just said."

I nodded again, though I was still planning to run or get help the first chance I got.

"All right, I'll let you go now, but you better behave now."

He removed his hand from my mouth, and I immediately spit in his face.

Wiping it off with the back of his hand, he said, "Oh, come on, you didn't have to do that."

"Give me my phone back."

The adrenaline made me feel more alert. I was probably still over-drugged but I felt more like myself.

"First you're going to sit down and relax."

I hocked up more saliva, but I didn't spit. Instead, I said, "Where's Michael? What did you do with him?"

"I didn't do anything with him, but I can help you find him. That's why I'm here."

"Did you kidnap him or not?"

"No, but I know who did."

"Who?"

"How about we sit and I'll tell you everything I know?"

I didn't want to sit; I wanted to run. I could go for his eyes again and knee him in the balls, then get to the door, bang on a neighbor's door. If I was screaming in the hallway, someone would help.

Then I thought, *But what if running away now was a huge mistake*?

While I had no reason to believe Colin about any of this—for all I know, he was completely insane—what if he really could help me find Michael? If Colin, or whoever he really was, took off and disappeared again, I might regret it forever.

"Fine," I said, "but you have to give me my phone back first."

"All right, but I'm warning you—if you try to use it, or take a photo, or try *anything*, what I said before remains true. You'll never see me again, Michael will die, and you might end up dead too."

I stared at him. His hazel eyes didn't seem nearly as compelling and sexy as they had years ago. Had they changed, or had they always just been normal hazel eyes?

"Fine," I said. "I'll sit. But you better not be wasting my fuckin' time."

We went to the dining area. I sat in the chair at the end of the table, with one leg out, and toes facing the front door. I'd hear him out, but if I thought I was in any danger I'd try to get to at least the hallway. I glanced around for something I could use as a weapon. There was a vase on the table—I could grab it and smash his head if I had to. There were butcher knives in the kitchen if I could get there fast enough.

He smiled, like he was trying to reassure me, and said, "I have to say, despite the odd circumstances, it's really great to see you, Vanessa. I mean I know I haven't made the best exits or entrances into your life, but I promise you if you hear me out—at least you'll begin to understand. Are you sure you wouldn't like some water?"

"Stop with the fucking water, okay? I don't need any water."

"All right, no water. Got it."

Actually, I did need water—my mouth was extremely parched—but I didn't want any favors from him. I traced my tongue around my mouth. My teeth hurt from biting on his watch, but I didn't think I'd broken or chipped any.

"You still haven't told me how you got in here," I said. "I locked and chained the door. I know I did."

He reached into his pocket, took out his wallet, and showed me a blue-and-gold badge: FBI.

"You're an FBI agent?"

I wasn't shocked. At this point nothing about this guy

could surprise me.

"The badge is fake, but it got me past your doorman. Your lock was easy to pick, I'm afraid, and a simple chain is never a problem—I don't know why people bother with them. Sorry, I couldn't call first and meet properly. I knew it would be a shock for you to see me after all this time, but I must say you're quite lucky I got here when I did."

"I'm lucky you broke into my apartment?"

"Yes. Yes, you are in fact. Time is running out—for Michael and for you."

I let out an aggravated breath. "Do you know where Michael is or not?"

"No," he said, "but we can find him together."

He disappeared for nineteen years, now he wanted to team up?

"How are we going to do that?" I said. "You said you don't even know where he is."

"I don't know, but I know who he's with. Look, I've made some bad—well, very bad decisions over the years, got mixed up with some very bad people, and now Michael is mixed up with it too. Michael and I, you see, are old mates."

"Yes, I know."

"Really?" He seemed genuinely surprised. "How did you—"

"The police showed me video of you and Michael having coffee in Tribeca."

"Ah, makes sense. These days nothing goes unnoticed."

"I also know you've known Michael since way before we met, when Michael was in Amsterdam, and that you've used the names Kevin and Adam too."

"You've figured out quite a lot, haven't you? Very re-sourceful, I'm impressed."

He was waiting for me to smile along with him, but I remained deadpan, glancing toward the door, wondering if running was my best option after all. Yes, I wanted to hear what he had to say, but the police probably had a better chance of saving Michael than I did.

"I know what you're thinking," Colin said, "but you need me. You want your kids to see their father again, don't you?"

I stared at him, thinking, then said, "Go ahead."

"The short of it is, yes" he said, "everything you said is true. I have had to change my identity many times, including when we were together. I'm afraid it's par for the course in my line of work."

"Okay, I'll ask. What's your line of work?"

"I'm a thief."

"Of course you are."

At this point, he could have said he was a Nigerian prince and it wouldn't have surprised me.

"No guns, masks or that sort of thing," he said. "I steal research—clinical trials, drug data, IP. You know, the stuff worth billions."

"What about med school? What about neurosurgery?"

"Back then? I was actually working on a cancer research study that I was hired to steal."

"So you weren't studying to be a neurosurgeon? That was all bullshit?"

"Believe me, I'm the last person you'd want operating on your brain, Vanessa." He was so calm, matter of fact, like he thought all of this was totally normal.

"I *was* working at Mount Sinai, though," he said. "We were studying a treatment that was supposed to be the next big thing—they all are until they crash and burn. This one seemed promising, though. It was tailored to the specific

DNA of each patient."

I had my phone out, googling. "What was the name of the drug?"

"C-twenty-six, but keep the phone where I can see it please. It was a long time ago, you won't find much about it now. As I said, the drug ultimately failed, but that was after I had to bail. It wasn't my intention to leave—I swear to you. I thought it would be my last gig, but the operation was compromised. Someone recognized me from another job, which sometimes happens."

I swiped through several search results. There *was* a cancer drug called C-26 and a mention of research at Mount Sinai, but how did I know he was actually involved in the research? It could have been another lie.

As if reading my mind again, he said, "I'm not lying. Today you get the whole truth and nothing but the truth. Isn't that how it goes here in America?"

He laughed. He'd always loved laughing at his own jokes, even when they weren't particularly funny. I remembered how this used to seem endearing.

Putting the phone down, I said, "Well, I guess that's why you never introduced me to your med school friends. Always kept me at a distance. I was too young and naïve and okay, oblivious, to spot a red flag even if it was waving right in front of my face."

"I planned to tell you eventually."

"Oh, well, that changes everything. I'm glad you had a *plan* to tell me the truth, that's very comforting and *so* noble of you." I rolled my eyes. "So how were you working on this study if you weren't actually in med school?"

"Oh, I *was* in medical school, just not in New York. I was a first-year student at UCL in London when I was recruited."

"Recruited?"

"I was originally going to take a straight path, you know, become an actual doctor, when I was approached with an offer and, well, it was for a *lot* of money, and I was in my early twenties. I was looking for excitement, thrills. My first job was in Thailand, loved it there. Then I moved on to Greece, Japan, then to New York."

"So you decided to quit med school and steal medical research for a living. That's normal." I rolled my eyes again. "So who are you working for?"

"No particular entity. Intermediaries normally give me assignments. Sometimes it's corporations, sometimes individuals, sometimes countries. It's often a don't ask, don't tell sort of profession."

"So you're an equal opportunity asshole."

"Basically. But, hey, it's a career."

"Unbelievable," I muttered. Then I said out loud, "So this is what you've been doing for all this time? Stealing research?"

"It's been my life for the past twenty-two years, yes. I've tried to get out at various times, including right now, but I can never seem to break free. There's always one more job."

"And one more woman."

"It's not like that, Vanessa."

"I really don't give a shit." I gestured with my phone. "Tell me what any of this has to with where Michael is or, I don't care what you say, I'm calling the cops right now. Is he involved in stealing research too?"

"Put the phone down, Vanessa."

"You're not in charge here, okay? You're in *my* apartment, and I can do whatever the fuck I want—I'm not afraid of you."

Colin smiled. "Ah, you haven't changed, have you? Same stubborn, feisty Vanessa I knew and loved. It's that Staten Island in you. God, I love it."

"Fine." I stood up and opened Randle's contact info, ready to make the call.

"Do you want Carson and Harrison's father to die today?" Now he was glaring at me seriously—I could see the whites in his eyes below the pupils. He waited a few seconds to make sure I knew he was serious, then said, "Sit, Vanessa. Now."

"Don't you dare tell me to sit," I said. "I'm not a fucking dog. And don't you dare call my children by their names. You don't know them."

"Feisty Vanessa. Please never change."

I wanted to run, but realistically I knew I wouldn't make it to the hallway without him stopping me. I had to wait for a better opportunity.

I sat again.

"Smart decision." Colin suddenly seemed calm, friendly again. "What were you asking me? Right, Michael. No, he is not involved in my work. He's an old mate, that's all. It's true, we did meet in Amsterdam, and we backpacked together for a while in Germany and Italy. It was a wonderful time. Have many fond memories."

The image of these two liars bonding in Europe thoroughly disgusted me.

"Why were you meeting with him at Gallagher's last Thursday and at a Starbucks in Tribeca on Saturday?"

"Wow, you really did learn a lot. Impressive."

"I saw you at Columbus Circle too."

"*That* I knew."

"Really? You saw me there chasing after your cab?"

"No, Michael told me about it."

"Really? Did he also tell you I've seen you at other times, or at least I thought I did."

"Yes, he's mentioned it, and it's possible you actually did see me somewhere. I've had to travel to New York several times over the years."

"I also thought I saw you in Jamaica, Miami. Once in Paris."

"Paris and Miami are possibilities, as I did meet with Michael in Paris once and I've gone on holidays to South Beach. Jamaica, I'm afraid that must've been my doppel-ganger." He smirked at himself.

"So why New York now, and why Michael?"

"He was doing some legal work for me. He's helped me from time to time over the years."

I flashed back to the times, just over the past year, when Michael went off to have hushed phone conversations, or closed his email windows when I came by. I'd thought these were signs he was cheating.

"Where did you come to New York from?"

"St. Louis."

"St. Louis?"

"That's where my current job was centered."

"So that's all I was to you? A *job*?"

"Of course not. That came out all wrong. You were—"

"Save it, I really don't give a shit. What estate work was Michael doing for you?"

"You learned that too, huh?"

"What was it about?"

"He was organizing the probate process for my will."

"How can *your* will be in probate when you're not even..." Then it clicked. "Wait, *seriously*? You did it *again*?

You disappeared? Faked your death? Did you go for a swim again and not come back?"

"Actually, this time I fell off a bridge."

I could tell he was serious.

"My life is extremely complicated, Vanessa. Feel fortunate you're not a part of it anymore. I did you the biggest favor I ever could've done when I left you."

"No, you would've done me a bigger favor if I'd never met you in the first place."

"Touché. But if I'd never met you, you might have met someone else, and you wouldn't have your family now. Butterfly effect and all that."

"So what's your name in this current life? Are you Kevin now?"

"No, I had a different name in St. Louis. I can't tell you what it was, for your own protection and for mine."

"That's normal." I couldn't have sounded more sarcastic. "And you have a fiancée there too who you ditched?"

"Wife actually."

I noticed he was wearing a platinum wedding band. It was so thick I didn't know how I'd missed it earlier.

"Congratulations." My tone oozed sarcasm.

"And two children."

"Wow, a family, good for you. I guess you stuck around for this woman, huh?"

"I was doing the best I could to change my life, Vanessa, but there's a limit to how much control I have over any of it."

"Oh, so if things had gone according to plan you would've waited to squeeze out a couple of kids before you ghosted me?"

"No, back then, I wanted to get out with *you*—quit, live a normal life. Maybe I'd actually finish med school, but not to become a surgeon. Podiatry maybe, or physiatry. My intention wasn't to leave you, ever."

"But you did. And you went on to the next woman, the next fake life, and you didn't give a shit about what you were putting me through."

"That's not true, I *did* care, but I can't undo what I've done. Despite what you may think I'm a good man and I've tried my best, but at times I know that hasn't been enough."

"I hope telling yourself all that makes you feel better about yourself."

"Would it make you feel better to know that I feel tormented and miserable most of the time? Part of the reason I came here this morning was to let you know how awful I feel for putting you all through this."

It was amazing how sincere he could make himself look and sound. He did so effortlessly, too. He was a natural bullshit artist.

"Oh, stop it, you didn't come here for *me*. You had nineteen years to reach out if you wanted to, but you were obviously too busy, stealing secrets and meeting other women under all different identities and doing whatever the hell else you've been doing. Worse, you were in touch with my husband the whole time, and both of you knew what was going on while I was dealing with depression and anxiety, being lied to and gaslit, feeling like I was losing my mind."

"I felt awful about all of that, Vanessa, but I didn't have a choice. I didn't want to leave you the way I did, but if I didn't do it that way I would've been killed and you probably would've been killed too."

"You mean you were really thinking about my well-being when you ditched me?"

"Yes. Actually, I was."

"Why did you get involved with me at all?"

"What do you—"

"Come on, was it just for sex? Or is this just what you do? Lure women in, promise them a life together, then disappear? Is that how you get off or something?"

"It wasn't like that at all. I thought you were amazing, Vanessa. I *still* think you're amazing. I genuinely fell in love with you."

"Wow, what a great love story. Girl meets liar, liar hands girl off to his secret friend, liar returns years later and acts like he's a saint. You have a white horse parked outside we can ride off on?"

"Who said I *handed you off*?"

"Oh, stop. Just admit what you did. Fucking own it."

My phone vibrated. I glanced at "Andrew" on the display and sent the call to voicemail.

Colin—or whoever he really was—must've seen the display too because he said, "Who's Andrew?"

"No one. Just a friend…I mean acquaintance."

"An acquaintance you're obviously not happy to hear from."

"No, actually, because he tried to attack me the other day. Sorry, you're not the only asshole in my life."

His eyes narrowed seriously. "What do you mean *attacked* you?"

"Never mind. Forget it. So what happened that night you disappeared on Shelter Island. Where did you go? How did you pull it off? And why did you pass me on to Michael?"

"I didn't pass you on to…" He let out a deep breath as he stood and began pacing. "When I left the house that day I went to the beach, yes, but I didn't go for a swim. I walked along the shoreline for about a half mile to a prearranged location. A motorboat was waiting. I was taken away across the Long Island Sound to Connecticut where a larger boat was waiting for me."

"You were 'taken away?' Where to?"

"Canada, then Newfoundland, then Ireland. Eventually Turkey."

"How did you travel under…oh, that's right you have a gazillion identities."

"Not quite a gazillion, but many, yes."

"And was this your plan all along? To get engaged to me then run off to Turkey?"

He stopped pacing. "No. Not at all, V. I told you, I wanted that to my last job. I planned to get out, marry you, live happily ever after."

V? Was he serious? Calling me by the cutesy nickname he'd used nineteen years ago, acting like that was yesterday.

"Don't call me fuckin' V, and you seriously thought I'd never figure out you lied about being a neurosurgeon?"

"I knew I'd have a lot to explain someday, but I'd thought we were strong enough to get through it all. But, of course, that never happened. The job I was working on got compromised, my cover was blown, so I had to leave immediately. There was no other way out. Believe me, I was devastated when it all went wrong, but I had no choice. I would've been in immediate danger and you would've as well. We never would've gotten off Shelter Island alive if I didn't leave when I did, the way I did. And if you ever mention this to anyone, especially the police, you could still be in danger. These people have long memories and you have no idea how powerful they are. They can pretty much do whatever the hell they want, and get away with it too."

"Did you know you were going to take off before or after

we shopped for the shellfish for the paella?"

"What's all this about paella?"

"So you forgot you were going to cook paella? You don't remember that at all?"

"What difference does it—"

"It's important to me. I need to know."

"It was before, I believe."

"So you had no intention of ever making that paella with me. When you told me how you were looking forward to making it and eating with me that had been a total lie, like everything else?"

"I couldn't let you in on what was happening. I had no—"

"No choice, I know. You're just a poor victim."

"I was crushed for days after I left you."

"Days! Wow, you really suffered. You know how long it took me to get over it? I'm not talking about being happy. I mean how many years until I could just function fully again?"

"I wanted to reach out to you many times, but I—"

"I know, you couldn't, because you didn't have a choice, you're such a victim. Meanwhile, you missed me so much you passed me on to Michael."

"No, I absolutely did not. I just…I just wanted him to check up on you."

"So how exactly did this go? Did you call him and tell him, 'Hey, there's this cute chick I just ghosted on Long Island, told her I'd marry her then went for a swim and never came back. But she's great in bed and really gullible, want her number, dude?' Or did you say 'bro?'"

"No, it was *not* like that at all. Michael is a great guy. I have enormous respect for him, he's like a brother to me actually."

"A *brother*? Seriously?"

"Yes, and I know how odd that must seem to you now, but I was not, I repeat *was not* trying to set him up with you. I was surprised when he told me you too were a couple, but I actually was happy about it. He's a good man and you're a good woman. I just wanted him to—"

"Get laid."

"Look after you."

I fake smiled. "You really thought I needed a man to *look after* me? Or else, what? I'd be lost, floating around aimlessly and manlessly forever?"

"No, that wasn't it at all. I knew I'd put you in a horrible position, Vanessa. And I knew you were a suspect in my disappearance, which I did not expect. And, yes, I knew it was hard on you after I left, and I was just trying to make things right."

"You're right. You were so kind and thoughtful. I've been looking at this the wrong way for years."

"Let me put it this way, V…Vanessa. I did what I thought was best at the time, but I assure you, I wasn't trying to hurt you in any way. That was the last thing I—"

"I'm curious, what exactly did you say to him?"

"It was years ago. How could I remember what I—"

"Did you tell him to marry me? To have kids with me?"

"Of course not. I thought you might be, I don't know, become friends, he'd be a supportive person in your life."

"*Friends*?"

"As I've said, I felt incredibly guilty for leaving you the way I had to, and I couldn't reach out to you, so what was I supposed to do? I guess I could've done anything, but that didn't seem right either. Try to put yourself in my position. I could've just vanished, but I thought it was better if I could do something positive for you, for your life, and I knew Michael was a good man."

"I don't need Michael or any man to take care of me."

"Look, I understand why you'd think it was all a game for us, some big plot against you, but that wasn't the case at all. Think about it. How could I have possibly arranged anything, or expected you'd actually marry Michael and have children? *You* made those choices, not me. And weren't they good choices, weren't they? Don't you love your family much more than you ever loved me? In the end, aren't you happy that I did what I did?"

I let this all sink in, then said, "Now I get it. Now it all makes sense."

"Good. I'm glad."

"Yes, yes, I understand everything now. All those times I told psychiatrists that I felt like my life was out of control, like I wasn't living my own life, like things were *happening* to me, it was all true, it wasn't really about *me*, it was about *you*. You've been manipulating me since the day I met you."

"Oh, for God's sake, Vanessa—"

"I'm curious, did you still think you loved me when I was a suspect in your disappearance? Or when I almost killed myself and had to get psychiatric treatment? Did you even care about the hell you were putting me through?"

"I felt awful about all of that. I still do."

"Then you *knew* all along what was going on? How exactly? Was Michael giving you updates, a full play-by-play of my psych issues when he was telling me I had 'let go' and 'give myself closure' and all of that other bullshit?"

"He kept me up to date over the years because I was concerned. I wanted you to be okay. And look how it worked out. You have two wonderful kids and you have Michael, a great man and a great husband."

I tried to stifle a laugh but couldn't. "Despite what you think, Michael and you are not *good* people. You're both psycho and twisted and pathetic."

"I'm sorry you feel that way, I truly am, but it's far from the truth. We both care about you deeply." He glanced at his phone, then said, "Maybe if we had more time, I could try to get you to understand my position better, but unfortunately time is running out. If we want a chance to save Michael, we have to move fast, and I already have an idea that I think—"

"Are you serious? You really think I'm going to help you or believe a word you fucking say about anything?"

"Fair," he said. "You're entitled to believe what you want to believe, but the fact is if you don't help me, Michael will die today and you might even be arrested for his murder."

"I have a lawyer. I'll be fine."

"Really? Are you certain of that? The police love to arrest wives when their husbands disappear and there's a good chance Michael's body will never be discovered. But, hey, it's up to you. If you want to roll the dice with your life, maybe it's your lucky day."

He could be lying, or how could I know for sure?

"Why would these men want to kill Michael?"

"Two men and one woman. The woman, Lena, is in charge, and they don't want Michael, they want me."

"How do you know?"

"After I met Michael in Tribeca on Saturday, they tried to kill me. That SUV that's been following you? It tried to run me over. So I suspect that Michael is their plan B— they're using him as leverage to get to me. I've been trying to find Michael, to save him, but it seems like they're trying to up the ante, kidnapping you as well, figuring that if they have you and Michael I'd be more likely to give myself up. And, while I know you'd find this hard to believe, if they had taken you last night I would have given myself up to save you. No question."

"You're right. I do find that hard to believe."

"Well, it's true. The big question is how have they been able to track you down with that SUV? You say you've seen it several times, right?"

"At least. So?"

His eyes shifted as he looked around the room, then his gaze settled on the console in the foyer where I'd left my handbag.

"Do you take that with you wherever you go?"

"My handbag?"

"Yes."

"Usually."

"May I see it?"

"You want to see my handbag?"

"There's probably a tracking device in there. May I?"

Figuring at this point I had nothing to lose, I brought him the bag. I watched as he felt around the lining.

"Feel that?"

I felt where he was feeling and sure enough there was a small hard object stitched into the lining.

"What's that?"

"What do you think? Do you have scissors? Don't worry, it won't cost much to repair."

The object did seem unusual, so I went into the boys' room and returned with scissors. After a quick snip he showed me what he had removed—a tiny tracking device, like a mini AirTag.

"This explains how an SUV has been following you

around."

"How did that get in there?"

"Could've been planted there at any time."

"Okay. So why shouldn't I just report all this to the cops? Clear my name."

He looked at me. "If you're going to trust me on one thing, trust me on this—if Lena and her crew get spooked, Michael will die. Our only chance is to find Michael as soon as we can and this tracker will help us enormously."

Now he seemed to be reinserting the tracker into my handbag's lining.

"What're you doing?"

"This is our best chance of finding Michael, if you lead me to him."

"And how am I going to do that?"

"Just by doing what you're doing, except next time you'll allow yourself to get abducted."

"Allow myself to get abducted."

Saying it again didn't make it sound any less insane.

"Yes. Then I'll follow you and free you and Michael."

I fake smiled like I thought this was all a joke, though I knew it wasn't.

"You seriously think I'm going to do this?"

"Can you think of a better idea?"

"Yeah, you go rescue Michael on your own."

"I'd do that if I could, but I can't. Not before time runs out unfortunately."

"So what am I supposed to do? Let them kidnap me, risk my life, and trust that you're not lying to me *this* time, that you're not going to just ditch me, you're going to *follow* me, and that you're right, or not lying, about Michael and everything else you told me?"

"Yeah, pretty much."

Looking into his dull, empty eyes, which still looked nothing like the glowing eyes of the man I once knew, I said, "And how exactly are you going to rescue us?"

"Leave all that to me."

Remembering how Jennifer has warned me that he's "dangerous," I said, "Are you planning to hurt these people? Because I'm already a person of interest, and if anything else happens—"

"The less you know the better. But this is it, Vanessa—your only and final chance to save Michael. If you don't help me, I assure you Michael will be killed. And you probably will be eliminated too, to be completely honest. These people don't like loose ends."

He sounded sincere, but he'd also sounded sincere on Shelter Island when he'd told me he was going for "a quick swim" before he'd make a big paella. Meanwhile, he knew what he was going to do, his plan was already in place. That sincerity was all an act, just like it might be an act now.

"How do I know this isn't all a set up? Maybe you're working with them, trying to find Michael, and now you want to use me to get to him?"

"Think about it. If I was evil and wanted Michael dead I could have killed him that day in Tribeca, poisoned him. Come on, what're you going to do, Vanessa? Will you help me or not?"

I didn't want to believe him *again*, I didn't want to get sucked in *again*, especially now that he was nonchalantly talking about poisoning, but it also seemed like an equally huge risk to *not* trust him.

"You expect me to risk my life to get Michael home safely when I don't even know your real name?"

"All right, in the spirit of full transparency, my name is John—John Adams. You know, like the second President of the United States."

John Adams sounded like more bullshit. While I didn't have a plan yet, I knew that somehow, some way, I'd get even for all of this. Until then, I'd play along, put my acting skills to work.

"Fine, 'John Adams,'" I said. "I'm in."

TWENTY-ONE

After we went over the plan several times he said, "Well, I should be getting going now. As I said, time is short." He glanced at his Rolex, then said, "It's nearly eight-thirty. Wait until ten, then leave yourself, all right?"

"Why do I have to wait?"

"I don't want anyone to see me leaving the building. And if they do I want to make sure that they think I'm gone. You won't be able to contact me, so the most important thing is you have to make sure you're not being followed. Later—and this is important—do *not* contact the police until you and Michael are at home safely."

I nodded slowly.

"And no more drugs of any kind today and keep drinking plenty of water. While I never had the opportunity to practice medicine or receive a degree, I do know a thing or two."

"Fuck you."

He smiled, "Ah, I've really missed you, Vanessa. I know you don't believe it, but it's true. Someday I hope you can see that I'm not as awful as you think I am. Despite what you might think, I care about you very, very much. Much more than you can ever imagine."

He went to the front door and opened it. I didn't follow him, stayed in the dining area. He knew he'd turn back to look at me the way he had before he'd left for his swim on Shelter Island, and sure enough he did.

"Well, this is it. After I free you and Michael, you'll never see me again. At least I can say a proper goodbye this time, so there's that. Goodbye, beautiful Vanessa."

I hated that, despite everything he'd done to me, and everything I knew, I was still attracted to him. Or at least my body was. I remembered how he used to kiss me, running his hands through my hair, biting on my lower lip a little…

Stop it, Vanessa.

Then he turned, the door shut, and he was gone.

IN MY BATHROOM, I got naked and turned the water on, but before I got in the shower, I thought, *What the hell am I doing?* I didn't trust this guy at all, I didn't even know his real name—John Adams, yeah right—and I was going along with his plan? For all I knew, this was a trap. Maybe he'd kidnapped or killed Michael and he was afraid I'd go to the cops so he was planning to kill me too. *He* could've planted that tracking device in my handbag when he broke into my apartment this morning, to make it look like someone else was tracking me, but maybe *he'd* been following me around in the SUV. That would make sense if he showed up at my place, a few hours after I was almost kidnapped. Maybe he'd come to finish the job, but he didn't want to kill me in my apartment where my body would be discovered, and he was planning to kidnap me, along with his "friends" in the SUV. Then he could dispose of my body and Michael's body and disappear to go scam somebody else.

Still naked, I sat on the foot of my bed, about to call Detective Randle. But before the call connected, I ended it.

Yes, trusting my serial lying ex-fiancé yet again after everything I knew about him seemed insane, but calling the police seemed just as risky. Even if I wasn't paranoid, if my fears were real, what would the police do? Since Michael had disappeared it seemed like all Randle had done was try to build a case against me. If I told him that my ex-fiancé had broken into my apartment, he probably wouldn't believe me. Or by the time I was able to convince him that I was telling the truth it could be too late to save Michael.

I had no choice. It was probably too late for the police to help anyway. I just had to hope that John Adams wasn't lying to me yet again.

Oh, yeah. And that I didn't end up dead.

WHAT DO YOU wear to your own kidnapping? Apparently pre-ripped jeans, Asics, and my favorite *Wicked* T-shirt, emblazoned with a pic of the wicked witch on her broomstick with the slogan: *Defying Gravity.*

Feeling queasy and anxious, I drank water finally, but it didn't seem to help. I knew I should probably eat something. I was tempted to take more Klonopin, just for the "hair of the dog" effect, to feel centered and stable again, but I didn't want to risk OD'ing and passing out. My children needed a healthy, sane mother, especially if Michael didn't survive.

It was only a little past nine and John had told me not to leave until ten, but I felt antsy. Didn't Randle say the more time that passed, the more likely that Michael would die? I felt like I was wasting valuable time in my apartment, but maybe there was a reason why John had insisted that I wait. I killed some time neatening up the bookshelf in the living room, moving around some books and doing some reorganizing, which at least made me feel a little more centered, then I left the apartment. It was only nine-thirty, but I couldn't wait any longer.

My elevator stopped on the sixth floor and Kim got on—a single mom in the building whose son Tyler was Carson's age. When the kids were younger, we used to go on play dates to nearby playgrounds, the park, and to kids' birthday parties.

"Good morning, how are you?" I asked.

"Fine, good." She seemed extremely uncomfortable. After barely nodding hello, she avoided eye contact, staring at the digital display of descending floor numbers.

I was going to ignore it, but I couldn't resist saying, "You know, none of what you heard about me is true. I'm a thousand percent innocent."

Still watching the numbers, like she couldn't wait to get away, she said, "About what? I didn't hear anything."

I knew she was lying. She'd heard and was obviously afraid of me now, or afraid to be associated with me, like everyone else.

I was beyond cancelled. I was radioactive.

When the doors opened in the lobby, Kim rushed out without saying bye or even looking at me.

I got out too, noticing that there didn't seem to be a crowd in front of the building this morning.

Carlos, who'd just started his morning shift at the concierge desk, said, "I saw one woman out there before, but now

I think they finally got away."

"Well, there's some good news," I said.

Maybe the reporters had moved on to the next big news story, but I knew they'd be back in full force if Michael's body was discovered somewhere and I couldn't prove I was innocent.

I walked to First Avenue, looking around for reporters, or the SUV, or John Adams, but no one seemed to be following me. If John really was a spy, stealing medical secrets, he probably knew how to be discreet so just because I didn't see him, it didn't mean he wasn't here somewhere.

I continued downtown on Fiftieth Street, then continued into the Forties. There was still no sign of anyone following me. Yesterday, I would've thought this was a positive thing, but now it only fueled my anxiety. This was ridiculous—I was wasting time, but maybe that was the whole point. Maybe John didn't want me to actually get abducted. Maybe he was just trying to distract for a couple of hours, have me walk around aimlessly while he killed Michael and disappeared. I regretted not calling Randle when I had a chance, but it was too late now—if John wasn't following me, he was long gone.

I walked uptown a few blocks, then went east to Sutton Place, and continued uptown. I was trying to be discreet, glancing at my phone occasionally, looking around mostly with my peripheral vision, but there was still no sign of an SUV or John Adams. I was imagining the police discovering Michael's body in a river or the park. John probably knew how to leave no DNA or physical evidence behind, but he could have already gotten my DNA, maybe from a strand of hair on one of my hairbrushes before he woke me up. He could leave the hair, or whatever, on Michael's body, and implicate me, and I'd be arrested for Michael's murder. My lawyer would probably tell me that I might as well plead guilty because there was no way a jury would find me innocent, especially with public opinion against me. I'd have to go to jail and leave my boys with Stella and Joe. No matter what I said, I wouldn't be able to convince anyone I was innocent. Eventually, I'd die in prison, miserable and alone, and they'd live the rest of their lives believing their mother had murdered their father.

One major side effect of paranoia—it's distracting. I kept telling myself, *Don't resist, let it happen.* I wasn't aware of the SUV approaching—it was suddenly just *there*—and then someone grabbed me from behind. I got a quick glimpse of the abductor; it seemed like it was the same guy from last night, except this time he was much more aggressive. As he lifted me up and then shoved me hard into the SUV I ignored my instincts to fight back or scream or do anything. If this was the last thought I ever had, I wanted to think about my kids, but instead I was picturing John Adams looking back at me with a weird, ambiguous smile as I felt a prick in my right shoulder and everything went black.

TWENTY-TWO

WHEN I OPENED my eyes, I couldn't see anything. For a couple of terrifying moments, I thought that I was blind, then I realized that something was covering my eyes. I tried to speak but my mouth was covered too. I wasn't in an SUV now, or at least I didn't seem to be. I wasn't moving and it was totally quiet. I was sitting up, in a chair, but I realized that I was bound with rope or tape because I couldn't move my arms or legs.

Okay, John Fucking Adams, where the hell are you?

John had said that I'd probably be sedated and tied up, but he also said he'd move quickly to free me…and Michael. My memory seemed okay. I remembered everything that had happened to me, up until the guy grabbing me and injecting me with something, but I had no idea how much time had gone by. Seconds? Hours? Days?

At least I was thinking. At least I was alive.

I tried to scream again, but I could only make a faint growling sound. Then I tried to wiggle my arms to try to loosen the ropes of whatever was restraining me. In movies this always worked—people wiggled around for a while then freed themselves—but when I did it, it seemed like I had *less* room to move around.

Struggling, trying to get free seemed like a waste of time, except that John Adams had told me that this was part of the plan. He'd told me to "make it look convincing" by screaming, trying to get free. Had he been lying to me after all? Had he set me up to be killed, maybe by him?

I tried to scream again, but again I could only growl, straining my throat. I tried to free my legs, but I couldn't get them loose. I desperately needed some meds because full-blown panic was setting in. Was this how I was going to die—alone in the dark, tied to a chair? What if I was never found and just disappeared, and what if Michael was never found either? My kids would live the rest of their lives, wondering if their parents were still out there somewhere, until the mystery drove them crazy. I didn't want them to go through what I'd gone through but that's exactly what was going to happen. Fuck, I should've called the police when I'd had the chance. Better yet, I should've killed John Adams, that lying, scamming son of a bitch. I could've made an excuse, said I needed a glass of water, and gone into the kitchen and grabbed a butcher knife. He might've caught on, tried to stop me, but if I moved quickly, I could've gotten to it in time. Then when he burst into the kitchen I could've stabbed him right in the chest. I could see it so clearly—the knife cutting into his heart, his wide-open eyes, like he'd be thinking, *How is this possible? I was always in control, at least one step ahead of her. I ditched her, set her up for murder, arranged for her to meet her future husband? Now she'd turned against me? How is this happening?*

But I hadn't killed him, and was tied to a chair, in darkness. There had to be some way out of here—some way I hadn't thought of yet. Panicking wasn't helping. I had to stay calm, breathe, and the solution would come to me. Maybe I could knock myself over—maybe if I was on the floor, it would be easier to free myself somehow.

I didn't want to just disappear from their lives, the way John Adams and Michael had disappeared from mine.

Then I heard something. A creak, footsteps, then faint voices. I couldn't make out any words, but a conversation was taking place with at least two people, maybe in a different language. One of the voices sounded female—could it be that woman John had mentioned, Lena? Maybe John was out there talking to them. Were they talking about how to kill me? Where to dump my body? Again, I saw myself jamming the knife into John's chest and the blood seeping— no, *pouring* out of him. It seemed so vivid and real, like it was actually happening.

Now the footsteps were getting louder—they were heading in my direction. Did they have a gun? Was one of them about to execute me?

Then a door opened—it sounded like an industrial steel door. The footsteps were echoing now. The people stopped near me. I tried to scream again, but only a guttural growl broke out. I thought about those awful terrorist videos everyone had seen and braced myself for whatever was next. I just hoped it would be quick, that I'd be dead before the pain kicked in.

The woman was speaking—in another language. It didn't sound like Russian, but it sounded like some Slavic language. I didn't know if the woman was speaking to me or to someone else. I figured she must've been talking to someone else, because how would she expect me to respond? Was she ordering someone to kill me? I braced myself again, but nothing happened—not yet anyway.

The conversation continued. In addition to the woman there seemed to be two guys—they both had deep voices that were hard to tell apart. Someone reeked of cigarettes. I thought I smelled onions too. I gave up trying to speak or trying to get free. I had no control any longer; it was all up to fate.

Then there was a loud, hissing sound—it seemed like it was coming from someplace low, maybe the floor—and the people began yelling, panicking. It seemed like they were scrambling frantically, trying to get out, and then there was a new, familiar odor in the room, like a permanent marker. It reminded me of the endless art projects I'd worked on with my boys.

But it wasn't permanent marker. It was gas.

It explained why everyone was so frantic and why I was suddenly light-headed and dizzy. I tried to hold my breath, though I knew this was pointless—I wouldn't be able to hold it for very long. Was John Adams responsible for this? If so, this wasn't part of the plan, and if he'd lied about the gas, what else was he lying about? I still had no idea if he was trying to save me or kill me.

For several seconds the screaming continued, then I heard a body fall, hit the concrete.

Then another body dropped.

Then another.

Although I was still holding my breath, I was feeling more dazed, probably from whatever I'd breathed in already. I thought I heard Michael screaming too, but maybe I was just hallucinating, the way people start hallucinating before they die, seeing dead relatives. Maybe that's what was happening to me—did this mean Michael was actually dead? Would I see other deceased relatives too, like my father and grandparents?

The screaming subsided. I only heard one of the Slavic voices and it was getting weaker, fading out. Then there was total silence. Did they all pass out? I couldn't hold my breath any longer, I didn't have the strength, so I inhaled more of the gas. I knew I'd pass out any second and strangely I didn't care anymore.

There was no point in fighting.

BRIGHTNESS STUNG MY eyes. At least I could see—unless I was hallucinating. No, I was definitely *here*, alive, breathing, but there wasn't that odor anymore. I could see and think and, holy shit, my arms and legs weren't tied anymore. Someone must've cut me loose.

I stood—too quickly because I still felt effects from the gas, and I felt queasy and unsteady, like I might pass out again. It took a few seconds to let myself feel stronger and to try to process what had happened. I was in a large, cavernous building—it looked like an industrial warehouse. The walls had to be thirty feet high, and some sections of the floor were missing. Rays of sunshine were coming through a dirty skylight; it looked like it was afternoon. Squinting from the brightness and maybe from irritation from the gas, I noticed that the cords that had been tied to the chair had been cut or untied, and the gag and blindfold were on the floor too, along with my handbag. I noticed that my wallet, phone, and keys were there, and my phone was getting service.

I had a missed call from Elana Krauss, the defense attorney. I was about to call 9-1-1, but if John was telling the truth, that call could get Michael killed.

Okay, but where *was* Michael? Oh, and what had happened to the people who had kidnapped me?

"Michael? Michael, are you here? *Michael*?"

I tried to scream but my voice was weak and a little hoarse from all the straining earlier.

I tried again, "Michael! Michael!" But a faint echo was the only response.

There were two industrial steel doors in the space—one was open slightly, so I went in that direction.

"Michael? Michael?"

Still nothing.

I pushed the door open slightly.

There was another space, even bigger than the one I was in. There was also a dirty skylight, and several overhanging fluorescent lights were on. On a table there were empty beer and soda bottles, and there were a couple of larger bags filled with garbage.

"Michael!"

No answer.

I had no idea how I was supposed to find him, or if even staying here looking for him was a good idea. John had told me to leave with Michael after we were freed, but he hadn't told me about the gas, so maybe he'd lied about this too.

"Michael!"

Suddenly I felt ridiculous, screaming for him. Was this part of the plan? Did John, and maybe Michael, want to humiliate me more than they already had? What if there were hidden cameras here and they were watching me? Or not just them. What if I was being live-streamed and the world was watching? Maybe the people who had kidnapped me had been killed and the murders were going to be pinned on me? At any moment, the police would burst in, and I'd be taken away in cuffs, hanging my head.

While I knew that I was probably making this all up and that it didn't make any sense, it still seemed very real. To hell with Michael. Despite the horrible things he'd done to me, I'd gone above and beyond trying to save him, because he was my children's father and it had seemed like the right thing to do, but now I had to save my own ass.

I was heading toward the exit when I glanced back at the other door. I wanted to leave, run, but I figured I might as well check just in case.

I stopped several feet away from the door and said, "Hello? Anywhere in there?"

No answer. Maybe whoever was here before had escaped during the gas attack, or John had taken them somewhere, but no one was here. If the door was locked from the inside, I would have just left, but when I pushed it, it opened easily.

It looked like another empty, industrial room. There were some empty boxes and pieces of plywood, and an empty, tipped-over paint can. Like in the rest of the building, the floors and walls were old and corroded in spots. I was about to leave when I sensed something to my right, beyond the open door. I peeked around the door and sure enough there was a metal chair, like the one I'd been tied to, and Michael was sitting in it, with his head slumping to the left. He was in the same clothes he'd gone jogging in and he was very scruffy, as if he hadn't shaved since he left our apartment last Sunday morning, which seemed like weeks or even months ago, but it had only been two days ago.

My first thought was: *Michael's dead.*

Strangely, this didn't make me feel sad or angry, or really feel anything. I was totally numb, even okay with it. If he was dead, it would be sad for the kids, but after I planned a funeral and cashed his insurance policy, I could move on with my life with a clean slate and focus on supporting my kids and building my business—"hobby" my ass. There was no chance that we could fix things and save our marriage and, at this point, did he even deserve my sympathy? I knew it was a horrible thought, but things would be much "cleaner" if he was dead and I didn't have to go through a divorce. Michael was a lawyer and I knew how vindictive he could get when he felt hurt. Divorcing him would be a nightmare and would cost me a fortune in legal expenses.

"Michael?"

I didn't say it very loud, just loud enough that he should have been able to hear me if he was alive. Wow, he was really *dead*? I had to admit, the idea felt more exciting than scary. I hadn't felt this excited about the future in a very long time. For years, I'd been trapped, with Michael and John manipulating and controlling me. Was this really it? Was I finally *free*?

I was about to leave—I'd rush out of the building, then run as fast as I could—but then for some reason I looked back at Michael again and saw him stir.

Shit. Seriously?

Maybe I'd just imagined it. That probably happens all the time—someone imagining a dead person moving? Although that was due to wish fulfillment. This was the opposite.

Then his eyes opened—okay, he officially wasn't dead—and he shifted manically back and forth several times. Nope, not imagining it. But I *was* still imagining sprinting away, toward the sunlight, when he saw me standing there and he said, "Vanessa...what, what are you doing here?"

The letdown hitting harder, I said, "You're alive?"

"Something happened, there was gas." He looked around frantically again. "Where…where is everyone?"

"I don't think there's anyone else here."

"*What*?" He sounded more frantic. "Where did they go?"

"I'm not sure. I thought I heard them falling from the gas, but I guess I'm not sure."

"How did you get here? Were the police here?"

"No…I mean, I don't think so. I was tied up here just like you were. But what happened to you? Are you okay?"

I was aware of how I didn't sound as relieved as a wife should sound after her husband had been missing for two days. But Michael didn't exactly seem thrilled to see me either.

"I'm fine, I'm fine." He stood. "Are you sure nobody's here? What happened to them?"

"I said I think they're gone. I didn't look all over, but we should probably get out of here."

I took a step away.

"Wait," he said.

I turned back.

"How did you get here?" he asked. "How did you find me?"

"It's complicated. We should probably just—"

"Did the police help you? Are there cops outside?"

"No, but I *am* a person of interest in your disappearance. I'm not sure if you knew about that or not."

"No, I didn't know. Jesus, I'm sorry, Vanessa. I was afraid something like that might happen. Don't worry—we'll fix all that. Are the boys okay?"

He was so full of shit; I didn't believe he was *sorry* about anything. And after all the lies and deceit, I didn't believe he cared about the boys either. Fucking narcissistic prick, I hated this man so much. I had to resist an urge to lunge toward him and scratch his eyes out.

But I said, "The boys are fine. Or at least they were when I left. They stayed with your parents last night." I went on Find My iPhone. "Yeah, they're both at school now. Come on, let's get out of here."

"No."

I glared at him, then said, "Um, yes."

"I have to figure out what's going on first."

"We'll figure it out when we get out of here. Stay if you want, but I'm going."

"Just tell me what you know." He was practically yelling. "How did you find me?"

I didn't owe this man anything, and I certainly didn't need to be yelled at.

I marched out of the room, through the main part of the building.

He rushed up alongside me. "Okay, I'm coming, I'm coming." He was looking around as he walked. "You sure they're not here?"

I ignored him.

I found the exit and pushed the door open and we were outside. It was great to breathe in fresh air and get any of that remaining gas out of my lungs. There were other warehouses around us—some looked abandoned—with graffiti and chain-linked fences. On my phone, I opened maps.

"Okay, we're in Queens, not far from the river."

He had his phone out too. "I know where we are." Then he looked at me. "What're you doing?"

"Getting a Lyft."

"Not yet."

I was still tapping when he grabbed my wrist. I was so sick of men grabbing me.

"I said wait."

"Let go of me."

"Not till you tell me what's going on. How did you find me?"

"Let go, you're hurting me."

He wasn't actually hurting me, but he didn't let go.

He said, "You have to trust me right now because there are things I know that you don't."

With my free hand I smacked him in the face. That got him to let go of my wrist.

"Jesus Christ, Vanessa, I'm on your side. I'm just trying to keep you safe and keep our family safe. That's what this is all about."

"Keeping me safe by gaslighting me since the moment I met you?"

"Huh? What're you talking about?"

"You want to know how I found you? Your *friend* arranged it, that's how."

He seemed fake-surprised, like he knew he'd been caught but he wasn't ready to confess yet.

"My friend. What friend?"

"Okay, let's cut the bullshit, all right? You know exactly who I'm talking about…John Adams. Or you might know him as Colin or Adam or Kevin. I'm sure there are dozens of other names he's used."

He absorbed this then, said, "So you spoke to him. Like in person?"

"Yes, *like in person,* and now I know everything. Well, not *everything.* I'm sure there are plenty of more lies out there, but I know way more than I did before you got kidnapped."

"Shit, I was worried about this. He's so fuckin' good. But what does he know? What did he say to you? This is extremely important."

"You want to know what he said? You mean after he broke into our apartment?"

"He broke in?"

"Yes, and he came into our bedroom."

I could tell Michael seemed jealous, though he was trying to hide it.

"Okay. And what happened then?"

"Sure you wanna know?" Yeah, I was enjoying this.

"What did he say about me, about where I was? How did he find out where I was? What did he want from you besides sex?"

"I didn't fuck him," I said, "but I'm glad you think so highly of me."

"Just tell me what happened, what did he want?"

"Are you serious? Now, after all these years, you seriously think you deserve *communication*? You deserve *honesty*?"

"We can all wind up fucking dead if you don't tell me everything you know right now."

Michael rarely got this emotional; it took a lot to jolt him out of his comfort zone, so I knew he was seriously frightened. I told him what had happened this morning but leaving out that I'd almost OD'd on a cocktail of antianxiety meds and painkillers I'd been hoarding. I knew Michael would only judge me or, much worse, file it away to use against me.

When I was through, Michael looked even more frightened than when I'd started and he said, "You made a huge mistake, Vanessa."

"I had no choice. If I went to the police, he said you would've been killed. I was trying to save you and you're lucky I even went out of my way to do that after everything I found out about you."

"You didn't have to do anything. I had it under control. You should've just let it play out."

"Play out? You mean go to jail for your murder? Because that's what might've happened before John Adams showed up. If that's even his actual name."

"Yes, it's his name and I'm surprised he told you that. I don't think I've ever heard him reveal that to anyone."

"Wow, great. I feel so special now."

"You have no idea what you're dealing with, Vanessa. These people—they don't fuck around. They're extremely dangerous. *John* is extremely dangerous."

"You're the second person who's told me that."

"Told you what?"

"About how 'dangerous' he is. Your ex-girlfriend Jennifer told me the same thing, though she knew him as Adam."

"You talked to Jennifer too?" He seemed surprised.

"Yes, and she had a lot to say—I mean *a lot.*" I didn't want to get into it all—right now or probably ever—but I said, "She definitely had some interesting stories about you and your good friend."

"He was never a good friend, or *any* kind of friend."

"Well, he considered *you* a friend. That's why he chose you to look after me as he put it, though I think he was really just passing me along to you."

"What?" Michael looked surprised, but I knew he was just faking it. "I have no idea what you're talking about."

"Oh, cut the bullshit. I know everything. I know I didn't

meet you randomly at that supermarket. It's funny, something has always seemed off about how we met, but I just thought it was because I was in such a bad way, missing Colin—I mean John. Also, I guess I was just naïve back then, or my guard was down, but that's when I believed that there were good, honest men in the world."

"I am a good man."

"Yeah, a good man who made me feel like I was insane for thinking my ex-fiancé was still alive. A good man who was lying to my face every time he said 'I love you.'"

"That's not true. You know I love you."

"Go fuck yourself."

I rushed away, toward the sidewalk, and he followed alongside, saying, "I know I have a lot to explain, but there are reasons why I couldn't tell you the truth, and the truth isn't as bad as you think."

"Wait, so let me guess, you did it to protect me, right? You didn't want me to get hurt? Making me feel like I'm losing my mind is okay, but God forbid I get hurt."

"It didn't happen like that. It wasn't premeditated. I got in deeper and deeper, then I couldn't get out."

"Is that what you tell yourself to put yourself to sleep at night? You believe all your lies and you fall asleep blissfully?"

"It's the truth." He paused, like he was trying to find the right words, then said, "When I was with Jennifer, I distanced myself from John, who, yes, was going under the name Adam then, because I knew she didn't like him. I didn't even know about his Colin identity, or about you or anything that was going on in his life, until he contacted me and told me what had happened, and how bad he felt about losing you. It's true he wanted me to connect with you, but falling in love with you and starting a family—that was all genuine, organic, from my heart."

His eyes were a little glassy. His acting really was amazing. Maybe *he's* the one who should be interviewing managers and trying to become a Broadway star.

"That's good," I said. "You've really gotten yourself to believe all that, huh?"

"Look, I know I have a lot of explaining to do, but—"

"Honestly? I don't give a shit. I just want to go home, hug my kids, and go on with my life."

I had my phone out again. He grabbed my arm—not as aggressively as before, but I still didn't like it.

"Wait," he said. "I need to know what else John told you."

"He didn't tell me anything, that was it." I yanked my arm free.

"Did he tell you anything about me? About what he knows?"

"What he knows?"

"Yes. This is extremely important, Vanessa."

"Well, I know you were helping him with some estate planning because he was ghosting yet another lover, oh and two kids."

"He told you all that?"

"Some of it. The rest I pieced together from Jennifer and Russell?"

"You spoke to Russell too?"

"Yeah, even though you told him not to help me—I know, for my own protection. The care and concern you have for me is truly astounding. Oh, and I also know you met with John at a Starbucks in Tribeca on Saturday before Harrison's show. You know, when you told me you were having drinks with Rob Heller."

Michael had a dumb look.

"How did you find out about Tribeca?"

"The police showed me surveillance footage—you know, when I was being interrogated."

"I'm so sorry."

"Bullshit."

"It's true, I didn't want to cause you any pain, I really didn't. But I should've figured you'd put it all together. I'm impressed, but I'm not surprised. You're a very smart woman."

"It's amazing."

"What is?"

"How you can't even compliment me without sounding patronizing."

"Vanessa…"

He tried to grab me again, but this time I swatted his hand away before he could touch me.

"How could you do this to me? How could you do this to your family?"

"There was no good solution."

"Oh, I get it. You *had* to lie to me again and again? That makes total sense."

"Yes, it *does* make sense."

"Oh, stop it already. I don't even understand what this big fear of John is all about, I mean, he's a thief, right?"

"Not just a thief. He's killed people. Many people."

I flashed back to being in my apartment with him, alone. He easily could have killed me if he'd wanted to.

"Really?" I said. "A killer yet you maintained a friendship with him for years?"

"We aren't friends."

"Acquaintances, whatever."

"I understand how crazy it must seem to you, but none of this was premeditated. It started with a favor, then another favor, and, before I knew it, we were embroiled."

"Embroiled?"

"Yes. You have to understand, Vanessa, you weren't the first one John did this too. There have been others—many others. He has relationships as covers while he's doing his jobs, then when he has to disappear he calls it playing the goodbye game. Because that's what it all is to him—a big game."

I didn't know if this was true or not, but the hypocrisy was incredible. He fakes his kidnapping and abandons his family and accuses *John* of playing games?

"Very interesting," I said, "because between you and John, it's *John* who's actually been the straight shooter lately. I mean, you've been lying to my face, but meanwhile everything he'd told me would happen, happened. He said I'd be taken here and he'd follow me and free me and you. He didn't mention the gas, but he still kept his word."

"Did he say anything about coming after me?"

"Wow, now look who's paranoid."

"Seriously, Vanessa."

"No, he didn't, but you should be thankful that I met up with him or you'd be dead right now."

"I wasn't going to die."

"How do you know?"

His look was his answer.

"Wait, what's going on? What aren't you telling me?"

"It's a lot," Michael said. "Let's get that Lyft. We should get home now."

As I tapped around the app, I said, "How do you know those people in there weren't going to kill you?"

"I'll tell you, but not now."

The car was three minutes away.

"Just tell me. Have you met these people before? John seemed to know a lot about them. He told me about the woman—Lena. Did you…Wait, you knew them, didn't you?"

"Knew *of* them. Just from talking to John over the years. But I never met Lena, or even planned on ever meeting her, until I was approached. It was Saturday night, after I met with John downtown. Remember you saw me on the phone?"

I recalled him slipping away to make a phone call at Harrison's show.

"Who approached you? Why were you approached?"

"I'm getting to it. How far's the car?"

I looked at my phone—two minutes. "Not far, go on."

"Lena contacted me. She and her crew were hired to kill John because of something that happened in St. Louis. I don't know all the details, but I know she's working for an Eastern European government."

"He didn't mention that."

"I'm sure there's a lot he didn't mention. Lena told me if I didn't help her I'd be killed and from what I knew about her I believed she would. So my kidnapping was staged, it was a setup. The idea was to make a trade—me for John. I told Lena that she was making a false assumption, that John had no real loyalty to me, he's always been out for himself. Predictably I was right. He wouldn't go for it. I was a loose end and I heard them talking, they were planning to kill me, so I came up with the idea of kidnapping you too. I know that, unlike other relationships he ditched, John actually cares about you, and he'd do anything to save you. But the idea was for him to give himself up, not for him to rescue us."

"Wait," I said. "So you *arranged* for that SUV to follow me around? That was *your* idea?"

"It was desperation, Vanessa. Didn't you hear what I said? I would've been killed."

"I get it. So your life is in danger, might as well endanger mine too. Not to mention John who you *knew* would be killed."

"They would've killed John anyway. If they didn't use me they would've found another way."

"Whatever," I said, "but I actually think you misjudged the situation. John wanted to save you, and seemed to legitimately feel bad about what happened. That's why he came to me, and that's why he actually saved us."

"What John says and what he does are very different things."

"But he did it. He saved us. Here we are. We're free."

"No, we're not free—that's exactly what I'm talking about. I don't know where Lena and those men are—maybe they're still inside there somewhere tied up, or maybe John took them somewhere, but John wouldn't just kill them. He'd torture them first and find out the truth, that I was involved in setting him up, then he'll come back, to get revenge. It's not a matter of if, it's a matter of when."

It was still hard to believe that the man I'd been engaged to, or even the man who'd broken into my apartment this morning and saved me from OD'ing, was actually a professional killer, but admittedly it was nice to see Michael so terrified.

"What's funny?" Michael asked.

I didn't realize I was actually smiling, but said, "Nothing. Nothing at all. But, look, maybe none of this is as bad as it seems. Maybe John won't interrogate them and find out anything, maybe he's on his way out of the country."

"Extremely doubtful," Michael said.

Looking at my phone I said, "Car's around the corner."

"Wait, one more thing and this is extremely important." As Michael's eyebrows furrowed, the skin between them formed a deep, vertical wrinkle, and his lips were quivering a little. "We can't tell the police anything about John or how we escaped."

"Why not?"

"Because I was fucking involved, that's why. I'll go to jail, maybe for years. We'll just say we don't know who kidnapped me, but I was released in Queens and you came to get me. That's the simplest way, and if John doesn't find out the truth, maybe he'll let it slide. It's our best chance to get out of this."

I didn't know why it was "our" chance. It seemed like this was mainly *his* problem. He'd probably get arrested for a fake kidnapping, and maybe other charges, but I hadn't done anything wrong. Also, if he went to jail my life would be better than if he *didn't* go to jail.

But I had an idea.

"Okay, fine, I'll say whatever you want."

"I'm calling your phone right now. Pick up, count to ten, then end the call. I want there to be a record that a call was placed."

My phone chimed and I did what Michael wanted me to do.

"Great," he said, seeming a little relieved.

This was perfect—let him get comfortable and believe I was the kind, thoughtful, empathetic loving wife I'd always been. Then, when his guard was down, and the time was right, I'd strike back. I wouldn't have to divorce him or get him sent to jail—that wouldn't be painful enough. No, I wanted to make him feel the way he'd made me feel throughout our marriage—confused, desperate, angry, crazy, alone, gaslit. That would be *true* revenge.

A white Honda Accord was approaching.

"Come on," I said. "Let's get home to our boys."

TWENTY-THREE

BEFORE WE GOT in, I asked Michael if it was okay with him if I texted the kids and told them that he was safe, and that we were on our way home.

"Yes, that's fine."

I could tell he liked that I'd asked his *permission*.

"But keep it brief," he added, "and no phone calls."

Great, let him think I was "same ol' Vanessa"—believing his lies, always trying to smooth things over, giving him endless "second chances." It would make it even sweeter when he finally got everything he deserved.

In the car, I tapped out a message to the kids:

Dad's safe!!! Heading home. Can you come right home after school?

Before I sent the message, I showed it to Michael and he nodded his approval. Again, I could tell how pleased he was that I'd "calmed down" and was "obeying."

Within seconds, Harrison and Carson both replied with exclamation points. Then Harrison called, but I sent his call to voicemail and tapped out another text—also showing it to Michael before sending:

Can't talk, in a car. See you @ home!

The traffic wasn't bad on the 59th Street Bridge, and we made it back to our building in Manhattan quickly. As we entered, Carlos was happy and a little shocked to see Michael.

"Wow, holy shit, it's really you."

"Yeah, it's really me."

"See? I knew you were okay, no matter what people were saying. So where were you? What happened?"

"Long story, man."

"I'll bet. Great to see you home safe, Mr. Rizzo."

In the elevator up, I looked up at the digital display of the numbers and didn't make eye contact with Michael or speak to him. In the car I hadn't interacted with him much either. He probably thought I was just upset or anxious and needed "an appointment with Dr. Stone," but actually I was excited—more excited about the future than I'd been in ages—already working out details of my big plan, game planning a strategy for how to pull it off perfectly. It was going to take a while—a few weeks or even longer—to put everything in place. Mainly, for maximum impact, I had to make Michael feel safe and secure, believe one hundred percent that I forgave him completely, that I was all-in. Then, when the time was right….

"I think…" Michael cut himself off, probably realizing that it was possible for Carlos to listen in on the conversation via the elevator's intercom. He waited until we got out on our floor and were inside our apartment before he continued, "Okay, here's what we need to do now. Call the police now and tell them you just got home, that I reached out to you from Queens and you came to meet me. All you know about what happened to me is that I called you and you came to meet me—say you took a taxi and paid with cash so there's nothing to trace about that trip. That's all you know—leave the rest to me. The important thing is that you don't mention anything about John, especially John contacting you. You still haven't seen John in years. Okay?"

"Fine," I said obediently. "I'll do whatever you want me to do."

Michael seemed so pleased. It was going to be so easy to string him along for as long as I wanted to, and it felt great to feel so in control of everything. It was like when I was working on one of my organization projects. I had a plan, a strategy, a *vision*, and now it was just a matter of implementing it.

"God, it's great to be back," Michael said, grinning as he walked through the kitchen, into the dining area, then back into the foyer again.

Sparkle came out of the living room, meowing loudly, and rubbed his head against Michael's leg. Usually, Michael didn't show much affection for the cat, so it seemed weird when he knelt down and started rubbing him under his neck. Sparkle seemed to think it was weird too because he freaked out and scampered away.

"Okay," Michael said, "you can make the call now."

I called Randle, expecting to get his voicemail.

I was surprised when he picked up and said, "I've been trying to reach you."

"Sorry," I said, "but I have some very big news."

I told Randle exactly what Michael wanted me to tell him, as Michael stood next to me.

"When did you get home?" Randle asked.

"A few minutes ago."

"Aha," he said.

I wasn't sure what this meant, but I assumed Randle was surprised that Michael was home safely, because now he had to shift gears and stop building his murder case against me.

"I'll be by shortly," he said, and ended the call.

"Perfect," Michael said. "I'm sure there will be a lot of questions, but as long as we stick to our story we'll get through it—*this* part anyway. Then our only problem will be John."

There he went again with "we" and "our." Fine, if he wanted to believe he wasn't alone in this now, let him believe it. But he'd find out soon enough what the *real* situation was.

"Well, let's hope so," I said.

Michael said he wanted to take a shower, which I agreed was a good idea as he smelled disgusting. I didn't smell, but I needed a shower too, so I took a quick one in the boys' bathroom. When I returned to the bedroom, wrapped in a towel, Michael came out of the master bathroom naked. I was hoping he would just get dressed but, making eye contact with my cleavage, he said, "Come here."

I wasn't attracted to him at all—actually, I was re-pulsed—but I went over and let him hug me. His hands over my ass felt like clamps and I could feel his hard-on poking against me. But when he kissed me, I kissed him back.

"God, I missed you so much," he said with hot, minty breath as he stared downward at my lips.

Then I tried not to cringe when he reached under my robe and caressed my breasts with his rough hands. I even moaned a little like I was enjoying it.

"I wish we had time for a quickie," he said, "but that detective will be here soon."

"Yeah, it's too bad."

"But there's always tonight." He kissed me again. "And

the night after that, and the night after that, and the night after that. I swear on my life, if we get through this, I'm never going to stop appreciating what we have, Vanessa. I'm also going to do whatever it takes to make you happy. We'll work out whatever we have to work out in counseling, then I want us to have an honest marriage. No more games, no more secrets."

I was dying to ask him what *games* he thought I'd been playing over the years, or what secrets I'd been keeping, but I didn't want to do anything to make him think I was unhappy, or wasn't on board with whatever fantasies he wanted to believe.

"That all sounds wonderful," I said.

I took some clothes with me into the bathroom and got dressed there and put on a little makeup. While I was still in the bathroom the intercom buzzed. I finished getting ready, then left the bathroom and heard Stella's grating voice. I couldn't make out everything she was saying but I heard her screech, "Thank God!" and "It's like a miracle!" I should've figured Harrison and Carson would tell their grandparents that Michael was home safe. She and Joe had probably gotten right in the car and sped over here.

I entered the living room in my comfy pre-ripped jeans and a baggy T-shirt, my still wet hair up in a bun. They were in the living room, on the couch—Michael between Stella and Joe, with Stella's arms around Michael as she sobbed. Joe said "Hey" to me, but Stella didn't even make eye contact. Then she glanced at me quickly before resuming fawning over her son. This was going to be the hardest part—being nice to Stella—but I'd have to suck it up to pull off my plan.

She was saying to Michael, "I want you to tell me everything that happened. Where were you? How did you get away?"

Michael gave his parents the bullshit version—tearily telling them he was kidnapped, held somewhere where he was blindfolded the whole time and only had his gag taken off to eat, how he had to sit up all day except when he slept on a bare mattress, and how he was released "somewhere near Long Island City" before he contacted me and I came to meet him in a taxi. It amazed me how believable Michael sounded and how comfortable he seemed lying. It made me realize why I hadn't caught on to Michael's bullshit years ago—any moral, compassionate person would have believed the lies that I'd believed. But, most of all, it was startling how Michael didn't seem to have any concern for the hell he'd put his family through, including his parents. I doubted he even cared or knew what it felt like to care. I'd always known that I was married to a narcissist, but this dark side to Michael's personality had never seemed so blatant.

"You poor thing," Stella said. "I hope the police catch the people who did this to you, and I hope they go straight to hell."

"Thanks, Ma," Michael said. "Hope so too."

Michael shot me a glance, checking in on how I was taking all of this, whether I approved or not. I faked a loving, supportive smile, as if saying, *Way to go, love you so much.* He responded with a similar expression.

Joe and Stella continued to tell Michael, seemingly in every way possible, how much they missed him and how happy they were to have him back safely.

It was getting harder to hide my nausea, so I said, "Can I get you something to drink? Maybe some coffee? We don't have much food, but I could order in."

Stella didn't respond or even look at me, but Joe said, "Coffee would be great, thanks. Light and sweet if you can."

As I was preparing Joe's coffee in the kitchen, Stella went in to get something from the fridge. To pull my plan off the way I wanted to, I needed everyone at ease—the more guards down the better.

"Stella."

She ignored me.

"Stella," I said, not louder, in the same tone.

With the fridge still open she looked back over her shoulder toward me.

Continuing to suck it up, I said, "I just want to apologize for some of the things I said to you. It was an emotional time, and I didn't mean to take it out on you."

Ugh, I couldn't believe that I was *apologizing*. I half wanted to say, *Sorry, changed my mind, bitch, you actually are the mother-in-law from hell.*

"Whatever," she said. "It's over now."

Well, that was the closest she'd ever come to finding any fault in her own behavior, but I'd take what I could get. It wouldn't matter soon anyway; soon she'd be out of my life for good too.

I brought Joe his coffee as the doorbell rang.

Popping up from the sofa, Michael announced, "That must be the detective."

I went to answer the door, looking in the peephole at the tiny, serious face of Detective Randle, then let him in.

"Hello, Mrs. Rizzo."

Before I could answer, Michael appeared behind me, extending his big, meaty hand toward Randle saying, "Hey Michael Rizzo, nice to meet you."

Typical Michael—inserting himself into situations, wanting to micromanage every detail and be in charge, especially in situations that involved me. It had always seemed rude and annoying; now it just seemed laughable.

"Randle, NYPD. Nice to see you're alive and well."

They shook hands quickly.

"Yeah, it's been an eventful few days, that's for sure," Michael said.

"I'm sure it has been." From his tone, it was obvious that Randle was skeptical and suspicious of the whole situation. "I'll need to hear everything that happened, including any information you can give us on who you might think might be involved in this."

I saw Randle's gaze shift toward me for a millisecond.

"No worries," Michael said. "Happy to help out any way I can."

"I'm going to need to speak with you and your wife separately."

"Fine," Michael said. "Whatever you need."

"That's all you got?" I sneered at Randle. "You make me a person of interest behind my back, trying to humiliate me and frame me for a crime that didn't even take place, and I don't even get an apology? Nothing?"

Michael gave me a stern look that I knew meant, *Calm, down, Vanessa, and just let me handle this, okay?* I wanted to hit back with, *You can go fuck yourself too, asshole,* but instead I acquiesced, like a good, polite wife who "cleans up nice," and said to Randle, "Never mind, it's okay. Do whatever you need to do."

Randle wanted to talk with Michael first. They left the apartment and headed down to the doorman's lounge where Randle had questioned me. While I wanted to be amicable with Stella, I still didn't want to *talk* to her. I put on CNBC for them, then went into the bedroom and distracted myself with straightening up my bedroom closet, bagging clothes I'd been intending to donate to thrift shops. I needed to get rid of as much stuff as I could, pare down our lives as much as possible.

Michael and Randle were gone for longer than I'd expected, nearly an hour. Finally, they returned, and Randle said it was my turn. As I left, Michael gave me a cocky glance that I knew meant: *It went well.*

The elevator ride down with Randle was silent as neither of us had any reason for niceties or small talk. When we were sitting down in the lounge, I explained that I'd gotten a call from Michael and came to meet him in Queens by taxi, and then we took a Lyft together back to the city. I included approximate times that I knew made sense with the time of Michael's fake phone call to me.

Randle tried to poke holes in my story and seemed frustrated that he couldn't. He asked me a lot of questions about the SUV, which was ironic since he barely gave a shit about it the other times we'd spoken. He also asked me a lot about "Colin Grant" and other names he'd used, but I didn't tell anything new—I only repeated the information I'd already given him. At one point he asked me point blank if I was lying and looking right at his eyes I said, "No, I am not." I felt so calm, so in control—I bet I could have passed a polygraph.

"Something seems off about this." Randle got up. "I'll get to the bottom of it, though. I always do."

We left the lounge together, then I watched him exit toward the street. Reporters, camera people, and curiosity seekers had gathered again, maybe the largest crowd since Michael had disappeared. I hadn't checked online today, but I imagined there were thousands of new posts about Michael and me.

When I got back to the apartment, Michael met me and

motioned for me to follow him into the bedroom, out of earshot from his parents.

"So?" He was almost whispering. "How did it go?"

"Seemed fine." I matched his voice level. "I think he'd like it if I was going to jail for murdering you, so I think he's going to keep digging around."

"Well, he can look all he wants, but he won't find anything. I'm home safe, so where's the crime?"

"What about the Lena and the people who—"

"He won't be able to connect them to us. I've been careful about my communications with them, I used a burner phone."

Burner phone? Michael suddenly sounded like a full-blown criminal, like using burner phones was just another normal part of his life.

"Well, that's good, I guess," I said. "But what if they find the warehouse where we were held? Maybe my fingerprints are somewhere, or strands of my hair."

"It could lead to more questioning, but I don't think anything will come out of it. This was a missing person's case and I'm no longer missing—case closed."

It seemed like Michael was being too optimistic at the moment, maybe a little in denial, but I didn't care one way or another. The police investigation and any crimes that Michael might have committed were the least of my concerns. Now I had a plan and that was all that mattered.

Hugging me, Michael said, "Mmm, you smell good."

"Thanks, you're so sweet." My sarcasm was dry so he couldn't have picked up on it even if he'd wanted to.

Still hugging me, making me feel claustrophobic, he said, "My parents will be heading back to Jersey soon. As soon as they leave, I'm gonna attack you."

Did he really think he sounded sexy?

"Mmm, can't wait."

"You won't know what hit you."

I smiled, pretending to be turned on by his pathetic attempt at flirtatious banter, then I changed the subject, telling him about the reporters outside.

"Yeah, I saw them too," Michael said.

"We should probably make a statement with a lawyer. I got a reference for a criminal lawyer from Grace Moss."

"Why do we need a lawyer, especially from Grace? *I'm* a lawyer."

"What do you know about criminal law?"

"More than you think." He let that hang there, then added, "Don't worry, I've got it under control, babe?"

Babe? Yuck.

He kissed me again, then we joined Stella and Joe in the living room.

"Is everything okay?" Stella asked Michael.

"Yep, it was just some routine questioning."

Joe, looking at his phone, said, "You're in the news again."

"Yeah," Michael asked, "what does it say?"

"Just that you returned home safely. Not much more info."

"Do you think you can identify the people who kidnapped you?" Stella asked Michael. "Do you have any idea what they wanted?"

"No, and who knows? Maybe they would've made a ransom demand at some point, but the main thing is I'm back home with my family. Nothing else matters."

I was thinking, *Does he really believe that shit?* when the front door opened and Harrison shouted, "Mom, Dad?"

I admit I cried real tears when Harrison rushed over to Michael and hugged him, sobbing, saying, "Daddy, Daddy, thank God you're back, Daddy."

A few minutes later Carson came home and there was a similar scene. Joe and Stella were crying too.

Watching Michael and the boys made me happy too but not for the reasons anyone else could possibly suspect. It made me happy to see Michael so happy, only because I knew that soon I was going to take that happiness away, just like he'd taken away my happiness. It also excited me to imagine a future without Michael, *and* Michael's parents, when they would be gone for good, deleted, and it was just me and the boys. We could have a happy, calm life, with only drama happening on stage. Was it cruel of me to have these thoughts? Maybe, but it also seemed fair.

Michael caught the kids up with his bullshit version of what had happened. It seemed like the more Michael told the story, the more real it sounded, maybe because he was starting to believe the lies himself.

At around seven, Stella and Joe finally left and Michael, the kids and I ordered in Italian from Tony's Di Napoli. If this had been a few nights ago, I would've been genuinely happy to be at the dinner table again with my family.

After cannolis, the kids settled down and were hanging out in their room, when Michael suggested we go outside and make a statement for the media.

"I still think it's a good idea to get a criminal attorney," I said.

"Then we'll have to wait till tomorrow, and it'll be an even bigger zoo out there," Michael said. "I'll be brief, and I know what to say and know what not to say."

I was against it and thought he was being a total idiot,

but I said meekly, "If you say so."

I went down with him. By his side, holding hands, we spoke to the cameras.

He said, "I'm just happy to be home with my family, and I have nothing more to say at this time."

Then I said, "I feel blessed too, and I hope everyone will respect our privacy."

As people shouted questions, we returned to the building, still holding hands. We'd pulled off the photo op beautifully. We looked like the perfect, happy, reunited couple.

Unlike the previous time I'd made a statement to the reporters, I didn't feel any need to check social media, the Citizen's app, or Spectrum News, just to see myself, or to find out what other people thought about me. Now it didn't matter to me what anyone thought because I was in total control, and it felt amazing.

The kids had quieted down. I peeked into their room and Carson was asleep, and Harrison was curled in bed, watching something on his phone, and he looked like he'd be asleep soon too. Remembering the panic I'd experienced yesterday when I'd thought the boys had been kidnapped, I felt calmness travel down my spine as I shut the door quietly.

I went into the master bedroom. The water was running, and I heard Michael brushing his teeth. I knew when he came out he'd want to pick up where we'd left off earlier and "attack" me. While I knew I should have been repulsed by the thought of his naked body against mine, no less attacking me, weirdly I felt turned on by the thought. Now that I knew that our marriage was through, that we had no future together, all the pressure was off. I could just use him, the way he'd always used me.

I washed up in the kids' bathroom then returned to my bedroom and put on my sexiest Victoria's Secret negligee—a silk and lace slip dress that I'd worn once or twice, but not in years. Then, from the drawer in my night table, I took out my favorite scented candle—champagne rose. I lit it, then dimmed the lights.

"Alexa, play The Weeknd."

As "Blinding Lights" began, Michael exited the bathroom in boxer briefs, and I saw his eyes widen.

"Wow," he said. "All right. That's what I'm talking about."

"Get over here," I said.

He was surprised that I was taking charge—I was usually submissive.

"Oh…okay," he said, and was about to get into bed.

"Wait."

He stopped.

"First, take those off." I glanced at his crotch.

"Now?"

"Yes, now."

He hesitated, then took down his boxers.

"Okay, now get hard for me."

"What?"

"You heard me."

He was touching himself, but he wasn't getting hard. I could tell he was nervous, not used to this kind of pressure, but I liked seeing him uncomfortable; it made me feel more in control.

"Come on, hurry."

"I'm trying."

"Try harder."

His forehead was glistening with sweat. He was stroking

himself harder and faster, finally making some progress.

It took a couple of minutes, but he finally got a hard-on.

I knew he wanted to get on top, but I said, "On your fucking back."

Usually, I needed foreplay to get turned on, but him struggling to perform for me *was* my foreplay. I climbed on top and started gyrating, but I wasn't thinking about him at all. I was using him, like a sex toy. Occasionally I said, "Oh my God, Michael" and "You feel so fuckin' good" only because I knew it would keep him hard. When I could tell he was about to come I slowed down—to prolong my pleasure, not his. After I came three times—almost four—I finally let him finish. I still wasn't thinking about him at all. As he grunted and moaned my name, I was thinking about my future, where I was happily alone, and he was out of my life for good.

It was total bliss.

"FUCK, NO. GODDAMMIT."

I was deep in a dream—on a sailboat alone, in the middle of the ocean, on a spectacular sunny day—when Michael's voice jarred me awake.

"What's wrong? What is it?"

Michael was sitting up next to me, looking at his phone, saying, "Shit, this is exactly what I was afraid of. Motherfuck-er."

He was usually even-keeled, stoic. It was unusual to see him so angry, especially after he'd just woken up.

"What is it? What's wrong?"

Still staring at his phone with an intense expression, he didn't answer.

"Is it—"

"Wait."

I hated the way he was talking to me, like I was a child, or a pet, but reminding myself that I wouldn't have to take any shit from him for much longer helped keep me calm.

After about maybe a minute of glaring and cursing under his breath, Michael got up and headed into the bathroom, still without speaking to me. I remained in bed, looking at my phone, but I didn't find any news stories or posts that mentioned Michael, except a short *Daily News* article about how he'd been released by his captors and had returned home safely and how the police's investigation was "ongoing."

Then Michael exited the bathroom, still naked, still looking preoccupied and distraught.

"I don't see anything," I said. "What is it?"

"They found the fuck…" He realized he was talking too loud in case the boys happened to be listening in, and in a quieter voice said, "They found the fucking bodies."

I didn't know what he was talking about.

"Bodies? What bodies?"

"The people who were holding us hostage."

With a hollow sensation in my gut, I asked, "What…what about John?"

"No, not John. Of course not John."

His tone was still disgustingly belittling.

"Okay. So then you think John—"

"Killed them? Yes, he killed them. It's as bad as I thought, maybe worse."

I tried to picture John killing three people, but it didn't compute with my memories of the sweet, kind man I'd been engaged to.

"Well, you said he's dangerous, right? Then why're you so surprised?"

"Because the bodies were discovered, that's why. In a Dumpster in Queens, it sounds like not too far from where we were held."

"So?"

"*So* that's not a John move. John's a pro, he doesn't leave loose ends. Don't you get it? He *wanted* the cops to find the bodies. If he didn't want that, trust me, those people would've vanished without a trace. He probably interrogated them, found out how I was involved, and put those bodies in that Dumpster to send a message to me, that I'm next. Dammit, Vanessa, why did you have to bring him into this? Why couldn't you just let this unfold?"

I'd never seen Michael act so paranoid and, admittedly, I was enjoying every second of it.

"I was just trying to do what I thought was best. I wanted to save you, and maybe I did. How do you know those people wouldn't have considered *you* a loose end?"

Good, let him think I was still on his side.

"Maybe you're right," he said. "Maybe I'm just fucked."

I put my arm around his waist, like a supportive wife, then said, "Maybe it's not as bad as you think. If John actually killed them, maybe he was just in a hurry, trying to get away, to leave the country or whatever. And how do we know the victims are even the people from the warehouse? Does the article you read mention their names?"

"No, but it's two men and a woman—so far unidentified, but that's intentional too. He doesn't care if the police can ID them, he just cares about *me* IDing them."

"Look, I think you're jumping to a lot of conclusions. You said John was in danger from these people previously, right, that they wanted to kill him?"

"Yeah, so?"

"So maybe that's why he killed them, if he killed them—so they wouldn't come after him. Maybe he never interrogated them or found out about your involvement."

Several seconds passed, then Michael said, "I guess anything's possible."

"Of course it's possible. It's even *likely*. And it makes sense you'd be paranoid after everything you've been through. You know what I think? I think you just have to stay in the moment, enjoy time with the boys. Everything's going to work out perfectly—I can feel it."

I didn't believe any of this crap. Yeah, things were going to work out perfectly—for *me*. But I wanted to keep *his* fantasy going for as long as possible, because if there was one thing I'd learned it was that fantasizing leads to complacency, and the more complacent he got, the easier it would be for me to get whatever I wanted.

"Yeah, I guess you're right," he said, still sounding worried.

"I think I know how to distract you." I pushed him onto his back, then crouched between his legs.

"Wow," he said. "Okay."

He was already mostly hard.

Maintaining eye contact, I said, "Watch me."

I could tell he thought *he* was in charge, saying things like "Yeah, baby" and "Keep going" and "Just like that," but *I* was actually in control. I could do whatever I wanted to him now—withhold the pleasure, or take it away whenever I felt like it. And I *would* take it all away—at a time of my choosing—and knowing this made me feel even more powerful. Did he really believe that John was the only one who knew how to play the goodbye game?

"Oh my God, Vanessa."

As he climaxed, my eyes widened with a different kind of excitement.

TWENTY-FOUR

WHEN THE KIDS woke up, Michael made them breakfast—banana fritters. The conversation was lively with the kids still very excited to have their dad back, updating him about everything that had been going on at school and with their extracurricular activities, but mostly asking him about what his time in "captivity" had been like.

"Were you tied up the whole time?" Carson asked. "How did you go to the bathroom?"

Michael explained how he'd been bound and gagged "most of the time," but how they took off the mask to feed him meals and how he was allowed to sleep on a cot. Again, it amazed me how easily and convincingly Michael could lie. If I didn't know the truth, his story would have sounded totally believable.

When the kids left for school, Michael's anxiety returned as he kept checking his phone and watching the local TV news on a loop, trying to find out any new information. His behavior was so similar to my past behavior that I knew he was getting obsessed with John and the idea that John was "out there somewhere." But I had no sympathy for what Michael was going through. Actually, I enjoyed seeing him overwrought. It was also enjoyable knowing that there no relief ahead for him—just more panic and anguish.

As the news spread that Michael was home safely and that I was totally innocent, I received texts from some friends and clients who had turned against me. While I was still angry, I didn't see the point of burning bridges. I wanted to stay open and focused on the future, rather than dwelling on the past, so I thanked everyone for reaching out, acting like I was willing to forgive and forget.

When I finished texting friends and acquaintances, I was tempted to go online, to see what those trolls were saying about me today. Were they still touting rumors and conspiracy theories about me or had they done a full 180? But, since I was in such a better place today—calmer, optimistic—I didn't want to do anything to ruin my mood and the new path I was on.

It was amazing how much my overall mood had changed in the past twenty-four hours. Yesterday at around this time John Adams had broken into my apartment and possibly saved me from a drug overdose, but today I had no panic or anxiety at all; I felt pretty much normal. I didn't feel like I needed any drugs of any kind; the idea even repulsed me. Revenge was my drug now.

I spent the day catching up on work and doing chores around the apartment. I went on the balcony and filmed a short, upbeat TikTok video I called "New Beginnings," about moving forward and not dwelling on the past. As soon as I posted the video, it was incredible to see the likes and follows skyrocket; within a few minutes it became my most popular video ever. Well, at least there was some benefit from all of the notoriety I'd gotten lately. Going forward I wasn't sure if I was going to continue with my business or start something new—maybe get back into acting—but I definitely felt like I was back in my groove and, even better, I knew that from here on things were only going to get better.

Michael, on the other hand, was an anxious mess. Pacing, fidgeting, checking his phone constantly. I offered to make him lunch, but he said he didn't have an appetite and said he needed to catch up on some work. He went into the bedroom and sat at his PC all afternoon, but he didn't seem to be doing work. I passed by a few times and saw that he was viewing news sites, probably searching for news about John and the police investigation. He looked so distraught that it was hard not to smile a little.

The kids came home from school, which distracted Michael for a while, but later, when they had gone to sleep, his anxiety returned in full force.

"I think I'm having a panic attack." He looked shell-shocked. "I can't get my heart to stop racing."

"Try some square breathing." It was the same lame advice he used to give me when I was so anxious I could barely function. "Breathe in for four seconds, hold it, then breathe out for—"

"I tried that already, it's not working."

"Okay, lie on your stomach."

He lay on the bed face down, and I climbed onto his ass and began to massage him, starting with his shoulders and neck, then moving down along his spine.

"I can feel how tense you are," I said. "It's not healthy to walk around with this much tension. Your dad has blood pressure issues, you have to watch out too."

"Yeah, I know."

I continued to massage him for about fifteen minutes, then sticking to my role of the loyal, supportive woman, I told him to turn over. He already had a hard on, so I climbed on and used his body for my pleasure, enjoyed my three orgasms immensely, and didn't pay attention to him at all.

Afterward, he said, "Sorry I've been so out of it all day, but you've been so awesome. I don't know what I'd do without you."

Thinking, *I know exactly what I'd do without you*, I curled up against him until we both fell asleep.

IN THE MORNING, I was on my balcony, getting ready to film another TikTok, when I got a call from Detective Randle.

"We need to talk again right away. There's been a development."

I asked Randle what it was about, but he said that he wanted Michael and I to come into the precinct to discuss it in person.

When I told Michael about the call, he had visible panic symptoms—shaking and sweating.

"I'm sure it'll be okay," I said, "but it might be a good idea to at least consult with a lawyer this time or at least—"

"I can handle it."

I hated how he was talking to me. Old Vanessa would've snapped back at him and it would've led to a blowout argument, but New Vanessa remained calm and patient.

"Whatever you think is best."

I could've added "dear," but the sarcasm would've been way too obvious.

Michael and I took a cab to the precinct. I felt so different from the last time I was here, when I thought Michael's life was in danger. Now I was cool, confident, but Michael still seemed extremely agitated.

Like last time, Randle wanted to talk to us individually. He led Michael away to the back of the precinct and told me to remain in the waiting area, on a wooden bench. They were gone for much longer than last time, then a Detective I'd never met before—a woman named Wang—came to get me. I thought she'd lead me to the room where Michael was being held, but instead she took me to an empty room and said that Detective Randle would come to see me shortly.

Maybe another half hour passed, then Randle entered and sat at the table. He said, "Tell me your exact whereabouts yesterday, beginning when you woke up."

No hello, or sorry for the long wait, or any attempt at any sort of nicety. What a total dick, but I believed that karma was real and that he'd get what he deserved; it was only a matter of time.

I did what he asked and told him everything that happened, but leaving out any mention of John and my almost overdosing. He asked a lot of questions, trying to poke holes in my story, but I wasn't at all concerned because I knew that no matter what, nothing drastic could happen to me. There was nothing to *arrest* me for. Michael, on the other hand, had staged a kidnapping that had possibly led to three murders. I expected Randle to ask me about the murders—if I knew the victims or could ID them—but he basically asked me the same questions he'd asked me last time, maybe trying to see if I'd answer them differently. Then he told me that a black Highlander SUV had been found in Queens near the East River—abandoned with no license plates. Maybe this was the "new development," but it seemed like it was just a tactic.

"How do you know it's the same SUV that I was in?" I said. "I mean, there are a lot of big black SUVs in New York City, right?"

It was fun, throwing his own words back at him.

"True," he said, "but you said you thought it was a High-lander."

"Yeah, but I also told you I don't know a lot about cars. Did you find any fingerprints or other evidence inside it?"

I knew the answer was no, or he would've led with this.

"No. No, we didn't."

"Well, that's unfortunate."

Leaving the precinct, Michael still seemed extremely nervous and overwhelmed, and I suggested we take a walk in Central Park. It was unusual to see Michael so scared and vulnerable, and I loved every second of it.

As we rehashed our Q and As, Michael kept re-asking me questions he'd only asked a few minutes earlier and he kept looking around to make sure no one was following us. Randle hadn't mentioned the location of the warehouse to either of us, but Michael didn't know if this was good or bad.

"Either they haven't found it yet, or John returned to the warehouse and covered up evidence that anyone had been there. Knowing John, I'd vote for number two."

A little later, as we walked around the reservoir, his paranoia peaked, as he suddenly stopped walking and said, "He could be following us right now."

"You really think so?"

"Lemme see your purse."

"Why?"

"There could be a tracking device."

I let Michael search through my purse, finding it inter-esting that Michael knew about the tracking devices. He probably knew that the kidnappers had planted a device on me and had been following me around the city.

Michael didn't find a device, but he got quiet, and I could tell he was preoccupied, inventing paranoid scenarios about John. I loved watching him suffer the way I used to suffer.

Over the next several days, Michael's anxiety intensified. He hadn't been back to the office yet because he wasn't sure he could handle it. He didn't seem to be getting much work done. I overheard a few conversations, including one with Russell, but mostly he was pacing, or just on the balcony, staring out at the city with a lost, helpless expression.

In bed, I initiated, but he didn't have much interest, saying he was too tired, and he always slept fitfully and had nightmares.

He wasn't leaving the apartment much, but one afternoon he announced he was taking a walk up to Carl Schurz Park. Then he returned about ten minutes later in a nervous frenzy.

"I think I saw him."

The irony was so obvious, Michael had no awareness. I guess it made sense—he was so self-absorbed that all he could think about was his own terror.

"Oh, I'm sure you're making a mistake," I said, mimicking the exact crap that he used to tell me when I thought I'd spotted "Colin."

"No, I really think it was him. I told you, he doesn't leave loose ends, he's going to be relentless, playing the long game. He probably wanted me to see him, just to fuck with my head. That's what John does. He plays mind games; he gets off on it."

I was dying to launch into a tirade about what Michael

had done to me, but I had my own game to play, so instead I said, "I'm sure you made a mistake, which makes sense given all the stress you've been under."

I was pretty sure that Michael had once made this exact comment to me, after one of my "Colin sightings" about ten years ago, but this didn't register with him at all.

"Don't you have a Klonopin I can take?"

With a straight face, I said, "It's really not a good idea to take drugs that haven't been prescribed to you." Then I added, "Hey, I have an idea, how about you make an appointment with Dr. Stone?"

For the first time since he'd returned home, Michael gave me a look like he realized I was fucking with him.

Covering quickly, I said, "Okay, not Stone. I know you shouldn't see *my* psychiatrist, but I'm sure Donna or your GP can suggest a great one. There really is no reason you should suffer."

Now he believed I was giving sincere advice and he said, "Yeah, you're right, I'll do it. I'll get an appointment."

"Great, sweetie."

I gave him a tight, loving, encouraging hug, while hoping that his new psychiatrist prescribed a drug that he'd get hooked on, and then maybe he'd branch out, start taking painkillers too. I wanted Michael to experience everything that he'd forced me to experience—except for him I wanted it to be much, much worse.

WE CONTINUED TO have sex, at least once every night, and an occasional "quickie" when the kids weren't around. We'd never had this much sex. Humorously, I could tell that

Michael thought the sex was a sign that we were getting closer.

One morning in the kitchen, Michael was staring at his phone, when I entered and said, "You know I really think we should continue couples counseling with Donna."

Michael looked up, surprised, and said, "Seriously? What for? I mean, things have been going so great with us lately."

Naturally his man brain thought everything was going well. He'd been getting laid and getting amazing blowjobs lately, so what could possibly be wrong with the marriage?

Good, that's exactly where I want you—in the dark.

"I think it's important to not be complacent. We're on a good path now. We want to keep it up, right? I really want our marriage to work out, Michael."

I delivered this so sincerely, he had no reason not to believe me.

At Donna's office, we sat on the couch holding hands.

"Well, this is a nice change," Donna said, her gaze aimed downward slightly, toward our hands.

"Yeah," Michael gushed. "Things have been awesome. Well, with us anyway."

"That's great to hear," Donna said, smiling. "The *us* is what we're here to talk about, right?"

"Well, not *everything* is great," I said.

Michael's expression darkened as he became concerned about what I was going to bring up.

Without looking at him, focused on Donna, I explained everything that I'd learned about Michael and my ex-fiancé. I referred to John as "Colin" because I didn't want to upset Michael *too much*, but I told her how my ex had lied to me about his background and that he'd arranged for Michael to meet me, and that Michael had lied to me about his involvement with Colin for years. At first, Michael seemed surprised, blindsided, by what I was saying. He tried to interrupt a few times, but Donna instructed him to "let her talk," and then he mostly listened calmly as I explained how Michael knew my ex was alive and led me to believe that I had a problem "letting go" and "moving on." I didn't mention anything about how Michael had arranged his own kidnapping, but I alluded to it by saying, "And recently I realized that the deceit went even deeper."

I had to hand it to Donna. I knew therapists were supposed to hide their personal feelings, but it was amazing how she appeared so detached as I spoke, even though I knew some of it must have been shocking for her to hear.

When I was through, Donna was quiet for several seconds, then said, "This is some extremely heavy, weighty information. It's brave of you to be open to discussing it in here, Vanessa."

I took a tissue from the box in front of me and faux dabbed a couple of "tears"—my eyes were actually dry.

Then Donna said to both of us: "It's particularly weighty given past experiences that Vanessa has had with men, including her father…How do you feel about all this, Michael?"

"Honestly? I feel awful," Michael said. "I love my wife so much. I love my family too. All I can say is that it was never my intention to hurt her. It was an accumulation of bad decisions that I made, if that makes any sense. But I swear, I'll never do anything to hurt her again."

I continued to hold hands with Michael even though I knew he was full of shit, that he didn't regret anything. The only thing he regretted was that his relationship with John had been exposed and that I wasn't in the dark anymore.

Then Donna looked at me. "And how about you, Vanessa? Are you willing to forgive Michael, despite everything you've learned?"

Although Donna was still maintaining her flat affect, I could tell she was surprised I was willing to let go so easily and move on, as this wasn't typical behavior for me. But this was the whole reason why I'd wanted to return to counseling—for this moment. I wanted to make Michael believe, without any doubt, that I was all in on us and our marriage.

So, with an appropriate sincere expression, I said, "I know it's a lot, and that there will be more challenges ahead, but yes, I absolutely want to continue on this journey."

Ugh, journey. *Did I really just say that? Could I possibly sound any more fake?*

But Michael bought all of it. Grinning, he squeezed my hand tightly, then kissed me.

Donna had a look that said, *The hell's going on here?* But she managed to cover it with a forced, yet warm smile.

At the end of the session, Michael seemingly had no idea that now *I* was the one with the big lie in this marriage, that everything I'd said had been total bullshit.

Walking along Fifty-Seventh Street, he said, "I feel so lucky right now. I don't know if I can get through this, but I *know* I can't get through this without you."

ALTHOUGH I HADN'T gotten my revenge on Michael yet, my life continued to improve. I was eating better and taking better care of myself. My anxiety was decreasing every day, and I resumed SoulCycle and barre classes.

I didn't want Michael to notice any red flags, so I kept to my normal routine—staying involved in my work and the kids' lives.

Harrison wasn't in the next show at Encore, but Carson had a small role as The White Rabbit in *Alice in Wonderland*. I had a great time running lines with Carson, then Harrison and I went to the dress rehearsal. In the lobby of the theater, it was great to catch up with my friends, especially the ones I hadn't connected with at all recently. Kathleen wanted to recommend me for a project—to help her sister's son who was having executive function issues. I didn't want to tip off any of my friends about my big plan, so I expressed high interest, saying, "Oh my God, yes, I'd love to connect with her," although I knew I'd never actually follow through.

I was chatting with Isabella about upcoming shows Encore was planning to produce when I saw Andrew arriving with Laurie, the woman he'd claimed he'd stopped dating. I hadn't heard from Andrew since Michael had returned and, while I was surprised he had the balls to show up at an event where he knew he'd run into me, I was more surprised by his appearance. His eyes and one side of his face were badly swollen, the way some boxers look within a few days after a fight.

Isabella saw me looking at him and said, "What do you think happened?"

"No idea," I said, wondering, *Could John have done it?* I'd mentioned to John that Andrew had tried to assault me. Would John have stuck around in New York, with the police investigating him and what had happened in Queens, just to track down Andrew and get revenge for me?

Andrew saw me looking at him. Our gazes locked for a second or two, then he went into the theater, holding his girlfriend's hand.

Harrison, who'd been hanging out backstage with Justin who had a small role in the play, came over to me and said, "It's so messed up."

"What happened?" I asked.

"Some random dude attacked him, around the corner from his building, near Park Av."

"Wow," I said. "That *is* crazy."

Harrison gave me a look as if he suspected I was somehow involved, probably because I appeared happy to see Andrew all beaten up.

"Is it true what you told me the other day? That Justin's dad did something to you, that he tried to—"

"He did. Yes, it's all true."

Putting an arm around me, Harrison said, "I'm so sorry I didn't believe you, Ma, and I'm so sorry that happened to you."

"It's okay, sweetie, but trust me—your mother can take care of herself. I'm so proud of both of you."

Harrison squinted. "Is something going on with you and Dad?"

I looked around, making sure no one was close enough to overhear us, then I said, "I'm not sure what you mean."

"I don't know, there's something…I don't know…weird about it all. I mean you guys seem happy, but almost like *too* happy."

"There's still about fifteen minutes before curtain. Let's take a little walk outside."

We went toward Lexington and headed around the block.

"What is it?" Harrison asked. "What's going on?"

"You're very perceptive. I can't slip one by you, can I? It's one of the many things I admire about you."

Then I told him about everything his father had done to me—from lying about knowing about Colin, who was actually John, to making me think I was crazy, to faking his kidnapping, and to arranging for me to be kidnapped. I stressed that I was telling him all of this in confidence and that he had to swear not to tell anyone.

We stopped walking as Harrison began to cry.

Hugging him, I said, "It's okay, sweetie. We'll all be okay."

"I don't want *him* to be okay," he said. "I want him to die."

"You don't mean that," I said, though I believed he did.

"I'll never trust him again. Why would I? He probably was lying when he said he was okay with me coming out— that seemed super sketchy, like where the hell was *that* coming from? I guess I wanted to believe it, because he's my dad and all, but...And *then* he made us think he was dead, put us through a fuckin' nightmare, and what's gonna happen to him now? He just gets to walk away, like nothing happened, and we're supposed to just like forgive him, pretend we're all *happy*?"

"Yes," I said. "That's exactly what we're going to do."

"But why? I don't get it."

I held his hands and squeezed them tightly and looked right at his teary eyes and said, "Trust me. I have a plan, a *big* plan, but it's important that all of us just act as normally as possible and go on with our lives. I need you to be strong and supportive for your brother. But by the end of the summer, it'll all be over—we'll all be free."

"What're you gonna do, Ma?"

"Trust me," I said, eyes still laser focused. "Just trust me."

TWENTY-FIVE

SCHOOL ENDED. AFTER a few weeks at home, it was time to take the kids upstate to French Woods, the performing arts camp they'd been attending the past few summers. They were eager to see their friends and Harrison had been doing exactly what I'd asked him to do, pretending that everything was normal.

Michael seemed excited about having time alone with me. After dropping the kids off, driving with one hand on the steering wheel and one hand on my leg, he said, "It's gonna be a great summer."

His hand felt like a clamp, but I rested my hand over his anyway and smiled as naturally as I could.

This was perfect. I wanted Michael to remain complacent, thinking we could rekindle our relationship, that there was hope. Meanwhile, I didn't care how much time we spent together or how much sex we had; nothing could prevent my forgetting what he did to me—the lies, the manipulating, the gaslighting—and nothing could change my mind.

Maybe Michael believed he was happy with me, that we

were on a good path now, but I could see the stress taking a toll. He'd been losing weight fast—at least ten pounds in the past few weeks. His face looked drawn, grayish, and he seemed generally unhealthy. He'd been seeing a psychiatrist and was taking meds; I didn't know if it was helping or not, but I could tell he was getting dependent on them. Although I enjoyed seeing him struggle, like I had struggled for years, I wanted to maintain my role as a concerned, loving spouse and I told him that he should make an appointment with his GP.

"Maybe you can get a referral to see a nutritionist. Eating right is so important."

Years ago, when I was dangerously thin and riddled with anxiety, Michael had told me that "eating right is so important." I didn't think he got the passive-aggressive dig, but I sure as hell enjoyed saying it.

When Michael was busy with work, I tended to financial and logistical details for my plan. I thought I had a good handle on most of it, but I wanted to make sure I'd thought of everything. I'd been doing as much research as I could— reading articles and blogs and watching YouTube videos. Most of the information was redundant, but occasionally I found a new, useful tidbit that I integrated into my plan. While I was eager to get on with my new life, I didn't want to rush or force anything. I knew I had one chance to get this right and I didn't want to blow it.

On YouTube, I also found it inspiring to watch videos by women who'd escaped their marriages and relationships with narcissistic husbands and boyfriends—men who'd lied to them, gaslit them, and abused them psychologically, and sometimes physically. Parts of their stories resonated with my experiences, and I applied their advice, and lessons they'd learned, to my plan. I also felt empowered by their stories. These women made me feel like I wasn't alone. While none of them had experienced the level of deceit that I had, they'd all been trapped in miserable situations, yet had found ways to get rid of the horrible men in their lives and move on. I felt like if they could do it, so could I.

TOWARD THE END of July, everything with my plan was in place, but I knew, for maximum effect, our last night together had to be memorable, so memorable that Michael would become obsessed with it, analyzing and reanalyzing every detail, wondering what had been going on in my head, what was I *really* thinking about that night, and how he'd been so oblivious to all of it.

I wanted to look my best and I needed to feel pampered, so I got a cut and color, telling my hairdresser Ari, "I want to look as sexy as possible." He did a great job, going lighter than usual, and I loved the blowout too. Nearby, at Bloomingdales, I splurged on a new outfit—a Halston emerald sequined gown and perfectly matching Jimmy Choo glitter pumps.

When Michael came home from work I was fully dressed, makeup applied perfectly.

"Whoa," he said. "You look phenomenal."

It was unusual for Michael to compliment my appearance, even in this semi-smarmy way. Managing to not roll my eyes, even a little, I said, "Why thank you."

After he showered, changed into one of his nicest Hugo Boss suits, and slicked back his thinning hair, we headed out.

We had sushi at a new expensive place in midtown I'd said I was dying to try—I wasn't—and then we went to see

Wicked, one of my all-time favorite shows and one of the few shows that Michael seemed to enjoy too. He'd seen it twice and I'd seen it five times, though neither of us had seen it with the current cast. Afterward, we walked back uptown around and alongside Central Park, holding hands, singing lyrics from "The History of Wrong Guys" and "What a Woman Wants", and stopping occasionally to make out like in-love teenagers. I could tell that Michael believed my emotions were real and, more importantly, would remember this night for the rest of his life. Hopefully, he'd become obsessed with the memory. Maybe it would even haunt him.

Later, in bed, I knew it was the last time we'd ever have sex, and I wanted to make it as memorable as possible, so I was louder, more energetic than I'd ever been before. I was so excited about the future that it was hard to focus on sex. I couldn't come because I was secretly so repulsed, but I faked a few intense orgasms just to please Michael's ego.

We slept naked, intertwined for most of the night.

In the morning, as we got dressed, I asked, "What time will you be home tonight?"

"I have a light day. Around six."

"Perfect. I think I'll cook a big paella tonight."

He looked over his shoulder at me. "Paella, really? I didn't know you know how to make paella."

"I've been reading a lot of recipes online and I think I found the best one. I can't wait to make it for you."

"I'm sure it'll be amazing." He kissed me. "Six o'clock it is."

As Michael left for work, it was hard to not flash back to the morning he left to go jogging, when he was really heading out to stage a kidnapping and make my life hell.

Son of a bitch.

I let the anger pass and snapped into action.

I packed essentials mainly—clothes to last me a week to ten days, practical shoes and sneakers, only necessary toiletries. I was an excellent packer; it was all about organizing space efficiently. I placed rolled items at the bottom, folded items in middle, and shoes filled with socks and other small items on top, with dry cleaning bags between each layer. In the end, I managed to get at least three suitcases worth of stuff into two large suitcases. One of the suitcases was Michael's favorite Samsonite that he took on business trips—oh well!

I went down to the lobby and told Carlos that the movers were coming soon. Carlos was surprised and annoyed because maintenance was supposed to be notified to prepare the elevator, but I explained that "due to all the stress I'd been under lately" it had slipped my mind to follow the building's protocol. He was sympathetic and said it would be no problem. The real reason I hadn't notified the building in advance, though, was I had to make sure Michael had no clue about any of it.

"No one told me you were moving," Carlos said.

"Oh, you'll hear about it today, I'm sure. The deal closed last night."

"Wow, where're you moving to?"

"Westchester," I lied.

"Nice," he said. "I love it there."

The movers arrived at ten sharp. I instructed them what to pack and what to leave. Basically, everything that belonged to me and the kids got packed, and Michael's stuff didn't. I also had them pack a lot of "mutual possessions," like my favorite photos of the kids and a couple of paintings, and items that had any value, like the dining room chandelier, an expensive set of China, and the Persian rug in the living room.

When the truck was fully loaded, aside from two suitcases with clothes and personal items, I felt an adrenaline rush—was this actually *happening*? I'd spent so much time anticipating this moment that I wanted to make sure I experienced it fully, so, after I brought the suitcases down to the lobby, I strolled around the apartment for one last walk-through. I let the emotions soak in, hoping that someday I'd remember how amazing this had felt.

Lastly, I put Sparkle in his box, put my keys on the kitchen table, and left the apartment without looking back.

CARRYING SPARKLE, I picked up the rental car, then stopped at the building to get my suitcases.

"Have a great trip," Carlos said. "Enjoy the new place."

"Oh, I definitely will. Thanks for everything."

During the drive upstate, the weather was gloomy, with occasional downpours, but the mood inside my car was anything but bleak. Showtunes blasting and I was singing along with them, really letting it rip for Sweeney Todd's "Not While I'm Around."

After I checked into the motel where I usually stayed, about ten miles from the kids' camp, I took care of some final financial details, then I texted the boys that I was going to make a surprise visit today, and that I'd "explain everything" when I got there.

Harrison, who was always incredibly perceptive, responded almost immediately: Everything okay?

I wrote back: **yes everything's great, sweetie, I promise!! See you soon! Love you!!!**

I opened the bottle of Prosecco I'd brought along and chilled in the hotel fridge. I poured myself a glass and sipped it leisurely. At around five-thirty, I logged on to my iPad to the spy camera app I'd downloaded. I'd also placed several cameras in different rooms. While the cameras weren't important for the plan itself, in a way the cameras were the most important part of the plan. I needed to *see* the pain I had caused for Michael. Just imagining it for the rest of my life wouldn't be enough.

I checked every view, and the apartment was just the way I'd left it. I knew Michael would be home any minute because he'd texted me about fifteen minutes ago saying he'd be "home in 15." I responded that the timing was perfect because "the paella's almost done." I loved how he'd added an exclamation mark to my text.

Staring at the iPad, I was as nervous as I was before one of Harrison's or Carson's shows, and the analogy made sense because I knew this was going to be great theater.

Then, with my pulse accelerating, the show began.

The camera facing the front door showed Michael entering. He already looked frantic and confused, probably because the doorman had told him about the move. As the reality of what had happened slowly set in, his expression morphed to full-blown rage.

Pacing the apartment like a caged, enraged gorilla, he said, "Vanessa. Vanessa, what the fuck?"

I had to change to another camera view to see him enter the dining room and living room.

"Jesus Christ, Vanessa. What did you do? What the fuck did you do?"

Then he went into the kids' room and saw that their stuff was gone too. Not only had he lost his wife; he'd also lost his family. He looked hopeless, devastated—this was so perfect.

"Vanessa, fucking Vanessa, what the fuck? Are you crazy? Are you fuckin' crazy?"

"Yeah, I'm crazy," I said to the screen. "And you messed with the wrong girl, bitch."

On his cell, Michael called his Financial Advisor, Gerald at J.P. Morgan. I chuckled when Michael said that he had "a very serious matter to discuss." Then Michael was silent as Gerald was undoubtedly telling him how I'd withdrawn all the money from that account and that there was one cent left. Leaving one cent had been a last-minute idea of mine, the perfect final "fuck you."

Enraged, Michael screamed, "What do you mean one cent? How's that possible?… Yeah, I know her name's on the accounts, but how could she have…"

Then he spotted the tiny camera that I'd placed in the far corner of the bedroom, near the ceiling. He ended the call abruptly and approached the camera. He got as close as he could to it, staring up at it, his face looking all ugly and distorted. I could tell he felt like a total idiot, thinking, *How did I miss all this? How could I have been so oblivious? How did I misjudge this situation so badly?*

"Vanessa, get your skinny ass back here? Did you hear me, damn it? I said get your skinny fucking—"

"Buh bye, motherfucker," I said, swiping the app away.

Ah, it all felt amazing, even better than I'd anticipated. The best part—Michael didn't realize yet *how* badly he'd gotten screwed.

This morning I'd drained all our accounts, including brokerage and crypto, and transferred the money into accounts in my name only. Because my name was already on every account, there was no fraud trigger. By using the power of attorney Michael had signed years ago, I'd transferred the deed to the apartment into my name by forging Michael's signature. Then I sold the apartment, sight unseen, with an expedited cash investor service, to a buyer in China at a steep discount. I didn't care about getting the best price; I just wanted out—a cash deal, as quickly and seamlessly as possible.

Michael was homeless now, and soon he'd be jobless too, as I'd sent a long WhatsApp message to Russell, describing everything I knew about his relationship with John, and how he'd had a secret, criminal client for years. The best part was Michael couldn't go to the cops about any of this without incriminating himself for the fake kidnapping and other crimes.

I left the motel and headed to pick up the boys. The rain had ended, and sunshine had broken through. It had become a perfect summer day.

I entered the camp's grounds, then pulled up in front of the main entrance and texted the kids: **I'm here!**

I knew when I broke the news that we were leaving their father and their lives in New York, Harrison would be thrilled. Carson would understand too, especially after Harrison and I told him about everything his father had done to us. Once we got settled in California, I knew the boys would love it there. I'd already found a couple of possibilities for schools with terrific theater programs. I'd informed Harrison's new manager about the "upcoming move," and he'd arranged to have a manager colleague in L.A. start working with Harrison. Hey, maybe I'd start auditioning too.

Meanwhile, Michael's life in New York would be hell. Knowing that John was "a pro" who didn't leave "loose ends," Michael would live in constant fear, searching for

John's face in every crowd. Hopefully he would get obsessed and develop serious anxiety and paranoia issues, and he'd have to up his meds until he developed a full-blown addiction. Then, on some mundane evening, he'd be walking along a dark street, and he'd see John, except this time it wouldn't be his imagination—John would be there.

The boys exited the building with concerned expressions. I was in a great mood, still imagining Michael on that dark Manhattan street—terrified, trapped, alone. When Harrison saw me smiling, I could tell by his expression that he knew I'd kept my promise, that I'd got rid of his father for good, and then both boys sprinted toward me, glowing in the sun.

THE END

READ MORE

Too Far
Panic Attack
Fantasies
The Follower
The Manhattan Trilogy

Join Jason Starr's newsletter:
jasonstarr.com/newsletter

ABOUT THE AUTHOR

JASON STARR is the international bestselling author of more than twenty crime novels and psychological thrillers, including *Vanessa's Men*, *Panic Attack*, *Too Far*, *Fantasies*, and *The Follower*. He has also written original graphic novels including *Casual Fling* and *Silicon Bandits* and has written for Marvel and DC Comics featuring Batman, The Punisher, and Wolverine. He has co-written several novels with Ken Bruen for Hard Case Crime. Many of his novels are in development for film and TV. He has won the Anthony Award twice. He lives in New York City.

For news and updates visit jasonstarr.com